CALLED TO DRAGONS NEST

Madison Hinko

First Edition

Fulton Books, Inc.
Meadville, PA

Published by Fulton Books 2020

ISBN 978-1-64654-313-7 (paperback)
ISBN 978-1-64654-314-4 (digital)

Printed in the United States of America

I wrote this novel for my little sister, Sofia, who owns my heart.
I hope one day you live in a world of prosperity and fantasy.
To Ms. Hollowell,
my dearest inspiration were your lectures,
and I will cherish the unique lessons you
taught in your classroom forever.

To believers!

Rose

It was almost December again, thought Rose mindfully while her long full bronze hair raced the wind. Almost a full year had gone by since she arrived at this mesmerizing place. After a three-year-long journey, Rose and her brother arrived at this natural preserve thought to be the safest for them, the place where their aunt and her three children lived. Rose loved it here. She loved the lake in the middle of the big woods, where light reflected off the water to make the sun's light shine throughout the whole dark forest. She loved the way the deer came and drank from the water then hurried off to tend to their young. *Even they have families,* thought Rose. Her brother was her only real family, and yet she felt different from him. Sibling rivalry was one thing, but Rose's intuition about a huge war being fought between their blood was something entirely different. The water always let her escape from reality. She felt safer here than anywhere else.

The ripples in the water danced for her, then later stopped to rest. The birds sang their usual evening songs, then left to explore the sky. Their long wings had always interested Rose, for she had always wanted to fly with them. She felt she could see all the water from the clouds and see all the world from that high up. Rose had only been to two places in her whole life, Nava and the Red Islands. She was born in Nava, but then she and her brother traveled to get to a cottage in the Red Islands.

She stood up from the edge of the water and dipped her feet in to clean off the dirt. It was freezing, and the blue-and-crimson water covered her feet and held tight at her ankles. When she finished her first foot, she went to wash the next. Her left was much dirtier; she had to step all the way in, and then the water grasped firmly on her midcalf. She lifted her ripped brown dress up so she wouldn't get it wet, even though it was just as dirty as her feet. Then she felt a hard force on her back. She hit the water with a large splash, and her bronze hair turned black. She wiped her mouth with her hand. She looked behind her, and there stood her brother, smiling down at her with a mischievous grin. His red shirt was spotless, and his black pants didn't look touched.

"Jason! Why would you do that?" asked Rose as she began wringing out her hair.

"I pushed you because it looked easy. You need to learn to keep your balance, Rose."

Angrily, Rose stood up. Her dress was drenched. She didn't mind, though, because she didn't like the dress and preferred to wear her trousers. But she knew a way to get back at Jason.

"Let's race home," Rose said, tricking him.

Jason nodded and smiled wickedly.

He was always in the mood for a challenge, even if he was destined to lose. Rose was much faster than Jason. She knew this woods front to back, all its secrets, twists, and turns. She felt the woods clearing a path for her to win, the roots moving to flatten the surface, the rocks scattering out of the way, so her feet only felt the soft texture of the mud. Jason suspected nothing, looking forward, trying to intimidate her by stretching aggressively, which made Rose almost laugh.

"Three…two…one!" yelled Rose.

They took off, her feet gliding on the ground. Her face felt the wind, and she looked in front of her to see all the trees move away. Jason, not running nearly as fast, tried to keep up as he had to jump over high roots and skip over large pointy rocks that were stabbing his feet.

Rose pushed her way through the dark trees and started heading northeast, a shorter way to her house. Jason was trying to follow her, but she was too fast. She was quickly slipping out of view. She was breathing fast, her heart racing toward victory. At this speed, her clothes would be completely dry by the time she reached her cottage. Her feet moved so fast. The green leaves followed her shadow, her feet skirting the surface of the dirt. Her hair was pushed back by the wind, bounced on her back by gravity, and then was cleaned by the air. She heard Jason catching up but breathing heavily, so Rose knew she would win, even if it wasn't by much. She had no cramps, no pains, no heartaches. She felt great. Running was one of the few things she was good at. She felt if she could run, she could be free from whatever people wanted to hide.

As the race came to an end, she was almost exiting the woods. Her brother was not far behind, but she could tell he would not get any faster. So she decided to get faster.

Faster, faster, she thought. *I want to be first.*

The quicker she got, the more she was losing her balance. She'd never had good balance. She skidded more, glided over more land, and then a great red fire burned out of her feet. She paused and completely stopped herself. Jason stopped too. He called for an end to their extravagant race. He breathed heavily while he walked toward her. She would not move. Never in her life had she created fire. Never had she ever felt so hot that she created heat. Strange. Her feet didn't hurt. Her feet felt fine.

Jason walked up to her and felt her feet. His hands were cold. His worry moved through him and into her body.

"What is going on?" she bellowed to her brother.

He remained still, but she could see something different in his eyes. He knew something was wrong.

"We need to get you to our aunt."

"No, we don't. It probably was just my speed. If it happens again, then we can tell her. I don't want to worry her. She already thinks I'm odd," Rose protested.

"She doesn't think you are odd."

"Yes, she does. She always frowns when she looks at my red lips and my dark eyelashes and my bright-blue eyes."

"She doesn't think you're odd. She knows something you don't."

"What is that?" she asked.

"About the war," he said. "Anyway, if this fire happens again, you can be certain that I am going to tell her. I'm worried the stories might be true."

"What stories might be true?" Rose demanded, getting impatient.

He ignored her.

She asked again, "Which of your stories might be true, Jason?"

Still no answer, like she was talking to a wall, but she knew he was thinking about something. His brown eyes showed fear, worry, and concern. Her older brother's dark-brown hair looked a little grayer, and his hands were fidgety.

Rose groaned, then jogged up to their cottage.

Once Rose climbed the low thick hill, the small cottage appeared to her eyes. It was a small building with two stories and a deck. The main floor had a little kitchen and a large dining room. She walked closer. Her heart still shook with the fear she could catch her little home on fire. Yes, to Rose this was home. She never seemed to understand why she had to be there, but that was because in her brother's and aunt's eyes, she was way too young to know. She knew so little and wanted to know so much. This world frustrated her curiosity. Even when she got answers, they seemed incomplete, so she would ask more questions. Why was she different from everyone else in her family? It nagged at her that she could not figure it out. She decided that she would never know what it was like to meet other people, because of her oddness. It was little comfort, though, because she could not accept that she would never know why she was different.

"Rose, there you are, my dear. We were looking all over for you!" screamed her aunt from the inside as she waddled outside.

"I am always at my lake," Rose told her.

Her eyes twinkled. Her long black hair and her gray roots reminded Rose of her mother. Her warm smile looked the same as her mom's. But Katrina, her mother, was much younger, her hair warmer. But Rose was slowly losing the feeling of her touch, the sound of her voice, and the look of her face. These memories were slowly being replaced by the image of her sister, Rose's aunt.

Jason stumbled up the hill in exhaustion from the race.

"And you ran home?" Liza asked, pursing her lips foully.

"Yes, Aunt Liza."

"Rose, you need to gain some weight. You are too light," mumbled Jason. Liza nodded.

Rose was undoubtedly skinny, but that was because she refused to eat any food that came as the result of harm to an animal. It drove her new family crazy, because she never touched fresh meat. The only things she preferred to eat that came from animals were milk and eggs. She guessed it didn't do too much to the poor, innocent, helpless animal, so she drank lots of milk for protein and ate lots of eggs to grow strong. She also, unlike her cousins, ate fruits and vegetables with all her meals. She loved picking vegetables from their garden and pretending she was the maiden in a fairy tale. Eventually, she would grow bored of that and return to the water and just sit.

"You need meat," finished Rose's aunt sternly. She patted Rose's head and began to waddle the other way. She was postponed by the dread of her niece.

"For a whole year, you have put up with it!"

"Rose, you will eat one slice of ham tonight for dinner. That is all I ask of you."

"Fine," Rose agreed, surrendering.

"Oh, that dress is terrible! What did you do to it?" asked Rose's aunt swiftly.

"I fell in the water, and the mud from the ground stained it," Rose told her.

"I told you, Jason, this girl has awful balance. You must help her with that."

"My balance is fine!" Rose protested.

"No. Rosie, go freshen up. I want a clean outfit on you for supper. And throw that ugly, filthy thing away. Go on," demanded Rose's aunt.

Rose walked up the stairs. She wrung out her hair once again, and very few water droplets came out. She stepped in front of her mirror. She looked beautiful. Her long bronze hair came to her waist, and her bright blue eyes glowed. Her black eyelashes transformed the light into dark. Strikingly, one of her strangest features were her lips. They were the most natural dark red imaginable. Sometimes, even though she knew better, she thought she was wearing lipstick. But it was all real. She was born with them. It always confused her, because no one else in her family had red lips—not her mother, not her father. Her brother did not have red lips, and neither did any of her cousins. *So why me?* thought Rose as she vigorously took off her dress and put on a black top with a black skirt. She felt that dark suited her because of her eyes.

"Everything must complement the eyes," she had heard her cousin Celia say to her once. "The eyes are the first thing a man notices."

Rose hurried down to supper, her nose filled with the smell of fresh ham, clean berries, warm bread, bright-green and red apples, and cut corn. The smell of well water also filled the room. The nice and hot potatoes lay politely in a stack on the table. A dab of butter was given to everyone for the bread. To Rose's surprise, a plate of sugar was set enticingly in the middle of the room. Fresh lemon was squeezed into everyone's water to change the taste of the dull well fluid. Small mints were also passed out to keep everyone's breath smelling fresh. Rose's aunt cut off a chunk of ham for everyone and didn't skip Rose this time. Rose felt uncomfortable sitting down and seeing this poor animal being eaten by people. Animals were worth just as much as any other living creature, including people.

They each picked accompaniments for themselves after being given the ham. Rose managed to grab a potato and some sugar. They each had to take fresh berries also or risk getting the look from Rose's aunt. As for the vegetables, everyone took corn. Rose grabbed a piece of bread and an apple. She ate her corn and apple first. She refused to gulp down the meat before the plants, which gave people food willingly. Rose also ate the bread before it grew stale. She stabbed the butter into the center of the roll to get the most taste. Everyone was eating happily. Still, they all looked different from Rose. The forks and knives clanked against the glass plates. No one really talked at supper, which always shocked Rose, since this was such a bubbly little home. She cut her ham last, while everyone else had already finished their meat. Rose had a hard time getting it to her mouth. It looked sad and greasy, but she knew she didn't want to let her aunt down. Instead, she started a conversation.

"Can you tell me about the war?" Rose asked her aunt hesitantly.

"I told you about that when we traveled," said Jason, who was aggressively chewing on his stuffing, his mouth crunching and drooling.

"Not Red Lips or the twelve jewels of Remular. Tell me about the war between the Red Lips and Nomads."

"Why do you want to know about such violence?" asked Celia.

"Because it involves me, doesn't it?" Rose informed Celia and the rest of the table. Her little cousins went silent.

Finally, her aunt spoke. "You know as much as you have to."

"No, I don't. Please, Aunt Liza, please." Rose tried to look innocent and just curious, but really, her eyes were full of pain. The pain of an unquenchable curiosity that no one seemed to know how to fill.

"Well, you're older, I know, but not tonight, love," said her aunt.

Rose felt sick. Her head felt hot, and her eyes felt red. She wished she still had a mother to cry to and a family to support her curiosity. Once again, no one seemed to have the patience to fill her head with the truth about who she was and why she was different. She dreamed thoughts of what it meant to be a Red Lip.

ASHBEL

Rose woke up early the next morning, completely skipped breakfast, and headed toward the lake. She jumped through the forest, where she raced her brother the day before, but this time the big woods didn't know she was coming and made the travel hard on her bare feet. Rose stepped over hard and sharp minerals and snapped her feet upon broken twigs and sticks. The deer ran away from her this time instead of racing her through the morning mist. The dew on the late-November ground also made her travel harsh. It had an icy, wet burn on her toes, which gave her the urge to stop running and walk carefully to her favorite spot on her lake. But her grit would not let her down, and she ran speedily through the poison ivy and leaped through the thorns. She felt alive, but her heart and head hurt because of the dinner the day before.

She made it through with bumps and scratches that let out blood. Her face was red and her breath was cold because she ran against the chilling, sharp, and then dull wind. She held her head high, though there was nothing to be proud or ashamed of except who she was. Her fate denied her, and her mind kept shifting on what to do next. She took comfort that, in all the stories she heard from her aunt, she was supposed to make up her own mind about her future. No one else would decide for her. Rose's mind was telling her to get answers, but with no resources faithful enough to inform her, she sat sulking at the edge of her lake, wishing for something different.

The water was warm that day; it stuck out from the cold atmosphere and the dew on the ground. Her hand could stay in longer without having to pull it out because it got too cold.

The warmth of the water gave Rose an idea. *I wonder if I can create it with my hands.*

She started moving her hands fast, mimicking her feet from the other day. No use. Rose then moved her arm with less speed and then slowly, calmly, and with ease. She felt relaxed, but it was still no use.

For the next week, Rose tried anywhere she was alone to at least create a spark, but the magic wouldn't work with her anymore. Rose felt more frustrated than she had ever been in her whole life. Her frustration rarely got the best of her, but this time Rose was a mess.

She gave up on the small thoughts in her head that she would ever be able to recreate the magic fire she once could create. She went back to being herself and playing with her younger cousins, letting Celia braid her hair, eating all her food, waking up early ready for life, and racing her brother. It was normal. Her aunt stopped worrying about her and started leaving her alone. But she still felt funny, and the memory of fire started becoming plastic, while her dreams slowly turned more tragic. She would fight in her sleep against the demons that would mock her glorious fire. She would feel whips against her pale skin and wake up with black-and-blue stains on her flesh. She knew it was not demons doing this to her but her fighting with herself at night to push the fire out. She loved the idea of fire being created from her body. In the winter, quickly burning wood without the labor of rubbing sticks together to create heat fascinated her. Thoughts like these would pop up in her dreams and shred her. Thoughts of dazzling fire left her head to return to the dreams of little children of vast dragons breathing breathtaking fire in the midst of a beautiful princess.

No, she thought, remembering the little heat of fire that burned from her fibula, *it will never happen again.* She let loose and slept more after her heat memory left. She couldn't be burned in the middle of the night by a fake monster threatening to convert her peaceful life into ashes.

"Do you know why my mother died, Celia?" Rose asked softly to her cousin as she braided her long luscious locks.

"Mother never told us, but that's probably because it was her sister. Mom knew her longer than you. I'm sure it is hard, Rosie, but one day she'll tell you. It is a sin for any child not to know of her parents."

Celia sounded older to Rose when she talked like this. Celia's mature smile, actions, and personal ways were so comforting. She had long blond hair and brown eyes. Celia's eyes were identical to those of her mother. Her tan skin matched nicely with her freckles. Her bony legs could do athletics but were not made for running, like Rose's legs. At the same time, Celia was the master of hair and beauty and rarely looked uncomposed. Celia's handiwork with hair was swift and a little cunning. Her idea of fun was playing with Rose's long hair, because Celia always got bored of her own. She hated the lake, for it was too messy, and hated when her little sisters didn't have their boots on the correct feet. She was a perfectionist and needed order every step of each day. She would make a fine wife to any lucky man, and a lovely mother, and Celia tried to convince Rose of that too. But Rose loved getting dirty, swimming, running with wolves, playing magic, dreaming of sword fights with knights, and anything else far from beauty or hair. But Rose loved Celia and let her do what she wished with her hair, face, and clothing, because Rose was always going to mess it up in the end. Oddly, Rose had no hate in her whole being.

After getting her hair done in a nice flat braid by Celia, Rose walked toward the fence of her aunt's garden and picked strawberries, blueberries, and grapes from their vines. The apples hung low from their short thin trees, just high enough to reach from her toes. Rose picked only the ripest fruit that the vines and trees bore. Then she hurried off to the vegetable garden and picked the corn growing from stiff stocks and the potatoes from the thick network of roots on the ground. Her hair stayed perfect all through these chores, but when she was done, Rose knew exactly where her hair was heading. She ran back inside, past the fences, over the steps, leaped over her flowers, and marched her way to the cottage. Rose was bored with these civil chores. She slammed the baskets of fresh produce on the dining room table and ran off to her forest.

Rose felt happy again to be in her forest, which seemed to be calling her as she ran straight through the entrance. She dashed through the air, now racing the dragon spirit inside her, fighting off any worries she had. The trees in her woods looked bright and green, not quite prepared to submit to the coming winter. Snow never touched the soil on the Red Island lands, which made it green all year round. Rose preferred running barefoot in her own little woodland. She sprinted down the small river that headed into her fancy pond, bouncing forward to her favorite spot. The trees moved once more to fit her straight-lined run, the rocks were out of her view, and the deer pranced after her and followed her trail. The midnoon fever hit her cold forehead as she danced her way through the sunshine-lit grounds. The strands of light beamed against the fallen twigs that lay idle, dreamless, and yet content.

The hot sun of the Red Islands shone brightly that afternoon, making it easier to see even for a late-December day. The wind carried a chill that caused Rose to hesitate during her run, not wanting to catch a bad cold. As she was adjusting to the temperature change, a second thought returned to her head. As she sat there, freezing, the word *fire* flowed through her thoughts and went away just as quickly. Rose was puzzled by this reflex and sat on the ground, sulking about her one-word thought. A warm fire would have been perfect right then and would have put off this chill for another hour. She couldn't turn back, for the sun was setting and she would be running against this increasingly harsh, new, icy wind. The sudden chill shocked Rose, for the forest normally mimicked her feelings. She didn't feel cold or unhappy. She started to relax because the thoughts of fire, which came like demons, stopped haunting her. Maybe this was their return, Rose thought angrily. She was no longer content, but annoyed that the night terrors of pride and torment had once again felt unsatisfied by her newfound happiness. The anger pushed inside her and forced the chill to get harder and duller. The forest once again began reflecting her every feeling. She relaxed herself, which she had always known how to do, and the frost calmed its attack. The refreshing feeling of the warmth came back to her when she finally calmed completely down. She stood up from the leaves and nuts that were burrowed under her bottom, and gazed around, preparing for another short run inside her happy place. Thinking of her lake made her feel excited and hyper, so she ran with all her might. This time, Rose galloped over the thorns in her path and jumped mightily over logs and a few huge stumps that did not yield. The atmosphere was gay, and the physical activity made happiness flourish inside her torso. She ran and ran and ran faster and faster to her nearby destination. The lake appeared again within her view. She was shocked that only moments before she had been locked in place by a chill that threatened the woods with cold and misery. Now, by the lake, the wind dissipated so quickly that the woods looked untouched by this adversity and even this hate.

She ran up to her lake and sat down near the little frontage, where the lily pads liked to grow and the neon fish loved to swim. This natural preserve was a paradise filled with life, love, and family. She saw the deer, young and old, find their way to the water and drink from it willingly. Rose smiled at her animals feeding off her water and the birds singing off her trees and the wind running through her air. It was like this forest was celebrating her name. Rose always called this land hers, but she never knew to whom it really belonged. Whoever hunted in these woods never showed themselves, if they even existed. Then again, Rose never actually encountered other people outside her family. She was always hidden because of her uniqueness, as her brother would say when they had passed through towns.

Rose watched the water dance for her again, and the birds sang once more. Her hair was far from perfect. She pulled out her braid to reveal curly locks draping down from her scalp, breathing freshly in the air.

She thought to herself, *Maybe one more try at the fire. Maybe this time it will work.* She stood up again and did her movements, but nothing happened. Was it her stance? she was asking herself to try to reason the answers she needed. Was it her hands?

Then, because of her awful balance, she fell face-first onto the ground. The unforgiving ground bloodied her nose and scraped her face. She dived in the water to clean off her blood and sat there in the water, thinking how to recreate the fire. What was it about the fire that made her want to create it so urgently?

As she scraped off the blood from her pale skin, the water creatures that dwelled in her lake swam up to her and gave her a welcome. They watched intently as she gently scrubbed at her face. Her nose stopped bleeding, and she knew, even if she had just gotten there, it was time to head back. She was tired and needed more sleep, so she walked back instead of running. Rose gazed at her beautiful forest and stopped to visit every tree that loved her so much. She returned their love to the trees by blowing a kiss of thank-you.

She continued her walk back. This time, it took much longer to see her cottage. She arrived, and the anticipation of warm food again filled her mouth with delicious favors. But she was not hungry, and the chilling wind surprised her. The idea of food sounded awry, and somehow eating would have been wrong. The table stared at her dully. Something about the piercing chill that had just passed drew Rose's attention.

"Where are you going?" Celia asked after she placed a bunch of the blueberries Rose had picked earlier into her mouth. Rose ignored the question and walked up the stairs. Rose realized she was also much too exhausted to even create words. She heard forks clanking against the beautiful plates. She heard soft murmurs and then heard rhythmic footsteps that bounced between sides. One's clank was much lighter than that of the other, whose clank sounded bolder. Rose marched into her room, which was shared with her cousin Celia, and lay in her bed.

Sleep sounded wonderful to think on things. Maybe her mind would clear things out. The chill was something her mind needed to focus on, too, but focus was another one of her minor flaws. She was a born multitasking person and rarely could ever give her full attention to any one thing. Rose recognized that her two best personality traits were her grit and her compassion. While Rose's family might also describe her as unique and optimistic, they also knew that Rose cared deeply and was not to be trifled with when she was committed to doing something, anything really. This memory made her recent frustration with making fire even more vexing. As she lay there, gritting her teeth to the sound of the low breeze, she remembered everything she could about the time she made the fire—all the feelings of fire, of heat, and of warmth. Rose desperately tried to remember the individual motions and actions that brought the fire out of her feet. Her head was spinning, and it just go to bet too much for her. She shut her eyes and breathed slowly. In and out. In and out. Relaxing her mind let her run away from anxiety for a short thirty seconds before a soft beating noise from her bedroom door awoke her from her light slumber.

"May I come in?" It was the sweet voice of Celia, the rapping, tapping, smacking on the door following her little voice. Despite her works in hair and grace, she was a very impatient girl. Celia hesitated just for a second or two on the other side of the door as Rose responded, "Sure."

Rose, though her heat was throbbing and her heart was sore, truly did want Celia to enter. She wanted to hear more of the sweet words Celia would kindly whisper into Rose's ear.

The door creaked open. The face of Celia became clearer by the inch as the door opened wider. She stepped in slowly, obviously feeling slightly awkward, and her pace got much slower as she closed the door behind her. Celia moved over, and her elegant blond hair bounced with every move she made. She smiled a touch toward Rose, then the smile broke, leaving the blank face with freckles sprinkled on her nose. She sat on her bed, which was directly parallel with Rose's bed, making it easier for them to talk.

Rose sat up, still feeling slightly light-headed, and looked at her feet, then sat her face up to look in the eyes of Celia Mensch.

"Tell me what's going on," demanded Celia.

Rose looked down, trying to decide whether to lie or tell the truth. She did not know how Celia would respond to either of her stories.

"I'm fine," Rose replied, trying to lie. "I think."

"No, you aren't. For a while you seemed depressed, and then for another while, you were fine. Today you aren't fine," she complained. "We are all worried for you. You're such a pain. Just tell me."

"If I told you, you would be far from believing me."

"No, I wouldn't. It has been a full year that you've been with us. I would never believe you lied to me, because you never would." Celia sounded mature and kind and concerned and compassionate all at the same time.

"Okay, I'll tell you, but you must promise not to tell Aunt Liza."

She nodded.

"A few weeks ago, I created fire. I've been trying to recreate it, but it's not working. I think it means something."

Celia started laughing.

"What's so funny?"

The laughing continued. She snorted a few times, and then once she finally calmed down, she told her. "The reason you haven't been eating is that you rubbed two sticks together in your little park?" she said in between laughs.

Rose was confused; she had never been made fun of in her whole life. She was stressing, and she gasped. "No! I created fire with my feet."

Celia scrunched up her nose and arched her brows.

"I was racing Jason, and fire—*real* fire—burned out of my feet. I've been trying to remake it, but it hasn't worked. I felt depressed because demons in my sleep were trying to mock me because I couldn't do it again. They returned today in a chill."

"They are not demons," Celia said simply. "They are called fears."

"I don't get it," responded Rose swiftly. The puzzled look on her face made it clear to Celia she needed to explain further.

"What do you feel toward this fire?"

"I love it. I want to create it again," Rose said. "I barely remember the feeling of it, but I believe it would make our lives better. I feel it needs to happen."

"Rose, those aren't demons in your dreams. They are fears. You fear you'll lose the magic, and your fears are getting the best of you."

She is right, thought Rose. *Demons aren't real.*

"You love it. Love is something no one can take away from you. In the same way, no one can choose what you love for you. If you love that fire, go make more. Love is the source of all life. If you really feel it, you can really make it happen. And besides, in January, it will start getting cold, and a fire sounds really good right now."

Her influential words really made a difference for Rose.

"Tomorrow I'll come back with a hand of fire," swore Rose. Her spirits were lifted, and her happiness filled her. She knew she would get very little sleep that night, but she knew everything would eventually come together.

The sleep she got that night was scarce. She slept for minutes at a time before being reawakened by her endless excitement. Celia had already gotten in bed and been fast asleep before Rose even got her first full hour of sleep, and only that by adding up all her small minute sleep pauses. She would twist and turn all through her sleepless hours and stay still for small moments and then kick herself into a comfortable position, trying to add rest to her night. Her hair was in a wad, and her clothes would be wrinkled in the morning, but that didn't bother Rose. Her mind was, for the first time, completely focused on her cousin's words, and all she wanted to do was test them out.

She decided, putting her mind to it, that she would get out of her nightwear and run to her lake. She slyly slithered out of bed and slipped off her nightgown soundlessly. She put on her favorite red shirt and her black leggings. Then she pulled on her old winter boots, the ones that she wore in Nava during the harsh, snowy winters there. She silently walked down the stairs, thankful to her lightness that she didn't make a single creak in the wooden stairs. She marched out the door into the moonless night, running quickly through the field and onto her small lake. Without the moon to guide her, she screamed in her mind, telling the woods to move all impediments that could harm her. She watched the trees shift in perfect sequence. She sprinted through the line that opened, untouched by rocks and twigs. She broke apart leaves into little pieces, and little squirrels lurking in her path were pushed away by the wind that wished Rose a nice travel with no interruptions.

As she ran her way through the wilderness, she felt the heat return to her.

Tonight is the night, she thought to herself desperately.

She begged the forest to let her pass. It acceded. She was almost to her destination, with only a huge log in her path. The log was so long and thick it must have once been the biggest, strongest, and largest tree in the whole forest. She leaped over it with all her might and landed on her knees. The fear of failing again hurt more than ever before, but she knew in her heart that her determination mattered. She had to know if she would ever make fire again. She ran farther and farther, faster and faster. She swallowed the wind and slammed anything else that tried to slow her down in the hard mud. Images of the fire danced in her mind. Her stomach smiled, and her throat was dry. She saw her lake. It was right there. The night made it look more blue than purple and made her feel colder than the night air. Her fire would make her feel warm again.

She slowed down as she got closer, then started to walk. Her heart pounded with nervousness, and her head raced with wild thoughts of the magic she would soon create. The amazement in her brother's eyes when she would show him played games in her own mind. The gratitude Celia would feel made Rose blush. All these thoughts piled one on top of the other in her head. She thought of how to start.

She was breathing heavily. She took her stance, arm shoulder length apart. She put her hands out in front of her body. Her mind was racing. All the mind racing went to a buzz, and then the noise went completely black. It was just Rose and the water.

"Please. Please. Please work!" she implored herself out loud. Taking one last breath, she pushed, begging the fire in her to come out. With all her force, she pounded the air. She opened her eyes and felt nothing. Her fist felt colder, and the air felt less alive. She yelled. The frustration inside her made her red lips swell. She felt stupid. Her back ached from the running she did so late at night. Never in her life again would she trust Celia. She felt ignorant, betrayed, and embarrassed that she wasted her night by running to her lake to do absolutely nothing.

Then, the woods shook. Rose's head whipped around each direction as she tried to discover what created the commotion.

Nothing appeared. The stomping shook the ground again. She felt a hot breath exhale down her back. Though scared to look back, she did. Once again, nothing was there. She heard the sound again, and Rose's heart raced. The repetitive stomping of this huge force shocked Rose again. She looked everywhere for whatever created the earthquake.

She looked around once more. Peering everywhere, she moved one of her feet. As she made her first step, the stomping shook the ground again. Out of the mist, an enormous head emerged from an opening in the trees. Two huge nostrils breathed vigorously on her face. She flinched. The beast was more than twice the size of her cottage. The beast moved, so Rose saw its whole body. It was a dragon. It was huge, and it was red. The maroon color covered its whole body. The scales blended in and made it shimmer. Its large red-yellow eyes glared at her, and then the dragon spread out its wings and flapped them together. It brought her more fear than ever. The wingspan had to have been one hundred feet long, and its mouth opened wide to show off the rows and rows of sharp, pointy teeth. After the yawn, it shook its head. Rose stood in awe, mesmerized by the mythical beast. Rose was speechless. The animal spoke merely one sentence to her at first.

"You are doing it wrong," the beast said. It had a raspy voice that was deep and magnetic.

"What?" Rose questioned, her face beaming at the dragon.

"Your form is wrong. You're doing it too hard. To create fire, move your hands in a circular motion, then push out slowly. Control your fire by staying still. If you show fear, your fire will be less powerful."

Then Rose's dragon coach sat and watched her as she stood, trying to put together the words it had just said.

She finally moved. Rose swirled her hands in a circular motion. After a while, Rose felt some heat and pushed her hands out. She stayed steady, and a little spark burst out of her palm and burned above her flesh. She laughed in excitement, her hand staying steady so as not to scare the fire. Rose was shocked that she wasn't being burned.

"You can't get burned," said the dragon. "As a Red Lip, you are immune to fire. It has been such a long time since anyone has seen fire like yours. Notice that it is red. It has been generations since a Red Lip that could control red fire was born."

Rose was shocked, happy, and her breath was taken away. She wanted to make fire repeatedly forever. She felt her differences made her feel important. She asked the dragon a question.

"What is your name, dragon? Where are you from?"

But the dragon never responded; he vanished from the forest with one little flame of fire, which took out her small burn. She looked at her hand, and nothing was there. No burn, no red, and no heat left over. She stared at where the dragon once stood, and a few words popped into her head.

Ashbel, king of Dragons Nest.

Rose

The fire that burned on the logs that next evening burned brightly. The fire was a dark maroon shade, with no yellow or orange ombre mixtures. The heat it created was thrilling. It made Rose feel pleasant and safe, even though it was large. It covered their whole fireplace, and the smell of the burning wood overwhelmed the smell of the magnificent cooking of Rose's aunt. That fire belonged to Rose. While no one was looking, Rose stealthily crawled up to the fire that was dying and created her own. The look of her fire was the same color of her lips, and the small sparks that burned out of her fire reminded Rose of the long sharp scales on the dragon that visited her the other day. Rose's bright eyes stayed staring at her luscious fire as it bounced up and down, remaining still. For small moments, it was completely calm, then as Rose would move, the fire would jump again and start dancing to the crackling noises it was making.

She didn't tell Celia about her fire, even though Rose swore she would. Rose decided to tell no one. The fire would cause worry to her whole family, including Celia. Rose's cousin hadn't asked about the trip to the woods meant to make fire, and Rose didn't mind not having to face questions from Celia about the result of Rose's efforts. Rose assumed that Celia thought Rose had failed and didn't wish to make Rose feel worse. Rose hoped that was what Celia thought.

Small moments during the day, Rose and Celia locked eyes, and Rose was always the first to look away. Fire was all she could think about and was worried Celia could read her mind through her eyes. Fire was something she wanted to keep to herself.

Rose sat there, yearning to create more of her fire.

Maybe I'll add a little bit more, thought Rose. But she didn't, because Rose was worried her family would see. What if someone caught her creating her fire? What would they do? Rose sat there thinking of these problems and watched her fire go up and down, burning the logs to small splinters. She smiled like a proud parent, watching her creation in the fireplace. More than a month of dying to feel the heat one more time had finally left her in peace. All this thanks to a mysterious dragon who visited her in her forest. The last words the dragon said caught her off guard. Dragons Nest was a phrase she knew she had heard before. She didn't want to mention it to her brother and have him worried, but she needed to know where she remembered it from. Sitting in front of her fire, she decided she would ask him about the Red Lips.

After dinner and her stomach was filled, she skipped up to her older brother, Jason. He looked at her once she got closer. Rose noticed his hair had gained back its color and his pale lips looked chapped. His eyes got darker, but they still looked sweet, and he welcomed her with a low smirk.

"Rose," he queried awkwardly, "do you need anything?"

"Yes," she responded. "Do you remember the stories you would tell me when I would get scared as we traveled?"

"Yes."

"And the stories you would tell me to get to sleep?"

"Yes," he said, getting annoyed.

"Will you retell me them, all of them?" Rose inquired, begging for his approval. Rose locked her hands together and gave him the innocent look.

"Fine," he said, sitting down and getting comfortable. He looked at Rose and motioned for her to sit on the ground and listen to him with her full attention.

Rose sat and looked up at her handsome big brother. He smiled at her and began his story.

"A long, long time ago, four dragons by the names of Candice, Edan, Vulcan, and Ashbel ruled the four kingdoms. Candice ruled Ceptem; Edan, Nava; Vulcan, the Red Islands; and Ashbel, king of dragons, ruled Remular. They watched over the Nomads with peace and prosperity. They judged with a keen eye, and a time came when they decided that they should create a special race of Nomads who, by science, were kind and never felt hate or envy. People of this race avoid the urge to kill or harm others and are known as Red Lips.

"The dragons were proud of their children and never wanted any harm to come to them. The dragons protected their people from all evil. Initially, the Nomads thought the Red Lips were divine and needed to be worshipped. The Nomads were amazed by the talent of the Red Lips creating and manipulating fire. At that time, several generations ago, the king became very jealous that the Red Lips were being worshipped more than he was. At about the same time, the Nomads realized that the Red Lips were entirely unable or unwilling to protect themselves. Out of jealousy, the king allowed the Nomads to mistreat the Red Lips.

"Matters got worse for the Red Lips when the heir of that king took the throne. The new king gathered his guards and recruited men to massacre these 'beasts,' as he would call them. His armies became so strong a war grew between the two.

"During this time, the dragons retreated to a hidden place in the Red Islands that they called Dragons Nest. There they called for the strongest Reds, and these Red Lips were given the will to kill the king, but in the end, the nature of the Red Lips prevailed and the Red Lips failed to kill the king. Some Reds who didn't get the blessing to kill did do harm to others and were called to Dragons Nest to be punished. Some say the king had a daughter after his two sons. They say the king was so angry because his daughter was a Red Lip that the king threw her over the castle walls. The story continues that the dragon Vulcan caught the ling's Red Lip daughter before she hit the ground and saved her life. Vulcan is said to have taken the daughter to Dragons Nest and turned her into a princess. Some say she is the princess of Dragons Nest and she is the judge at the dragon trials.

Legend has it that she will kill her father one day, but most Reds think someone greater will end the war."

"But how did she become a Red Lip?" asked Rose.

"Ah, that is my favorite little side story! There was a little well found at the edge of Nava where any Red could go. If a Red Lip puts his or her face inside the well, the water would wash away all the person's Red Lip traits. The queen wished to marry the king, but she was a Red Lip, so she went to the well and washed away what she thought was a flaw and married the king. They had two sons with the Nomad traits. It was only when they had their only daughter that the queen's ruse was discovered, as their daughter, sadly, was born with the queen's flaw."

"So is she still alive?"

"For all I know, she may never have existed," he said. "The princess of Dragons Nest."

"You've never told me her name."

"Aya."

His voice was little now, like he was worried what Rose might think of this name.

"Why did you say that?" Rose asked.

"Say what?" he replied. "I answered what you wanted, didn't I?"

"No, the way you said her name."

He hesitated. "Rose, the reason we had to flee from Nava was because the king believed you and I were a threat to his reign and ordered us to be killed. You are the special Red Lip who can stop the violence and protect the Red Lips. Not Aya! You! Don't ask how I know, but I have been meaning to tell you. I just couldn't find the words to tell you."

"Jason, I really do not know what you mean about violence and protecting Red Lips. What are you saying that I am supposed to do?"

"Rose, you have known all your life that you are special. You may be the most special Red Lip ever born. At some point, you will need to decide if you will fulfill the stories and try to end the reign of the king."

Rose didn't know how to feel. She never wanted to be a part of the war, and now she was right in the middle of it. Rose was so overwhelmed by the flood of emotions that she felt like she was going to faint. Rose felt her mind go clear, her eyes roll back, but she was still standing up. Rose's eyes were covered with small visions of her childhood. Little noises of her mother and father echoed in her ears, then she heard a conversation she must have overheard when she was very small.

"Hide her!" The distant voice of her mother said. Her eyes rolled back farther. She saw and heard nothing from her conscious self.

Then her brother's younger self spoke. "When do I tell her?" But all she could hear from her answer was the low scream of her mom. They must have been attacked because of her red lips. Then the faint words of the dragon spoke to her again.

Come to Dragons Nest.

It was more of a whisper each time it was said. Once it finally stopped, her eyes rolled back up and she stood and looked at her brother. He looked into her eyes, and then Rose dropped to the floor, coughing and crying. She heard a plate break, and then all Rose could hear was a buzz.

*****

Rose awoke the next morning numb all over her body. Her eyes burned from all the tears she shed the previous night. Her hearing was still fuzzy, and her head still spun dizzily. She looked over at her cousin's bed, and Celia was not there. The bed was freshly made, and Celia's pillows were laid out nicely against her wooden bed board, her nightclothes smoothly folded on her rocking chair, which sat in the corner of her room. Rose sat up, and immediately a scorching pain burst inside her chest. Rose collapsed back into her pillow and tried to regain her strength. She knew why she was so frail. The dragon had tried to send her the small message of her coming to Dragons Nest, but that message arrived with the faint childhood memory. The thought of her mother telling her brother to run and hide was so painful. Almost certainly, that was one of the last memories Rose had of her mother. Rose had blocked out all sound and tried to forget it so much that she actually succeeded.

I must go, Rose told herself. *Perhaps the dragons can explain how my brother knows about these things. Maybe the dragons can answer all my questions.*

Rose sat up, this time more slowly. Her muscles ached, her stomach burned with hunger, and her veins pounded because her pulse was throbbing from her anxiety. She slipped on fresh clothing and her winter boots. Her hair was put into a tight ponytail with a rubber band. Her red lips looked like lipstick had been applied; however, her whole face was a blank canvas.

Rose walked down the wooden steps and slid out of sight of her family. Nevertheless, one person noticed Rose's actions. Unaware, Rose quickly burst into a run and then darted to the forest. Rose's hair fell all around her eyes. She didn't know where Dragons Nest was, but she just knew, one way or another, the dragons would find her. Rose had barely even reached the forest when she heard the yell of her brother.

"Rose! Where are you going?"

"Away," Rose said.

"Not to your dumb forest again? Every day, it's you going back and forth to that place. Give it a break. Those trees are probably exhausted from shifting for you."

"My forest isn't dumb, and I'm going to Dragons Nest," responded Rose weakly.

"Why do you want to go there?"

Rose sighed. "Jason, I have to go. I'll be back for you, and we can go stop the king together. Just let me go. Make an excuse to Aunt Liza. Just please don't tell her."

He nodded and turned around to walk back inside.

Rose stood alone. She started walking the opposite way. Facing her forest, she breathed and walked on. Rose was going to the place where four dragons awaited her and where the princess Aya lived. The place was called Dragons Nest.

Samuel

"Busy, busy!" Samuel shouted at the door that had a tattoo that made his chamber shake. "Quiet!"

He carried his royal body to the gold door and opened it with a face of disgust, only to see his loving wife.

"Myra, what do you need? I am busy."

"Oh, I am sure you are. Planning to kill a young girl that you find threatening."

Her face was covered in expensive powders of all different colors. It was a way to show her wealth. Her dress was purple with gold patterns and other talented hand workings. Her crown was tightly fitting, a gold circle with four spikes at the top and four purple jewels. The queen looked like a queen.

"I don't find her threatening. She is a distraction for the people," announced the king proudly as he paced the halls of his study. Purple curtains were draped over the tall stained glass windows. The floor was covered in red carpeting. The chandeliers hung high above them in heavy gold. The couple stood, reviewing their plans to advance south into Ceptem. They had made known that they had already moved, to see what the enemy lines would do, although the attack wasn't planned for months.

"That wretched girl is leading that Red, flying on dragons, of all things! My daughter is a disgrace. I should have made sure she died and not left it to chance. I should have stabbed her right in the—"

"Samuel, please," interrupted Her Royal Highness the queen. "Aya is doing what she thinks is right. We will wait."

"You still love her," whispered the king. He rose from his chair and walked over to his wife, to see her eyes. The queen had dark-brown eyes, long black hair, and tan skin.

"You still love her," Samuel repeated. "No!" he shouted and slapped her across the cheek. A stream of blood flowed down her nose.

"I won't have that. Not my wife. That damned girl will die, and I will make you watch her life leave her body! And you will be grateful that you are still breathing out of that worthless nose!"

A sniffle came out of the queen as she whimpered. She loved that man, sacrificed so much for his happiness and pleasure, even her own daughter. But this man had no love, nothing good in him.

The king, covered in riches of fine jewels, the finest robes, and the most expensive perfumes, turned his royal head to face three men who were burdening him with their data. One man stood proudly in the middle, a purple sash around his chest and bracelets around his wrist. He pointed his finger down at the table all four men surrounded and touched the southernmost detail.

"The Red Islands," he said. "Too many to count, but they are all crawling with Reds. Warm all year around, and they can farm there too. It is a great place to raid while we travel, for the army."

"And the child?" Samuel spat.

"She is hard to follow. Her identity is still a mystery. My men have been searching."

A tall man with long brown hair swallowed hard as his hands were firm to his chest. He seldom looked at the king. Another man, fat and old, nodded leisurely at his king.

"The people keep talking," Samuel said, clearly displeased.

"Yes, my king, we know. The Reds, heathens they are, keep whispering their rumors about the girl."

"After all my attempts to be rid of them, they still exist in great numbers. They thrive in their treasonous joy. They breed and birth like rabbits."

The king sighed as he looked at his map. All the heavens they had made mocked him. Every place they had claimed as their own to rise in numbers. They had poisoned the land, *his* land.

"There is to be a festival, in Ashbelle," the wise purple-cloaked man said. "They are planning a large celebration."

"What does Amos say of this?" the king asked.

"Why, he encourages it!"

Samuel pounded his fist into the table. "You! Fool!" He pointed his fingers to the man whose hair was long and greasy. "Meet with your friends in Hope. Plan a surprise in Ashbelle."

"My king," the fat man declared, "they are dangerous. My most wicked instrument. They cannot be trusted with our will. They will rebel. They are not tamed!"

"Then tame them. They can be a weapon and a curse, as we all know. Use them, I say!"

He nodded and rushed out of the room, leaving the three men to their plotting.

"Now you, Sallemanno, I want a new group. How quickly can you gather?"

"I sail through the Forgotten Ocean in the morning. You may join."

"Indeed I will. Gather my wife. Gather my sons. I am going to create chaos!"

Aya

Rose followed the low sound of the wind, which seemed to be guiding her. She would stop, wait, and listen to hear where the wind would point her to next. Rose saw that the midday light had slowly started to leave her, with only the light of the moon to soon care for her. The day had gone by so quickly, with no sign of Dragons Nest. The wind just showed her the way, but the dragon didn't show up to fly her there. She had always had to struggle to find her answers. Now she was struggling to find Dragons Nest. She was far away from her little cottage and had long passed her lake. She had not eaten her breakfast and couldn't find lunch. It was almost suppertime, and no food had entered her stomach in over a day. She felt sick and needed sleep, but she had an intuition that a dragon was close. Maybe Rose needed this time to prepare for what would come next.

Rose finally stopped to sleep when she knew she was close to the edge of her island. She made a small bed out of leaves and soft twigs. Only a few hours of sleep would grant her peace. Upon her waking, her body was sore because of the unforgiving ground. She lay back down even though her back already ached. Stopping did refresh her feet, even though her body refused to move into a comfortable position. Rose lay there with her arms over her chest, breathing heavily with nerves. She heated herself with her fire. She had a warm red glow around her whole form. Her body glowed, and she was still learning all the different things that she could do with her fire, sometimes without even trying. After the fire in her body went out, she felt cold and empty. She couldn't create more fire because her body was too tired. She shivered because of the coldness in the air. She heard leaves break, and she used all her might to sit up. It was just a small squirrel that had scurried out of one tree and into another. She felt stupid and blind. Grayness covered her eyes, and she felt light-headed again. This time, it was serious, and she collapsed back onto her uncomfortable bed with her eyes sealed shut.

Her dreams were filled with nothingness, and her sleep was filled with pain and aching. She woke up with bumps and bruises in the shape of sticks that had been carried into her slumber during the night and had stabbed into her skin, hard. She woke early the next morning with the urge to fall back asleep, but she had already lost a night on her journey to Dragons Nest. She sat up and sighed. Rose wished she had woken up to her cousin's smile and that she had her brother with her. Most of all, Rose wished a dragon would show up and save her. When Ashbel did not greet her, she got up and found some berries growing in a bush not too far from where she had collapsed. She ate those as her breakfast and drank from a small puddle of water. The water tasted disgusting, like mud and ick mixed into water. There were leaves that floated on top of the puddle. Rose questioned her judgment when she noticed that the leaves were covered in moss and mold. To make matters worse, the small rocks that bordered the puddle were coated with dirt and other filth. Rose choked, gagged, grew light-headed, and then the fluid she drank hurled back out of her mouth. All the mush in the water appeared worse. Rose screamed in frustration. She heard a crack, and hoping it was Ashbel, she flinched happily. But the sound was made by a stag wandering the wilderness. Feeling once again gullible, she got up and walked on.

Her back was hurting more and more as she walked. It was like dull knives took turns poking her in the veins. She screamed when a hard pain burst in her back. One of the twigs she had slept on had left a splinter in the middle of her flesh. Crying, she tried reaching back to pull it out. As she moved her back, it got worse. The splinter started bleeding, and her agony grew. She screamed again. It was a mournful yell that shook the ground around her. She put fire toward her pain, and the heat incinerated the splinter. She screamed and cried as her body expelled the ash from the splinter and her skin resealed above the wound, and she fell to the ground. The little piece of bark made her fall to her knees. She lay there, pale and bruised, tears scattering down her dirty cheek. All she wanted was to find Dragons Nest, find where she needed to go, and find the dragon that so badly needed her to come. Again, her eyes rolled back. She lay there and saw again the words flash through her head. *Come east, the farthest island, the largest volcano. Inside you will find Dragons Nest.*

Her eyes rolled back, and in the distance she saw a faint image of Ashbel. He looked directly at her. She jumped up in pain and ran toward him, running faster and faster, but as she got closer, he would move farther away until the great reptile faded away. She stopped running as she passed through the small dust of smoke where the dragon Ashbel once stood. Her face was dull and confused. With water in her eyes, she put her hands on her head and sighed. Rose brushed her fingers through her long bronze hair.

"Which way is east?" she quietly asked herself. She moved one way and felt her senses. Not east. Again, she moved. West. She turned around, faced the opposite direction, and saw in her mind that it was east. She walked farther, slowly, trying to find where she needed to go. The twigs she stepped on snapped and cracked. These sharp sounds startled Rose, causing her to realize how very frail she was. Looking back toward where she had come from, Rose noticed that she had been walking uphill almost the whole journey, gradually at first, but with even steeper slope now.

"Ashbel, please help," she pleaded to herself, shaking. Only a day away from home, and Rose was going crazy. Going home was an option. The other option was to just keep walking. She begged again for the help Ashbel once gave her.

So close...you are so close, little Rose. So close.

She walked again, to the east.

Rose crested the last big hill, only to arrive at the edge of her island. She looked out over the ocean and saw many other big islands. The Red Islands were so named because the combination of active red lava flows, reflections from the surrounding ocean, and haze born when red-hot lava met ocean water created the appearance of red islands hanging in a sky of clouds. The islands glowed red from the fresh lava streaming from an inexhaustible source. The lava flowed from every island without regard to size. As the red lava would cool, harden, and then crumble, black dirt would form, which was rich in nutrients and made a perfect home for the native plants. The islands were lush with thick vegetation, including beautiful bushes and trees growing to their very ends. Many of the islands had flowers growing from the rocks, and in some areas, a nice bed of sand reached out to the ocean, making playful beaches. Rose could see blue and green flowers with intricate patterns. On one of the nearby islands, roses grew farther in the forests, and beautiful sunflowers stood watch in a field like an army of scarecrows. After staring for a while, Rose noticed that all the islands grew to look the same. Rose was in shock how she lived on an island that had twins that looked just as beautiful. Rose wondered if all the forests could do what her forest could do. Rose turned her head to face the island where she just knew she needed to go. This island was the largest, having the largest volcano and standing big and brown. Rose breathed a sigh of relief and stood mesmerized at the sight of it. The volcano lay at the center of the island, with many cuts and cracks carved into it, allowing passage inside. The rocky and jagged face of the island bore piles of ash and soot, which must have been deposited from earlier volcanic activities. The brown rock made a shell for the nest at the center of the volcano, with molten stone glued onto the volcano's warm blanket.

How do I get there? Rose questioned to herself. She shifted, and some grounded dust and rock fell off her island into the water below. She looked down and gasped. Rose was on the tip of a rocky cliff, and beyond her weary feet was the blue sea. She watched some waves crash against the rocks below her, and she smiled as she wished to touch the water to clean her hands. She wiped her sweaty forehead and coughed. Her red lips were throbbing as her eyes focused on the nest. She touched her lips, and she felt her pulse pounding faster than ever. Rose knew for sure that she had arrived at the correct place.

She started walking slowly down the coast of her island.

"Red fire, green fire, blue fire, purple fire," she said calmly, dreaming of the magical flames.

As Rose was walking, her foot caught on the side of a rock, breaking the rock and causing Rose to trip. As she was falling down the steep cliff, Rose grabbed ahold of a vine, which stretched from her weight and threatened to snap entirely. Frantically, Rose searched for a place to anchor her foot. She was so excited when she found one that fire accidentally radiated from her hand and burned her little vine to a stem. She quickly grabbed onto a nearby rock. One of her feet was dangling, and the other was slipping. Rose's only choice was to jump at an angle and slide down to the sand. Rose believed so truly and deeply that her dragons would save her. She was not afraid of the tumble below her. She began to think of ways to safely escape from the cliff. Fire was one thing that couldn't kill or harm her. She pushed herself up, grabbing as much solid land as she could grasp. With all her might, she launched herself back up the cliff and landed hard. She stood up and looked down. She did her motions, and fire sparked. She pushed it to the edge of the land, where, if she jumped, she would die. She made more fire, and it spread rapidly. She calmed it before it brought harm to trees. She looked down, and with her hand, she made the fireball form into a cushion. She breathed, with her arms stretched out. This action could kill or save her, maybe even do both, and Rose would know in the next few moments. She looked down and cried.

"Oh, please!" she repeated unevenly to herself, her hands shaking as they floated above her middle. She looked down again, and the last thing she saw was the vision of her brother.

As she fell, she gripped the fire and safely controlled her fall. The fall was a large one, and it took ages for Rose to reach the ground. She felt the fire circle her being. The fire sealed everything else out. It covered Rose from her head down to her toes like the stretchy blanket on her bed in the cottage. She could feel the slight warmth, and she also felt the air pushing against her ears. She screamed as she saw the ground rise to meet her body, all while she was covering her face. The fire spread out around her again and pushed her upward when her feet were inches from the ground. Once she stopped falling, Rose's fire collected itself from around her body, shrinking to become as a bracelet on her wrists, then flowing back into her palms. She was left standing alone, with no fire and no way to get off the island. She had made it down to water level. Behind her the red glow shadowed her, and she walked forward to touch the water. It was cold, but not icy. She swayed her wrist in the water, letting her fingers collect the water and feel refreshed. She cupped water in her palms, then splashed her face. She felt relaxed now that she knew she was so close to the nest.

Rose sat for another five minutes, analyzing how she would cross the sea to Dragons Nest on the near horizon. She didn't have a boat, so her only real option, other than sitting around, waiting for help that had not been given to her on the journey so far, was to swim. She took off her boots and took a big breath, hopping into the water. The cold came as a shock and caused her to shiver. It was much colder when she got all the way in. She scooped herself up to the surface and whined. She was freezing and now her clothes were drenched, but she warmed herself with fire in her inner body. The water on her skin evaporated by her heat, and everything around her stayed warm. She felt the water disappear from her clothing, and before long, she was completely dry. She watched as, when she treaded the water, nothing made her wet.

How could someone so young be so talented at fire? she questioned herself mentally. She smiled and then swam on, her hair staying completely dry, as well as the rest of her body. She kicked underwater, which made big splashes. She looked ahead every breath to see the huge brown volcano, keeping this goal as the focus in her eyes. Her fire kept her warm, but as she swam and breathed and watched the volcano, it was hard to also use her powers. But she pushed through it. Staying focused on many things at once was not one of Rose's strengths. She needed to keep calm to control her fire, but she was so excited to see Ashbel again that she was slowly scaring her fire down. She felt herself getting colder and the water touching her clothes. She pushed her guts inside her until they hurt to create more fire. Rose was so exhausted from all the effort that her arms quaked and began to collapse. Water was being pushed up her ears and nose, so her hearing and smell went away. She breathed through her mouth, and water funneled down her throat. She paused and coughed. The coughing continued and turned into choking. Her coughing got harder, and Rose started to drown. Her fire was all gone, and the water was drenching her clothing and her skin. She was surrounded by water and only halfway to her destination, the island with the huge volcano. Her voice couldn't even be heard by the fish in the sea. Her coughs hurt and made her throat dry. It was becoming harder to breathe. Her coughs became closer together. Her throat ached, and so did her fragile head. She splashed all she could around the water, trying to get anyone's attention, but it was no use. She filled herself with fire, and the fire evaporated the water in her throat, so she no longer coughed but the fire reached her head. The pain caused her brain to ache, but all fire burned out when she lost focus.

Her eyes and attention shifted, following a magical beast in the sky. She didn't see all of it, until it became much closer. The sight took her breath away, which was a problem, because she had been in the process of drowning. Renewed with energy from knowing that help was on the way, Rose focused on treading water and staying afloat. She took a deep breath and regained her calm. The dragon flew high above, and the dragon flew fast. The dragon's roar was sharp and magnetic. This dragon was blue, and the shimmer it had was just like Ashbel's. The dragon had the neck of a tree trunk, and the light blue was as light as Rose's eyes. She looked up, and the fire softened on Rose's command. She watched, treading water, as the oversize reptile flew gallantly in the air toward her. The long blue tail was much darker than the rest of its body. She heard it roar so magnificently as it started to descend toward her. It started its fall with ease and cunning toward her.

She was soaking wet, and she had a feeling that the dragon was there to take her to Dragons Nest. She felt sharp claws grab her shoulders, and then she was flying in the air. Rose was carried higher and higher into the sky. The dragon made a sharp turn and nearly threw Rose in the process. Rose's stomach began to become sick again, and her thoughts turned to what would happen next with the dragon. The beast roared again, and it was much louder with Rose much closer to the source. She felt excited, goose bumps lining her arms and legs. She thought she could feel them growing on her pale face.

She bit her red lips to center herself, but her mind raced, trying to calculate and prepare for what would come next.

The magnanimous dragon held her shoulder tightly. The sharp claws grasped her pale skin. She was more aware of the risks from the sky above her than from the water below her. The proximity to the sun boiled Rose's skin, though the apparently still water that shimmered under her dangling feet made her stomach grow queasy. Catching herself, Rose decided that this dragon must be friendly and sent to help her. After all, if the dragon meant her harm, it could have just let her drown or flung her against one of the sharp cliffs nearby. Rose looked directly at the dragon above her, attempting to remember the colors and the coordinated names of the dragons.

"Which dragon are you? Did Ashbel send you? Why didn't Ashbel come to my aid? Wait! Better question! Why didn't any of you dragons help me while I was drowning? Instead, you pushed me to the brink of death!" Rose gushed out. The words became less audible as she spoke, as the sound of the strong winds dominated.

"Your questions will all be answered by Ashbel soon, little flower. The only question I can answer now is Vulcan. I am the dragon Vulcan," said the dragon sympathetically. Rose heard his honesty and honored it.

"I don't understand," she mumbled.

Vulcan did not hear her and instead flew faster to their destination.

*****

Jason woke up the next morning after Rose had departed into the woods. He barely got any sleep. He stayed up, waiting for a blood-curdling scream, a cry of help from Rose, or a plead. One sound. Just waiting. The silence destroyed Jason. Rose could be so far away, and he couldn't help her. He wasn't fast like Rose, and he wasn't special. Jason did not have a connection to the dragons like Rose did. He had only seen the war once, on the day his family was attacked. His mother screamed at him, and his father disappeared. All he had left of his family was Rose, and he wasn't going to lose her too. He had not met his aunt Liza before the journey to this cottage.

To be blunt, Aunt Liza was not the most welcoming toward the two children when they first arrived and claimed to be her niece and nephew. Aunt Liza's demeanor only changed after Jason had broken down in tears while explaining to his aunt, his mother's sister, what happened. Aunt Liza knew what and whom his mother was long for before Jason did. He cried to Aunt Liza. Cried because all he could hear in his head were the screams of his mommy crying for help. He didn't even get to have a proper goodbye. It had been years since he left his mother, but Jason still cried that night as he remembered escaping with Rose. The silence brought him to tears. He quieted his weeping, but then another flood of tears made their way down his tan and perfect skin. He cried because he had a feeling Rose was gone forever and he had no way of helping her return. Rose was calling him. She needed him. She was dying, but Jason could do nothing.

His aunt knew immediately something had happened to Rose.

"Jason, honey, where is Rose? I haven't seen her since yesterday, and she wasn't in her bed last night."

Jason stood. He couldn't come up with a story fast enough. He just plainly looked at her like she was crazy. Then he thought of a response she would never question.

"She needed alone time. After everything that happened yesterday, she went to her lake. She must have fallen asleep there."

"She must be freezing," Celia said, worried. Jason locked eyes with Celia. She had a plate full of fruit. Jason looked farther down the table. There were two empty seats. The seat next to his aunt and a second one next to Celia with a plate of just fruit, no ham or bacon, for Rose. He bit his lip, and he could feel his eyes burning.

This is my fault, he thought.

Believe me, she is not cold, he thought further, remembering her power. He walked on, taking his seat down next his aunt.

"Jason, go get her. She needs to eat," Aunt Liza directed. She looked worried, and Jason knew she knew something was awry. "It is so unlike her to miss breakfast. I know she loves that lake, but not as much as her own bed," his aunt joked, and his younger cousins laughed. His aunt looked at him and gave him a look and winked. He bit into his food ambitiously, trying to end the conversation.

"Jason, may I have a word with you?" asked his aunt abruptly. Jason nodded, and they both got up. Celia eyed her mother and mouthed "Sorry" to Jason.

They moved to the living room, out of earshot of the rest of the family. Jason looked at his aunt with innocent eyes. His hair was still all messy from his tossing and turning during the night. His eyes had saddlebags underneath from the restless sleep. His muscles bleeped out from his white cloth shirt. He sat down, but his aunt stopped him.

"Get up, Jason. Talk to me like an adult. This is serious," she said very powerfully. Jason jumped, his hair flying up and bouncing in his eyes. The brown in his hair looked more copper, like his sister's, in the daylight.

"I know that Rose is going to Dragons Nest. Tell me, why she is going there?"

"Rose went…," Jason said, stuttering from a loss of words. "Rose left because she had this feeling that the dragons wanted to talk to her. I think. She didn't exactly tell me."

"Well, if she feels that way, I mean, she probably isn't wrong. Those dragons love her. She is special to the Red Lip kind," Liza calmly told Jason. Jason was in shock. He looked all around but couldn't find a way to look at his aunt. Her eyes seemed too serious. But he wanted to give her his attention. She deserved his attention. Rose was her niece and relative too.

"How do you know that?" Jason asked, looking at her nose.

"When your mother had her second baby, Rose, a dragon by the name of Ashbel talked to me about how she was going to be very powerful and special. He would not stop explaining to me how important she was to the war. So I knew then that the dragon loved her. He wouldn't call her for no reason. He is probably going to tell her what I'm telling you now and what you told her the other day."

Jason didn't know she knew all this, but she had known from the moment little Jason and Rose entered her home who they were. This confused Jason. All his life at her home, he felt all this was just as much of a mystery to her as it was to him. When they entered her home unannounced, Aunt Liza had such pain in her eyes when he told her that his mother had died. He just thought the rest of the story was all a mystery to her as well.

"Believe me, I know Rose. She is special and the best of the world. I can't imagine losing her. She is all I'm worth living for," Jason pronounced quietly. He knew Aunt Liza saw the wetness and worry in his eyes. Jason could see it in her eyes too. But why? Why was this one time that Rose left home so emotional for them both? Had they both had a feeling she was gone forever, like the rest of Jason's family. Why was this one runaway so impactful on his aunt that she told him her story? All these questions bounced around in Jason's head before those thoughts were interrupted by the one word his aunt said.

"Jason," said his aunt moments later. Her brownish hair had waves through it. Her clothes were freshly washed, and she still smelled of the fragrances that she had when she bathed. Jason looked at her, waiting for her to finish her sentence.

"Yes?"

"Promise me you'll protect her," she said, starting to cry. "She is all I have of her. She is all I have left of Katrina, you and her."

"I will."

ROSE

Before the dragon landed, he hovered above the ground for a moment, spreading and beating his wings to slow his speed. His hind legs landed on the huge volcano that was Dragons Nest and absorbed most of the shock from the impact with the unforgiving ground while his front claws tenderly placed Rose on the ground. Their landing sent the island trembling. His blue scales shimmered as the dragon walked along the side of the volcano into a hidden entrance. Rose was dazzled by all the forms of the rocks and the beautiful imprints the water had made while crashing in waves upon the rocks. She saw the heat from the lava as she walked. Her body was aware of the dangers from being so high on a rocky surface and compensated with additional focus. The dragon huffed and puffed as it walked in front of her. The smoke poured out of his large and beautiful nostrils like gas leaking out of a cauldron. The scales shimmered while the sun sparkled on them. She felt calm looking at the beast. His blue features looked like the sea. Vulcan was a gorgeous dragon. His sharp claws dug in and out of the solid rock surface on which they both were standing. He appeared more majestic with his every move, but the volcano, on the contrary, appeared more unstable because of the motion. Rose couldn't decide whether to watch the dragon or the fresh lava flowing from a vent somewhere in the volcano.

Her selection process was interrupted by Vulcan when he spoke to her. "First things must be first. This place, the volcano and the home inside, is called Dragons Nest. Originally, it was called Dragon's Nest as the possession of Ashbel, who is the oldest of the four of us.

As it happens, I am the youngest, and Candice and Edan are both middle-aged, for dragons. Anyway, not too long ago, in dragon years, the four of us got into an argument about who possessed this home and whether or not it shouldn't be all of our home instead of just being recognized as the home of Ashbel. Let's just agree that the competitions we engaged in were, frankly, quite dangerous *and* counter-productive," expressed Vulcan, flicking the wrists of his front claws, "to say the least." He paused. "Anyway, I remember it was Candice who suggested that it would be *healthier*," continued Vulcan, flicking his wrists again, "for the four of us to view the name of this place as a declarative instead of as a possessive. Instead of arguing over who *owns* this nest, we agreed on that dragon's *nest* here and call it *Dragons Nest* and have since avoided any further drama on the topic. We came here because of the war."

Rose responded with a chuckle, then a stutter and hesitation.

"The words you speak confuse me. Who else is there that wishes to contact me, and why didn't they help me sooner?" She wondered if her vocal tone would sound too fierce for the creature. After all, he did save her, but he also probably watched her suffer throughout the journey.

"The rest of us dragons are here of course, and Aya, the princess of the dragons, lives here. Erik, the chief of the Blue Lips, has also come here to meet you," said Vulcan politely, trying to be a good host. His hips swayed in front of Rose, as if to intimidate her.

"I beg your pardon? Blue Lip?"

"Yes, child," Vulcan explained. "Erik was born with red lips, much like yours. The king personally ripped them off his face when Erik was a teenager. Erik is middle-aged now, and the wound has healed, leaving blue bruises where his red lips had been. Try not to stare at them."

"If Erik is chief of the Blue Lips, then there are others like him?"

"Oh, my child, you Red Lips are so needy. Why did we even create you in the first place?"

Rose felt taken aback by that comment. What was that supposed to mean? Did he regret making the Red Lips, because they asked too many questions?

As they curved around the volcano, she saw an entryway to a huge open cave. It was very round but had some sharp ends to the surrounding barrier. The curve of the entryway was huge and a dark, oily brown. The structure looked ancient but also brand-new, since from Rose's view there were no cracks or molding or age erosion. She was awestruck by all the beauty in one hole in the side of a mountain, but all she could think about was the beauty it held within.

"Come, little rose. This is where you must climb on my back," said the beast with no hesitation. His body stopped moving, and he was waiting for Rose to climb on to it. She slowly moved forward, her hair shifting to in front of her eyes. She pulled the strands back to behind her pale ears. She used them to listen to the slow breath of the dragon. His back went up and down, slowing as it sighed in and out impatiently. She took her first few steps cautiously, then moved more quickly when she felt safe. Her boots sanding the floor. When she touched the dragon, her hands glowed with fire. Fire that she had not used in a while. She burned into him, politely, since she knew the dragons gave her this fire. She returned it into him. She could feel a warm smirk coming from Vulcan. He shifted the weight from his left foot to his right foot, making Rose pull back. He felt bumpy, and his texture was rough. You couldn't pull back on the scales for fear that would rip them, and pulling forward would imprint them into the second layer of his body. She went back in for the pet, after his feet had shifted. She touched him, then, after a millisecond, moved her hand gently around the area where her hand could move. She petted the beast in a circular motion, calmly. She wanted to show, not tell, the beast that she trusted him. Then she took down her hand from his side and sighed. She tugged her beautiful brown hair back into a fake ponytail and then let it go. Her blue eyes stayed concentrated on one part of his body. Once her pale hands dropped to her side, she lifted them up and placed them higher on Vulcan's body. Then she took a firm grip on some fur the dragon had on his back and pulled herself up onto his back. It was a struggle. Her muscles were weak and were barely useful, but she found a way. She placed her left foot on the side of the dragon, feeling his bone, with her heel still in the air. She gave one last yank, and her knee was balanced at the top of the creature. Then she pulled her right boot over to the opposite side of Vulcan and she was sat on him like riding a horse. She sat waiting for him to move. She was excited and impatient. She was just outside Dragons Nest. She couldn't believe it. She was so ready to fly like a dragon, while properly riding one. She waited in anticipation for the show to continue. She collected her hair and put it onto her left shoulder. She smiled with her red lips. She could feel the dragon get ready to take off. Her mind raced, again, with thoughts of the dangers and how she might compensate to prevent the chance she would fall. Rose balanced the exhilaration that came from flying with Vulcan against the control she maintained by walking and decided to challenge the dragon.

"I don't want to fly, Vulcan," she said with determination in her voice. Her hair moved from her shoulder back down to her back. The sound of the blue waves crashing against the volcano filled the background. Seagulls chirping also made the cut for her ears.

"Yes, you do, little rose. Don't overthink this and let those demons enter your brain. That will be your downfall, just like your father," he said.

My father, thought Rose. She pondered what that meant. It had been such a long time since anyone had mentioned her father.

"Vulcan, let me down!" she said after remembering that her father, according to Jason, had died. She didn't want to die like her mother and father so heroically did years ago. To protect her. Was that to mean they died in vain? No. Rose would not accept it.

"I'll walk down," Rose continued, but Vulcan insisted.

"No, child. Impossible. Come, you are wasting time. Ready?"

"Fine," she said simply. She felt the small smirk of Vulcan grow. He trembled.

"This should be fun," she heard him whisper.

His wings spread from each side. Roughly they pounded, flapping repeatedly until the wind grew so strong that he lifted his feet off the dirt ground. The sea looked the same. The entrance looked the same, but slightly deeper. Rose's heart raced with excitement. She looked around and back at her home island. It looked so small and far away. She mapped out where she had just been and had nearly drowned. It all looked so beautiful. The sky was a bright blue, and the sounds of Vulcan's wings made the sea sound like a small cricket humming. She smiled, and rapidly her smile turned into a roar, a roar of victory. She was going to conquer and save this world. She laughed hysterically.

Then Vulcan dived.

She spun forward, screaming with joy like a small child on a roller coaster. The adrenaline filled her veins. She burned and put fire inside herself, so she glowed. She wanted to enter Dragons Nest glowing with fire. As they twisted and turned through the tunnels, she yelled louder. She bled with happiness. She was doing this for real people. She enjoyed herself at that very moment. She yelled again. Vulcan enjoyed himself as well. He was flying very fast and challenging gravity. His tail sharply cut through the air to control his direction. Rose coughed and lifted her hands off the fur on the beast's back. His hair flowed wildly, and so did Rose's. The next turn they faced, her hair spun that way, and the sharp ends of her hair whipped around and poked her in the face. She yelped, but still her red lips and pale cheeks beamed. It was as if Rose were a newborn child again, without any pretense of controlling her surroundings, having that illusion replaced with a simple confidence that those responsible for her would care for her. She let Vulcan control her every movement. The tunnel sank deeper and darker until she finally saw the smallest light.

As they got closer to the light, the light got brighter and bigger. Vulcan slowed down, and once they entered the room, Rose realized how grand the room was. They circled the inner walls of Dragons Nest. Rose calmed her yelling and only adjusted her posture on the dragon. She pushed her toes forward and lunged backward with her shoulders. Her hair jumped on her back as she extended her arms back out to grasp his beautiful blue fur. She pulled herself closer to him. Her skinny chest bumped his back. She bent her pale forehead to the neck of the dragon, calming and steadying herself, preparing to land.

As they circled the walls for a second and third time, they got closer to the ground. There were five other beings on the floor awaiting their arrival. From the air, three of them looked to be dragons, and two others looked like people. She couldn't make them all out since they were still very high up, but as they circled the fourth and fifth time, their relationship with the ground became one last circle away. Her heart skipped a beat when she realized this. The final spin around was the longest one because all Rose wanted to do was meet all the other beings in the room. They hit the ground with a large bang. Vulcan silenced his wings and then stood up with all his beautiful, sharp, dazzling blue claws on the ground. Clouds of smoke circled Rose and Vulcan because he had flown so fast. He huffed through his nose and nudged for Rose to get off him. Rose sat mesmerized.

She was in Dragons Nest. It was an enormous one-room cave inside the volcano. The brown walls looked painted with slight shades of red and blacks and copper. The walls had curves and structure. She had never seen anything like this place before. It was the grandest room she had seen. It had the shape of a ballroom but the capacity of hundreds of thousands of ballrooms. It was big and brown. At the top of the nest was a huge ball of fire. The fire was red. It looked like Rose's fire, and Rose saw the comparison too.

She looked ahead of her, and there, all in a row, stood three more dragons. They were all sitting powerfully on huge golden thrones. The thrones all had different patterns on them. One had some vine imprints. Another throne had water imprints. Ashbel's throne showed the story of how the Red Lips came into being. The history lesson began in the back of his throne. It showed Ashbel creating his first Red Lip and a Nomad watching from the sides. It was beautiful. All the thrones were, but not as beautiful as the beasts sitting on them. The one farthest to the right was a dragon Rose had not seen before. She was mighty and looked buff. Her scales were a brilliant shade of green. Her eyes looked like emerald stones, and her lashes looked like dark black waves. She didn't show her teeth, but the low cheekbones she had showed she wasn't one for smiling. She was wise like Ashbel and not free-willed like Vulcan. Rose could tell all this just by looking at her. Just by connecting eyes with this dragon, Rose knew that her name was Candice, the only female dragon. Candice's tail had curly fur at the bottom, and small roses were imprinted on the sides like a tattoo. She sat at the throne with vines.

Next to Candice was a beast Rose recognized. Ashbel, king of Dragons Nest, was how he had titled himself to Rose in the forest. So much had changed since that first encounter, even just in the last day. Rose smiled at him, but he did not smile back. Ashbel looked grave and worried. His red scales and fur matched the color of her fire. Both his scales and fur seemed grayer, and his eyes were pale. His giant throne fit him perfectly, but she knew he obviously didn't want to be here. Next to him was a beast sitting on the throne of waves. Edan, the dragon of Rose's home country, Nava, was purple and looked serious. He had shiny lavender scales that rippled all along his body, curving at every curve and ending at his long spiky tail. His eyes looked red, not purple. They seemed foreboding and dark, like they were hiding many secrets. Edan appeared mad, unlike Vulcan, who was taking his seat confidently. Vulcan knew his aerial show wouldn't be the last show of the day. He sat at a throne next to Edan on a throne of kings. It had an image of every powerful Red Lip on it, so they would never forget why there was still a war.

Rose's attention shifted to the Blue Lip Vulcan had referred to as Erik. The years had not been kind to him, and the dark-blue bruises that had formed where his lips had once been were an assault on the eyes. He had grown a disheveled beard as a partial disguise for the wounds and was otherwise quite average and unremarkable. He put little effort into personal hygiene and outward appearance, perhaps as a conscious admission that his only feature that mattered was the one he did not have. At the same time, his eyes were confident and could command any room. He sat unflinchingly when Rose noticed him and prepared to introduce herself to him.

Rose's introduction was interrupted by movement out of the corner of her eyes. This, then, was the moment that Rose had most anticipated. Rose saw her, the woman Vulcan must have referred to as the princess. Her long dark skin shimmered when she moved. She had hair down to her ankles, and it was even darker than her skin. She wore a dress only a royal could wear. The straps intertwined down to her fingers. Long gold vines of roses flowed down her torso.

Her face was clear and dark. She had a warm smile and appeared to be only a few years older than Rose. Her arms stretched out toward Rose. She walked toward her, getting up from her throne. She had been sitting on a throne with no imagery, just a blank backboard. Her dress flowed behind her. On her head was a crown sculpted to show the four dragons above the lands they ruled. Ashbel was above a castle, Remular, and Vulcan was above three huge volcanoes. As the woman got closer to Rose, Rose stretched out her hand to the princess. They touched, and a spark of blue fire gleamed in between them. The princess giggled, and Rose smiled. The princess's white eyes twinkled. She looked so beautiful, and her hair was perfect compared to the matted mop that Rose's hair had become. The princess's dress was the definition of stunning. The way she walked in it was like she was built to wear it. Rose did not know what to do, so she stood there with fire in her hand and the princess's fire across from hers. They both stood and smiled awkwardly at their creations, like it was the most important thing ever. They were spellbound, staring at the flames.

"My name is Aya," introduced the princess.

"Of course, it is. I am Rose."

Then the princess focused on Rose. The princess smiled a warm and contagious smile. The princess, who had once been the victim of attempted murder by her very own father, smiled at Rose.

Rose smiled back, her cheeks burning. She knew they were red. The blushing of her cheeks made the gums of her mouth rip. She felt light-headed and special. Her hair flowed timelessly down her spine, drooping like a fishhook. She stared at Aya, staring into her silver eyes. They had a tint of mint-colored blue in the center of her silver pupils. They appeared majestic, and mysterious, like a million secrets were hidden under their surface. But Rose knew that she, too, had secrets hidden in her eyes, secrets that she didn't want to be the chosen Red Lip, secrets that she wanted to just leave. Rose felt intimidated by Aya. Some secrets Rose would never reveal.

"Your fire is beautiful," Aya said, putting out her fire and placing her hand over Rose's. Her hands were cold, unlike the rest of her body.

Rose nodded in reply.

Aya nodded back.

She stepped a bit closer to Rose, softly gripping her wrist. She intertwined their knuckles until their hands were locked together as one. She grabbed her elbow and walked her on toward Aya's throne. Rose was shocked and speechless. What was Aya planning to do with her? The dragons watched intently, and the Blue Lip looked impatiently at Rose. Ashbel stared at her with a warm-eyed glare, his old fur curled around his eyes. Vulcan's new fur curved directly in front of them. The other dragons stared like they just wanted the entertainment of "princess meets warrior" to end. But Rose didn't feel like a warrior. She wanted to go back home to her brother and cousins, but she got distracted when Aya led her to the throne. Aya placed both hands on Rose's shoulders and pushed her down into the throne, her dress swaying. Aya looked confident but didn't lock eyes with Rose in the process. Once Rose was on the throne and comfortable, Aya did the unthinkable. She took off her crown, with all four dragons and kingdoms on it, and carefully placed it on Rose's head. It fit perfectly. The crown pushed her curls down, and some strands of hair were pushed in front of the corners of her eyes. Rose put her hands on the handrests of the throne and tightened her smile. Rose was confused why she was going along with all this. Rose wasn't royal. She didn't understand what it meant to save the world, and she certainly had not done anything of the sort yet. Why were they honoring her? She had done nothing except nearly drown on the way to Dragons Nest.

The dragons all got up and flew above Rose. When they landed, they all stood in a row behind Aya. The Blue Lip chief stayed still, with a bored expression on his face, like he had seen this same performance before. All the dragons looked serious, like this time was different. What surprised the dragons and even the Blue Lip was that Aya bowed first. Aya got down on both knees, on the floor, first. The dragons stood motionless as this was happening.

Then Aya said, "Ashbel, its's her. She's the one."

Aya stared up at Rose, like she was seeing the light, and smiled at her. Ashbel then nodded back toward her and bowed too. In rapid succession, Vulcan bowed, then Candice, then eventually Edan.

Once that happened, the Blue Lip looked toward Rose and put both his hands out, bowing his head while refusing to get up out of his throne. Then Rose made eye contact with Aya. This was what Rose was supposed to do. To be with them and help these six life forces was what mattered. At some point, Rose was confident they would explain to her what saving the world meant. Rose just felt a sense of belonging with these beautiful creatures while, at the same time, being terribly humbled by her modest credentials. While being with these beings in Dragons Nest mattered, what mattered the most to Rose was attending to her brother and aunt and cousins. Aya must have known that Rose's thoughts had shifted to Rose's family, because Aya nodded to her, approving, wanting to keep Rose's family safe too.

But she must have also seen how Rose was confused, because after the longest time, Aya said to Rose, "Rose, you are the chosen Red Lip. You are the one!"

Rose couldn't breathe.

CELIA

Celia, the eldest of Liza's three children, was very close to Rose throughout the one year that Rose was a part of their home. Their father was torn from them by the world's civil war. Some good Nomads would fight the battles against the king's army for the Red Lips, so they had more of a chance of winning. Sadly, he died in battle less than four months before Rose arrived. Celia always knew Rose needed extra protection from this war. When Rose and Jason arrived, Liza brought all her children into the main room and told her children all that Liza knew about who Rose was. Celia's mother made her children understand that they could never tell Rose, because other people owned that responsibility. Timing was everything, and Celia's mom explained to her children that messing up the timing would be like undercooking or overcooking a cake. Raw or burnt if they got involved, and just okay if they let others do their job. The children all knew that *others* almost certainly meant dragons. The children also knew that dragons created Rose and that dragons once ruled over the world with dreams of creating a Red Lip destined to be just as powerful as Rose. Celia never questioned the reality that, in the end, there might no longer be a Rose to be with, just like in the end, there was not to be a father to play with.

The lake Rose was obsessed with was once Celia's. But she gave it up to Rose because it was in Rose's name. The lake listened to Rose.

Celia's bedroom was once just hers, but she had to give that up too. Sharing a room with Rose was necessary so that Rose had a place to sleep, and it had its advantages.

Celia did so much for a person Celia might, in the end, never see again.

That was the pain her mother one year ago warned her about, the pain of losing someone to someone else. The king had been cruel to not only Red Lips but people who supported them as well. He was envious of their magic and connections to the dragons and how people, his subjects, loved them more than they did him. For he was the king, and no one could take that from him. Rose was supposed to be that person, the person to take it from him. Celia didn't believe she could do it. Until she heard Rose's side of the story. One early morning, during their first few nights in the cottage, Celia and Rose had a conversation starting with one question.

"Why am I who I am?" asked Rose. Her brown hair was shorter that day. Her red lips were pursed, and her muscles didn't exist. Celia sat in the bed next to her and listened for the sounds of her family and the courage to tell her what she knew without spoiling Rose's future. Celia knew Jason told Rose about the Red Lip heritage during their travels. Celia quieted down to make sure no one else was near. She heard the faint cry of her little sisters. They must have fallen and were waiting for their mother or Jason to take care of them.

"Do you not know who you are, Rose?" asked Celia. They were face-to-face with each other. Celia saw that tears were forming in the eyes of little Rose. Her mind must have been racing. Celia knew she had to lie to her, but a newfound respect for Rose gleamed inside Celia.

"I know who I am, Rose Hide Mensch, but like, *who* am I?"

"That's right! Rose Hide Mensch. Do you know what that means, Rosie? You are a leader, a lighthearted and fun person. But you know what else you are? You are a warrior, a fighter, and a saver. That's what you are, Rose. That is what you will be."

"I like that. I hope the war ends and no one else has to get hurt, not like my mother and father. And I hope the Nomads don't win the war."

"Just stay safe, Rosie," Celia said plainly. All Celia wanted was for Rose to live and come back to Celia after the end of the war. That was something her father did not do. Celia's mother would drown herself in tears if she was sent the fallen bodies of Rose and Jason. They were like her children now.

Celia shuddered at the thought of Rose having to kill the king to end the war. How was it that Rose, an innocent Red Lip, would be able to kill? Rose might not be loved by the Reds after the murder of the king, because it could go either way. The Red Lips could hate her, or they could love her. For Reds didn't kill. It was not in their identification. It wasn't normal for them. Many Reds had tried to kill the king and others like him, but none of them had had the stomach to do it. Rose could kill to save her kind, or Rose could kill and betray her kind.

Erik

Rose awoke with a start, her head with a heavy tattoo. The crown had slanted on her face, dipping over her eyelashes. The chamber she was in was different from the one with the thrones. The throne she was on had disappeared, and now she was sitting in a chair, above a large room. There was a series of chairs below her.

Ashbel, Vulcan, Edan, and Candice all sat upon their marked thrones.

There was a slight echo of words, spoken only between Aya and Ashbel, words Rose couldn't hear. They were powerful, filled with relevance, heated with the colors of passion. The Blue Lip, who was both short and fat, was dressed in a dirty robe. He chimed into the conversation, his voice jumping as he drank the final sips of his red wine.

"Rose," the strong voice of Ashbel announced. "I must apologize. Did we overwhelm you so?"

"The child is obviously frightened, fool. Should we offer her some wine to drink?" the Blue Lip suggested.

Rose denied the drink, her voice still shaking. She tried steadying her breath while watching Aya as the flow of Aya's hips waltzed through the grand room. Aya would occasionally glance up at Rose and smile her dark red lips toward her, in hopes to comfort her trouble.

There was a long pause as everyone in the great room shuffled to their assigned places, the dragons on their thrones, Aya on her golden chair, and then Erik, the Blue Lip, upon a small stool with a large glass of wine next to it. Rose then found herself tensing her pale back against the chair that looked over the other chairs. The feeling of the cool metal against her body relaxed her. She waited intently for any clue that something was about to happen. It was the sound of Ashbel's mighty voice that perked Rose's ears.

"Rose," he said again.

"Ashbel," Rose declared, her voice much louder than his. "Why did you call me here? I left my home in search of answers, then I nearly drowned. Please tell me why you have called for me."

"Rose," Ashbel began, his voice less mighty now, "you know your destiny?"

Rose shook her head in denial.

"A buffoon," the Blue man rasped. "You have put the fate of the world in the puny hands of a buffoon!"

He was promptly hushed by Ashbel with the quick whip of his scaly tail. The room was silent. Ashbel looked up at Rose with his yellow eyes.

"You have been told your role by your brother, haven't you?"

Rose stuttered. "I know that what I am to do isn't just, that I am to kill someone. Though I must be honest and say I don't understand what that means."

The Blue Lip laughed, his swollen lips stretched wide to expose the rusted, rotten yellow teeth he bore inside his hideous mouth. "The child is an idiot!"

"Erik!" Aya exclaimed. "She is as innocent as you once were!"

"I do know things die. Both my parents have died, and my uncle," Rose interjected, her hands crossed over her budding breasts.

"Yes, this orphan was raised by her brother. A brother who hid you from the wretched world and all the world's thieves and murderers and terrors. What a kind soul," Erik said, sipping another gulp of the wine. "Do you wish to know how my lips became the way they are? The king ripped them from my face after I told him my fire wasn't to be used for his envious desires! The world already has so much hate. Let's keep this one this way. She should stay the way she is."

"Didn't you just call her an idiot?" Aya's eyebrows arched, her dark fingers resting upon her hips.

"I doubt her in every way imaginable. That does not mean I do not care for the thing!"

"Erik, you are so naive. Let her decide which path she should follow," Ashbel said calmly, his breath heavy. "There is so much more to this than what is being spoken."

"More powerful people than her have tried and failed. The king still lives, and he will continue to live. There is no point in losing the innocent for the ultimate failure," Erik reasoned.

Ashbel interrupted impatiently, asking, "Rose, do you know how you came to be?"

Rose hesitated and admitted, "Ashbel, my brother Jason has told me tales that seemed like fairy tales about how different parts and peoples of the world came into being. It is difficult for me to know the difference between fairy tales and the real world."

"Let me help," responded Ashbel in the deep voice of a father to his creation. "We dragons have existed on this planet with the Nomads for a long, long time. Many generations ago in Nomad years, the four of us dragons decided to sacrifice parts of ourselves and to tie our futures to helping the Nomads evolve."

Rose watched intently with new focus.

Ashbel continued, "At that time, the four of us each infected one hundred newborn children with our dragon blood. Pathogens, or tiny organisms from our blood, traveled within the veins and arteries of these babies, making their way to the infants' brains. Once inside the babies' brains, these pathogens severely limited blood supply to the central or animal-instinct part of the babies' brains and proportionately increased blood supply to other portions of the brain. It is in these areas of the brain that love for one another, thoughtfulness, and connection with the environment are fostered. The additional blood supply also manifested itself in physical ways, making the lips turn a deep red and enabling these babies, once they matured, to create and manipulate fire."

Rose was spellbound and unconsciously touched her lips in acknowledgment of the special connection to the dragons.

Ashbel continued his story. "Rose, we dragons took this action to bring about an improvement and an evolution in the Nomads. We saw a world increasingly filled with gluttony, sloth, lust, greed, pride, envy, and wrath. We were committed to helping the Nomads be born again through the physical example of this chosen race of Red Lips. We knew that the pathogens in the dragon blood would enact a permanent change in the genetic makeup of these selected infants and that their progeny would continue on with these features and with different character traits."

Ashbel paused and took a deep breath before continuing. "We dragons have recognized the origins of evil in the central animal portion of the Nomad brain. This instinctual organ creates a false choice within Nomads when confronted with natural and unnatural forces. Instinctively, Nomads had come to fear dangers and reacted by either fighting or fleeing. If you live in harmony with nature, you have no need to be afraid of nature. You certainly would not need to fight with nature or run away from it. At the same time, nature has a way of noticing those organisms that are not in harmony. Nature responds in ways designed to return balance. Over time, the Nomads had posed real threats to the environment, so the environment responded to physically threaten the Nomads into more responsible and harmonious activities. Does this make sense, Rose?"

"Ashbel, I can see the things you are describing in the life I have lived the past year," Rose quickly shared. "In my forest, the living creatures respond to me with such strong alignment and support. I have to admit that I did not actually understand what you meant when you mentioned gluttony, lust, wrath, and the other traits of the Nomads."

"Rose, that is because you are a Red Lip," responded Ashbel. "The seven character traits I mentioned develop as a result of the animal part of the central brain. This portion of your brain has not developed because you carry the Red Lip genes. This part of the brain places an absolute priority on surviving and continuing to live. It is not like being without this instinct, we would all just perish. Living in harmony with the environment means that you accept death as a natural part of the life cycle and are not anxious about the recycling that occurs as a part of death."

Rose contributed, "I saw this happen with the seasons during the years when Jason and I were traveling to Nava. The winter freeze would terminate certain forms of life, only to have the spring thaw nourish their children."

Ashbel smiled gratefully at the wisdom of this innocent child and continued, "At its best, this instinctive portion of the Nomad brain helps them survive when confronted by dangers. At its worst, this portion of the brain taxes the environment by causing several mental disorders related to the priority Nomads place on surviving. Gluttony is the drive to consume much more than is required due to anxiety about not being able to get what will be needed in the future to survive. Sloth is the avoidance of physical work out of anxiety over not having the energy to take necessary future action. Lust is the excessive craving for pleasures of the body created by anxiety over what will be available in the future. Greed is the excessive desire to hoard wealth and other resources out of a belief that this will aid a Nomad's survival. Pride comes from the confidence in your own abilities at the expense of others, as survival can pit Nomad against Nomad in unhealthy competition. Envy is the desire for the abilities, status, characteristics, or situation of another and is driven by the anxiety that another person will survive better or longer than you will. Of the seven characteristics, wrath is the worst and is a rejection of love in favor of its opposite, fury. Wrath drives Nomads to hurt and even kill one another in the belief that it will help them survive longer."

Rose interrupted softly. "Ashbel, I know that the words you have spoken have meaning, and I do not understand why Nomads would act in these different ways."

"Little flower," Ashbel confided, "you do not understand because your brain accepts the natural order and priority of survival. The animal part of your brain has not forced you into the false choice of fight or flight when you perceive danger. Your brain acts in a third way. When you are put at risk of loss, your brain responds by trying to figure out a way to reduce the risk of harm, with compassion and love for your surroundings, and with an acceptance that if you do not survive, then it is to suit some higher purpose in nature."

"Ashbel," Rose commented with excitement, "you just described how I acted and responded when I was falling down the cliff on my journey to Dragons Nest!"

"Exactly, Rose," Ashbel affirmed. "You found a creative way down because your brain focused on solving the problem rather than being anxious about surviving. The problem with the animal brain is that danger limits Nomads' choices to fighting or running away. Over time, this stress can cause Nomads to only see these two actions as the real alternatives."

"Ashbel, my friend," interrupted Erik between sips of wine, "this history lesson is all well and good, but when are you going to break it to this innocent little girl that we need her to give up her life of peace and become corrupt like the rest of us?"

Ashbel continued patiently, seeming to ignore the outburst from Erik. "Rose, there is a problem between the Red Lips and the Nomads. We dragons had hoped the Nomads would see the peaceful and harmonious way that the Red Lips live and evolve. Many of the Nomads, particularly those with power and authority over other Nomads, like the king, have felt challenged by the Red Lips."

On mention of the king, Erik sank back on his stool and returned to his wine.

"Over time, rather than see a positive example in the Red Lips, the Nomads became jealous of the *special powers* of this *chosen race*. The Nomads also discovered that the Red Lips were neither equipped nor capable of defending themselves or protecting what Nomads might recognize as the Red Lips' possessions. Nomads found that they could take from the Red Lips without consequence and even kill Red Lips without any form of retribution. The king and those in power ostracized Red Lips, attributing weakness to the Red Lip genes and even directing parents of Red Lips to cut their lips off at birth and abandon these *abominations* in the forest with the other Forgotten Children."

"I cannot pretend to understand why a Nomad would tell another Nomad to hurt a child," Rose admitted. "Or why any parent would listen and comply."

"Which brings us to the reason that I called you here," responded Ashbel. "If you are going to help us protect your people, the Red Lips, you are going to have to sacrifice your innocence and become infected with purple fire. This infection will awaken the animal part of your brain, with all the anxieties that entails, and put yourself at risk of all the mental disorders I listed. I regret that it comes down to this, but you need to recognize evil to stop it."

"Rose, don't do it," counseled Erik. "You might very well sacrifice everything and gain nothing."

"Rose can handle it!" Aya fought. She didn't seem to enjoy the presence of Erik.

"Though she must choose to give up her innocence willingly," Vulcan advised, and Aya agreed.

Rose watched as they began to bicker over the small details of the situation. She laughed at some, though she was confused at others. She wanted to help, but she was confused by some of this discussions. She watched the brown walls grow taller into the sky, and the cave's carvings and red paints along the walls. She saw the polished floors and the winding vines that decorated her podium. She listened as she looked, her fingers tapping along to the beat of their voices.

"When is it all right to give up one's innocence?" Erik asked, his large, fat head leaning toward Aya.

"When the needs of the world are involved," Aya retorted, her strong feminine voice torturing his old ears.

"Why doesn't Ashbel just take over the throne?" Erik voiced. "People will follow whoever is in power."

"The world needs a leader, not someone who is a threat to their lives, like a great dragon would be," Aya countered, a little proud of herself.

"Is it moral to kill for one's family?" Erik triggered.

"Erik! This isn't your choice!" Aya exclaimed, her mind baffled. "Think of all the emotional and physical pain the king, my father, has bestowed upon our kind. The shaming of our people!"

"Rose, you must decide," Aya told her, the silver in her eyes looking up at her.

"It's for the greater good," Ashbel added, his face gleaming proudly yet solicitously up at Rose.

"What is good?" Rose asked kindly. "What makes something good, and what makes something evil?"

The room was quiet, then Erik began talking with a grin on his face.

"If it helps my people and hurts my enemies, it's good."

Aya scoffed. "Good is an absolute. It doesn't depend on the context. Good is good, and evil is bad."

"There are basic principles," Ashbel chimed. "Treat others the way you would like to be treated. Treat yourself with dignity. Treat others with respect. Don't take what isn't yours. Don't let the purple touch your veins."

"All people are equal," Aya concluded. "One shouldn't be marginalized. Everyone has something to offer."

"Unless they disagree with me." Erik smirked.

"If everyone is deemed equal," Rose protested, "then why is the king being treated so poorly? Why must we be reduced to an act of violence?"

Ashbel sighed. "Rosie, there has to be a great process to the decision to kill. First, you must decide whether you will be a part of it by giving up the innocence your genes have gifted you."

"Rose, just know you don't have to do this. We can find another way to handle this," Erik mumbled while pouring himself another glass of wine, wiping the wetness from his thumbs on his stained robe.

Rose, who was as curious as she was innocent, smiled down at the dragons below her feet. Aya fiddled with her fingers, awaiting Rose's final response.

"Come what may," Rose committed gleefully, "I will hand over my innocence."

The room cheered, for Rose was compromised.

Once the loud echo had fallen silent, the group sat back into their assigned chairs. Rose had ceased to smile. The sound of the wind outside Dragons Nest oddly danced in Rose's ears.

"As I had mentioned prior," Erik said, wheezing, clearing his throat, his hands adjusting his robe, "my fire has the mysterious properties of evil. I shall hand them over to Rose. The purple will infect her enough to bring her consciousness of the cruelties of our world, the dangerousness of the world, and she will never be innocent again."

Rose nodded down at him, her skinny body losing her balance while her mind was racing.

Erik walked over to Ashbel, gathering something within his hands.

"I," Erik reasoned, "have been cursed with the purple fire. I will bite into this plum, then Rose will, infecting her with my disease. Then we shall talk about the rules."

His dirty hands revealed a purple fruit, so innocent and pure, and held it up to the nose of Ashbel, who sniffed the juices. They agreed it was the best idea.

Erik folded the sleeves of his robe up his hairy blue arm. He exhaled loudly before lifting the circle to his mouth, his bruised lips surrounding the plum. The bite was oddly disturbing, his gross teeth sinking deep within the skin of the fruit, the juices leaking down his chin, dripping like blood. Purple blood seeped out of his gums, into the fruit, until he chewed off his piece. He then began eating the bitten fruit he had torn off the core of the plum. He swallowed remorsefully.

"Rose." His old eyes looked up at her. "You don't have to do this. You must know that after this, you won't ever be the same."

Rose balanced herself. "Yes I understand. Though you, I don't. You were so rude to me, and now you are trying to protect me."

"I understand you. You and I are the same. I want to preserve those who are good as long as we can. If you knew my life's work, you would believe the same."

Rose nodded and extended her hands to catch the plum when he tossed it up at her. It flew gracefully toward her and bounced lightly in her hands. She could feel his bite against her palm and the sweet wetness of the fruit on her skin.

She gathered her courage and watched the plum touch her red lips. Her teeth sank deep into the purple skin of the fruit. She could feel the cold against her tongue. It tasted good. She felt her body shift. She felt heavier, and her head throbbed. She licked her lips clean. Her teeth chewed on the soft fruit, drinking its juices, the purple entering her body willingly.

She gulped. It was in her. She did not need another bite. She was infected, and the plight of evil filled her thoughts.

The scenes of murder danced in her foresight. Rose saw visions of bloodstained walls and fingerprints against the corpse of an innocent child, the ripping off the lips, the abandonment of a person, and the abuse of an animal. Rose heard the screams of those being tortured with heated metals and whips. She could feel the ropes wrapped around their throats as their final gasps for air were frustrated and dissatisfied by the strangling. In her mind, Rose witnessed it all.

"Rosie," Aya said, whimpering calmly, her white eyes darting between Rose and Ashbel with much concern.

Rose was barely audible when she culminated her sentence, confirming her consciousness. Rose sat back down on her long chair, resting her head upon her dirty palm, watching the walls steady themselves. She nodded once more.

"Rose," Aya called, hankering for her safety, "may we begin?"

Rose combed out her long bronze hair and fiddled with it until it was out of her eyes. She nodded again for the final time while reaching down to her booted foot. She gathered the fruit in her hands. The plum was cold.

"You are as much as the rest of us," Ashbel orated profoundly, directing his intimidating yellow eyes at all those in the room before continuing. "Let us begin!"

Rose expected something to happen. She waited, but nothing happened. The room was the same. Erik continued drinking his red wine, and Aya continued braiding her long black hair, struggling to break the knots. The dragons continued to sway their large tails behind their thrones and huff boldly so that all could hear. Rose tapped her feet to the vigorous beat of her mind's twitch, impatiently waiting for the meeting to begin.

"The process of the murder of the king will consist of many rules and procedures that all Reds must obey. If rules are broken, those accused of failing to follow the rules will be called to Dragons Nest," Aya voiced. The rest agreed with slight murmurs.

"Why do we need a process?" Erik asked. "If I want someone to drop dead, why can't I just kill them?"

Rose sat back down in her chair. "When must we come to the decision to kill?" she asked, understanding the concept.

"A perfect question to begin with, Rosie," said Ashbel, ignoring Erik. "When is killing moral?"

The gulping filled the room, and a scrawny, hairy blue finger was lifted into the air. Erik belched out, "Killing is moral if I gain power." He seemed to forget his first comment.

Aya reasoned, "Then it would be fine for everyone to kill for power. Is that a world you want to live in?"

"Killing is an extreme solution, which should only be used on a limited bases," Rose decided.

The room went cold. A chill swam down Rose's spine as a light breeze tickled the small hairs along her arms. She was infected. She understood. She was knowing.

The paintings on the walls looked redder to Rose as she intensified her stares. The thoughts of murder and defilement clouded her thoughts.

"Let us not be hypothetical," Aya voiced out, her long brown hair resting upon her feet as they dangled from her throne. "The king has stigmatized the Red Lips by removing their lips. He is going to do more wrong. We shall end his life to end the madness."

Erik smirked. "Aya, my dear, are we killing him for something he has already done or for something he is going to do?"

"Erik, do you wish him alive?" Aya spat.

"I am trying to play by your petty rules and to help show our perfect Rose what the real questions are. Rose needs to know the real reasons people do the wrong."

"Good is how people act when they know others are watching," Aya retorted, rising from her throne to tower over the fat man, "and unless you desire to fool people into believing they are being watched all their lives, we must think of how they are going to act while they are alone. We must act upon their likely behavior. It is not worth the risk waiting to see how much worse the world could get." Aya sat down.

Ashbel then arose from his golden throne, stretching his beat body, gallantly flexing his red scales and pink underbelly. His thumps dominated the beats of the wind against Dragons Nest. He stood above the rest of the dragons.

"It is our job to prevent, which is the best solution, but not always the ultimate solution. Try to convince them to stop. Until their choices are made, they cannot be punished. We must choose to spend our energy convincing."

Aya growled.

"Is there a process to who decides who dies?" Erik asked while stirring his wine with his finger. "Oh, wise dragon, please enlighten our pitiful souls!" His voiced mocked those of the merciful, the beggars. No one found it amusing.

"The most important part of the process is to be transparent, fair, and fact-based," Ashbel enforced. "There shall be no biased opinions or judgments, and most certainly no unjust actions."

Aya, the daughter of the king, stood up from her chair again and began to wander around the room. Her steps were slow at first, then they progressed, becoming quicker and more determined. She never stumbled, and the gait was as graceful as if in a ballet.

She turned to face her audience. "Let us make a case against the king!"

She was rather pleased with herself, for Erik could no longer defend the rights of the innocent if the innocent was proved guilty. She waltzed around the room once more.

"The king has proved time and again that he is nothing but lies and evil," Aya proclaimed. "He ripped your lips off your mouth because you refused to give him your fire."

She bounced again.

"The king, when I was only an infant, threw me from his castle walls to die, though I was saved."

"How do we know he didn't throw you so you would end up here? Without him, you wouldn't be the princess of Dragons Nest." Erik laughed.

Aya glared down at his crusty double chin, threatening his overused throat. He didn't talk much more, only drank.

"He manipulated the parents of countless children to harm their child, in hopes of their purple fire as well dooming them to the pain of being a Forgotten Child," Aya said, though Rose wasn't paying much attention. She seemed to be more focused on how many drinks Erik could serve himself during Aya's testimony. It was quite substantial.

"Finally..." Aya paused after venting about all the other cruel things the king had done with his violent life. "The current war, the massacre of the Reds, the dream of genocide to all those pure and kind are all at the king's direction."

"No one deserves the cruelty the king has wrought upon my family, my true family. I am willing to fight for it." She smiled. "Is that enough to prove him guilty?"

Ashbel sighed. "Yes, thank you very much, Aya."

Aya skipped around once more before hopping onto her throne gleefully, sitting on her long black hair, smoothing out her long white dress. A blue aura haloed around her whole form. She was glorious, and Rose took note of that, admiring her beauty.

"If he has committed these moral crimes," Aya concluded, "he deserves to die. If we don't act in the name of justice, the king will continue to kill those who are innocent."

"This cannot be about making the Reds stronger," Ashbel strongly said, his deep voice chilling the breath that Rose exhaled. She was still adjusting to the staidness of his being. Ashbel continued, "But about the moral message."

Every one of them readily agreed with the dragon. Erik patted his beefy stomach with his thick fingers while drowning himself in the wine that was never ending. His feet hung loosely from the small stool he used. His chiefly crown dangled from his greasy hair, which was sparse. The scruff along his chin was stained red. He was very pleased with himself, though frustrated with everyone else.

"You powerful sons and daughters of bitches and whores have voiced a concern with everything I have said so far," he smugly contributed, which made everyone cringe. "So can we all agree that the maiming or murder of another due to self-defense shall be moral?"

Edan proudly said, "I agree with self-defense. I would do it for any one of you."

"Even you, Erik," Aya slyly said, smiling caringly toward the Blue man, reaching out to touch his arm affectionately.

Rose shook her head. "How many of you have to die? Once we make the decision to fight, how do we balance the collateral damage? Say, ten thousand men must die so that I might get to the king? When is the sacrifice not worth it?"

"If they fight for the king, they are the king," Aya told her, her silver eyes stern.

"How does my army get to the king?" Rose asked. "Do we kill to get to the king?"

Ashbel smiled. "If they follow the process properly, then yes, they will be allowed to kill. The day of the great battle, whenever that may be, I will grant them all the curse to kill."

"Ashbel," Edan questioned, his purple tail thumping hard, "how do we limit the number of deaths the day of this great battle?"

"We can't control that," Erik said simply, spilling another full glass on the front of his robe, cursing at the sudden wetness. "In the end, do we want a whole army of men who are willing to kill our kind the way they are willing to eat food still walking the dirt ground and wandering the palace walls while we rule the world? Or would it be better to wipe them out while we have the chance?"

"The king's army are combatants. If they die, they die," Ashbel declared, the force in his voice turning to empathy. Rose felt it. Ashbel continued, "Though we want to limit how many have to die. The less blood on our hands, the better. If they rise again, we shall deal with it then. It is a fool's dream to make detailed preparations for something so uncertain. If we just get the king, we may be able to change everything else for the better. We might reverse the manipulations they have been so accustomed to."

Edan, who was filled with tremendous guilt for what his fire possessed, asked, "As for our kind, when they fight in this great battle, how shall we know they know the rules?"

Ashbel chuckled to himself, smiling down at his dear, paranoid friend. "When I gather those who are willing to fight, I will tell them. I will tell them of the powers they will possess and the responsibilities that will come with it."

"And if they break the rules?" Aya implored.

"Then they shall be judged in the dragon trials," Ashbel responded.

Aya's smile turned to a pale frown, and fear drowned her face.

*****

Rose reappeared beyond the safe walls of Dragons Nest. She was on the grassy ground surrounded by trees and bushes. The wet mud mushed against her pale hands as she stood up. She wiped her hands off slowly. Rose trotted around the greenery, inquisitive as to the ecosystem around them. Rose tapped her feet on a stick and then hummed to herself before sliding down the crusty bark of a tree and sitting back down.

"Rose," the grumpy voice of Erik said behind her. Rose jumped.

She looked at the fat old man and studied his waddle as he stumbled over to her. His robe dragged in the grass behind him. He frowned.

"Where are we?" Rose asked, her hands folded across her chest.

He laughed, as he tended to do with stupid questions.

He led her along a steep path filled with stones and sticks, red leaves, and brown twigs. Fallen nuts and berries cramped their feet as they waltzed. He grasped her hand and swayed it slowly, feeling the warmth of her fire. The forest was dark and dead. No wolves howled. No birds sang. No trees danced in a breeze. It was just the two of them.

They finally stopped in the open of a pasture, the sky visible above the tops of the trees. Rose sighed.

"Erik," Rose began, looking over at the fat man. He was stationed away from her now, holding his hands within his own palms.

"Purple fire used to be a great fire, worshipped among many," Erik told her. "Until it possessed dark magic. Then people feared it and feared those who controlled it."

Rose nodded. She loved stories.

"People never fear what they do not themselves have. They only fear what is different and imagine how it can be used against them."

He smiled. "You look so pretty standing there, and so innocent from afar."

"Am I not pretty from close up?"

"No one is ever pretty from close up. Everything that come from people is rotten."

"Reds aren't rotten," Rose told him.

"Yes," he sighed. "I suppose that is why Ashbel made you. He never liked things that were cruel."

"Are you cruel?"

He hesitated for a long moment, smelling the meat and wine on his robe and gagging. "Yes, I suppose I am."

The ground began to tremble, and the trees pushed one another back. The bushes lost their leaves, and the branches became so light that the wind carried them away from the open field. Erik stood and watched Rose fall to her knees when the field began to rise. The flowers exploded into petals. The bark from the nearby trees flew loose in splinters and cut Rose's eyes. They continued to attack her eyes, which were now wet with defensive tears. The loud smashing and forging in front of her dominated her ears.

A rustic domicile rested upon the pasture now. Rose rubbed her eyes in agony. She felt the new feeling of heat wrap her skin, warming her. Erik exclaimed joyfully. The barn flung itself forward and behind itself, quickly, before settling below Rose's nose. Erik clapped. Rose opened her eyes, collecting the wood shards from within her lashes.

She saw the last of the barn torn in flames, purple flames. The terror ate the barn alive. The wails of those inside taunted Rose. She began to cry, her hand reaching out to run to the walls.

"It is only a vision!" Erik yelled over Rose's screams.

Rose coughed, looking anxiously at Erik.

"A future, your future!"

Rose wept louder now. "Who could do such a thing?" she wailed.

Erik shrugged his fat shoulders. "I am only a messenger bringing the truth of purple fire," he said.

"People are dying in there!"

"Oh, yes, quite right. I suppose that will have to be avoided when the time comes. No one likes death."

Rose nodded, wiping her tears. The endless burning passionately ripped apart the barn. Purple fire lashed out angrily at the walls and frames of the barn.

"Rose," Erik said, instantly killing the barn and returning the woods as they had been. The flowers collectively bloomed below their feet. The grass was freed of ash and soot. The branches and twigs returned to the trees, and the bushes regained their leaves. Erik continued, "Use this as a warning."

Rose didn't nod, nor did she even shake her head. She only stared at the man as he disappeared into the forest. Erik sulked away with his shoulders burdened by the weight of another child who had lost her innocence.

*****

Rose found herself staring blankly into the white walls of the bedroom she shared with Celia. Rose touched her hands along the padded sheets and covers. The room was in disarray, from the chairs and desk to the brushes that were tossed onto the floor and the cheap beauty powder spilled on and staining the ground. Rose marched down the wooden steps to be greeted by her aunt and her cousins. Rose's brother sat comfortably on the sofa.

"Where were you?" Liza scolded.

"In Dragons Nest," Rose told Liza, beaming down at her.

"I hope you found what you were looking for and learned what you needed to learn." Liza scoffed at her.

Rose nodded.

"There is a letter addressed to you on the table. I found it on the doorstep earlier," Liza said, avoiding Rose's eyes.

Rose touched the piece of parchment carefully wrapped in lace and gold rim, engraved with red ink. She touched it to her heart, then scurried to sit at Jason's feet to open it. Those she loved gathered around her.

Rose's skinny hands cut the small wax that sealed tight the paper, and she smiled happily when she began to read it out loud.

"Dear Rose," she began, her younger cousins looking up at her, "the dragons and I are terribly excited to begin this journey with you. The lives of our kind are in your hands, where they should be. We begin in the summer, when we will travel around the world. We will seek those who need our help the most. Our journey is best fit for us. My love and happiness, Aya."

Rose looked daintily down at the signed name. The clear and concise form of Aya's lettering caught Rose's attention. Rose noticed that below Aya's signature was a symbol, drawn in red ink. It was a circle with three slashes down the side and three more down the center. The claws were curved and uneven. Rose laughed because she instantly knew the meaning of this symbol. It was the symbol of Dragons Nest.

Dear Rose,
The Dragons and I are terribley excited to begin this journey with you. the lives of our kind are in your hands, where they should be. We begin this Summer, when we will travel around the world. We will seek those who need our help the most. our journey is best fit for us.
My love and Happiness,
Aya

ASHBEL

Aya sat in her study. It was a dark-brown room with a clock and a small desk with an ink bowl and many pieces of parchment. She finished writing her letter to Rose. Aya needed to explain to her all that was untold at their meeting. The reason Rose was so sleepy at their meeting was that Ashbel was feeling weak. So Rose felt weak. If only Aya knew why.

When Rose fell asleep, Aya left to her bedroom. The bedroom was not much bigger than her study and had a golden bed, a large mirror, and dragon print painted across her walls. In the far east corner of her chamber was a full-scale map of their world, with all the geographical features from the mountains in Nava to the volcanoes in the Red Islands. Aya stood in her mirror, staring at herself, looking into her silver pupils. There, in her eyes, a flash of purple covered her vision and the laughter of her brothers corrupted her. She cried and wanted the purple to leave her. She knew it was growing close to her veins, but she didn't want anyone to know that it truly was in her. She opened her eyes again and stared into her darkness. Funny how the darkness was not only physical but that there was also an emotional and magical darkness that lay beneath the layers of her skin. The mirror was outlined with a rose gold trim. There were faintly embossed small wings resting at the curving top of the mirror and a small tail extending from the bottom. She grasped her long black hair and took the small knife, slashing at the hair and cutting it in half. This left only hair to her chest. She did this knowing the purple was in her blood. Cutting off so much of her dark hair might rid her of some of the darkness. Then anger filled Aya, and she took the knife, ripping her beautiful dress, fiercely cutting at its edges until the dress barely covered her thighs. She took the blade and chucked it at the mirror, shattering it completely in an explosion that left sharp, cracked pieces of glass scattered on the floor. She screamed once again and fell onto her bed. The red bed was overcomforted with pillows. The gold trim around it made her feel royal, although that right was taken from her when her was thrown from the castle walls by her father.

So Aya returned to her study, short hair and ripped dress, and finished the symbol at the bottom of the letter to Rose. Aya let the letter fly out of her window and took her blue fire and pushed it in the direction of Rose's cottage.

*****

Darting out of their cottage, Rose sprinted for her woods. In her mind she commanded the woods open to her will, and they obeyed. Every brown tree shifted in its place to leave an open field cleared straight for her lake. The wind was soft that morning. A light breeze filled the air, leaving Rose a steady journey. She stepped where twigs and leaves quickly moved out of her way, so she didn't trip or make a crack in the forest. Her feet sank into the moist dirt, closing in on her bare ankles before she jerked them back up for momentum during her run. The process of the forest adjusting to Rose's thoughts took less than a second. Rose continued running forward, while all things dodged her, just like she commanded through her mind. This convenience was more something Rose discovered she could do the very first time she and her brother came through these very woods, trying to find the cottage. She remembered the way younger Rose had no knowledge of the war and wanted to know everything. Now that she knew so much, Rose wanted to know less, have less responsibility, and not be involved. It was like the plum had poisoned her dreams, filling them with nightmares. Rose thought of these things as she arrived at her lake. The crimson water hadn't changed in color. The lily pads still sat firmly near the edge. Small fish were dancing at the bottom of the water. Deer, young and old, visited the lake but now left as they saw her. Truly, it wasn't her they were afraid of, but the great beast that lingered in the shadows.

"Little Rose," Ashbel said, greeting Rose. He came out of the trees, where he had been waiting, and showed all his red, all his scales, all his teeth, and his yellow eyes. His wings were held closely at his side, resting upon his waist. The bright woods felt darker in his presence. Rose held her smile.

An early bird chirped. Rose sighed and stared into the overgrown reptile's yellow eyes. Ashbel looked relaxed, focused, and more leisurely than he had been at Dragons Nest.

"When you do fulfill your promise, you will rule the world and be a great leader. I am sure of it," Ashbel offered soothingly.

"Ashbel, I won't be ruling," said Rose. She had sat down on the shore of her lake and played in the water with her feet while listening to the calming but stressful words the dragon was saying. "This world belongs to my brother. My brother will be crowned king, and I will return here and live with my cousin Celia. Or maybe I'll return to my childhood home in Nava." Rose smiled. "When it is done, I want to never hear from or see you people again."

"If that's what you want," continued the dragon, sighing. "Celia? How is that dove?" asked the dragon.

Rose pounded the ground with her fist and stood up to face Ashbel, saying, "Not one of your puppets."

"I have no puppets. Actually, Erik is my puppet. What a stubborn little rat."

"The man who gave me purple fire?"

"Certainly."

"Why do you commune with people so rude?" Rose asked with a smirk across her red cheeks.

"I must tolerate him. He can be rather useful."

Rose laughed. The lake felt calmer and more joyful and lively. It reflected her emotions, commands, and desires. The deer ran back over to drink, as if they had been dying to hydrate. The birds chirped again, as if they did so for the first time. The squirrels scurried, and the raccoons followed. Far away hid Rose's worries, insecurities, fears, and problems. Rose hugged Ashbel and felt his warm body heat press against her chest. His red scales patted against her shirt, and his head lightly sat upon her shoulder.

"Will my aunt allow it?"

"I'll talk to your dear aunt."

All Rose could do was smile.

*****

Rose felt like she knew everything she was getting herself into, but none of that mattered. She was back home with her aunt and brother, with her dragon, agreeing to save the world. Her new darkness bubbled inside her head. She could feel a purple glow that did not feel warm like her fire. The purple infection was cold and empty, squeezing her blood and draining her of all goodness. Ashbel could see this new purple glow around her body and this violet shade of evil. He walked closer to her warm body, and his claw touched her little pale face. The glow around her body turned red at his touch. Their veins were pounding, with blood burning inside them. Their touch meant something. Something only Ashbel knew.

Rose smiled and gazed at the beast. Rose was thinking only the worst thoughts, and yet the lake still was lively, bright, and peaceful. The same emotions Ashbel was feeling. In the blink of an eye, Ashbel turned to dust and vanished. Rose gasped but knew he was safe, having gone back to Dragons Nest. She looked around, and the ripples on the lake grew larger as they got closer to her, spreading and growing until the ripples stopped on the shore, where Rose sat. Then more dead leaves left the trees and fell toward her lake. They landed safely in the water, creating more ripples in it, and repeated the cycle over and over.

Rose moved and sat down near the edge where the lily pads were and cupped one in her hands. Crimson water dripped out of her palms and left the leaf and the white-and-purple-mixed flower. The petals overlapped one another, with their sharp tips pointing out like rays of sunlight. Rose stared at the flowers until she set them back down in the crimson water. She pulled her hair back behind her ear and just admired everything in her view. The way life worked and how she helped that and how many lives she would save by killing the king. So she sat there dreaming of a peaceful world before thoughts of murder came back into her head. Rose pondered the thoughts of evil and darkness. The purple infection must have been growing close to her veins.

She felt a sharp pain in her foot. She screamed and squirmed, but for some reason, she could not look or touch her leg. Rose sat facedown in the dirt, squealing. Once the pain passed, she grasped at her right ankle and saw two symmetrical lines marked in parallel with each other, like an equal sign. She stared at it, and the words passed through her head. But is wasn't Ashbel's voice; it was that of Erik, the small Blue man, whose voice echoed.

"I am cruel," the voice said over and over.

She breathed heavily and stared into the deep woods.

Rose got up and ran back to her cabin. Quickly she darted past anything that would hurt her. The woods moved with her, so she had a clear path back to her cabin. How badly Rose wanted to be with her mother again. The same mother that the king took from her. So now she felt a sudden determination to end his life. How angry this man made her, making her blood boil. Her pure red blood, the gene that was in her, made her this innocent child that had no hate and envy or the will to hurt others. But now she was given the mark of the warriors that were sent out to kill the king before Rose. The sign represented equality, peace, and the ideals Rose represented and esteemed. As is so often true in nature, the sign also meant that Rose now had the will to kill.

Once Rose reached her house, she saw the faint image of her aunt. Liza was standing in the kitchen, making something delicious, as usual. Liza had a distressed look upon her face. Rose saw it as she grew closer to her beloved aunt. Rose finished running up the tall hill, entered their little wooden door, and was welcomed by the sweet, warm embrace of her aunt. The kitchen smelled of dinner—warm bread and fresh meat, fruits, and vegetables.

Rose hugged her aunt back lovingly. When Rose noticed that her aunt was crying, Rose pulled back. Rose grasped Liza's hands and looked into her old face, which reminded Rose of the way her mother's face had looked. The brown hair was similar, but her mother didn't have gray stripes and roots, nor did she have the beginning of wrinkles. But Rose stood there looking into Liza's eyes, gazing at the water that poured out of them and then flowed down her cheekbones.

"My dear aunt, why are you crying?" asked Rose, trying to smile as a comfort to the sorrow on Liza's face.

"Because, Rose, I know you made that sick deal with the princess and the beast," she told Rose, pinching her hands, leaving a scratch. The blood that flowed out was not just red blood, but small specks of purple blood ran down her wrist.

"Ouch!" panted Rose. "Aunt Liza, why have you hurt me?" asked Rose, running to get a towel. The cold towel felt nice on her new wound. It quickly became full of blood, but the blood also quickly stopped pouring out of her wrist.

"To show you that purple fire is truly in your blood. But why? Why, Rose, is there purple fire in your blood?" shouted Rose's aunt. Her face looked flustered. Her cotton dress was slightly tattered, and her shoes looked less polished than they used to be.

"You were touched by purple fire," Rose told her aunt. She looked into her eyes to find the purple, but it wasn't there anymore. It would have been washed out in the well when Liza and her mother lost the gene. Rose's eyes directed the conversation to the sofa. Liza followed her and sat down next to her and touched her skinny knee.

"I was more than touched by it, Rosie. I was able to control it. Purple was my fire color, and green was your mother's fire color. She loved watching my fire, but once I learned that it had evil properties and that the king was looking for us, I took your mother and we ran to the well where we could lose our gene. I thought it would be the safest thing to do, but obviously, some of my genes were passed to you," Liza cried, but she was cut off by Rose cupping her face and frowning.

"No, I wasn't born with this. I was touched by purple fire. Erik, the chief of your tribe, exposed me to all the cruel it does."

"Rose, that evil is the reason I don't want you to go on this *journey*."

"This journey is what is right," Rose said sternly.

"It's suicide!" Liza projected, throwing her hands in the air. Her eyes glowed up in hurry when she heard what Rose wanted to do. Rose saw all the tears empty from Liza's eyes and travel the entire length of her long face. Liza held Rose's hands, which were as cold as ice. They fought with each other to make eye contact. Rose searched Liza's kind face and saw there was no evil in any form in her precious body. She smiled and looked into her aunt's brown eyes.

"My husband, your uncle, never got to meet you or your brother because he went off to fight this war. He died months before you came. He fought for you and for everything we believe in. But I still lost him. My children still lost their father. And I'm not about to lose you, too, or lose Jason. I promised your mother, Katrina, your beautiful mother, that I would protect you. I promised that beast that I would protect you. I cannot. I will not break that oath."

She cried so hard, looking into Rose's young eyes. Rose felt so bad about everything she was about to tell Liza, but Rose told Liza anyway. Holding on to every word her aunt had just told her. She cherished those words in her heart and hugged Liza once more. She breathed deeply and pushed back her long brown hair.

"Liza," Rose started, looking into Liza's eyes while playing with her fingers, "I am going. I will avenge your husband. I will avenge Mother. I will avenge Father. I will protect my brother. I will do whatever it takes to make sure this family is safe."

Liza frowned and looked disappointed. Rose sat up and looked into Liza's eyes. Rose was becoming more confident and determined with every word now.

"My decision is final," declared Rose. She stood up and walked up the stairs, leaving Liza to sit on their sofa, with tears continuing to run down her old face. The only thought running through Liza's head was what Katrina would do in this specific situation.

"Katrina would have made a fantastic mother."

"I need your spirit, Katrina."

And the final words Liza spoke in that moment were for her dear sister when she said, "I'm so sorry, Katrina. I can't protect them anymore."

Liza wept as she faced the fact that she had disappointed her dead sister.

Meanwhile, Rose walked into the bedroom she shared with Celia, who she found was sitting and reading a book. Before Rose could even say a word, the door closed. Celia started to scream but was cut off, and a blue glow wrapped around her body as she fell to her bed, unconscious. Rose darted around to see the last person she wanted to see, Erik. She balled her skinny fists and ran toward him, but he used magic to freeze her. She could only blink and talk, nothing more, and she felt so powerless.

"Is being powerless one of your fears?" asked the Blue man.

"No, you are," she replied, trying to move her body to jump at him.

"Oh, I don't want to scare you, little Rose," he told her, and with the flick of his hand, he made a glass of wine appear. He drank a sip, then looked back at Rose. Erik's bruised blue-and-purple lips were pursed while he looked at her. He was dressed in the rags he called chief clothes and puffed his wine belly up at her. He was still shorter than her and had to look up at her, but he didn't seem intimated by that fact at all.

"Undo your curse on my cousin," demanded Rose while trying to create fire with her hands, but nothing worked.

"Yeah, okay. Once we are done with our conversation," he responded, smirking.

Rose scoffed.

"I need you to know about the evil in our world, and I'm willing to give you a secret tip on how this outside world works."

"Your advice has yet to help me. It just torments me."

"I disagree."

"You gave me purple fire."

"Of your own free will and at your request," Erik corrected.

"You showed me my future."

"Only to protect you!"

"You hurt my cousin!"

"She is in no pain!"

He swayed his hands all around her face. It made her flinch, but she just wanted to make sure Celia was okay. So Rose acceded and pushed to get the conversation moving forward. Rose's frozen body started hurting, but she relaxed and just focused on the Blue man in front of her.

"Speak!" Rose commanded him.

"My advice, first, is to not trust everyone you meet," he said plainly.

"I know that because of my lips, people who fight and support the Nomads will want to kill me," Rose told him with every ounce of patience she had. The purple was controlling her choice more often now. Patience was one of the qualities of the Reds.

"I see the fire I placed in you is working," he told her, sipping another drop of wine. His fat belly wiggled as the wine entered it. His Blue form got really close to Rose, and he smirked while she wanted to cry.

She breathed deeply, and every time she did this, the border would fog up and then be cleared away. This process repeated many times before the Blue man gathered his thoughts.

"If you want to face what is out there, you have to know it. You have to know the evil and unpleasures that lie in the world of the Nomads. To know it is to be it."

No.

"By doing this to you, I'm trying to help and even prepare you."

No.

"Now you can understand everything because you can live it. You can be it and feel it."

No.

"It's growing close to your veins now. I can feel it," he said, touching the border around her arms.

"No!"

"I wonder what will happen when the purple grows into every ounce of blood you have to the point where you bleed only purple."

"No! No! This won't happen. Goodness is in our nature! No matter how dark the magic, it is in our genes. We breathe goodness!" Rose said, warming up. The fire was becoming easier to use, which meant his spell was breaking.

"Just know that I warned you about everything in you and out there," he said, pointing toward Celia.

"No! She is good! She is a good person! She would never harm anything! Celia is good!" But before she could finish anything, Erik had left and both spells had broken. Rose jumped up and burned fire from her fists. She wanted to fight that man for all the pain she had to endure, but Celia was the main focus right now.

She ran over to Celia and held her hand as she sat up, not knowing what happened. Her curly blond hair was a bit tangled from her lying on it. Rose's blue eyes looked into Celia's brown eyes, which were filled with fear and worry. Rose calmed those emotions by warming Celia with some heat.

"You can create it now," Celia said with a smile. "I never doubted you would." She giggled, and their bodies touched in a friendly embrace. Once they spread apart, Celia's eyes searched Rose's eyes urgently. There was real confusion in Celia's eyes this time.

"Rosie, who was that man?" Celia said, sitting up more. Her blue cotton dress made slight ruffling noises as she moved carelessly about her dress.

"That man is someone you will never see again. I will make sure of that," Rose told her. "Do you believe me?"

Celia nodded in agreement and belief. "Is it true you are leaving?" she then asked.

"Yes," Rose said. She was surprised by a strong hug from Celia.

"Rose, please, for me. Use your powers to stay here in peace with me."

"If I stay, who will make the peace?"

"If it is meant to be so, why cannot it be so through someone else?"

"Haven't you and I always joked with each other that if we want something done right, we always need to do it ourselves? Hiring someone else to do the difficult tasks does not make the result any less cruel."

*****

The rest of the day was left for Rose packing. She packed a long leather bag with extra clothes and weapons. For food, Rose packed apples, berries, bread, and other sundries that would not spoil. She packed ink, parchment, and a brush so she could write home to her aunt and cousins. She smiled as she left the room that she had shared with Celia. She smiled at the quilts that were made to keep them warm at night. She looked at the desk that Celia would sit at to fix her always-perfect hair. She thought this was the final goodbye, but that thought was stopped when she heard the yell of her aunt, the usual yell around sundown.

"Dinner!"

Rose groaned and dropped her bag and ran down the stairs. Her little cousins were already situated, and Jason followed behind her down the steps. Celia was helping her mother set the food down on the table. There were fresh meats, blueberries, strawberries, and watermelon, which they must have purchased from the market. Bread was laid across the table in two small baskets. The butter was on a plate next to it, and next to that was a basket of potatoes. The plate of sugar always made a smile grow on the younger cousins' faces. Grape juice was poured into everyone's cup.

Once everyone had arranged themselves, Rose's aunt raised her glass in front of the table and said, "To family! We always stick together." Everyone else raised their glasses and sipped the tasty juice that it held.

"What a nice phrase to end on, Liza," Rose told her. She drank her glass like Erik would do. She felt so foolish, but she needed to do this. It was the purple in her. It was spreading.

"Whatever could you mean, child?" asked their aunt with a stern face.

Rose fixed her bronze hair and then smiled a toothy smirk and told her plainly, "I'm leaving tonight to go save the world. I'm so grateful that I could have this one final dinner with my family."

"I thought I made my words quite clear. You are not to leave this house." Liza kept her voice calm, but everyone in the room knew it would not stay that way for long.

Rose's eyes glowed blue as she shared, "Ashbel said he would talk to you!"

Liza saw the flash and flinched. She looked stunned at what Rose could do. Rose then proceeded to spread out her hand and showed everyone her bloodred fire. It was a small flame, but everyone but Jason looked shocked. Jason sat, eating his food. He, too, knew that this was his final meal with them. Rose raised her eyebrows at Liza.

"I'm leaving to save everyone's lives. It's the honorable thing to do."

"Is that a threat?" Liza said calmly again.

"Would you like it to be?" said Rose, standing up. Her skinny body was soon put down by Liza standing up and looking her in the eyes before shouting at her.

There was a knock on the door. Celia went to answer it, and when she opened the door, she just stared and looked at Rose.

"Who is it, Celia?" asked Rose.

"Rose, it's for you," she said, walking away, leaving the door wide-open.

Rose slowly made her way to the doorframe, taking every step with caution, but she stopped dead in her tracks when she saw who it was.

Aya and all four dragons were standing outside, in full battle attire. Aya looked disapprovingly at Rose, as if to say, "Why aren't you wearing battle armor?"

"Rose," Aya said, "are you coming?"

Rose

"Aya," Rose told her, dumbfounded.

Her pale skin lit up at the sight of Aya's short black hair and dark skin. Rose missed Aya. And now Aya had shown up, ready to take Rose to a war where they both could die.

All the worries of the past evaporated, however, and Rose ran up and hugged Aya's mature body. Once they touched, all the red blood in them statically exploded, as if their veins were pumping into one another. Their touch was filled with magical chemistry. The reds of both worlds blended together in a warm embrace.

"Rose, Ashbel told me everything, and we have to go soon. The king has advanced, which means he knows you're coming. The upside is that it's our move."

The war talk made Rose warm her hands with heat. Anger flowed in Rose, then purple flashed up against her eyes again. She gasped at the red-and-blue mixed flash that covered her pupils. It was true. The king was moving. It was likely it would be close to where they were this very moment.

"In a week's time, the king could be here, if he's moving from Remular," Rose told Aya, looking deeply into her silver eyes. The white lens blended into the outer part of Aya's eyes.

"Yes, we believe that's where he is," Aya told her. Rose looked back to face Celia, who looked worried. Celia's beautiful blond har waved down her chest as she stared fearfully at Rose.

"Celia, get Liza and your sisters. Move somewhere else. The king will be here soon, looking for me. You have to leave!" Rose shouted at her.

Aya moved closer to Ashbel, and while hopping on his red back, she yelled for Rose.

"I'm going to search the land for hideouts. I'll be back. Help your family, Rosie." And with that, Ashbel jumped into flight, racing the wind and touching the clouds. Rose heard a distant battle cry from Aya, and she laughed at the confident noises she was making. Rose ran back inside and faced her furious aunt. The looks they gave each other as they stared each other down were both pure and livid.

"Rose, stay safe," said Liza quickly before Rose could say anything.

"You're letting me go?" asked Rose, confused. Rose's face was all scrunched up as she waited for an answer, as she implied.

"Yes, Rose, I am. I have faith that you will do this and stay safe. Have Jason protect you. Protect Jason. I will move farther up toward Dayton, where the village is, and see if we can find shelter there."

Rose stared at her, confused. "Dayton?" she asked.

"Yes, Dayton is the village above us. We send Celia there occasionally to trade for our harvest."

"I didn't know there were other people here besides us and the hunters from Nava."

"No, Rose, dear, the hunters come here from Ceptem, where there is only farmland. There are no forests like ours in Ceptem," Liza told her.

"I'm still confused. Why wouldn't those from Ceptem just hunt in Remular?"

"Because you have to pay to hunt in the royal forests in Remular. It is quite expensive to purchase a hunting permit. The king likes having plenty of targets when he hunts. Also, riding on a train can be a real hassle for travel back and forth, especially if you are returning with a hunting prize."

"A train?" asked Rose again.

"Have that beast explain geography to you while you kill men and fight battles you might die in," Liza said, suddenly sobbing. She was interrupted by a tight embrace from Rose, whose skinny pale hands wrapped themselves along Liza's thick waist. Rose's head snuggled up against Liza's breast, and she talked while taking deep but silent gulps of oxygen.

"I will be safe. I promise."

Liza patted her hair and laid her head on the top of Rose's, saying, "I know you will. You are a strong girl."

Rose pulled out of their embrace and looked back up at the brown eyes her aunt had. They were soft, and little drops of water were forming within them. The gray roots in her hair were carefully pulled back behind her ears. Rose saw the faint image of her mother as she stared at her mother's older sister. How similar they looked, yet how different they were. They both, as blood relatives, shared the most important thing, their motherly heart. Their touch was soft. They wanted to protect their children with all their heart. And Katrina knew that Rose and Jason would be safer with her sister. Katrina knew that Liza was a good mother and would do what Katrina could not do. What every mother wanted to provide, protection. And now Rose was making that job even harder for Liza as she walked out, facing dangers, including death.

Rose felt the strength of her mother in that moment. She felt the bravery her mother possessed. It was all coming to her. She could feel the purple trying to fight that power, that love away. Rose remembered that her mother used to say that love was the greatest thing of all and that love never failed. Rose was, in that moment, more than any other moment in her life, a Mensch.

"Rose, my beautiful flower, I wish to give this to you," Liza said, pointing to a jewelry box in the corner. Rose had seen it before but never knew what was in it. It was next to the fireplace, where Rose had once sat all day, staring at her fire. Liza walked straight to that little wooden box with the pretty wooden trim. She opened the box to reveal a simple rose gold bracelet. It looked very expensive, like a royal person would own it. Rose liked the simplicity of it. No diamond was placed in the chain. No charm hung loose from it. It was just a circle, with a snap button that one would press down to open the circle so it could fit around the wrist. And that was exactly what Liza did. She opened it up and tightened it around Rose's wrist.

"This bracelet has been in our family for generations. One day you will know why, but I wanted to give this to you. It is important that you always know where you came from, and that is from the Mensch family."

"I will," said Rose, feeling her wrist as she looked at Liza one last time.

Celia came up to Rose and gave her a hug. As usual, her hair was perfect, and her dress was properly flattened on her body. She was crying the most beautiful tears as they fell down her perfectly sculpted face.

"Don't die," she told Rose as she rubbed her back.

"I'll try."

"I will miss you so much," Celia said, whimpering. She began holding Rose in a warm embrace. She sniffed her clean hair for the last time. She caressed her soft skin once more. She kissed the tip of her nose, smiling.

"I will miss you more."

Celia cleared the tears from her face as she released Rose from her arms, then began waving goodbye to Rose. The roar of the dragons blocked the noise of the two little children as they said their farewells. They, being very young, didn't know what exactly was going on or that they might never see Rose or Jason again. The same way that they hadn't known that they wouldn't see their father ever again.

"I love you," they told Rose.

"I love you too."

Rose left the cabin. Rose's mind began looking forward to where Jason was, standing next to Aya, and to talks about the journey to come.

"You don't have to go. You should stay and take care of Liza and her children," Rose told her older brother.

He smirked. "Are we just not going to say 'Aunt' anymore?"

Rose laughed. It was her first real laugh in a while. She loved her brother because he could do that, be positive in even the most serious and stressful situations.

"Aunt Liza."

"No, Rose, I am staying here, with you, forever. No matter where we go, we are in this together. Aunt Liza will survive without her favorite Mensch."

"I do believe that I am her favorite."

"And that, Rose, is where we disagree."

Aya came out of the cabin, probably advising Liza where a good place might be to find protection from the king. She walked up toward Jason and Rose and looked at them with her pale eyes and dark skin.

"We leave now. We are heading north, but I have people we should meet. They have been traveling south and are north of Toad's River in Freshwater. We should travel to Beal first to miss the king's troops, because they will be coming from the north. We will lie low there and, in about a week, head up."

Jason nodded, while Rose still was clueless on the geography of the Red Islands.

Rose felt powerful as she positioned herself on Ashbel, tightening her thighs around a small part of his long scaly neck. It felt rough against her body. The feeling was similar to being on a horse.

She grabbed firmly on the wild red hair on his neck and then gazed over his reptile skin.

Her anxiety built up right before he jumped into the sky. She could feel her body jolt down, as her heart raced up, once the beast took flight. Ashbel's angelic wings had them soaring through the white clouds. Shortly they would reach the edge of the island, her island, and soon the king would invade. He would make her home some war-torn battleground, just like her mother had feared.

Rose curled her neck and faced forward, with a slight bell ringing in her ear. That ring was the sound of a Purple heart beating. The evil was heating up and growing, watching and waiting for the perfect moment to set fire to her veins. She heard the knocking, and now she would forever hear the knocking and the ringing of the bell as it tolled. The Purple fed off her energy, devouring every life she held and painting her walls with its darkness. Rose resisted every urge to know who was knocking and ringing the bell. Forever not knowing—that is, of course, if she didn't give in. Because as most Reds, excluding Rose, knew, if a Red gave in to the purple fire and allowed it to touch the veins, that Red would gain full knowledge of good and evil, and therefore full access to the game that is life. Those fully infected Reds could feel and do evil and cruel things. They could feel anger, envy, hatred, and the lust for corruption to begin. As the Purple grew, the Red would lose the conscience of the once-good and once-pure Red, slowly devouring all that life. Rose could see that she needed to be careful with her Purple or risk losing herself and becoming someone she would detest, a powerful Red Lip who could create fire and use it for whatever purpose, good or evil, she chose.

So Rose flew through the sky, all the while hearing this ringing.

Ring...

Ring...

Ring...

The echo was like that of a bell tower in a faraway field. Rose could hear this ringing and, at the same time, the sound of Ashbel's wings as they glided through the air, cutting it in halves like a knife cutting butter. Aya, behind Rose, was calling her name.

"Rose!" she shouted, catching up with her, the blue dragon meeting the red.

"This is your land. Save it well. This is your country. Don't let that damned king take it from you! Call your battle cry!"

Rose shouted, calling for the king. She screamed and yelled passionately. The trees shook, the ground quaked, and the echoes thundered from the valleys below. With that triumphant war cry came the first knock.

Knock...

Knock...

Knock...

It replaced the sound in her ears. The reality of the Purple was there, truly, awaiting the first breath of life in her veins. There it was. The first urge came as a sharp pain. It guided itself throughout her body, nibbling at every muscle. The physical adjustments Rose proceeded to make to be more comfortable didn't help. They only moved the pain forward. Her eyes were numbed to the point that only gray and black circles covered her view for a short time. All this repeated until the urge stopped. The vibrating left, and the hazy dimness evaporated so she could see light. The red of the dragon appeared again in her vison, and she heard Aya still shouting. Jason flew behind her, and the fourth dragon lay empty, carrying no person. They flew on until the day's end and stopped to rest at the edge of the Island of Beal.

"Here, Rose, have some," Aya told Rose, handing her a container of water. Rose gladly took and drank the liquid, which relaxed the tension in her mouth. The liquid would have tasted better if it had been cold, but it must have warmed up from the travel.

"The dragons are heading back to Dragons Nest, for now. The troops could possibly see them if we head too close to the edge. The red of the islands would make them very obvious."

Rose nodded to show that she understood the plan.

"We will continue on foot. There is a village in Beal, much like all the small towns here, which are Red sanctuaries. Plenty of unwanted Reds come to places like Beal and hide in their towns."

"What is the name of the town that we will be voyaging to, Aya?" asked Rose, pacing ahead of her.

"Witchdell."

The two girls walked on until they reached an enclosed forest range with over a dozen cottages like Liza's and many people talking to one another. The houses had brick and stone exteriors, some having flower beds with lilies and daisies, while others had horse and donkey mangers out next to the outhouses. There were bread bakeries and something that would resemble a schoolhouse. Rose saw pig farms and other fertilized grounds that were growing harvest. Beal was a bigger island, which was much bigger than Rose's island. The diversity really excited Rose.

When they arrived in the town, Rose instantly decided that she loved being in Witchdell. It was fascinating. All the women were wearing brown and white dresses. Some men wore fancier clothes, while others remained lying on the ground, wearing rags. Other men had patches over their eye sockets. The group of three children looked alien to these people, who all looked like merry townsfolk.

As they gazed on, Rose noticed the number of people who had red lips. Men, women, and children all had pale faces, light hair, bright eyes, and dark-red lips. Not one was quiet the same as another, but all were very similar. Rose's lips were the farthest from theirs. Her lip color was a deep shade of maroon, while they had a light red that some could even confuse for pink. Aya felt the most awkward of the group, for she had dark skin, pale eyes, and dark lips. But Rose had beautiful red fire, and Rose knew that her fire was more talented than any of these people's.

They became noticeable and were stared at by all the people who walked nearby. Aya led the group, pretending not to notice the townspeople's stares. Rose stared back at them, making them feel uncomfortable. Jason was being whispered about because he himself had no red on his lips.

Past the bakery and the homes they walked. Some children voiced loudly their opinion on the group, and their mothers hushed them, forcing them to walk on. The color and liveliness of the town seemed darker as they made their way deeper into the town. Near the center of the town, the trio arrived onto the doorstep of an inn.

"Witchdell Safe Haven," Rose read aloud as she judged the old broken building. She smiled, remembering her little cottage with Celia.

"Yes, I believe this is the place," Aya mumbled to herself as she walked through the wooden doorway, creating the sound of an old dying peal. An old man with a gray beard sat at a desk in the right corner. Aya motioned for the Mensches to stay back as she greeted the man. Rose couldn't hear what she was saying, but eventually the man left and Aya returned.

"We are getting a room, and he is bringing out my friends."

"Who are your friends?" asked Jason quietly.

"Nice people, Reds, who want to help," Aya told him, placing money in a pocket and staring him in the eye. Rose's mind drifted for a bit, and then the man returned. The innkeeper walked up to the group of the kids. Aya ever so quietly gave the innkeeper the rest of the money. Two kids came waddling behind the innkeeper and shyly waved at Aya.

"Hello!" Aya greeted them. "How are you?"

"I'm doing well," said the female of the two. This girl looked older than Aya, perhaps Jason's age, and Jason took an interest in her as well.

"Fine," said the boy.

They both had curly red hair and green eyes. They both had gray roots in their hair, probably brought on by stress that the king would march in and take their home. A clear face and a small nose covered the girl's head. Muscle was popping out of the girl's green tank top, and you could see the shape of more muscle in the torso of her body as well. The boy's looks were very similar to hers, so Rose guessed the two were siblings. He also had a clean face and large biceps. His hair was curly at the top, so his hair stood straight up.

Rose observed all this as Aya talked quietly to them.

When she finally introduced the two to Jason and Rose, she said, "Jason, Rose, meet Andrew and Camilla. They are Reds who journeyed from Ceptem in hopes of peace. They both really want to help us defeat the king."

Camilla took out her hand for Rose to shake.

"Rose, Rose Mensch."

"Camilla. It is lovely to meet you."

And they talked, then the boy came up to shake Rose's little hand.

"Andrew," he said, his voice very deep and manly.

"Rose," she said again. Her eyes gazed over at Jason, who blushed very hard when Camilla introduced herself to him. He was slightly taller and slightly more buff, but the slight giggle she gave meant they were having a nice time. Aya watched intently as her friends were meeting, and then the day carried on.

All the planning and strategizing took up most of their evening. They ate pork and other meat over an open fire. Rose didn't eat the meat and instead ate leaves and berries she went off to pick by herself. The woods in Beal were nothing like her woods. They didn't move for her or scatter the leaves for her to find only the red berries. They didn't do much for her, but they did move once. Rose, to her surprise, saw Camilla standing behind her.

"This might sound weird, but the woods do as I command them to do. In my head I say it, and it is like they can listen," Camilla said. Her eyes glowed in the moon as she viewed the wonders of her own wood.

"No, not crazy at all," Rose told her empathetically. They walked on, talking.

"Water is hard to find here, unless you want to drink the ocean water. So I command the woods to give up some of the nutrition they get into this small creek right here," she said, pointing to a little pond of water much smaller than Rose's lake. It bubbled clear water down little frothy bumps.

"The people say that it has magical properties to heal, but it really is just reused water from my little forest." Her red hair flowed, the curls bouncing as the pair continued walking. Her lips were a bright red, almost like the sunrise. Here and there appeared a pile of different fruits from all over the forest. Camilla must have been telling the forest to do that the whole time. Rose was so grateful. All she could do was hug her and thank her for what she had done.

"How long have you been wanting to kill the king?" Camilla asked abruptly.

"Not long," answered Rose. "It took me a while to realize what I needed to do and to put aside what I wanted to do. It's hard, you know. One day you wake up and you are being told what you have to do. I have lived my life traveling and living by my own rules. Jason and I look out for each other. Then I learn that there is more to this game we call life than me, you know?"

Camilla looked at Rose and smiled at her. It was the same beautiful smile Celia had, with bright white teeth and her lips big and luscious.

"Yes, I know. Andrew and I are twins—interconnected, you could say. I have always had to share with him. My parents were poor, so we could only have a few things. Everything I got, Andrew got, too, but then I had to put aside what I wanted to look out for what he needed, and eventually he did the same. That was when I knew I wanted to help other people. So I came here, with my brother, to live with my uncle. We traveled from Relor in Ceptem, took the trains down to the edge, took a boat down to the islands, and ended up in Witchdell. We met Aya somewhere along the way, and she told us about you and how special you are. She expects great things from you, Rose Mensch. Don't let the princess down." She laughed.

They both walked back and talked, watching the sun set and the night grow black. They parted, and Aya and Rose entered their room, and Jason went into his.

While the girls wandered the halls of the inn, a man stood quietly in a corridor, watching them. His eyes darted between Aya and Rose quickly, studying them intently. He growled at their smell. Aya confidently walked up to the man and smiled at his pale lips and brown eyes. She whispered a message into his cold ear, then whistled. His shoulders grew upright, and he watched Aya apprehensively, squinting at her. He ran once he had studied her enough. Aya walked back to Rose, and they silently entered their room.

Cozy white comforters covered the areas of the two beds in the room. They pampered themselves and then snuggled into bed. Thoughts of dragons raced in their heads, while the sounds of cannons and shouts of men teased their ears.

"Aya," Rose said quietly.

"Yes," Aya responded. The night was growing very dark and did not allow enough light for them to see properly.

"How do people live like that?"

"Like what?"

"In fear? Fear that one day an evil man is going to come in with hundreds of armed troops that will burn their homes to the ground along with everyone they love?"

"They rely on hope. Hope in one thing. Do you know what that is, Rose?"

She shook her head no.

"You," Aya told her. "They hold on to their hope in Rose Mensch, the Red Lip who will defeat the king and end all this madness."

"Yes, but Reds don't kill."

"But you will, Rose."

"No, let me speak," Rose said before Aya could continue. "Reds don't kill. It is not in their nature. So by killing, am I really saving my kind, or am I betraying them?"

Rose and Aya pondered that thought for a good while. The morning would come soon enough. Neither of them answered it, nor did they continue the discussion. They stared up at the gray ceiling until their eyes closed. They stayed still as their brains moved to other places, forgetting for the moment that the king was on his way.

Samuel

The city was bright, filled with the different shades of orange and red. The people that walked the streets were all the same. They had red lips, light eyes, fair skin, and dark lashes. They dressed in modest clothing, never stole or cheated. They raised their children with a tender heart and taught them to behave with kindness toward everyone. It was typical for a Red haven to be a prosperous city, to engage in the equality and industry of those around them.

The king, with his golden robes and shone shoes, gathered his ships and his army near this little village. They docked on the small harbor, forcing their way aggressively by the small trade ships filled with beets and cabbage. With their swords and shields, the soldiers marched into the small city. The soldiers glared with disgust at those who bore lips the shade of red.

"Pigs," the guards would spit, their drool clogging the eyes of the children who played in the streets.

The gait of the soldiers was heavy and sophisticated, with a touch of authority. Their heavy metal spears and swords helped them advance. They banged their silk-covered hands on the wooden doors of the small apartments that filled the city. A woman would answer, lips dark red. She and her children would be ripped from one another and thrown into the small wagons the soldiers had brought. The Reds, who had no reason to not be proud, were easy to spot. But the Purple some bore was much harder to discern.

As they were thrown, a talent show was performed, their feet clanking in chains, to see which color their fire glowed.

"Wrong man!" called out a fierce fat old soldier, throwing a young Red onto the ground. "Green is his fire!"

"We shall find them. I know they make life here," Samuel said, walking slowly up to the soldier, stepping over the fallen man. "And if we don't, I will have every one of them hanged, for they are not useful to me." He slid closer.

Samuel's jeweled hands ran through the dirty face of the young man, touching his red lips.

"They are filthy," Samuel hissed, slapping the poor boy. His hands reached deep within a coat pocket, lined with silk, and retrieved a dagger. The sharp dagger had his name engraved on its side. The king looked deeply into the hazy, bright eyes of the pale man who lay helplessly on the ground. The man had his feet wrapped in piercing chains, his ankles bleeding out in the mud. Samuel gripped the man's waist.

"A waste of a life."

The man gulped when the dagger smoothly penetrated his flesh, draining him of his red blood and causing an end to his life. The man's face flushed red, and then his skin turned yellow. The burning of the king's eyes was malevolent. The organs that seeped through the long opening created by the dagger now swam in a pool of blood. The man slammed hard on the ground after being released from Samuel's hand, his cheek splashing in the gore.

Samuel stood and wiped the stains off the end of his cloak before walking along the path and watching as the final colors were burned from the palms of the Reds.

The next men and women who burned blue and green fire were placed in a dump off the streets of their homes. They were bound in chains, awaiting their next instruction. They would weep and begin to crave Ashbel. They would beg to be reunited with their loved ones. They would hold hands with their sorrowful neighbor, and they would sit still and listen to the king speak to his army. As quickly as they came, they left with only a cart of people, and the Reds, with one key, slowly clicked themselves free.

Samuel led the wagon full of tightly muzzled Reds, who had been bounded by chains lining even their fingers, to a small room within a large stone building. There, they were ordered to step behind one another and sit on the small benches made of wood, beyond the metal doors. The room was lined with ice and snow, kept cool by cold steel that replaced the walls. The wood benches had icicles under them. There was frost even within the cracks of the hail-filled seats.

A man who was dressed in a white gown that fell to his toes sluggishly stepped out of the room, shaking the hand of the king. His hair was greasy and white. Over time, his back had twisted into a hump. His nose was large, gnarled, and pointy. Red blotches covered his cheeks and forehead.

His weak grasp was crushed by the ring-dominated fingers of Samuel and the booming of the king's voice as the final clanks of the Reds hushed.

"Dr. Sallemanno!" the overjoyed and deep voice of the king exclaimed.

"My king! My king!" he cried, his raspy tune cracking and shaking.

"Is the room ready?" the king asked, gesturing to the closed door beyond. The doctor nodded vigorously, tripping over his own feet as he turned around to look at the door.

"Yes, sire. Very cold, sire!"

"Lead them in!" Samuel demanded to the guards who waited wordlessly beside the Reds. They began to march collectively, slowly, and took their place on the benches, shivering.

"As king, I own everything in this land. You mere peasants have something that I so dearly want to have: your fire!"

The Reds began to shake tremendously.

"I have concluded that to kill all of your useless kind would be rather-exhausting work. Instead, I have mercifully decided to infect your kind in a rather simple manner. In a separate yet related conclusion, I have decided that those who can control the evils of the purple fire must willingly infect those who can be infected. So I have made this unbearably simple. Join me and be rewarded, or die a dreadful death here in this cage."

The Reds shook their heads in immediate denial. The king, who wished so terribly to gloat, relished in his power. He chose to violate them further, laughing to himself.

"No one wishes to help me?" he said in a whimper, a false tear slipping down his face. "I suppose that is all right. Doctor, please enlighten them."

The guards, who had supported this exercise many times before, paired up one-on-one with Reds and led them into the chamber beyond the door. The chamber was filled with rows and rows of long metal tables, like what might have been used to perform surgical procedures. Each table had a series of straps, which the soldiers used to restrain the fingers, hands, feet, and heads of the Reds, who were now to be referred to as Dr. Sallemanno's *patients*. Once the straps were attached and checked, each soldier returned to the outer room to gather another patient and repeat the routine. The room itself was cold, not so much as a part of the doctor's treatment, but as a learning from the first few trials. Those who supported the doctor's treatment complained about the overwhelming stench on the last day of the treatment. The doctor made this concession regarding the temperature in the room, realizing that the cold kept vapor pressure lower, an efficient way to address the smell issue.

The king chuckled mercilessly as he watched them squirm. Some of the Reds began to let tears drip from their bright eyes.

Dr. Sallemanno paced inside the door behind the Reds, smelling their fear even in the cool temperature. He threw snow onto their laps joyfully before looking deeply into the youngest child's eyes. He smiled. The doctor dug his dirty pink hands into his gown's deep pocket, revealing a wicked instrument. It was a metal clamp with sharp teeth, with a fingerlike post opposing the hinge. There was frostbitten flesh stuck to the sharp teeth of the clamp. The black of the metal was dotted with red.

Dr. Sallemanno began checking the straps to make sure the young girl's head and neck were fully restrained.

"Edgar, my dear friend, has designed for me a device that could very well kill you!" the king bellowed with glee.

Edgar violently clamped the teeth on the red lips of the girl, watching her muffled squeals as the teeth bit into the flesh around her red lips.

"The rules are simple," Samuel explained while Edgar moved onto the next Red Lip. "You have three days to rethink my offer. In the meantime, you rot here, cold and wet, thirsty and hungry, with nothing but your tears to mock you."

After all the patients had their lips clamped and their heads fully restrained, Dr. Sallemanno left the room for the refrigeration chamber. The doctor efficiently returned with a bucket of frozen metal washers. He then began placing two washers each on the fingerlike post of each patient's metal clamp.

"Warm yourself with your fire and your clamp shall be ripped from your shiny faces," Dr. Sallemanno described as he finished putting the frozen washers on the last patient. "It is so cold that your lips will grow numb. If the clamp is ripped early, as punishment for bodily warmth, your lips will be torn off with the clamp and you will bleed to death on the ground below you. Stay cold the three days and just maybe your lips will be blue enough to let you survive. Either way, it will be delightfully painful!"

Edgar slapped the face of the child, kicked her knees, and bit her fingers before cuffing them tightly together. He slowly left the room, shutting and locking the door behind them, and then beamed up at the king.

"And if they do not give in or warm themselves?" Samuel asked.

"My king, they belong to you. They fear you. It is for you to decide what use to make of their gifts, not themselves." His hands twisted, he bowed before the king.

Samuel began to strut out of the small lair. "I will have your eyes gauged out of your disturbing face if you lie to me!"

"Of course, sire!"

The first day, the metal doors were heavily guarded with soldiers. The rooms to the side of the large cooler were filled with gadgets and torture mechanisms of every kind. Edgar worked tirelessly, imagining ways to pry out the most satisfying cries from those who deserved it the most and least. He didn't really care.

He was shuffling his feet back and forth by a small drawer full of a variety of knives when he was interrupted by the rhythmic tapping of gloved soldiers at his wooden door.

"Dr. Sallemanno," one of them called with a stern voice. "One is glowing."

Excitedly, Dr. Sallemanno abandoned his drawer and unlocked the door into the cooler, his white gown flowing behind him.

A woman who had grown skinny and whose face was tearstained had an aura of purple surrounding her form. Her eyes were closed. Her breathing grew normal. The eyes of her fellow Red Lips beamed at her with anxiety. Her eyes opened to the ugliness of the doctor looking at her with pure admiration.

"Do you wish to give up your fire?" he asked, touching her face and feeling her pulse.

She shook her head.

The doctor hopped like a rabbit, racing to tap on the king's guest room, which was where the king resided on weeks when Dr. Sallemanno had patients.

Samuel, still in his nightclothes, followed closely behind Edgar. They arrived at the woman in question. It was odd how the king's admiration mirrored that of the doctor.

"Rip them! Rip them! Quickly now, my king!"

Samuel saw the tears drip down the patient's face as those who sat by her tried to reach out for her hand. Alas, the Red Lip's hands were all tightly bound.

"Does no one else wish to warm themselves up?" Samuel asked around, looking at their fearful faces. "It is always more fun when I can do two or three in a row!"

Still, no one dared to heat their freezing bodies. Samuel himself was getting a little uncomfortable in the cold room.

His manicured hands gripped neatly on the top of the clamp. Bending down, the king quickly yanked the clamp across her face from left to right. The lips of the Red were now fully contained in the clamp, and the patient's face instantly was awash in blood flooding from around her mouth. The gaping hole offered quite a disturbing view to the uninitiated.

Her face contorted in pain, while her limbs struggled against her restraints, as she tried to reach her face, blood gushing out of her mouth. Her cries of agony slowly turned to moans, then whimpers.

She cried for help. She dreamed of simpler times. She could feel the blood dripping down her chin and neck and the red falling down her body. Her chest was now red, and the blood began pooling around her table. The smell of blood filled the room. Mercifully for the other patients, her ordeal ended in lifelessness in minutes and not hours, with the clamp holding her lips displayed as a trophy to the other patients.

"No one else?" Samuel asked, looking at the woman's corpse. "Would you like to give up your fire now?"

Every patient in the room waited for someone to volunteer, but no one did. They all remained solemn and silent.

"How disappointing."

*****

The second day was filled with rage-drawn dialogue between Edgar and Samuel, whose fits grew more violent as the hours progressed.

"No one! Not a single one has yet to comply with me! *Me*!" the king yelled, throwing the knives from a drawer around the room.

"Sire!"

"Don't you dare call me sire, you idiot!" Samuel barked. He walked around the room and searched for anything else to throw, now targeting the doctor.

"My apologies!"

"You have been successful in every other case you have committed your pitiful self to. You have burned, scalped, raped, flogged, whipped, hanged, skinned, and performed countless other exercises! Tell me why!" He shivered. "Tell me why I am the one you make to look the fool!"

Dr. Sallemanno fell hopelessly to the ground on his knees.

Samuel, dressed in dark-blue robes and shawls, paced around the room, his face flushed and his blood heated with anger.

"Am I a fool? Tell me, old friend, am I a fool?"

Edgar stuttered. "No, Your Majesty, never!" In his big head, he wished to know what would happen to him if the king grew angrier.

"Lies!" Samuel cried. "You lie to me!"

"How? How do I speak falsely to Your Grace?"

Samuel laughed in frustration. "I have worked with you in many groups of Reds. Dozens! Yet I am still here, with the same routine, without my Purple army! Tell me, how does that not make me a fool?"

Edgar had no way to reply. Words had betrayed him.

"They are starving in there, Your Grace. Surely, they will want food."

"Every day they don't eat food, my enemies grow stronger! My daughter is out there, prancing around with the girl *destined* to kill me. She might just succeed in killing me and taking everything we have worked for!"

Samuel threw himself onto a chair snuggled up in a corner, resting his head in his palms. "Sire, there are other ways to conduct a murder than to birth a genocide," the doctor informed him. "We could make it more personal."

"What about the souls in the cooler? If we make this more personal, as you say, what shall we have with them?" Samuel asked.

Edgar smiled. "Fun."

*****

The third and final day was packed with many events. Edgar began his day as he always did, in his study, plotting and conversing with a customer. The Reds had been quiet and only wailed every few hours, when the doctor replaced the frozen washers to their clamps. Efficiency dictated that the doctor replace the washers with newly frozen washers every two hours. The *patients* would struggle against their restraints, especially if their stomachs ached.

Samuel was walking in as an older woman was walking out. She had dark hair and cruel eyes. She wore a tight veil around her face and head. She solemnly wandered out, her eyes never meeting those of her king.

"How did it go?" the king asked, shutting the wooden door behind him.

"I assume well," Edgar answered, polishing an empty jar. "She took the poison."

"When shall she go?"

"Whenever the girl is on a train. That is when she will do it."

The king smiled and brought his hands together in a satisfied habit. The room was dimly lit with candles. A metal chandelier made from animal traps hung low from the ceiling. Samuel poured a glass of wine.

"So…she will be exterminated?" Samuel questioned, sipping the red wine from his glass.

"Absolutely not! I merely gave her the poison to frame her," Edgar corrected.

Samuel's face turned grim. The king forcefully gripped the robe the doctor was wearing, passionately spitting on his nose.

"What?" he exclaimed, ripping his teeth into his lip.

"I thought you would like to kill her yourself!" Edgar whimpered, choking on his collar.

"And give her the opportunity to kill me first?" Samuel yelled. "You dim-witted swine! You idiot! You buffoon! You oaf!"

"Sire!"

"You are so wise in how to kill! I wonder how it would look if you died from your own invention! How poetic to see you choke on your own poison!"

He dragged Edgar across the room by his greasy hair, with his other hand loose on his throat. He tied him to the wooden chair snuggled in the corner, ignoring the doctor's pleas of mercy.

"I have waited," Samuel began. He looked furtively at the different chemicals and potions.

"I have been patient!"

He shook one of the different bottles, black and red sparkles floating above the dark-green liquid. He swirled it around and around, pondering whether to give it to the doctor. He chose in favor.

The strong clamp of Samuel's leather boots rubbed against the wooden floors. He strutted slowly, to torture the doctor.

"Sire! Sire! Please no!"

The king smirked. "How sweet! The master manipulator is pleading for his life."

"Yes, yes, so I am a fool. I have not been a good manipulator. Please spare me!"

"I spare no one."

Samuel parted his yellow teeth, opening his rotten mouth, pressuring his defiant jaw. Dripping the poison, drop by drop, he forced the doctor to swallow.

The doctor whined and tried to spit up, but the king would not let him. He forced the poison deep within his body.

"You will die here, fool!" he spat once the bottle was emptied.

"My king!" he cried once more, begging for water.

Edgar's tan face turned yellow. His pupils turned red, and the blood within his body began drooling out of his nostrils. The sweat he bore dripped intensely down his face. The yellow swiftly turned to red, then purple, and then blue. He coughed and wheezed. His hands began to burn, then they became freezing cold. His chest spasmed wildly, and then he lay there, still.

The king laughed and held his body closely, feeling the life leave him.

Once he lay still, foam spilled from his mouth. Red and black sparkles mixed within the white. Samuel patted his loose hair, brushing it out of the way. The king hesitated before getting up and fixing his gowns. Dr. Sallemanno had taken the lead in so many of the king's different efforts, but disappointment had consequences. The requisite reflection period being satisfied, the king then waltzed to the table where the doctor's notes were kept for safety.

He shuffled through the different leather books and white pages filled with black ink. The drawings of dead bodies and murder equipment flooded his brain. The ingredients for the worst potion brews danced within his consciousness. He collected the data for dark magic.

Samuel left the room with one final kiss upon Edgar's head. He carried the books as he skipped through the halls. The king decided to take a rest and lay upon his bed at his temporary residence during these exercises.

Before midday had begun, a man had pleaded to meet with the king. He stressed to the guards that he had information the king would be pleased to hear. When he finally gained his attention, they sat at a wooden table with a golden map below their eyes.

"I am a poor man from Witchdell, Your Majesty. I have been a spy for years. I have worked and served you for most of my life, so please trust me when I say to you that I have seen her. I have laid my eyes on the witch."

Samuel stirred. "Where? With whom?"

"Your daughter, Aya, and a few other Reds."

"The girl, who is she?"

"Rose. Rose Mensch. A brunette with fair skin and blue eyes. Her lips are as red as her fire. She is fast, my king. She is smart and fast. But I sense that she is scared."

"Mensch!" Samuel cried. "A Mensch! She is the daughter of Ekon! How dare he! How dare he!"

The king wept in betrayal. He fell to his knees as he dismissed the man. Surrounded by traitors, he was. He snatched the map from the table and read it through his tears. Witchdell was another young city near the king himself. He began to cry in fear of her. He called for his generals to aid him in a decision.

Once he collected himself from the tense pressure of the Mensch daughter, he said, "There are only two directions the bitch can go from Witchdell, at least only two directions that make any sense. Fortify troops here and here." He pointed on the map to Remular City and Ravens, Nava.

"My king, may I burden you with a request to improve the positioning of our troops?" begged the senior military man.

"As you were."

"My king, I can understand Remular City, but what is the importance of Ravens? That city has no relevance to you and this plan."

The king laughed. "Fool! She is a Mensch and may just need to go home first. I will arrange for additional security. There is no time to waste. Men, begin your plans!"

They led themselves out of the room, and Samuel continued searching through the books.

Later in the afternoon, there was a swift knock on his door. The palace guards wanted to inform him that three days had gone by.

Samuel closed the journals and walked out with his soldiers and pounded on the metal door. The banging frightened the Reds, who were nearly asleep. Their lips had long since lost circulation. Their pale faces had turned red. They sighed of relief, knowing their ordeal might soon be coming to an end.

They had all been humiliated in a singular fashion. The chamber reeked of feces, sweat, and dead flesh. The soldiers mocked each patient for choosing to suffer.

The soldiers unstrapped the patients one by one and then chained them together both by hand and by foot. The clamps remained in place on the patient's frostbitten lips; however, the frozen washers were collected in a bucket to be reused with the next batch of patients. The soldiers then marched the patients outside to the great yard, which was behind the small building in which Edgar Sallemanno once worked. The patients felt warm in the Red island sun, their hands showing through their metal restraints. The patients pouted and were anxious, both realizing the damage that had been done to their faces and worried about what further action the king might take.

"You know why you are here, you dirty Reds!" Samuel called.

They grunted.

"I have kept you, bound you up, and refused to feed you. For three days you have sat in your piss and shit. You have slept in your saliva. You have sniffed your morbid odor and have tasted your breath."

The soldiers laughed as they pointed at the stained clothes the patients wore. The king stood straight and watched as cannons were being lined up behind the patients.

"I killed Dr. Sallemanno, a friend of mine, because he did not give me what I wanted. I hate you! I will do much worse to you. I want to do much worse to you!"

A soldier, who was young and bulky, hooted.

"I will ask only once more," Samuel warned them. "Give me your fire!"

A grave silence hovered over the field. None of the *patients* nodded. No head muffled an agreement. They all stood still.

"I understand. You fear what I will do. You should. But you should fear more what will become of you. Perhaps I can persuade you to enjoy fear. For fear is what all men want and is the easiest to obtain."

After he finished his argument, the sound came from a large salvo of cannons fired from behind the Reds. The artillery shells nearly missed the Reds, flew into the trees, caused the ground to tremble when they landed, and set some of the trees on fire. Some soldiers prepared to get buckets of water to put out the fire, while others remained to guard the Reds. Then another round of cannons roared, and another, making the Reds feel even more uncomfortable.

"Having fun?" Samuel asked with a large grin across his face as the Reds squirmed and panicked. The soldiers cheered their approval.

The last few cannons were the loudest; they pounded deep within the forest and banged on the ground with might. It made the Reds cry.

Samuel, after the last cannon was fired, walked up to the Reds and watched them as they flinched at his every step. The breeze was light, and the sun was beaming. The king was wearing his full black gowns and robes, golden ropes, a large crown upon the top of his head. A drip of sweat fell down his face.

"Have I persuaded you?" he asked a very pretty girl who had grown rather hideous in the past three days. He touched her sweet face, caressed her neck, and fiddled with her hair.

She shook her head with confidence. She wished to burn him. She wished to burn the metal around her fingers. But she feared for her life. They all did. You could not bet on reason at a time like this; however, most Reds calculated that the worst of their ordeal was over. The Reds standing in the great yard behind the building where they had been tortured began to consider that perhaps the king was out of ways to hurt the Reds more.

Without regard to whatever hopes the Reds might have, the king punched the pretty girl in the stomach, with her doubling over. As she recovered and stood back up, he spat in her eyes and slapped her arm.

"You watched your friend die, you saw her body begin to decay, and you still wish to stay as you are?"

She nodded.

He gripped the clamp on her lips tightly and slowly, even exquisitely, peeled it off her numb face passionately. She cried as she began to open her mouth. It was blue and cold, frostbitten and dead. The rest of her face had begun to look blue as well. The lips had turned blue due to blood loss. She fell to the ground, whimpering and whining.

"No one shall ever want to kiss those lips again!" the king taunted while throwing her clamp at her feet, where she could look at her lips still tucked inside.

She cried some more.

He walked over to the next man, who was fat and young. He ripped his clamp off with indifference toward the man. Then the king moved on to the next, and the next, and the next, all the way down the line.

They were all on the ground, crying and holding one another, comparing scars. Samuel looked pleased with himself.

"You shall never use your fire again. You will be too ashamed."

The soldiers cheered their king on with plain faces. Their long white capes were on the ground. Their metal armor covered their feet and beer bellies, for being a guard on this detail was a select assignment. Their long brown and black hair was combed to the side, under their helmets.

"Where do you wish us to take them?" one asked while gripping his golden sword.

Samuel thought to himself.

"Send them where the rest are. Send them to Erik, the chief of the Blue Lips."

Rose

"Ready…set…go!" yelled Rose. Andrew and Jason were competing in an obstacle course in the woods. There were climbing ropes, mud ditches, jumping logs, poison ivy, and other dangerous factors. They had been training ever since they met for this. Aya and Rose planned their attacks but also helped build the track and map out Jason's way to victory.

Camilla was certain that Andrew was going to win, but with all the racing Rose had put Jason through, Andrew didn't stand a chance.

The two boys started to climb a long yarn-like rope up into the treetops, and there they swung across different vines and tree branches, until they landed on a wooden platform. There they jumped down into a pile of dead brown, red, and yellow leaves, sprinted across the center of Beal into a mud bath. As they slowly made their way out of the sticky substances of mud, they jumped over three logs, each one bigger and bigger than the one before it, and first one over the last one won.

All three girls, screaming at the end of the finish line for their favorite to win, coaxed them on to run faster. Jason hopped over the first log, Andrew barely trailing behind. Andrew bolted, cracking twigs and other ground items. They had tied up, getting ready to pass the last log, when Jason tripped over an outgrown root and Andrew took the winning place.

Camilla giggled mischievously.

"No. No. No. Not fair!" Rose shouted playfully. Camilla and Rose had grown quite close over just one week, realizing different features of themselves in each other. Aya was still the leader of their tribe and was worried all week that her father would attack. After recognizing Andrew and Camilla's uncle was a watchman for the king and sending the king a threatening message through their uncle, Aya was certain the king would arrive very shortly. The five kids finished their exercises in the green woods and returned to the town of Witchdell. Rose hadn't had much time to really see much of the town, since she was always with Aya. Aya was relentless when it came to preparing battle plans. Although Rose wouldn't be formally fighting anyone, she had to know the battle plans in case the battle did not go as planned. Rose would only be killing one person, maybe. The thoughts of the first night's dreams filled her brain every time she thought about the war. Aya never helped her cautious eye either.

"Rose, what's going on?" asked Aya at week's end. They were both in their room, looking over a map, something Rose had never seen completely.

"What I said that night, it still haunts me."

"Why?"

"Because I don't want to do something I think is good and then have everyone I did it for hate me. I know I sound immature, but it's true. It is eating me alive, this whole philosophy."

"Is it also home?" Aya asked, putting a hand on Rose's shoulder.

"I just don't want to let them down," Rose said, a tear leaving her eye. "I miss them so much." She twisted the rose gold bracelet her aunt gave her. She wanted to see Celia again. She wanted to know if they were okay, if the king had advanced, and if he was hurting them like he did her mother.

"That man will pay for what he did," Aya told Rose quietly.

"Why do I have to make him suffer? Why do I have to cause pain to people?"

Her new tattoo on her ankle burned, like it craved to be satisfied with its purpose. A heartbeat could be felt if a finger was placed against it.

They stared at the ceiling of their shared room at the inn. They planned attacks on the king's army for a while and then walked outside into the hallway. Across from their door was a door that looked very similar to their own. A wooden frame and a lighter, wood-colored door with a false silver handle that, when twisted, opened. The hallway was painted an off-white color. The ground floor had a lumber tile, and stairs were at either end of the way. They walked together down the east-side stairwell and entered the lobby. There was an open area with a small seating place and a front desk, where Andrew now worked after his uncle left to betray them. Outside was the town, and there all the people were crowded in a bunch. Some were sitting in chairs, while others were sitting on the grass or in a gravel path. All were there to listen to a speech from Rose, a speech of hope given to lighten the hearts of the hopeless Reds.

Jason was there to usher in all the people. There weren't a lot, as it was a small trading center that got all its water from a stream redirected by the mind of Camilla, a sixteen-year-old girl. About three dozen people, more or less, entered the main grass area. Many children were held upon the shoulders of their fathers so they could see Rose properly. Her bronze-colored hair was done in a nice braid by Aya to show her dedication and her seriousness about the matter.

"Good day," Rose started, the whisper of the folks quieting down. "My name is Rose." She gulped. All the people's bright faces, their red lips, and their skinny flesh were mesmerized by the girl in front of them. For a moment that seemed to be an eternity, the only audible sound the chirping of birds.

"Red Lips are a people I never knew too much about. My brother, who ushered you all in here today, told me about them when I was young. We traveled from Ravens in Nava down to Dayton in the Red Islands. My parents were both killed by the king. My extended family is being torn apart as we speak, and I know that I don't want to lose my kind too. And hey, I know it sounds hard to believe, but I know that hope exists. It's real, for sure. I wouldn't be here without it. I know that dragons are real, for I have seen them. I know that things that to others may seem impossible have been done. I know all these things, but that doesn't matter. What matters is if you know. If you don't believe, no one can. Whether we are the lowest of the low or the highest of the high, we just need to know in here that our situation in the war is changing. We deserve to end this war, which has gone on for too long, and make the peace that we all deserve. The evil king knows that we are coming for him, and he is afraid. All I ask is that you keep hope in your heads and in your hearts and have courage that your hope—"

Boom.

Cannons were fired not far from where they stood. Screams of horror from the mouths of the people of Witchdell blended with the sounds of war. To soothe the panic, Rose commanded the people to leave the gathering, enter their homes, lock the doors, and close their windowpanes.

The people quickly gathered their belongings and ran. A few children appeared to be abandoned as parents of larger families ran out of hands to pair with children. The homeless beggars were left to endure the full commotion. Aya grabbed on to the little hands of two kids and ran with them to the inn. Jason ran over to an elderly man and helped him move inside the inn. Rose and Camilla ran to see what was happening and were surprised by the booming sound of another cannon as soon as they entered the wooded area. Another cannon was fired. They followed the sounds of shouts and yells from far away. Surely, a battle was going on.

"What other cities are there in Beal?" asked Rose, running faster toward the noise.

Camilla, who commanded the trees to move to make it easier for the girls to pass, answered, "On Witchdell, these noises I have never before heard. The explosions and the sounds of destruction are not native to my ears."

They ran faster through the moving forests, getting closer as they heard more of the noises. Finally, they reached the battleground. Rose had never before seen battle.

In a plain open field with trees surrounding it lay men in shallow trenches. The men wore iron armor covering their entire bodies. Men, covered in dirt and blood, covered the east side of the field, while fewer than five armored men lay motionless on the west side.

More cannons took fire. More people lay dead. More families lost loved ones. The math was simple. The outcome was always tragic.

Rose then drifted into a light memory. During the week and before going to bed one night, Rose and Aya had shared their deepest, darkest secrets with each other. Rose remembered every word Aya told her that night. She remembered the way Aya's hair looked all cut off and uneven. Rose realized that the battle Rose was watching right now was the very battle Aya had described. Erik was right. These were their futures. How much closer would Rose come to her own darkest fear? Rose was paralyzed in thought, remembering the burning barn.

"Rose!" Camilla shouted as she touched the arm of the hallucinating girl.

"Y-y-yes?" Rose responded.

"Come! We must leave. This battle is too close to my home."

As they left, one more thought came into the mind of Rose. An image of a man entered Rose's brain, much like the day Ashbel entered her mind.

The man had a shaven face, deep black eyes, a young look to himself, and a golden crown on his head. The man was passing into the waters of the Southern Bend, the Forgotten Ocean, as Camilla and Rose ran. She fell to the ground, cracking many twigs and leaves and bruising her back in the process. Rose shook and trembled. Her body moved, but her heard was dizzy. She could only see the face of the man and the way he appeared to her to be looking right at her. Her back moved up from the ground, shifting, but not intentionally. The man terrified her. She wanted to break free of his hold, but all she could do was stare and squirm. He whispered something loud enough for Rose to hear. It was almost as if he wasn't talking to Rose but instead merely cautioning to himself.

"Beware the purple veins," he repeated over and over.

The echo was pounding so. It would have driven any man crazy. Suddenly it all paused. Rose stood up and noticed that time was no longer moving around her. Rose saw the beautiful body of Camilla looking at her, pleading for her to get up.

But Rose wasn't dead.

"Enjoy the show?" asked a familiar voice.

"Erik," said Rose, infuriated.

"I quite did, not that you care or anything."

"I'm sorry, but you almost killed me. You enjoyed watching that," said Rose, "so please excuse me if I'm not entertained."

"Wasn't me, Rosie," said the Blue man simply. His fat old body giggled as he spoke these words.

"Then who was it?"

"Either yourself or someone you hate."

"What does that mean?"

"It means," whined Erik, "that the king is near."

"That is not good," said Rose, sprinting away. She could hear the shouts of her name from the Blue Lip. She didn't turn around but ran until she saw the town. It, too, was also frozen. Time itself had stopped.

"Can't escape that easily," Erik told her, now with a glass of wine and a chair.

"Please unfreeze it."

"Please let the Purple enter your veins."

"No!"

"Then I can't help you."

"You're pathetic," snapped Rose.

"And the king is near," replied Erik, disappearing.

Rose woke up instantly from the ground where she lay, and Camilla had green tears falling from her face. Camilla's hands were holding Rose ever so carefully. Camilla was attempting to pick Rose up right before time itself stopped.

"Are you okay?" asked Camilla in a hurry, rushing to walk up next to Rose, who had stormed off in embarrassment.

"The king is near," Rose told Camilla, with time for nothing more. Camilla thought about this in the way of a normal, pure, non-Purple-exposed Red. For the first time, Camilla felt something new. *Anger.*

They both hastened their pace, sprinting back for Witchdell, where many lost and terrified people had gathered.

The city looked deserted; only Jason and Andrew walked the middle of the grounds, where dozens of people had recently sat.

"What happened?" asked Jason, grabbing Rose's arms and pulling her close. He looked worried, as if he had seen and felt true fear.

"The king. His men. Fighting. Up there!" Rose responded, panting, pointing one skinny finger up to the trees, where the pines stood out and the leaves bore a dark-green shade.

"We should leave, then," Aya told her. "If my father is good at anything, it is thinking and acting quickly. Over my years at Dragons Nest, Ashbel has told me many different things about my father. He can be really foolish when he gets emotional, which is happening more and more lately. He is less of a threat if we move fast. Let's get out of here."

Then there was a large *swoosh* and a *bang* hitting the ground, causing the trees to bend and sway from the sudden jolt. The group of children turned to see both Vulcan and Edan standing behind them, looking quite proud of themselves. Their blue and green scales shimmered in the light. Their hair flowed down their backs. Edan walked forward on his five claws.

Strutting his way over to Aya, Edan said, "We both have strict and direct orders from Ashbel to safely and directly move you from Witchdell to Ceptem."

"Who said anything about safely?" blubbered Vulcan. Rose remembered the last time she rode his blue body and how he loved to be reckless in flight. She giggled remembering it and the adrenaline he brought her.

"Ashbel told you this?" Aya inquired suspiciously. "Why isn't he here himself?"

"Having a meeting with the big brute, no doubt," Vulcan replied.

"Erik, the attitude-having little prick."

Rose laughed, also having a dislike for the Blue. The relation made her smile.

"You must not like this poor man," said Camilla, who had never had the pleasure of meeting the sad, gruesome fat old man that was Erik.

"Erik is not a man but merely a parasite that feeds off of Ashbel," Aya said cautiously, knowing Camilla has not been exposed to cruel words.

"Hop on my back," commanded Edan a short while later.

Rose was not hesitant to jump up on the back of Edan instead of Vulcan. She had had enough excitement for one day. Aya and her short hair and dark skin followed, with the bright-red hair and green-eyed Camilla next up behind Aya.

The boys got on the back of Vulcan, gripping firmly onto his blue fur. The dragons both fluttered their great big wings, which matched their sorted colors, and took flight. The dragons glided in the air, soaring high above the green trees. Only moments later, they were past the dangerous battlegrounds. Rose heard men shouting at the reptiles, but no action was taken. Surely, to the king, it was a sign that Rose was here and that Rose was prepared.

Flying over the water, they looked down at the blue liquid that covered most of the area. Rose's faced beamed in front of the others as she looked at the water.

"The Southern Bend, or the Forgotten Ocean, is hated by people down there, so it has a different name. The others are so-called the North, East, and West Oceans, but none like this one with the Red Islands," Aya whispered in her ear. Her breath was cold, like ice. The air was colder to breathe in, and Rose shivered. She warmed her body with her red fire. A glow circled her body, resembling a warm and red halo. She breathed again, and this time she was warmer. Aya grasped her body to warm herself as well because the winds of the atmosphere had remained frigid.

All alone they were, in the sky, drifting above home en route to a foreign place. The king would have already passed Ceptem, leaving it safe and hopeful. Not even birds would travel so high above the clouds, but dragons would so dare. The great big reptiles could fly beyond physics and time, defying all laws and seeming to require little oxygen. They could cover the whole world in a single day. Once in a great while, the dragons would sit on high mountain peaks, where they could see their own place and the world they once ruled. How could things get this bad?

The pace the dragons set with this flight was impressive. In no time, the dragons made it past the Southern Bend and reached the land of Ceptem.

The dragons landed in a large plain field, with no trees or bushes to be seen all the way to the horizon. Ceptem was a paradise of farmland. The dragons rested in a vast valley with sowed grounds and green grass growing to touch the knee bone. Dead stalks of corn rotted on the ground, and far in the distance, Rose saw horses.

"Ceptem is known for their farmland," Aya had to say, high-stepping past Rose to move over the corn. Jason and Andrew were just now ending their torturous roller-coaster ride on Vulcan. Both of them were shaking and trying to regain their balance.

"And you said my balance was bad," Rose said, mocking, with a full laugh as her brother fell to the ground from being dizzy. Andrew grasped the grass, pulling on the little stems to carefully make his way over to the girls. All three of the girls giggled. Even Vulcan was laughing hysterically to the point that he risked setting the field on fire with an unintentional breath of fire.

Eventually, the dragons flew away, gracefully soaring in the sky while cutting the wind with their sharp wings. The group of teenagers was left to fend for themselves in Ceptem, a land they didn't know. Ceptem was also a land far more dangerous than Beal, where friendly Red Lips were plentiful. The closer to Remular the group traveled, the more loyal the people and more dangerous the journey.

"Horses," Camilla said abruptly, pointing toward the herd. "We should get horses."

"Right. I'll keep watch while the rest of you steal the good ones," Jason told them.

"No!" interjected Camilla. "We shouldn't steal them. We should pay the owner for them."

"With what money?" questioned Aya logically. It was true. Not only were they wanted by the king, but they were also without money.

"Aren't you a princess?" Andrew asked her while tying his bootlaces. They continued to creep closer to the herd.

"Yes, Andrew, I am a princess, but I am also supposed to be dead on the will of His Majesty. I am also the daughter of the dragons. Who wouldn't want to help me?" she replied sarcastically, quietly, knowing they could be heard if they were too loud.

"Sorry, Camilla, but I think we are going to have to be bad," Rose told her, patting her back. "I'll tell you what? I will get you a horse and you can stand back, do nothing, and look pretty."

Rose smirked and laughed dryly. Rose skipped over to the top of the herd gate, which was where they would exit if successful.

The sky was blue. Rose loved the sky, loved birds, loved flying, and dreaded purple fire. Stealing was exactly what purple fire would want her to do. Purple fire could suck all the goodness out of her brain, telling her stealing was okay so long as she benefitted.

Aya, Rose, and Andrew came into the gated area, where three dozen horses stood, eating or galloping. There were all different breeds. Some were solids, black, white, or brown. Some were splattered with different colors and shades of colors.

They stealthily walked up to horses and, one by one, walked them back to Jason and Camilla by their mane. The two of them were watching the little farmhouse all the way in the distance for any sudden movement.

Rose grabbed a white one, a plain white stallion with a gray mane and blue eyes, and carefully trotted him through the gate in the fence, while not far behind her, Aya came walking alongside a brown-and-white spotted horse. Andrew came behind her with a black one.

Rose and Aya pushed through the gate opening as Jason quickly responded and took them out of the way, using both hands. Eventually, they were ready for Andrew's bronze mustang. Aya and Rose went back in to grab two more. Aya quickly pounced on one very close to the gate. It was a solid brown steed with black hooves, and his mane was the same copper color. Rose took slightly longer to find the last horse. This one was for Camilla, and Rose wanted one that fit Camilla's personality, the purest of all the herd.

Standing close to the middle was a solid white horse, with no spots or opposite shades of fur for the mane. This horse had long and overgrown fur at the hooves. The ears perked up as she patted the side of her neck.

"Beauty," she muttered, caressing her hair. Grabbing the mane, she led her out the gate opening.

Aya was there, leaving Jason to take the horse she chose out. Aya reached her skinny dark hands out to Rose. Rose picked up the pace, and so did the horse. She gorgeously trotted out of the gate and into Aya's arms.

Rose took charge of two of the horses, the jet-black one and the brown-spotted one, as the group walked out of view of the house. Once they were safe, thirty minutes later, they came upon a river. The river was flooded with black water, as if something dyed it this muddy fluid.

"Black river. Drink it. It is the same as any blue water, but black," Aya told the group as they hesitated to let the horses drink.

"It seems polluted," Andrew responded disapprovingly and in mild disgust.

"It is not," Aya had to say. She splashed her face with the black water. It dripped down her face like any liquid would. She then splashed her mouth and drank from her own cupped hands. The horses were already gladly drinking, all five of them. Their long tongues reached down into the water, and they gulped down.

"Should we decide who has what horse?" asked Rose after a swallow water. Everyone nodded in reply. Rose squinted as the sun came out of hiding from behind a cloud. She judged all the horses and then walked up to the black one. A solid colt that had black mane, black hooves, black eyes, black fur. He was beautiful. She petted his nose, and he puffed out air as he neighed. Camilla quickly chose the pure-white horse, and Aya picked a white steed with brown spots. Andrew chose an all-brown horse, casually petting his side before pulling himself up on his back using his manly muscles. Jason picked the white mustang with a gray mane and dark black roots. He, too, had the overgrown fur at the hooves that Aya's beast had.

Rose petted the mane of her jet-black horse, then hurtfully lifted herself on the back of her horse.

"What should I name you?" Rose pondered to herself out loud. "You are a male. A male beauty, owned by a Red running from Beal. Bealfire—a perfect name."

Close by, Aya muttered the name of her new friend. "Lords," she said.

The rest were being named out of earshot of Rose. They all called out the names of the animals as they commanded them to gallop into the open field of Ceptem. They were far away from where they were from, heading even farther away. Even as they grew closer to danger, Rose finally felt safe.

"We will sleep here for the night," Rose told her friends. She walked off, gathering wood for a fire. Aya was tying all the horses to the low long branch of a tree. Rose walked alone in the only wooded area nearby. Aya told her that they were far away from the nearest town of Relor. It was another trade city, but famous for its train tracks. Trains were nearly everywhere in Ceptem, transporting goods from farms to the cities and industrial equipment from cities to the farmlands. Only one train per day traveled into Remular. That train connected another city to Remular. Aya thought it would be too risky taking that train to Remular, so they were planning to catch a nearby train to a third city.

As Rose scoured the wooded area, she found small twigs, which were too little to burn, and long logs, which were too difficult to move. It was getting dark. The owls were starting to hoot, and the small wood was starting to echo growls and breaths. The wind and far-off wolves howled in harmony, and Rose walked faster. She looked back and could see the opening where her friends were. A perfect tree limb lay directly in the front of her. She reached down and held the prickly fallen branch. A second and third one were hidden nearby. For another twenty minutes, she collected more wooden sticks. She clicked her tongue and then snapped her fingers together. Out of her palm, a flame rose. A dark maroon fire brought the area to a glow. She followed her light and strutted back to the campsite.

"Finally," pronounced Aya in distress. The relief in her voice was palpable and welcomed by Rose's ears. Aya snatched the branches in Rose's hands and threw them into the firepit Jason had made. Camilla then used her hand to let a burn of soft-green fire rise and dissolve the wood.

"Lovely," Rose complimented.

Jason sat in awe of Camilla. He blushed when he was caught smiling too brightly at her. His eyes switched between the fire and her hair, eyes, and smile. He couldn't decide where it was better to look, so he took it all in. To him she was the most beautiful vision his Nomad eyes had ever fallen upon.

Jason went out to hunt and returned after not too long with two dead rabbits. He had lured them with berries and clicking noises. His father taught him how to hunt when he was very young, and he never forgot.

They tore the skin off the bunnies. Most of the group ate the meat after it was properly roasted above the fire. Rose ate berries and leaves she had freshly picked herself. She sat down with the group as they pretended to have adult conversation.

"Where are we going next?" inquired Camilla, who was absent when Aya originally told the rest of the group where they were going.

"We go next to Relor, a town just a few hours east of us. There we will take a train to Ashbelle, another safe place for Reds. Hope is large there. They are throwing a festival and parade in honor of Red Lips in a fortnight. We should go, to get our minds off things for an evening."

"Should we be risking losing focus?" asked Rose to challenge Aya.

"Well, yes, but a break can be nice. It will be fun," Aya told her, smiling.

"We haven't thought about anything since Beal!" shouted Rose, staring into Aya's silver eyes.

"Calm down, Rose," Jason said, scooting over toward her, comforting his little sister.

"We just left all those people there, with the king only fifteen minutes away. All those Reds are probably dead now!"

"Ashbel probably came by and took them to Dragons Nest, until the king was done fighting," Aya told her, trying to ease her Purple mind.

"But we will never know for sure!" exclaimed Rose. When she paused, everyone jumped up to help her. Rose was stuck in one place, but her head was somewhere else.

"Sorry to startle you and your friends," said a friendly, familiar voice.

"Ashbel!" exclaimed Rose, rejoicing, running up to embrace the beast. He curled his neck down to softly touch her back with his scaly red chin.

"Dear child, you are distressed on my behalf," the great beast told her with his deep, echo-like voice.

"Where are all the people we've abandoned in Beal?"

"Back in Beal," Ashbel replied to her. "The king saw you riding on the dragons and never thought to go farther in his battle. The fighting ended quite quickly after that. I was traveling down from Nava and heard the Blue Lip followed me down?" Ashbel raised an eyebrow.

"Yes, Erik paid me an unkind visit," Rose said with a sigh, facing the large dragon.

"He has taken a great interest in you, you know."

"Why?" asked Rose.

"Little Rose, because you remind him of himself when he was a Red Lip."

Rose had a look of disgust when she was told this.

"Erik was brave, selfless, cunning, and given the will to kill. Yes, the old brute was commanded to slay the king, but he failed, out of...well, I don't know. He is closely watching you to see if you will make the same mistake he did."

"Why couldn't he kill the king? He sure isn't innocent or pure." Rose scoffed, crossing her arms. Her red lips plumped out as she stared at the beast with her great blue eyes.

Ashbel waited and pondered the question, deciding whether he was going to tell the girl the answer to her question.

Silence ensued between the two, only to be interrupted by the noise of Ashbel talking.

"Little Rose," started the old red dragon, "the king and Erik are indeed brothers."

Rose was then pulled out of the state of shock and drifted back into the real time, where Ashbel wasn't present and where her loyal friends were. The only thing that changed was the new knowledge of the kin relationship between Erik and Samuel, the king. They were indeed, by blood, brothers.

AYA

Relor, the capital city of Ceptem, was full of life, love, and power. The city of wealth was a powerhouse within the food market and a perfect transit point for a group of wanted misfits.

The sky was a dark blue the day they arrived. Their muscles bulged through the cotton that made up their shirts. Clear water dripped from her hair down to Rose's dirty face. The horses looked dusty and sad, exhaustion showing in their eyes.

"Bealfire, stay here," Rose commanded her steed as she tied a knot in the rope attached to the bridle. Rose attached the rope to a log on the outskirts of Relor.

A small stream had clear flowing water, which poured out from a crack in the rocks. Rose didn't complain about the poor rock but merely pitied it and then celebrated its water. She dripped the water down her face, sucking little droplets as they flowed. Splash after splash, ripples danced far away, until more ripples were made by Andrew, who arrived next to Rose to also quench his thirst.

"The horses are tired. We should let them rest and walk a while," Aya pronounced to the crowd. Awaiting an answer, she cooed to her beautiful stallion and weaved her hands through his copper mane.

"How far is Relor?" inquired Camilla.

"Not far. Another few hours' gallop, so maybe double that on foot," Aya told Camilla, who just now got off her white pet, tying it also to the same log where Bealfire was.

They walked into the city, the biggest city Rose had ever seen. She had been accustomed to taking back roads to get anywhere, hence the reason it took Rose and Jason so many years. The city was loud, bright, covered in gold trim, and had a green glow. Metal rods were placed as distance markers to help foreigners navigate their travels around Relor. Large heavy carts lined themselves upon the roads to carry different provisions. Buildings circled the outside of the railroad tracks. The buildings were large and brown buildings, some of them three or four stories high. Dirt roads separated the buildings and intersected the railroad tracks. Outside every other home was a crop field. People with pale lips poked the plants with sharp sticks. Women carried seeds in aprons, having their children place them among the silt. Carts and barrels were being traded between the city-goers. Bells sang their songs, and merry people chatted along the dirt roads.

Draping the leads behind their shoulders, the misfits walked in front of the brick wall with a sign that read, WELCOME TO RELOR. Passionate green paint dried carefully on the stone. Without breathing, Aya took the first step in, taking a firm grip on the rope. Following behind her was Lords, then the skinny body of Rose, who was trailed by Bealfire. As they all gathered in, they looked down, hiding their lips. The king's spies were everywhere, waiting for sudden suspicious behavior.

The town was busy that day. Everyone was prancing behind, next to, and in front of someone else. There was so much food going to so many different places. The group went unseen. They walked past everyone and into a large cart on the railroad tracks.

"This is a train cart. Animals go on these. We will put all the horses here," Aya said, leading. One after another the owners bade their lovely animal goodbye. Jason was the last to wave farewell to his pretty beast.

"Goodbye, Liza!" he said, extending his arm. A large smile was sewn onto his face, gradually getting smaller as the cart door was closed by Andrew.

"Liza?" Rose inquired.

"Yes, Liza, after our aunt."

"Why not Katrina, after our mother?"

"Our mother abandoned us. Liza didn't."

"She had no choice!" yelled Rose, defending her mother and turning away from her brother. She walked onto a different cart, where Aya was. There was soft seating in every compartment. All five sat in one, girls on one side, men on the other. Payment wasn't required on this train. Taxes were used to pay for the conductor. The carts were covered in paint, ripped, and worn—not a first-class transport. The king would never be seen in such a place. The king relied heavily on the people of Ceptem to feed and clothe the well-heeled people of Remular. The people of Ceptem did not ask much for the goods they provided, which was fortunate, because the king did not give them much in return.

A second family went into the compartment next to theirs. Rose thought it was sweet that a mother, her three sons, and an old woman were all traveling together in the compartment next door. Rose noticed that the sons sat across from their mother and the old woman. They all looked very sad and weepy, colored in black clothes and solemn faces. Rose thought that maybe the reason for their travels was not pleasure.

"Don't look," Camilla half-whispered and half-screamed.

All five of them turned away and faced either each other or outside as the train started moving. Rose felt uneasy about the ground speed of the train over the land, but it wasn't nearly as bad as riding Vulcan. Jason looked brightly at Camilla. She smiled and then returned his stare. Moments later, Camilla stood up and moved to sit next to Jason, laying her head on his shoulder. Rose scoffed, imagining her brother in love. The thought grossed her out.

The train ride moved north and east, to Ashbelle, the city of Red. Bump after bump, the riders fidgeted as the train danced along the rails.

The family in the opposite compartment was quiet, gray, and dull. Happiness escaped their grasp, leaving nothing but boredom and tension. They were a family of pointy noses and unremarkable brown hair. They stared into nothingness and then stared some more.

An hour had gone by since the travelers were standing on the dirt. Rose started to feel empty in her stomach. Camilla was cuddled against Jason's shoulder. Her sweet little head sank onto his skin. Aya stared out the window, next to Rose, blinking rarely. Aya was mesmerized by the plain fields and open area. The train passed hour after hour of land, where people did nothing beyond pure manual labor. Andrew sat next to Jason, who had arranged himself closest to the door. Andrew refused to be anything like his swooning sister. He found it positively disgusting how *she*, a blood relation of his, found *that* attractive.

Moments passed, and neither one of the two carts was moving. Rose began to worry that the conductor had lost his way, which Rose admitted to herself would be difficult, given that the train rode on two simple rails that led to their destination. Still, Rose knew that other people had found ways to mess up even simpler tasks. Rose was relieved when the train suddenly lurched forward, continuing on its way north to Remular. A female steward for the train line also entered their compartment to deliver drinks to everyone in the cart.

"Heading to Ashbelle. Would you like some water?" she asked. She had long black hair, brown eyes, and pale lips. She was dressed in a long fluffy blue dress with buttons from the waist up. Her shoes were the opposite of the combat boots Rose was wearing. She had clean feet and red high heels. Her shoes only made her half an inch taller, but they looked cute with the outfit. Rose scoffed. Beauty was not Rose's thing.

Rose accepted the water, as did everyone else. One by one, the steward poured glasses of water from a container on the side of the cart she was pushing. She left the cart behind her, with one cart for every two compartments. Rose figured that this math made sense and had been determined by someone somewhere to be the most efficient way to perform this simple courtesy. Once all the people in Rose's compartment had received their drinks, the steward moved on to the next compartment, where the sad family seemed just as sad. The three sons smiled and accepted the cold beverage. The old woman drank as if she hadn't drunk in days. The mother declined the water and instead was poured a different drink that was red and purple.

Rose had taken an interest in the family and, from her somewhat-obstructed view, found it strange that the mother only appeared to sip her drink and never finished it. Moments later, the mother tossed it outside her open window. The mother had tossed the barely touched drink forward, which was not very smart, because the wind blew it in a mist right back at her and against the side of the train. The mother then returned to her stare at the wall.

Rose stood up, infuriated, purple running through her veins. The train danced on the tracks, causing Rose to lose her balance. She eventually got up, opened the two compartment doors, and stormed into the compartment with the sad family.

"Ma'am," Rose commanded, staring down at the woman. The whole family looked up at Rose in surprise. Rose realized that her own appearance looked disgusting, gross, and dirty. She could feel the family's eyes noticing Rose's skin.

"What do you want, girl?" the mother demanded. She sounded like the fat Blue man that Rose knew.

"You wasted your entire drink when you threw it outside the window. That is bad for the environment. You shouldn't do that," Rose began.

"Well, there is not much I can do about that anymore, is there? It has been thrown out the window and is long gone now."

"I just wish you hadn't done that."

"You need to leave, Red," the woman said, insulting her. She saw her lips. She saw her pale skin. She saw her blue eyes and dark eyelashes. She probably could see her purple veins too.

"I beg your pardon!" Rose insisted, shifting closer to the woman, who had barely made eye contact with Rose. Instead, the mother was attending to her youngest son.

"I don't speak to your filthy kind. You are all disgusting pigs. You trot around with your magic, trying to end the reign of my king."

"I believe in peace, not the war, which is all your king wants!"

"If you believed in peace, you wouldn't have shouted at me in front of my children. I am a good citizen and haven't raised my voice once to you, have I?"

"Rose, what is going on?" asked Aya, entering the compartment.

"I remember you. I remember your birth. You are the daughter of the king! The girl who was born a traitor! Leave my presence, you witch!"

The puffing and coughing sounds of the youngest son filled the ears of the women. The child, not much older than a baby, had turned yellow. He continued to choke and spit, until blood came out. Rose darted to the boy, trying to get him to stop. Rose pounded on his back, chest, anywhere she could put her hands. The boy's body spasmed, and his color rapidly changed from yellow to red and then finally to purple. Scared and confused, the boy started to scream, pain and agony filling his eyes. Blood started to drip out of his nose. Blood filled his eyes. Blood dripped from his mouth. Rose felt the temperature of the boy's hands change from hot to ice-cold. The boy's teeth were stained by a dark-green fluid, with his tongue sponging it in, even as he was coughing up blood. He was breathing, but barely. His screams horrified the girls pleading for him to live. The brothers stood in shock, the old woman barely moved, and the mother turned pale, trying to conceal her feelings.

Coughing, choking, bleeding, and then coughing again formed a repeating pattern, but the boy held on to his life. It was painful, but he tried. Spits of blood drained him, until his face turned blue and the foam containing red and blue spots stopped flooding out. His body spasmed one final time, and then he lay lifeless in Rose's arms.

"Witches! Witches! You killed my son!"

"He was poisoned, but not by us!" Aya pronounced, searching for the boy's drink. It was nowhere to be found.

"Witches!" the mother continued to shout.

The female steward returned and screamed in horror. Her dress nearly ripped on the doorway as she left to go get help. Rose knew that she had only tried to help the boy, and she began to wonder about his mother. A male train attendant came by and requested that the two girls leave and return to their own compartment.

"Rose," Jason said, standing up and pushing her into his arms, where she felt safe. His body against her own calmed her down. She needed his love and compassion. He was her best friend and her only family. He was always there to support her.

"Aya...Aya saw the woman put something into the mouth of the boy when she was attending to him. That was why she was so quick to want to go in there with you," Jason told her.

"We can't talk to the authorities, since they happen to be people who also want us locked up," Aya told them.

"I know," Jason said sadly. "That woman is disgusting, but we will have bigger problems with the authorities if we get drawn into this."

"More than that, she is a murderer!" protested Rose.

"Well, don't be too quick to judge those," Andrew told Rose. She knew what he meant. She was destined to be one herself and to kill the killer of killers. Her body felt heavier. She turned around to see Aya, but Aya pushed her back around so she didn't have to look at the body of the boy being carried away.

The commotion in the compartment next to Rose's only continued after they had left. The mother screamed at the male steward to arrest Rose for killing her son. The male and female stewards talked between themselves. Rose could hear the female steward explaining how valiantly Rose had tried to help the boy, while the mother had just sat there and watched. The male steward informed the mother that there was nothing the train line could or would do. He insisted that the mother quiet down or face having her family forcibly removed from the train.

Rose began to cry. Tears flooded down her face. In an instant, she became very, very scared. A worse fear than the death of her parents or the death of Liza and her children was the fear of her own death. This terrified her.

Rose contemplated her future as she drifted off into a deep sleep.

Rose woke up. She had been asleep for a long time next to Aya. Jason had placed Rose's dreaming body there. The train had just arrived with a lurch at Ashbelle, and there the boy was buried.

Rose thought, for a very long time, about what would motivate a mother to kill her child. Only she would know, and Rose would never see her again. Rose remembered seeing the mother on the platform before boarding the train and the mother taking notice of the appearance of Rose's group, particularly their lips. If this mother really detested Red Lips as swine, why had she chosen to take the compartment next to the one Rose took? Rose felt very fortunate that the train stewards had not pushed the matter of the boy's death and the Red Lips' involvement in it any further. She could only imagine what joy the king would feel if all five of them were arrested and presented in shackles and chains to him. With the only justice in the world at that time being led by a racist monarchy, the mother would get by easily. Rose's fate would have been much different.

Rose knew she was no killer, not yet at least. But in her dreams the boy gave her pain, and the pain would be the burden of not only witnessing a murder but of being a murderer as well. The king might find himself fond of the cutting of strings of life, but Rose loved only sewing things together.

"Rose!" Aya smiled, her dark skin wrapped around her own bones tightly. A solicitous smile assuaged Rose's pain. Rose became anxious that they were not somewhere safe.

"Aya," Rose started, but Aya quickly hushed her and pushed her back down onto the ground. Pleading for an explanation, Rose forced herself up and looked at Aya.

"We are in Ashbelle."

"So I gathered," Rose said, pouncing onto her feet and wandering the camp. "Just wondering where the city is."

"That way," Aya said, pointing at a band of trees.

Rose scoffed.

"In a mood?"

"No, just that I witnessed a murder and can barely remember walking off the train."

"You fainted," Aya began, breathing with a hit of a twitch, "on the train, so we got you off the train and made camp here. We figured it was far enough away from the city and out of the way that no one would track us or be interested in what we were doing. It was no small feat, because there were all the horses to gather and that wicked woman started raising a new commotion with the officials in Ashbelle about our involvement in the boy's death. Frankly, we were lucky to get out of there so quickly with you in tow. For the record, you didn't walk off the train, you were carried."

Rose asked, "Where are our friends?"

"In the city," Aya told Rose, her staid voice trailing off into the campsite. Rose followed the voice to find their home for the night. Aya continued, "We were worried about you, and I drew the short straw and was assigned to watch over you. Your behavior has been getting more and more erratic. Is there something I can do to help?"

A campfire was lit. The flames were a deep maroon color, the same color of Rose's lips. No ombre mixtures were present, just a pure red glow, a warm heat, and safety dwelled in its mighty presence. Cautiously, Rose sneaked around it and sat next to Aya, staring at the green trees. Rose laid her kind head on Aya's bony shoulder and drifted back into a deep sleep.

Myra

The large forest ahead of the lost dove that was Rose glistened in the sunrise. The sun continued passionately growing in light and in heat until, eventually, it peaked at midday and decided to begin falling back down to leave a blue nothingness on the canvas that was the sky.

Aya sat carving wood next to the sore body of Rose, who had once again slept far more than expected. It was becoming predictable.

Rose fiddled with her eyes and arms before fully arising from the ground to feel the diminishing sun on her pale skin. Her hair swayed in the light breeze, while her eyes held a firm gaze on Aya.

"Jason stopped by last night," Aya began after noticing Rose's conscious presence. "Was wondering how you were. How are you, Rose? Doing better?"

"Better," Rose replied, pacing on her feet and walking closer to the trees. "When do we leave?"

Aya didn't know how to respond. She herself didn't know when she would feel safe enough to bring Rose to Ashbelle.

"You told me Ashbelle was a safe place for Reds, or was that a lie?"

"It was not a lie, Rose," Aya began, moving her precious body closer to Rose. "You freaked all of us out the other day. We don't know if you are ready to see more people."

"The people I am going to save. Do they know that I am close?"

"No" was all Aya could bring herself to say. She wanted to say something to comfort Rose Mensch, but strangely, her clever mind was at a loss of words. Her cut hair draped over her prideful face. Her silver eyes shivered.

"I'm leaving," Rose said quickly, braiding her bronze hair to the side, leaving strands of blond and brown out.

"Oh, really? Where?" Aya spat while crossing her dark arms. Light freckles were dotted across the hair sprouting on her skin.

The leaves gleamed and twisted across the sky. The trees listened, waiting for an answer from Rose, but she said nothing. Just moved her arms into a circle. A ring of fire. The flames grew, then died, and a passionate red fire floated above the dead twigs and leaves.

"Bye," Rose said, waving her palm, gesturing toward Aya. Carefully she stepped in, bowing her head under the hot fire. Before Aya could mock her or laugh at her, Rose disappeared, as well as the ring. No trace of Rose was at the campsite, just a puzzled Aya and burned leaves.

*****

"I am here," Rose pronounced abruptly as she entered the main chamber of Dragons Nest. Casually prancing around the brown lounge, she locked eyes with a beast. Green were her scales, and emerald were her eyes. Rose's skinny body stepped back. Candice's great form looked down upon Rose, judging the thing in front of her. Behind the green dragon was a red king. His scales flowed down his back like the water current in a speedy river.

"Rose," Ashbel said calmly.

"You called me," Rose replied, staring into his eyes. He was perched on his throne. Ashbel looked mightier than any king Rose had ever heard and known. His magnificence was firm. His pride only grew when his tail curled around the girl's body.

"There is someone here that is just dying to meet you."

"Or should we say something?" corrected Candice, her radiant royal blood sitting on her throne as well. Vulcan and Eden were absent from the party. Rose's interest in the conversation with the two dragons was piqued.

"Follow us this way," Ashbel began, his voice trailing off in the direction of an inner tunnel. It led Rose down a great hall of paintings. Different artworks had been created directly on the walls. Some showed naked men and women eating grapes while trolls stole their gold. Some were of fire and Red Lips controlling that fire. One image, out of the many, had a young girl was standing by a lake. The lake looked very similar to her own but was filled with boiling lava. Both girls had long hair and skinny bodies. The resemblance between the painted girl and Rose Mensch was striking and uncanny.

"Aya painted them all. She has always had that talent," Ashbel told Rose, as he noticed the inquiring faces Rose was making. She squished her blue eyes together to try to get a closer look.

One thing Rose noticed was the color of the paint Aya had used to create the art. Red. Every bit of detail, including every curve, face, rock, and grape, was red. The detail in the image itself allowed Rose to comprehend what each figure was, without the help of color. Red hair was on the women who ate red grapes. The red trolls were stealing red treasures. The little red girl was standing over a red lake. The red lake was more than just the absence of blue or purple. It was a boiling pond of lava. The red steam was painted above it.

"I never knew Aya was an artist," Rose admitted, finally comprehending exactly what Ashbel had told her moments ago.

"I don't believe Aya would say she was either."

"I love it."

"Aya did too. She loved to sit here when she was younger and paint. All she ever wanted was to paint and meet you."

"She knew about me when she was younger?" Rose asked plainly. Her skinny feet stopped in her tracks, and she looked into the eyes of Ashbel, king of Dragons Nest.

Ashbel spoke calmly. "Everyone knew about you."

Rose breathed deeply. They were arriving near the end of the hallway. She opened her eyes to see a room smaller than the great chamber of thrones. It had candles all around, like in a worship space. Light flickered and flashed all around. Fire danced and swished, while some flames remained calm and sleepy. A dark shadow lingered over the roof of the room.

"Who am I meeting?" Rose inquired.

Candice decided to so kindly answer the question instead of Ashbel, shushing Rose. "Quiet!"

The hiss quelled the fire in more than a great dozen of the candles. Rose swayed her elegant hand, and each candle came back to life, holding a beautiful red fire. The others were blue or green, and even the glow around the corner was such colors. Now a red sparkle gleamed within their midst.

Candice swore at the child and continued to walk on. The room was large enough to carry two enormous dragons, a teenage girl, and hundreds of candles. The reason the room existed was unknown to Rose. Perhaps it was a room of quiet and peace for the dragons to escape.

As she walked out the larger room, she noticed a woman standing in the shadows. Her hair was a dark brown, her skin lighter. She had powders on her face, blue on her eyes, red on her cheeks.

"Myra, meet Rose Mensch."

The woman smiled a cold smile. She only glanced at Rose before turning away to face Ashbel and Candice. Her side profile showed a double chin, though it was hidden when turned forward. Her body was not too plump, though her curves were noticeable.

"Rose, my name is Myra."

"I know who you are," interrupted Rose, feeling her Purple grow. "You are the wife of the king. The queen betrayer. The born Red. The mother of my best friend. The mother who threw her child off a building."

"That was my husband, and it was a castle," Myra tried to explain.

"But you allowed it. Is that not the same thing?"

There was a great pause. Moments lingered, and time passed.

"I know of my mistakes," the queen finally said. Her body twitched but did not make a dramatic motion. She was unbearably nervous.

"And yet, you show your face here," spat Rose.

"I am here to form an alliance."

"How do I know this isn't some form of trickery? How do I know you don't want me to trust you just so you can go run back to your mad King and plan to kill us all while I trust you?"

"We don't," Candice told Rose, staring her beautiful body down. Her eyes glowed and her teeth roared. She moved closer to the little girl, "We trust."

"And your proof?"

"My sons were given purple fire when they were young. They were manipulated by the evils of the purple. I have seen dark Magic. I have seen how it is controlled."

"This is useful to me how?"

"I have magic. Magic of my own that I want to give to you and to Aya, but you must trust me."

"I do not want your curse," Rose declared, starting to walk away, but she was stopped at the feet of Ashbel. His sharp claws burned against her skin, as they dug into her bones, Rose winced in pain. Getting the message, Rose turned back around.

"I miss my daughter more than anything and I will do anything to make things right with her."

"You should have thought about that years ago," snarled Rose. In a conscious perspective, Rose knew that what she was doing was wrong. A Red would be patient. A Red would be kind. A Red would not be proud, rude, or self-seeking. A Red would always protect and trust. But Rose's purple wanted to be proud, to be rude, to hate, to torture, and destroy. Rose's new favorite color was purple.

"It will help you!" called out Myra. The long royal blue dress she was wearing shimmered in contrast to her dark lips. The queen approached Rose, her hand touching the skinny skin-wrapped hands of Rose. She looked into Rose's eyes pleadingly. Rose was taller than she was, so the queen's chubby chin looked up slightly at the girl.

"Let me show you," Myra's voice continued. Her hand detached from Rose's wrists and traveled up to her own lips. In a flash, her hand covered her own pale mouth. As the hands moved back down, her lips were a swollen red color. The queen repeated the motion with her perfectly manicured hands, and the color was gone.

Rose said nothing. She wanted to say something and was surprised when her own words were not forthcoming. The queen had been hiding under this mask for years. She had never traveled to the well and had never given up her magic. It made sense how the genes were spread to Aya and how she maintained a kind character.

"I want to show you something else," began Myra anew. Her hands found each other, and she burned the most beautiful fire unlike any color or tone Rose had ever seen. She saw red fire, a lighter shade than her own, but it was red. It was beautiful. She performed tricks and showed her power. She showed Rose that fire had a strange calmness to it and that red fire had a glow that outshone all the other colors. Rose was dumbfounded by the fact that Myra was a controller of red fire and yet she married the king of Nomad blood.

"Was the gift to be able to hide my lips?" Rose asked.

"Not really. I'm convinced that one day there will be an inescapable path, where your lips will get you killed before you can kill my husband."

"What do you ask for in return?" inquired Rose suspiciously, her red lips hidden and her palms beginning to sweat. The room was dull and cold, and as Myra spoke, it only got colder.

"When the time comes for you to murder my husband, I want you to kill me first," Myra told Rose.

The girl looked the older woman in the eyes and thought to herself, *Why does anyone have to go?* It was an admirable desire, to want to keep the sinners with the pure. *Can a lion lie down with a lamb? Can the dragon befriend a wolf?*

"I promise" came the surprising response from Rose.

After that commitment was made, the Purple got much closer to Rose's veins.

JASON

After the dragons had called her to their home, she found it difficult to converse with Aya. The budding secret inside her butterflied to questions for Aya. She worried, most of all, about Aya's vision of a future. Imagining that once the war was over and won, would Aya want a life with her mother again or with her brothers? Rose didn't want to think of breathing without Aya. They had grown so close over the journey that to exist without Aya would be like not existing at all. She didn't desire to share Aya either. Aya protected her, not Jason or Camilla or Andrew, but Rose.

Aya had decided to take Rose to the city on the day of the festival as a pleasant distraction. Reds from all over the world were coming to celebrate their culture. It was advertised as a safe place where they would all dance, party, perform fire, and embrace magic. Rose didn't know when she would get a chance to use the power Myra had given her, but she was nervous about Aya's reaction.

The forest looked greener as the sun looked more golden. They latched on to their horses and began walking. The slight chirping of the birds in the sky was a comfort to their travel. The taste of water was fresh in their mouths. Warm air traced their skin. Rose felt sunbeams on her pale, pale outer layer. The sun made her feel warm and secure. To Rose, anything warm, like fire, was safe.

Camilla, Jason, and Andrew had all taken their horses with them. They rode them into town as they let Rose relax. They all knew how troublesome the train ride was for Rosie, and they refused to let her be in a crowded place, like the city of Ashbelle.

"Rose, I think it is safe to begin to ride," Aya told her while latching on the mane of Lords. She pressed her dark body onto the great back of the beast. She then proceeded to situate herself while looking at the pretty stallion.

Rose did the same thing, on Bealfire, as she pounced onto his long arched back and straddled him. She kicked her legs together with her combat boots, and Bealfire took off. Lords tried to keep up as Bealfire darted into the wilderness. Together they ran, one ahead of the other, crushing all the different leaves and twigs into the ground. This wasn't Rose's forest, so the trees stayed in their path. The ride was like an obstacle course, which had them dodging firm branches and hopping over roots and dead logs. Passionately they galloped out of the forest and looked over a cliff.

Below the rocky overhang, a large city was celebrating. Red, green, blue, and purple streamers were hung from all the tops of the homes and buildings. People took to the streets with their homemade candles and foods, hot foods to celebrate fire. Performers, children, and adults sprung from their homes to watch and participate in the celebration of the dragons.

Aya and Rose trotted their steeds to the place Aya was told Jason was staying. It was a small home in the middle of the city, a redbrick building many stories high that had brown toppers hanging down from the roof. Each floor had two windows, one looking over the right side of the city and the other looking over the left.

They walked their horses up to the stable just outside the city, where they met the horses that belonged to the keepers of the inn. Their horses quickly found their friends, the three that Jason, Camilla, and Andrew had been riding. Aya led Rose up the stairs into the inn. Rose saw her friends laughing and giggling at a table without her.

Rose thought to herself about the time she had spent with Aya. She wondered if she was truly ready to share Aya again. Did she want to have everyone else compete for her attention? She was torn and flustered as she pushed ahead of Aya and raised a pale and skinny wrist to knock harshly on the door. It was a wooden door, and Rose found herself wanting to set fire to the door and let the whole home burn to the ground. She could then hide under the mask Myra had given her. Aya still did not know that Rose had such abilities, and Rose honestly thought that perhaps keeping it from her was the right decision. But when Rose heard the sound waves of the banging, she drifted from that thought.

They both faced the door, dark and light, blinking and breathing slowly, gripping each other's hands, until a friendly face opened the door. A brunette, masculine, and a teenager smirked, greeting them with pleasure beyond measure. Both girls gleamed at the sight of him, feeling more at home than ever. Rose was excited to see Jason and was filled with regret for ever worrying him and leading him to feel unsure of her state of being.

Jason greeted them with much enthusiasm. He desired to know of everything that happened during the time away. Rose and Aya told him, but she did not share Myra's stories.

"Rose, why did the dragons call you to their nest?" Aya asked. She had seated herself on a green love seat. The cousins were soft-spoken, and the lace in their clothing encouraged a visual of dragons dancing in the sky. The room was cozy. It was the only room at the inn without a bed. The five of them sat closely together, either on a chair or on the carpeted floor.

Rose pondered the question. She was in slight surprise with herself that she had not yet thought of the perfectly imperfect lie to tell them. She was slightly more surprised with Aya for not bombarding her with this question as soon as she returned form Dragons Nest.

As Rose sat there, viewing their stares and their need for an answer, she decided not to lie but to simply tell the truth. She denied her Purple and stayed close to her Red in the moment. She loved Aya and couldn't lie to her any more than she already had.

"Aya," Rose said quietly, "I saw your mother."

The room was silent.

"My mother?" Aya inquired. "The woman who helped my father try to kill me? Why was she at my home?"

"She was there to show me something. Something to give to you."

Rose stood up and held out her hand as she walked over to Aya's love seat. She looked into her white eyes and touched her dark arm. They remained in contact all through the shock as this burst of rapid energy came hurtling down to Aya through Rose. It only lasted a few seconds, but it was long enough for the group of teenagers to gather around the girls and feel their pulses, ensuring their health.

"My horrid mother tried to kill me through you!" Aya said, gasping with her mouth open and holding on to her lips.

"Aya, pull your hand away from your mouth," Rose said, squinting in the light. As dramatically as it came, the magic was there. Her lips were brown, not red. It was not because of the way the light hit them, nor was it because they had just been electrocuted, but because of the power Myra had given to them. Aya then moved her hand back up, and her red lips were back. She never again desired to kiss her hand. She wanted to stay Red, but perhaps her mother took that away from her. She was lost and confused with her emotion toward the witch. She felt passion and not weak, undeniable dislike, rather a burning hatred for her mother.

*****

The parade was the next day, and they had all gotten their first long sleep that night. All except Aya, who worried throughout the night that she would swing her hand above her lips for a long-enough time that her beautiful red would cease to exist permanently.

Rose had brushed her hair and her teeth with a comb and a bamboo stick, respectively. The combs she had run through her straight bronze hair until they finished the end knots. She chose to wear a short red cloth top and her baggy leather shorts, which fit comfortably on her thighs. Her combat boots gripped her ankles, and her toes felt so cozy in the fur that lined the inside of the soles. She felt the slight burn of her tattoo, which Ashbel had given her. It still ached with a desire to be fed.

Jason, Camilla, and Andrew all awaited Rose and Aya in the middle room, where they shared their meeting yesterday. Horrible nostalgia was layered in the room for Aya. Rose, on the other hand, remembered how just seeing Jason's welcoming face had helped her move back to Red from Purple. That and, for whatever reason, Rose really liked the furnishings of the room. They all gathered together and then left the green room. The city of Ashbelle was huge and very gorgeous. The red trimming followed every building, making each building appear to touch the sky. The buildings were tall and curved. The royal red stone was an element of the exterior of all the business buildings. Merchants rode the streets, yelling at passersby to buy their wares. The merchants offered green grass, purple flowers, red flowers, and even roses. They walked on a stone path, not a dirt path. There were fountains in the streets, and in the water were sculptures of bodies swimming and dancing. They all had red lips. Other visitors for the festival had washed clean of their travel dirt, and their children ran happily in cool silk clothes. Streamers were hung from the balconies of all the homes and stores. The doors had red paint on the brown wood. The white roses were painted red, and the men had red-colored stripe decals placed on their cheeks.

"Happiness is flooding in here," Rose said, dazed by the Reds.

"Not all fun and games here," Aya said, watching the children laughing.

"What is that supposed to mean?" Camilla asked toward Aya.

"They have the highest-security prison here. My father sends the top assassins here. The ones who have failed to kill him."

"But Reds don't commit crimes. How could this place be dangerous?"

"Nomads travel here and rob them, knowing they would never hurt them back. The most mass murderers of Reds are here too. Really evil people rot in those prison cells."

Rose was shaking with wonder and hurtful impulses.

Jason, the romantic he had become, gripped Camilla's hand when he heard of murderers. Rose knew, though very unconsciously, she was falling out of her brother's intense favor and being replaced by the beautiful but dull redhead.

They walked on without words. It was not a quiet stroll, though. People all around the city were bubbling and chatting with themselves and one another. The buzz about Rose had spread all throughout the city. Stares and smiles followed them throughout their walk. They assumed the people were enthralled to see them and weren't glaring at them or trying to solve their problems.

They heard a large bang up ahead in the distance and darted to the scene to find out what had happened. An old man stood on the stage in the middle of the city and talked proudly to the people.

"Reds, my friends," said the old man, taking off his brown top hat in greeting, "welcome to Ashbelle, the city of Red." He put his brown hat back on. His foppish, red-colored suit made it look like he was that wonky old man who put spiders in children's hair.

"I am Mayor Foxx, as many of you know. I am here to introduce the wonders of the red parade."

Aya and Rose shot eyes at each other, worried. Who was he?

"May the parade begin!"

A large red ribbon was strung from one building across the street to the next one. The mayor took one hand and made a wave of blue fire, which curled along his finger. The blue fire danced its way down until it touched the ribbon and burned it in half. The people cheered with great howls as they ran into the closed-off park of Ashbelle. A long stream of Red Lips with light hair and light skin trampled Rose's group. When the crowd subsided, Rose found her friends and they collected their thoughts.

"Should we go?" Andrew offered. Aya nodded slowly, hesitating for a moment.

Rose focused ahead. She watched the children pick the red roses and their parents kiss each other on their red lips. They smiled and walked, eating red sugar and singing hymns of proudness. She nodded as well, but less cautiously.

Jason and Camilla were still intertwining fingers, and they both nodded. Andrew didn't like any of it but seemed to enjoy their togetherness.

They entered and were greeted by a Red patting Rose, Aya, Andrew, and Camilla on the back. He didn't dare touch Jason.

"You aren't allowed," the Red said with fear. "The boss said so."

"I promise, I am no harm," Jason said in the most apologetic and sincere way possible, though Rose could tell he was annoyed.

"You befriended this Nomad?" the man asked Rose.

"He is my brother," Rose said, touching his shoulder. "Do you see the resemblance?"

Aya chuckled.

"And who are you? I have never seen you around here before," the man said, observing Rose.

"She is my friend, Petur," a voice said from behind them.

Petur, as he was named, lowered his head to a young boy who was walking behind them.

This boy had pure-brown hair and blue eyes, but no red lips. He walked in front of them and tipped Petur a good gold coin or two. He motioned for the five of them to walk behind him and get access without any further trouble. He smirked once they could not be heard by the inspector.

"Petur is always good fun," said the boy. He was quite handsome, very bony, and not as large as Andrew or Jason. He looked two or three years younger than them too; no acne or redness had hit his face. But he just looked gorgeous, at least to Rose.

"Who is he?" Aya asked the boy loudly.

"One of my father's interns. He doesn't like me all too much, but he has to put up with me." He laughed, quite hard, at that poor man, but Rose found some humor to it, even though it was a bit rude.

"I'm LeRoy," he said, putting his hand out for Rose to shake.

"I am Rose," she said, blushing at his strength. They stood there looking in each other's eyes before they coughed and he introduced himself to the others.

"I must go. So sorry to keep you this long. Goodbye. Goodbye, Rose," he whispered. He ran off into the parade.

Rose smiled and then looked at her brother.

"Well, at least he got you in!"

The parade included a train of people tossing things into the crowd. The street was covered in rose petals and cherries and red candies. The group loved to walk in the gardens. The horticulture was stunning. Shrubs had been chopped into art that replicated a dragon, and some even had been chopped to show scenes with historic Reds.

Rose and Aya found one that looked like Aya, or baby Aya. It was a symbol of the sacrifices people made for the greater good.

They were in the line to see the train. People were sitting in the windows, waving at the crowd. They had yellow eyes and red lips. Their hair wasn't usual, and they had long claws as hands. One scream, then another, was heard. Rose turned and saw a horrible sight.

A woman with red lips was being torn in half, straight through the middle. Large spurts of blood poured out of her as everyone ran away from her. The yellow circles in her eyes turned dark brown. Her skin melted to the ground. Her vestlike body became a puddle on the ground, and the form of another woman took shape from the puddle. The newly formed woman was ugly and old. Her long hair draped over her face as fangs showed from her mouth.

All around Rose, the people on the train were being split. Their guts and goo spilled out from their stomach, as well as blood, lots of red blood. Their skin fell to the ground and melted into the stone, until there was nothing left to stitch back together. Their eyes were just sockets that could been seen through, and their lips were just painted.

Men and women gathered around the train. Ugly men and women who had been formed from blood that day. They were covered in horrid smells. As they grew closer, the parade watchers screamed and ran. All the Reds fled. All except Rose and Aya. They had been training for fights like this. Fights where their fire would burn the people who tried to hurt the innocent.

The monsters ran fast, almost as fast as Jason racing Rose. Rose sprinted up toward them and burned their fighting arms. They held swords and daggers, small knives and large ones, bombs, and some just had their fists. Rose burned them all. They were still crawling out of their bodies, and some even had doubles.

An ugly monster smiled after Rose had attacked its face with fire. Then it shrank and crawled out of that body and showed Rose a bomb in its dirty hands. As it threw the bomb to the ground, Rose held her hands around her head, trying to shield it.

After the explosion, dirt and crumbled rocks covered the ground. The red roses and streamers no longer stood proudly. They were alone and broken on the stone path. Rose coughed as she opened her eyes in surprise. She had survived the bomb. She could see that many people did not.

All around her were dead bodies, coughing children, and widowed mothers. There was red blood surrounding the streets, and crying squeals of Reds flooded the ears of many. The monsters grew closer to Rose as she realized that they had come for her. They had scratches and cuts all along their horrible faces. Purple blood streamed down their cheeks. Their brows twitched in their brows twitched and their claws slapped at the air in frustration.

Rose sat up, her muscles sore and tired from the bomb's explosion. She gathered her hands the way Ashbel taught her, ready to spawn her fire as the monsters tore their skin once more. A third and a fourth person escaped from the skin of the monsters. A fresh-coated porcelain doll woman stood nearly ten feet from Rose. She had the yellow eyes and black hair they all had, but she had constructed herself in such a way that, to Rose, she looked harmless, broken, and lost. Suddenly, the doll woman grasped for a sword and struck Rose along her arm, gashing the flesh and tainting Rose's perfection. Aya came up behind Rose and struck the woman with a powerful blast of blue fire. It burned away at her skin, and she fell deeper into the gravel. The woman howled and panicked and was a real terror to watch. The truth in death is that pain is distributed unevenly. The more one deserves death, the more it hurts.

"Rose, let's leave," Aya told her, yanking her arm behind her. Rose wanted to stay and watch the yellow-eyed monster burn. She was quite intrigued by the way she melted so splendidly, so horribly, and so poetically.

"Rose…"

A second explosion was heard. Ashes and buildings fell near her feet, then a third one. The buildings smashed on the ground. The stone rocks left sharp debris on the ground. As the final sound hit, Rose and Aya were toppled out of the way by a fast force. An epic passion threw them to the side, and then the physical being came rolling out of the dust. LeRoy was coughing and wheezing near them as he rolled farther away. The building above them came crashing to the ground. The bodies of Yellows fell out. They had pushed the structure off its foundation and suicided themselves down to the rocky terrain.

The girls walked over to LeRoy, once the bombing stopped, to see his face, to check the pulse, to know if air still escaped his selfless lips. They touched his brown hair, so matted and tangled. His skin was layered with dirt. His eyes were sealed shut. Rose was on the verge of sobbing. Her eyes closed, too, as she imagined the boy lifeless on the ground below them.

"Rosie," Aya began to say, "he is breathing."

A gasp of true air seeped into her lungs again. They together picked him up by the shoulders and feet and carried him to a forest clinic. Many other harmed Reds had been taken there, some dead, some not. Many crying Reds stood by and observed each operation and each miracle being worked. Even Candice, the female dragon, flew down to Ashbelle to offer anyone she could the hospitality of Dragons Nest.

Rose found Jason, Camilla, and Andrew not too far into the city. They were all very scared but intact and not horribly injured. Camilla had sprained her ankle. She was walking with the aid of Andrew after having her foot wrapped in Jason's shirt.

Rose knew this was terrorism. This act of violence was a strategic plan to kill her and more Reds. It was a ruthless tactic to kill her kind, with Rose in mind.

Rose felt broken and alone, guilty and ashamed, angry and hurt. Aya held her hand tightly as they walked together into the woods. They desired to find a cave where they could sleep without rocks on their backs. Rose connected with the trees, and they obeyed and moved away from their feet. In no time, they found a large hole in a cliffside. It was deep, but not too dark, because the evening had just arrived and the sun had not fully set, although it was slowly falling.

Along the path near the cave, they found a watering hole that had blue-and-purple water. Steam was pouring through a nearby vent, and along the river was a waterfall that pulled green waters down to become blue and purple in the pond.

Rose, Aya, Andrew, Jason, Camilla, and LeRoy all found themselves naked and walking slowly into the water. Within minutes, they forgot about the troubles they had and were splashing and swimming in the waters. Playful screams could be heard nearby as the teenagers closed their mouths and eyes when they threw water at one another. The six children had fun in the water. Their fire slept in the coldness, resting its powers deep within their blood.

Eventually, they quieted down, and some sat upon the rocks. Others dried out and tried washing their clothes by the sand. Rose stayed in the water, swimming and dancing along to the sound of their conversation.

"LeRoy," Aya said, doting over the young boy. "What does your father do?"

LeRoy paused and then answered her question with much disappointment.

"My father damn near owns Ashbelle. That city runs on firewood. They have the best trees in the whole world. My father runs a business that cuts, sells, and manufactures these logs for all kinds of customers. He services customers from the islands in Nava to the tropical no-man's-land of the Red Islands. He's rich, and I was his heir."

"Was?" asked Rose.

"Well, not anymore. That city is dusted. Most of the people will move to Remular if they have the guts and money, or maybe Bear Cave, if they want to survive."

The group was saddened to hear of his great loss in Ashbelle. LeRoy had it the worst, though. His hands trembled and his skin grew rashes when the name of his hometown was mentioned.

"So that town of Reds was owned by a Nomad. How does that add up?" asked Aya, who seemed very skeptical of the father's business, which LeRoy described.

"My grandfather was Lorded by the king and was granted title to the city of Ashbelle. He took the company for his own and let everyone live in peace, at least those who didn't die trying to keep him out. He even kept a mayor in town, but that, too, was all the king. He, according to my father, wanted to keep all the Reds in one place so that one day he would kill them all. You, Rose, weren't part of that problem. It was just my father."

Solemnly, everyone headed out of the water, gathered their clothes, and walked back to the cave. All moved on except Rose, who decided to stay, wondering how dangerous the king truly was.

She moved her arms in the water. Reflections of fire burned against the liquid, and eventually steam rose above the cold. Rose was beginning to be hard to see, and no one could watch her movements in her dreamlike wonder. Her toes pointed outward, and her long arms followed until the splashes were too heavy, so she sank deep under the cold. She watched her hands move the water, and the red fire made sparks against it, like a flickering candle trying to stay alive after being blown out. She hummed as she danced alone and afraid, her bare skin bouncing against the light waves she had created.

"Rose…," the slight voice of LeRoy could be heard saying from beyond the mist. He made a splash as he dived into the water. She was startled but not frightened to see him. He was the heir to an ultraevil company, but his calming sounds echoed in her ears.

"LeRoy…"

One step was all they had to take to move out of the mist and see each other alone in the water. It was such a perfect moment for the two of them. They were both lost souls. Seeing each other's eyes enabled all the pain to surface in one spot.

How beautiful they looked together. How beautiful the steam looked from the sky.

"Rose, do you wish to know how I knew to be at the gate when I did?" he asked, stepping closer to her body and swimming around her elegant form. LeRoy could see her muscles and bruises, the scar from the sword strike, and her scrapes and cuts from the bomb explosion.

"I thought it was only coincidence," Rose said, smiling down at him and his perfect blue eyes.

"Perhaps," he said, grinning, sitting up to stand right above her, inches from her eyes, "but perhaps it's more."

"I am all ears," Rose told him quietly.

A long pause held them both breathless for the moment. Neither of them wanted to say anything, only to live in the moment. LeRoy had promised Rose a story, and Rose just loved stories.

"I was sitting in my room nearly an hour before you arrived in my city," LeRoy began, talking happily again, his tan face still close to Rose's, "and I heard a large banging outside my door."

Rose looked intently at LeRoy. He smirked at her, giving her a sense of peace about the story. They paused once again as a low chirp of birds was heard. The stream was rising, and they could see nothing beyond themselves.

"So as any normal person, I walked over to my wooden door and opened it right up. I had put my fist in the air for protection, and I saw nothing."

Rose frowned again with much disappointment. LeRoy moved his strong arm over to hers and pulled her closer to him. All she heard were the sounds of the water shifting to let her pass.

They stared into each other's eyes. His blue eyes. Her blue eyes. They matched perfectly.

"So I turned back around, and you know what I saw in my room?"

"What?" Rose asked quietly, her cheeks blushing pink.

"A dragon."

Rose stood up out of the water. Her eyes grew so large she had to blink multiple times to make them smaller again. LeRoy went straight-faced, too, in worry that he had startled her. It was darker now, and the moon was lightning up Rose's face. LeRoy used the light to guide himself closer to her again. He sighed as he gripped her hand and looked up into her pale face. He saw her blue eyes, her red lips, and her dark eyelashes.

"He told me his name was Ashbel, king of Dragons Nest," LeRoy continued. "I heard my father talk about dragons before, but I never really believed in them. The Reds in the town always blabbered, but I only thought it was a religion. Until I saw him. He was huge. His red spikes filled my entire room, and more, probably."

Rose laughed, remembering her first time meeting the red dragon and how terrified she had been. How he taught her to create fire and control it. How he was so calm and honest toward her. How he loved her.

"Please continue," Rose told him, intertwining her fingers with his. He was a flattering boy, with such a gorgeous smile and with such perfect hands.

"He told me barely anything, but this I remember: Find the girl with the cherry lips, whose skin is light, and on whom the sun shines graciously."

His hands traveled up to her lips, and he pressed his strong hands on that delicate red skin. Rose smiled up at him.

"Whose hair is the color of a bonze shield that danced in the wind," LeRoy continued.

His hands then made their way up to tangle into her hair, combing through the small knots in the wet places.

"The one who runs and plays in the wild. The one who travels with a pack of wolves. The one whose beauty outshines all the others. So I left."

Rose smiled up at the sky, looking for the stars of Ashbelle. So happy she was then, with a handsome devil and a dragon who would fight for her every desire.

"So," concluded LeRoy, "I walked into town until I saw you and your herd of wolves. You fit every detail Ashbel told me of, so I knew I found you. I found you!"

LeRoy took his hands out of her hair and raised his hand to her perfectly rounded chin. He leaned into her until their lashes intertwined.

Aya

Rose woke up to a strong poking in her right shoulder. It was Aya. Rose had fallen asleep right outside the cave and could barely remember how she got there or the night before.

"Rosie!" demanded Aya again, her short black hair getting all in her face as she poked Rose's arm repeatedly.

Rose sat up in annoyance, but an innocent annoyance, with Aya. Rose loved Aya and knew there was something more important than her sleep to be dealt with. Her skin ached from the gravel, and her eyes were sore. Her lips as well felt an uncommon swelling. She blushed as she remembered her kiss from the night before. Memories all flooded back to her, especially the story of Ashbel and LeRoy, the mist from the water, and the horrors of the city bombing. Rose fell back down to the ground in emotional agony, but Aya, in frustration, yanked her arm forward and dragged her until she walked on her own two feet.

"Aya!" Rose shouted before giving up and rising to her normal height.

"Rose!" Aya shouted back, looking not at Rose but in front of herself, beginning to create a circle of blue fire. It burned in a beautiful blue ring. Rose watched in awe as Aya worked her skilled fingers. Carefully, she stepped back. Rose watched it grow until leaves weren't being shown through but an empty, dark large room.

Rose and Aya looked at each other, knowing they were heading to Dragons Nest. Rose nodded as she grasped Aya's dark hands, and they walked simultaneously into the ring of fire.

They walked into a new room in Dragons Nest. It was one Rose had not before seen. It was large and brown, with leaves of red flowers draped from the ceilings. In a far corner, Rose saw a chair. It was a brown wooden chair that one person could sit in. Along the walls of the room, in more hidden detail, were drawings, like those in the halls that Rose had already seen. They had images of people being burned in red fires and red dragons glaring at groups of Red people. Red babies with red lips being carried on the backs of red dragons and being placed in the wombs of mothers. Aya drew them all, but these specific images looked newer. The drawings were more mature, showing that Aya's artistic skill had advanced since the hallway art. The cryptic history in the imagery was a mesmerizing story of many traumatic experiences.

"Why are we here, Aya?" asked Rose. She was quite excited to be there. She adored learning more of the secrets of Dragons Nest. Rose also was very inquisitive about her visit, because she wanted to be prepared, since the secrets she had learned the last few times here had really tested her. She looked over at Aya's short hair and clear eyes. Pain was written all over Aya's face, and Aya had an aura of extreme pain.

"Ashbel called me here, and I needed to bring you too. You need to see something."

Within a flash, the room shifted only for a second, and the once-empty room now held the four great dragons. Vulcan, Edan, Candice, and Ashbel sat in their claimed thrones in front of the lonesome chair. The air in the room became quite heavy, and with the sheer volume of the four dragons, the room seemed quite small and warm. For whatever reason, Aya moved away without informing Rose. She walked so gracefully, with her dark shadow caressing her every step. Her hips swayed against the air, and the brown rock melted at her feet. She walked to a chair Rose had not noticed above the vines and red flowers that hung from the walls. A balcony was resting above the thrones, and on the balcony, there was a great golden throne with large thorns impaling the armrests. The golden throne had a perfect view of the room, seeing both the dragons and the chair, as well as the halls, the doors, the veins, and the flowers.

Aya climbed the branches until she was high enough to throw herself over the balcony. She touched the throne with much relief and some anticipation. Her hair flew over the head of the chair, her fire burning its sides, leaving only her eyes staring at the empty seat. Rose watched as Aya's face trembled in want and desire to step away from the chair, but Rose did not know why. Aya leaned in and sat down. As she sat, her body sank deep into the golden throne. Aya took a deep breath, knowing that she would need to be comfortable and in charge to effectively manage what would come next. Aya loved the throne, even though she hated it. It was so powerful yet so cruel, and Aya enjoyed sitting in the golden seat, because it fit her so perfectly.

Rose found herself without a chair, alone, and in a room full of friends who had a secret that they had not yet shared with her. Ashbel guided her with a flame to a small stool next to his throne. The stool was blue and purple and quite uncomfortable.

"Bring him in," called Ashbel toward the halls. His deep, demanding voice echoed until Rose heard the slight shuffle of feet heading toward the room.

Rose saw a young man with long brown hair and brown eyes being forcefully pushed into the room. The man was heavily chained and even muzzled so that he could not speak. The man was being pushed by a shorter man Rose was not as pleased to see. Erik, the little Blue man, was using a dull spear to prod and direct the younger man.

Rose scoffed in annoyance at Erik but was very curious why they had all gathered for the sake of the brown-haired prisoner. He had a beard that covered most of his lips, with low cheekbones and eye structure. The prisoner's eyes looked rough and evil. His hair was greasy and battered. He was the lucky, or not so lucky, man to sit in the wooden chair. The prisoner sat down and faced the four dragons, the Blue man, and the two girls.

"Ashbel," began Erik. "He was not as fun as you led me to believe."

Rose rolled her eyes. She felt Ashbel did too.

The heavy breath of Ashbel shook the room as he began talking. "Erik, friend, we are not here for fun. We are here because this man has committed a horrible crime, and we must seriously and deliberately decide on the appropriate punishment. Now, please sit down."

"How can I? You gave the bitch my chair."

"How rude!" Rose said, rising out of the stool. "Do you have no common decency?"

A large clap echoed throughout the room. Aya, from above, had caused the bang, in hopes to end the bickering. Rose supposed that in that throne, Aya had that responsibility and power, commanding the room.

"Sit on the ground, Erik," Aya said loudly, her strong feminine voice echoing throughout the chamber. After her words, Erik said nothing more, not even a whine.

Ashbel turned his great neck toward the man in the chair, who had enjoyed the show Erik was giving him. Rose saw the man smirk when Aya put him in his place. The prisoner seemed to welcome the distraction in the same way that he visibly winced when Ashbel mentioned the horrible crime committed and the punishment.

"Aya," Ashbel said, interrupting the silence to continue the proceedings, "you know you are here to conduct an examination of the prisoner, who is accused of committing a horrible crime against the Red Lips. If you please, Aya, begin the session."

Rose stared directly into Aya's clear eyes and watched her as her hands moved along in front of her chest. Little flames of blue fire sprouted, and then one long burst of heat flew across the air, ceasing at the end of the room. This action was repeated thrice, until Aya stood up and began talking instead of moving.

"You sit in the presence of the almighty dragons, Aya the Undead, and Rose the Savior. State your name for all to hear," Aya said.

"Ekon," said the man, avoiding eye contact with Rose and Aya. His dark-brown hair fell in front of his face, covering most of his shallow cheekbones and his brown eyes.

"State your full name," said Aya again, stuttering and hesitating. This hurt her, because she knew the terrible fact of his name. The prisoner was dangerous and a war criminal.

He refused to speak. His jaws clenched. His lips stayed together. He blinked, and his throat dropped. He was tired, alone, and being humiliated by children.

"Ekon, what is your full name?" Rose asked the man quietly, her fingers shivering and her shoulders beginning to slouch under the weight of her anxiety. Her stomach turned over, and her forehead began to sweat. His brown eyes stared up at her body, her bronze hair, her blue eyes, her red lips. A purely evil smile escaped his face.

"Rose," Ekon said slowly. He tried to stand up from the chair, but the chains kept him secured tightly in place.

Rose stuttered her way through mumbles and confusion as to why this prisoner would know her name. Erik looked over at Rose in worry, and so did all the other dragons. She was very scared and confused, afraid of the truth that her own intuition already knew.

"I'm Ekon Mensch, your father."

"You're lying! My father's dead," Rose said loudly, her eyes full of anger. Ashbel curled his tail around her waist to keep her still and safe and out of reach of Ekon's hands.

"I'm not, Rose. I'm alive!"

"Don't look at her!" yelled Aya fiercely. She stood up and pointed out of the balcony, threatening the prisoner with the fire resting in her palms. "Don't you dare talk to her! Don't look at her blue eyes. Don't speak your lies and cruel words to her!"

Ekon stepped back, his head dangling from his neck. He was frustrated with himself for being the traitor he was.

"You, Ekon Mensch, organized a plan to murder thousands of Red Lips in Ashbelle. Do you deny it?" Aya asked, one tear falling out of her white eye.

Rose was caught off guard and reeled, mumbling words of shock and horror.

"No, I do not deny it," Ekon said, looking up at Aya.

"You tried to kill both Rose and me. Do you deny it?"

"I never knew the target was my daughter. I would never hurt my own daughter!" he pleaded.

"But you gladly killed your wife. Do you deny betraying the love of Katrina Mensch and murdering her in cold blood?"

"Yes, I never killed her!" Ekon said, pleading for his life, his eyes melting away. Rose cried, and Ashbel shielded her from looking at her father.

"Lies!" Aya yelled at the top of her lungs. "You killed your wife!"

"I organized a murder when I worked for the king. Yes, I did. The men…oh, how the men stomped! They banged on our door. Katrina went to hide my son and daughter, my baby girl, and I fled. I learned later that Katrina was alive, living somewhere in Nava, Ravens perhaps, but I never killed her."

Ekon was crying now. He regretted so many of the life choices he had made, including becoming a husband, fathering children, and attempting to murder all three of his loved ones. He regretted hiring the demons to rip apart Ashbelle. He looked like he was drowning in all the bad choices he had made in his life.

"Rosie," Aya said quietly, "look away."

Erik was very solemn now as he stood up and took Rose's pale hand from her lap and looked into her eyes. Rose's face was red and wet, with pain written everywhere. Erik wiped a tear from her cheeks. They walked away hand in hand, and as they walked, the heat of fire filled their backs and necks. Sweat dripped from their palms as it got hotter.

Behind them, every color of fire was being poured into the chair. Aya's hand rose, tears streaming much faster down her cheeks, seeping into her red lips. Cries of Rose's name and pleas for help taunted Rose's ears, but she refused to turn back. Her father, once dead, was alive and, once alive, became dead again.

The trials of Dragons Nest.

"I'm sorry," Aya told her. They were both back in the forests, where the cave was and where their friends were.

Rose was sitting on a log, looking away from everything. The woods had cleared of everything poisonous and every bug that could bite her, so she found herself sitting comfortably next to Aya. Her eyes hurt from crying so much, and her throat hurt from screaming and yelling at both her father's dead body and the dragons. She felt so alone, even with the new knowledge that her mother might be alive.

Rose was still traumatized by the experience of hearing her father plead her name while being burned by fire.

The two girls had been talking for a long while. Aya was doing most of the talking. She explained to Rose that Aya's most cruel job as princess of Dragons Nest was presiding over the dragon trials.

"It's called the dragon trials," Aya explained, her voice cracking and trembling. "As a part of being a Red Lip, a person would be faced with purple fire eventually. Those who fall into the darkness do terrible things. They fight, hunt, and kill Nomads and other Red Lips. Even without the equal sign, some Purples believe they have the right to end lives and the right to hurt. So an apprentice's job would be to find those rare Red Lips and bring them to us. I would sit on that throne, that evil throne, humiliate them, scare them, torture them with words, as the dragons watched. I was the judge, and the dragons were the jury. The dragons would kill them, either with fire or their claws, and I would have to watch. I only cried the first time. After that, I learned to love the chair and the power. I didn't know it was your father until he walked in. I wish now that I hadn't brought you."

Rose listened quietly to the story. Her fire melted in her hands and then bounced back to life every few seconds. She didn't know how to feel or even respond to the horrors that went on in Dragons Nest.

Her father was dead; that was all she knew. Rose wondered if she was better off knowing the truth or continuing to believe the lie she had believed for all these years. Aya contributed to the murder of her father, evil though he was, but still he was her father.

"I'm sorry about your childhood, Aya. You didn't deserve that," Rose told her, running her skinny fingers through her bronze-colored hair. Rose and Aya didn't want to talk. So much had happened in the last few days. It was just overwhelming. They were tired and at risk because Purple was close to their veins.

"Aya," Rose began, "can we go to Nava? Can we see if my mother really is alive?"

Aya lowered herself to be right at Rose's face. Looking into her sharp blue eyes, her trimmed eyebrows, and her clear skin, she smiled.

A small nod was the beginning of a long, perfect, friendly hug. Their arms intertwined, their heads on the backs of each other. They rested upon each other, so intimate and so warm. Their Red blood collided together, causing them to feel each other's power and capability.

They let go when they both chose. They wanted to stay still and to breathe into each other. They needed sleep. They needed to close their eyes and dream of the most pleasant things in their lives, so they could wake up and breathe again.

They walked back to the cave, still confused and angry with each other. At the same time that they were broken and lost, they were also warm and safe.

They woke up late in the afternoon. They changed their clothes, washed their hair, cleaned their teeth, shined their boots, and began walking. The sooner they were out of Ashbelle, as Jason told them, the better.

Andrew managed to corral their horses back from by the inn and bring them out of the bombings safely. They gripped onto their horses' manes and guided them safely out of Ashbelle's biggest woods, with the help of LeRoy, who knew the woods and instructed their every turn and step.

The green leaves dangled above their heads so perfectly, and they never had to duck. The shrubs in the back also contributed to the wonderland of greenery. The squirrels would run around the logs and up the trees, their bushy tails pointing in the faces of the teenagers. The deer would prance over their path, either before or after they walked on it.

Rose managed to clear every path they followed, moving the sticks, tree roots, and leaves out of the way. Instead of crunching and stomping, only the low click-clacks of the horses' hooves could be heard. To Rose, it was very relaxing. She focused only on moving Bealfire and the obstacles along the path. The group chitchatted and kept conversation on light subjects. No one asked Aya and Rose where they were in the early dawn of the morning. Rose planned to tell Jason everything she knew about her father and mother, because all his stories were wrong. Rose worried about him being more lost and broken when he found out the truth.

They had been moving for hours before they finally made it out of the woods. The sun was hot now, and the sky was clear of clouds to protect them. Rose stood up and stretched her perfect body, anxious to ride her horse for hours until they were in Nava. She knew that first she had to explain where they were going to the group. She told Aya that she would and asked Aya just to try to keep Jason calm. Rose was terrified, more than she had been in Dragons Nest that morning, of Jason's reaction. How ironic would it be, she thought, if Jason hated stories after he heard the one Rose needed to tell?

They were all mounted on their horses, Aya on Lords, LeRoy on the back of Katrina, Andrew on his Bear, and Camilla on Xenia. Rose, the leader, rode in front of all her friends. Her skin collected the sunshine so perfectly. Her blue eyes glowed, while her red shirt seemed redder. Her hair stuck to the back of her neck from sweat. Rose was drained from all the recent adventures and new knowledge gained. The experience at Ashbelle, which was supposed to offer a well-needed relief and celebration, had resulted in exactly the opposite outcome. Learning about the man who organized that tragedy, her own father, only made matters worse. Maybe it was naive of anyone, and especially the Red Lips, to believe that there could be normal and even happy lives so long as this king lived.

Rose was weak all over, from her arms, to her feet, within her head, and especially inside her heart. The weight of the story about her parents had become too much of a burden to continue carrying. While Rose's fire was weak, she knew that her words were still strong.

"I know what the king has done to affect all of you," she began, getting their attention to be on her and on her body. She saw LeRoy smirk. "And I could not be more empathetic toward you."

Aya hooted, the blush on Rose's cheeks was the color of her fire, and Jason smiled up at his sister talking so boldly, taking charge.

"But I can't kill him. Not yet. Not until I see someone. Someone I've barely met, whom I really only learned about when dead."

Jason's ears fluttered, his eyes widened, and his hair perked up. LeRoy saw Jason's back tense and switched focus back and forth from Rose to Jason, like he was in the wrong seat at a tennis match. Everything in the prairie was peaceful, except the misfits, who were all anxious and paranoid about what Rose would say next. Who was this person who had become so important than even the king? Why did Rose need to see them so impatiently?

"She is my mother," Rose said, looking straight at Jason. "Our mother."

Jason's face was pale, but not unreadable. He was dismissive and alone, but not broken. He didn't cry. He kept breathing. He didn't need to break eye contact with Rose, though.

"You knew," Rose said, squinting her blue eyes to focus in on him and his brown hair and brown eyes.

Jason kept looking softly in her eyes; apologetically he stared.

A wind rose, and the light breeze waved her hair across her back. Water began to form in her eyes. "You knew?" Rose inquired softly, trying to understand.

Jason nodded slowly.

Of course, he had known, Rose thought to herself. He would have had to remember watching her flee as she left them alone to die. Rose broke down and fell off her horse in such shock that Aya and LeRoy rushed to her side, while Andrew and Camilla watched from the side, in such confusion and disappointment.

Rose was being comforted in the arms of LeRoy, who was gravely concerned for Rose. The excitement for LeRoy of holding Rose again and feeling the warmth of her skin was instinctive and subconscious. He desperately needed to help Rose move forward and sort out her life.

Jason watched as his sister flailed on the ground, knowing she would be fine. He watched as she fell unconscious. He watched as Aya cried in shock. He watched as Camilla broke eye contact with Jason to focus on her friend. It was all his fault. He didn't tell her, and he knew it.

Rose woke up in LeRoy's arms. They put her back on her horse and let LeRoy hold her while controlling the beast. She was quite startled to be moving, but when she saw LeRoy, she was calm again. Rose rested her head on the crook of his shoulder. They rode to Nava, ready to meet Katrina, wherever she was.

ERIK

The backs of each person felt so sore when they reached the border of Remular and Nava. The fields were filled with nothing, and the smell of the pure air reached the noses of the teenagers. The sky was serene. The fluffy white clouds streaked the sky, giving a visual of a relaxing heaven.

"There are guards positioned all along the entrances," Aya said as they could see where Remular began. Beyond the land of Remular was a deep forest of evergreen trees. Snow was laced along the trees and the grounds. It got thicker the deeper in a person went.

"Do you think they would let us pass?" asked Rose, who was worried that she would not see her mother, that she would have traveled all the way to Nava to be turned away. She had been panicking the whole trip. The weeks they traveled through Remular. The times where she would cry herself to sleep in worry. She was very anxious, but not as anxious as Jason. Jason was worried that his dear mother would see how he had raised Rose and judge all his choices. When in doubt, Jason would remember that his mother was alive and still decided to not return to the Red Islands, where her children were.

Aya stopped her horse, out of the view of all the guards. Her beautiful short hair danced in the wind. Her silver eyes scanned Rose's face.

"I'm sure my father put them there to stop us if we went to Nava," Aya said with complete certainty. "He must know about Dragons Nest and your father."

"How?" Rose asked, astonished at his ears and eyes around the world. "No one was there except us."

"Maybe your father's friends, or perhaps he is still working for my father and died to get five minutes with you."

"How did he know she was going to be there?" Jason asked, staring at his sister. Perhaps someone was watching them, waiting to attack those he loved.

"He watched us, or maybe dumb luck," Aya told them. "Either way, no one can be trusted."

"You figured all this out by looking at guards far away from us?" LeRoy asked, doubting. He was still sitting behind Rose, holding her hips on the horse, taking in the scent of her bronze hair and the scent of her sweat. He felt so in love during that moment, but Rose was still uncertain about it all. She was far more focused on seeing her mother. Nothing was going to get in the way of her and Nava.

"Yes, LeRoy, I believe I have," answered Aya, glaring at LeRoy and his slight smirk on his pale lips. "But I have a plan."

The group of misfit teens shoved their horses as close together as they could to hear Aya talk about how they were going to get past the guards.

"The most they have are swords, and maybe some arrows. Rose and I will use that horrible gift my mother gave me and rid ourselves of the red lips, just until we can sneak past. Andrew and Camilla, they don't know you, so you guys are less of a threat and can wear this lipstick that I have in my bag."

Aya reached over for a small bag she had carried for months. Inside she pulled out a small tube of red lipstick. It wasn't the perfect shade for the twins, but it fit enough to give the effect of normal-colored lips.

She handed it to her friends, and Camilla helped Andrew apply it to the perfect edge. Their red hair and red lips complemented their light-green eyes. Their smiles were so big, and so were their muscles. Camilla had grown up the past few months, getting mud in her face and training with Rose and Aya every day. Her curves outshone both Aya's and Rose's. Though she was older, her long hair curled down her waist. Jason enjoyed running his hands through it.

Andrew and Jason had become friends, pushing each other's limits during training, racing through the woods, with Rose tripping them by commanding the roots to sprout up. They had matured in their months of seclusion from their homes, much like everyone else had.

"Jason and LeRoy will stay the same. You two happen to not have red lips." She glared again at LeRoy's pale face. "So stay on the horses and keep quiet. Let me do the talking."

Aya took a deep breath. She was rather worried about how the guards would react to these teenagers crossing the path, knowing that the guards were looking for teenagers.

They trotted up to the line of men, with trees lined behind them. Everyone shuddered when they saw all the swords and the armor, but Rose thought that her fire could melt the armor and burn the skin, a thought the Purple gave her.

Aya's and Rose's horses were right in front. They shuffled their eyes between each other and the men in armor. LeRoy had moved in front of Andrew, hiding his lips with his body, while Camilla was out in the open. She was the most terrified. The brutality to Red prisoner was rumored to be so cruel that she would rather drop dead before anything happened to her.

The guards shielded their swords when they caught the eyes of the group. The slight clanking of the metal on metal and the loud clacking of the horses' hooves were all that could be heard.

"We desire to pass into Nava," Aya told the guards. Her lips were pale now, and so were Rose's. They steadied their horses so that they weren't a moving target, and behind them the other horses paused.

"Names?" asked the guard standing in front of them. He was buff and had a shaggy voice that was rather raspy and tired.

"Why would that be a question to be asked?" Rose said firmly. "We are travelers from Kings Bay. Let us pass."

"Not without names. His Majesty's orders."

"LeRoy, son of Amos of Ashbelle. Tell His Majesty, his friend, that Amos of Ashbelle has died in an attack and that his guards are keeping his son from seeing his uncles in Nava," LeRoy said proudly, staring at the men in metal armor.

"You may pass, LeRoy, son of Amos. I am deeply sorry for your loss. Any friend of the king is a friend of his army."

"And my friends?" LeRoy asked impatiently.

"They may pass too," he began, until he stuttered and looked intently at Camilla. "You, girl, what is your name?"

"Camilla," she mumbled, losing eye contact with the man in the suit of armor. She closed her lips, trying to hide the color.

"What is on your lips, Camilla?"

"Lipstick."

"Touch them," he demanded, "and dismount from your horse. Come here and let me see your thumb."

Camilla breathed. Jason was close to yelling at her to stay put, but instead she dismounted and walked from her horse up close to the man. Her thumb was covered in red residue from spreading it across the bottom lip.

The guard grabbed her hands and observed the makeup. He smirked and then laughed, forcing all the other men in the guard detail with him to laugh as well.

He threw Camilla into the arms of the man to his left and drew his sword.

"Kill them all!" he called. All the men drew their swords and marched toward them as Camilla pleaded for them to draw back. She began screaming and kicking as the men toyed with her.

"What color is your fire?"

"How is Ashbel doing?"

"Sin for us!"

Aya jumped off her horse, and so did Jason. LeRoy ran toward Rose, and Andrew leaped for Camilla. They all marched toward an army of men, six against one hundred. Aya used her blue fire to burn the necks of all the men, kicking and punching them when she had the chance. Rose sprinted toward Camilla, outrunning all the guards. Rose took Camilla by the arm and made a flash of powerful red fire that pushed all the men down. Her pale hand intertwined with the trembling hand of Camilla as they darted into the woods. She controlled the trees as she sprinted, basically dragging Camilla as she tried to keep up. The trees tripped and cut the few guards following them until she was far enough ahead to hide Camilla from sight.

"Stay here. They won't find you. I promise," Rose said, barely out of breath, while Camilla was also gasping dramatically for some air. The snow was comforting yet very cold. The fire kept her warm as a green glow haloed on her body.

"Yes, they will," Camilla said once she could talk. "I can't camouflage with the snow!"

"Don't worry about that. I will have this under control very soon."

Rose's eyes flickered. She used her brain to move a tree from view and then back again. She darted back into the open field once she knew that Camilla was going to be fine. LeRoy saw her long hair and red lips and ran to embrace her. They touched for a moment, but then Rose saw men coming after her in the corner of her eyes. She managed a large ball of fire and spun it at them. Her space became very heated and blinding as the men fell to the ground in pain, not death. She watched as Aya took after the head guard and swung both fists at him. Rose continued to fight, with Jason, Andrew, and LeRoy by her side.

Aya fought hard against the man in charge. She took her hand against the metal of the sword and melted it in front of his eyes until nothing was left but the handle. Fist against fist, fire against flesh, she was close to closing his eyes in the deep sleep. He fought hard because he knew he was fighting for his life. Rage filled Aya's face. They worked for her father. They listened to the evils that he whispered in their ears.

"Who are you?" he asked, looking into her eyes.

"I am Aya, daughter of the king, princess of Dragons Nest, and you will die," she said, placing a hand on his chest plate. Her fingers began to get hot. Fire burned through the metal chest plate, getting near his heart.

"Aya!" called out Rose next to her.

Aya looked over, losing connection with the man, looking only into Rose's blue eyes. The head guard collapsed onto the ground, passing out from his near-death experience.

"We won! You can come over to me now," Rose said calmly. She began walking closer to Aya, gripping her arms.

"Rose?"

"Yes. Rose."

They found Camilla hiding in the woods. They were now in Nava, alone and scared. Jason embraced her, with a deep kiss. Holding her in his arms, Jason was aware that every touch might be the last one.

"We must keep moving. Grab the horses," Aya said, worn-out from anger and the fighting. Her silver eyes were widened and aware of every sight in the woods. Her hair was sweaty and in disarray.

Andrew ran out of the woods and gathered all the horses. He held on to their ropes and led them into the greenery of the trees. Rose was delighted to see that her Bealfire had not been hurt in the battle. She surveyed her own body and found no injuries, not even a scratch. She rubbed her fingers through her horse's black mane, feeling the thickness of the strands and whispering soft love words to her beautiful horse.

Aya did the same to her Lords. She felt her and petted her. She kissed her soft pink nose. The wetness from Aya's lips was dripping all over the face of Lords from their exchanging so many kisses.

They were all so excited to be with their animals again. It hurt having to leave them and find them so many times. They were beyond overjoyed at how smart the horses were to run and hide from the swords. How clever they were to leave the fighting to their owners.

"We ride on. We are heading into Blue Forest. Erik will let us stay there for the night," Aya told them after everyone was mounted on their stallions. LeRoy was behind Rose once again. Rose felt safe with his arms around her skinny pale waist.

"In case you have forgotten, we don't get along too well with the Blue man," Rose pointed out as they galloped down the path she was clearing for them. Her blue eyes were sore from staying alert for so long. Her arms hurt form punching and slapping, but she insisted on hearing an answer, so she focused on that more than LeRoy massaging her shoulders.

"Yes, but if I have anything to do with it, we will be more than welcome to stay for a while."

"You plan to call in Ashbel to make Erik behave?" Rose asked her sarcastically, smiling up at her silver eyes.

"Perhaps yes, but I also have the power to summon Ashbel anywhere and the voice to make Ashbel do something about Erik's rude temperament."

Rose laughed. She remembered how Erik had been frightened of Ashbel when Ashbel talked. Rose remembered how Erik froze Celia, how he gave her the purple fire, and how dangerous he was. She was apprehensive about sleeping in his territory, where he was far cleverer and more in control of the setting. Rose hoped that she could at least control the forests there, but perhaps Erik had a magical spell restricting that.

"So you grew up here?" LeRoy asked, whispering into Rose's ear. She watched him look around every now and then, while moving his fingers all around her back and muscles. He was very touchy and clingy toward Rose. She thought that was only because she was the reason he was on the journey with them. She found that a little cute.

"Not exactly," she began. "I was born here. When I was little, my parents died and then my brother and I had to pack up what few things we had and travel to the Red Islands. My aunt lived there with her daughters, my cousins, and it took us three solid years to get there. We had to take back roads with long detours and hide from every person we saw. We even built a boat to sail to the Red Islands. Once we arrived and found my aunt, we had only lived there for about a year before we left on this adventure. Now I'm back. I never thought I would be back."

"Does it feel nice?" he asked, whispering his words into her ears again.

"I wish it were under different circumstances. I never thought I would be back to see my mother, who I thought was dead for years. We are going back to ask her why she didn't find us and to understand what other secrets she has kept."

LeRoy sighed. His hands were now back around her waist. He thought about how sweet her lips had tasted. He wished they were back in the warm water, with her hands intertwined with his.

They rode on until they were farther into the forests of evergreen trees, which had recently been layered in snow. The trees were a thick color of purple painted with simple dye that dried and then rotted. Small fires could be seen up ahead along all the trees, and that was when they paused.

"Be careful. This place is filled with animal traps," Aya warned. She kicked the side of her horse again and wandered slowly off into the distance. Rose followed, and behind her were Jason, then Camilla, with Andrew trailing the group. They steadied their horses' paces, looking closely at their surroundings, aware that something dangerous could happen at any moment.

Little springs and ropes were heard snapping in the distance, but no one was too afraid of what was setting them off. They began to trot along the way, waiting for the fires they could see in the distance to be right in front of them.

Rose cocked an eyebrow up at Aya. "You sure you know where we are going?"

"Positive."

Rose scoffed, rolling her eyes to the back of her head.

"We have been moving for a while now. What is taking so long?" Rose asked Aya with much annoyance, her shoulders tensing again.

"The Blue Lips fear just about everything. They aren't just going to be in the open," Aya responded calmly, moving her eyes to meet Rose's face, studying her body language. "Are you scared?"

Rose's blank face stared back at Aya. "I have more problems than a mean old man."

"You were fine just a second ago. Is it because of your mom?" Aya inquired.

Rose paused. She was at a loss for words, her eyes dull from exhaustion. LeRoy patted her back, moving his fingers up and down the spine, until she began moving again, completely calmed down.

"You know me well, Aya," Rose told her, wanting to smile. Rose was nervous about how the Blues would react to her waltzing into their village. She was worried about how her mother would respond to seeing her as a mature Red Lip. All this reality was hitting her, and it was painful, sharp, and cutting.

"We are nearly there, and when we get settled, maybe we can talk?" Aya offered.

Rose nodded shyly, still easing into LeRoy's gentle touch, melting into his warm arms. He had braided her dry hair during the trip. He had twisted and combined the strands of her hair, until all the bronze hair on her head was in a perfect braid. She loved how he massaged her head when he braided the hair. She loved how safe she felt when he wrapped his arms around her waist. Sleeping on his broad shoulders and feeling the muscle, bones, and skin on his body were even better.

Aya, after a while, began to slow down her horse's trot, shifting into a very slow walk. Keeping a steady pace, the others followed, trying to understand why she had slowed so suddenly.

"Is there a trap?" Jason asked Aya, waiting for her to shake her head in response.

They stayed quiet, until Aya was right in front of a tall tree branch with green leaves. A strong breeze caused all the kids to bend sideways, while they watched Aya intently, observing what she was planning on doing with the branch.

Aya minded her head before riding underneath the lowest leaves, guiding Lords into the woods just beyond their view. Rose followed behind her, seeing just what she was so cautious about.

Beyond the bushes was a blue village. Huts upon huts were built out of blue trees and wood. Purple fires were burning among rows of fireplaces that stuck out of the ground. Large drapes were hung around the sides of trees so travelers wouldn't see the people who lived in the village.

No people were seen in the open, only their homes and fires. Aya looked around to see large beaming eyes staring at them from the tops of trees above them. Rose saw them too. Purple eyes, purple faces, deformed purple lips, rags for clothes, sharp teeth, and crooked smiles—all these stared at them with cruel intentions.

"Aya," Rose stuttered, "you got a plan?"

Aya mumbled something that seemed, to Rose, a confirmation that she did. The blue shade of the village made it hard for the group to watch the moves of the little Blue people. Rose watched them closely but was also scared of how many purple fires there were. How toxic that would be for all the Reds in the surrounding areas.

"We have to find Erik," Aya whispered to the group. Her horse began moving ahead, following the path that was laid out, dodging all the firepits, watching out for the people hanging above them.

The low hissing sound of all the beings above them could be heard as they rode deeper into the forest. Aya led the group into a large tent in the deepest part of the village, where Erik was supposed to live. It was purple colored with a red trim. A fire hole was made going out the top so that an indoor fireplace could be made. Rose found it amusing that the high and mighty Erik, friend of Ashbel, lived in a royal *tent*.

Rose pulled up the entrance curtain with a gentle finger to reveal a fat man sitting on a purple bed full of cushions. He was licking his fingers clean of wine stains when he recognized the broken faces of Rose and Aya. He was wearing the robes he wore any other day, just with more stains from grapes and alcohol. His stringy hair was greasy and lazily combed. Rose watched him intently, observing the way he moved when he realized they were here, judging how unprofessional and greedy he was.

He cursed loudly when he saw all the stains on his shirt, then cursed again when he looked at all the kids in his room. His fat feet carried him to the wineglass, and he poured himself and Aya another overflowing drink of the red wine.

Aya gladly took a sip and then passed it along the line of friends. She smiled up at Erik with the same perfect smile her red lips made for her. The group all walked in and sat on the ground. Rose hoped against hope that Erik would moderate his behavior in front of her friends, but that was not to be.

"They didn't kill you out front?" he asked Rose with a scruff in his throat, coughing and wheezing.

"No, Erik, but what are they? I have never seen children hang from tree branches without smiling and laughing playfully."

"They looked like demon? They are demons, aren't they?" LeRoy spat excitedly, his eyes widening at the thought of fighting demons or of even seeing demons.

"You're new?" Erik asked slyly, knowing that if LeRoy had been with the group in Ashbelle, he would never be that pleased to see demons again. Demons were a real headache.

"LeRoy, son of Amos of Ashbelle," LeRoy interjected, sticking his hand out for Erik to shake and continue the conversation.

Erik looked at the dirty hand that was being presented in front of his eyes, watching how the fingers moved in excitement to know him. He shook his head and shooed away the boy's palm, glaring at him until he decided to drink another sip of wine.

"No, you swine, they aren't demons. They are called the Forgotten Children."

"Jason told me about them. The kids who had the power to control purple fire, whose parents cut off their lips, who were banished to live here, with the punishment of never seeing the light of day again."

"You make it sound so depressing," Erik said with a sappy sound in his voice while gulping another taste of wine.

The rest of them were solemn about the thought of how these children were treated. The wineglass made its way back to Rose, and she took a big sip, tasting the sweet grape-and-sugar mix and then passing the glass into Aya's dark hands.

"What are you idiots even doing here? Shouldn't you be in Remular, killing someone?" Erik's tone changed, sounding more annoyed than stressed and lazy. His piercing eyes stared directly into Rose's blue eyes, leaving her unable to talk from his intimidation. It was beginning to become harder to breathe in the small tent, seeing as six people were squished into the shallow space.

Her head became light again, as she saw small dots every time she tried to focus on one thing. Rose became even more uncomfortable, watching all their heads spin, the wine bottles shake, and her vision narrow.

"Rose," Aya's gentle voice whispered into her ear as her strong fingers ran down her back. "Don't let him do this to you. Don't get anxious about *him*."

"Erik, why do you live in this tent and not out with your Forgotten Children?" Andrew questioned him, trying to distract Rose from how he was making her feel.

"They are an army of physically abused children. That is no place for me. Besides, they needed a king, so I became their king. A king doesn't engage in conversation with his people."

"Whose side are you on?" yelled Rose, triggered by Erik's impression of what a king should be. Rose knew Jason would make a fabulous king and he would do the opposite of what the current king was doing presently. "That is, what would make a great king? A loving and kind person whose humility would outshine his power and who would want personal relationships with his people!"

Aya held on to Rose's hand, feeling its sweat and her heartbeat along her wrist. She counted its beats to help relax herself and Rose.

"Is that what you plan to do when you take the throne?" Erik asked her, pouring himself a second glass of wine. The last one had been fully consumed.

"I won't have the throne. I would give it to Jason."

"Why would you do that? It would be yours, O King Killer!" Erik sang, smiling at the idea of this little girl ending the life of the strongest man in the world.

"I have a home here, in Nava, that I would return to," Rose said, arching her eyebrows and smirking.

"Doesn't Jason have a home too?" Erik questioned further.

Rose listened and breathed heavily. She saw his hand flicker and create purple fire, trying to lure her in with the drug that was in her vein.

She had never thought of what Jason wanted, just what she wanted. How she couldn't rule but how Jason was the nicest person she had ever met. Rose was certain that Jason as king would be the best for the people. He would bring prosperity to the world, and then she could go back home, either to the Red Islands or Ravens in Nava.

Jason stared into Rose's eyes, trying to get her to calm down. He tried to show her that everything was going to be all right. But to Rose, this wasn't how her life was supposed to go. This wasn't how it was supposed to end. This was the path she had to follow and not the path she preferred to follow. A reluctant savior she was.

She wanted everything to be back the way it was before she learned what she could do, what she was destined to do, and how she was supposed to accomplish it. She was realizing that her life would never be back to normal, and she hated that Erik had to be there to watch her and see her fall apart. He was happy that everything was going downhill for her, but he was ultimately shocked that she had made it this far. She had spent many months traveling the world and seeing all the evil it had to offer. Rose had not let her Purple into her veins, still denying the bad, only accepting the good. To Erik, this was an amazing accomplishment.

"You can stay in the tents outside. I will talk to the Blue people and ask them if they would move over for your lot. If they don't want to, you are welcome to leave and never come back!" He smiled as they walked out. Aya left to make a fire, while the rest of the group collected food and water.

Rose went for a nature walk in the woods to a little pond she knew she would find. The pond was not too far into the forest, and Rose hoped she could calm her mind, just like how she would back in the Red Islands.

The water was dirty with dead leaves and stains from rotting logs and animal bones. The pond was a dark-blue color and had no fish. The water was cold and uncomforting. No animal would drink from it. She watched as the trees that once surrounded the pond tightly shifted farther apart so she could sit nicely next to the water. For someone who was hot and fiery, she was attached to water, loving how calm and peaceful it was.

"Rose," she heard a familiar voice say. She looked over her skinny shoulder to see Jason's handsome body. She examined their similar features, and then his face and his brown eyes. He smiled down at his little sister, smiling at her blue eyes, red lips, and dark eyelashes. He smiled at her perfectness, smiling at the way she smiled back at him.

"Jason," Rose said to him back, patting a piece of grass for him to sit next to her, and he did. His shaggy brown hair shook above his eyes when he sat down. He stared at the water until he found the words to talk to Rose.

"LeRoy was looking for you."

"Let him."

"Are you guys…?" he questioned, smiling down at his little sister.

She scoffed. "I don't know. We kissed once."

Jason looked shocked, but he was happy for her. She was happy for him. He told her about Camilla and how they were in love, how her red hair was beautiful, and how her green eyes gave him his happiness.

"Do you want to be king?" she asked, interrupting his story about their first kiss. He paused before looking back at her. His breathing steadied, but his eyes sank into his face. He looked very tired.

Jason watched the ripples in the water before he looked back into the eyes of his little sister. He watched her twitch her eyes, lick her lips, and play with her hair. He watched her begin to cry and latch onto his chest. He held her close to him, wanting to help her.

"Rosie, if you kill the king, if we win," he began, touching her long bronze hair, "I will become your king."

She smiled, thinking of their future together, where he was on the throne and she could escape the world and live alone, with the dragons protecting her, with Aya visiting her, with LeRoy holding her at night. Being happy.

Jason held her as she cried tears of joy and relief. Her skin was so hot fire was burning in her veins. He hated seeing her so emotionally broken, but he had to leave her. He had to go back to help the others, to help them eat their food, to help them relax, and to calm their nerves about Rose.

Then Rose was alone again, sitting by the water. She dreamed about all the changes Jason would make in the world. She imagined how he would enforce rule to end discrimination against the Reds by the Nomads, and how he would give them both equal opportunities. She was excited about how many Reds would come out of hiding, and how they would be able to live without fear of their own lives being taken because of how they were born.

She smiled to herself, her cheeks hurting because they were stuck together from the tearstains. Some of the dirt was cleaned off her face by her tears. She felt less weight, too, like she needed to cry. All this pain had built up in her head, now all escaping through her eyes, dampening her eyelashes.

She sat at the pond for hours, until she managed to get comfortable and fell asleep. Sleeping recklessly throughout the night, rubbing herself against sticks and leaves, coughing and freezing in the cold atmosphere of Nava.

When she woke up, her nose was solid red. The pads of her fingers were also red and difficult to move. She had forgotten to warm herself up with the fire that burned in her veins. She could have frozen to death.

She walked back to the camp, and her brother found her a nice place next to the fire and put a warm blanket around her shoulders. He then put his strong arms around her so he stayed warm too. She fell asleep again on his shoulder, in the comfort of his heat, and Aya's blue fire surrounded them.

They woke up again in each other's arms. Behind them everyone was packing up, gathering all their items, walking past and back again. Rose walked and entered the small tent that was set up for the boys to sleep in and observed the eyes of the man inside.

She gleamed desperately at the small pillows on the ground, touching the grass on the dirt lightly. Her bare feet tickled against the leaves and sticks. Her eyes stared directly into those of LeRoy, who was caught still packing all his bags. Their eyes met perfectly. Those eyes, those perfect blue eyes that Rose had, pierced through LeRoy.

Her hands traced the skin of his chest. His hands grasped her hair. Their eyes closed. Their fingers intertwined. Their breathing stopped, and then it began again in deep gasps. Their energy belonged to each other, just as their lips stuck to each other. Their wet lips closing in on the other, until the breathing was impossible to be without.

*****

Aya's horse led the group once they were all packed. They wandered back into the home of the Blue Lips. There was more life in the morning. People were found wandering the fireplaces, walking into Erik's tent and walking out with full plates of meat and fruits. Their lips were all torn and bruised. Their faces were all pale and hopeless. Their fire would never be used properly.

The tents of all the people that lived in the forests were occupied by all their children, waiting patiently for their parents to come back with their food for the morning. What lips they had were red, but their faces were bruised and cut. Many had broken bones and other bruises. They seemed to be abused.

"The Forgotten Children are not the friendliest, especially to kids with parents. They find ways to torment the children born to adult Blue Lips. Erik seems to enjoy it. He does nothing to help fix the problems here," Aya told Rose after Rose asked her about all the scars on the kids' faces.

"That's horrible," Rose responded in disgust. "Jason and I will have to make some serious changes here in Nava."

"It must be horrible to find yourself with this place as your home."

"It still is," Rose told her, patting Bealfire's mane as they walked on, smiling at all the people who watched them enter their village.

"It doesn't have to be. You could live with me in Dragons Nest."

Rose looked deeply into Aya's eyes. How happy and safe she felt in those clear eyes. "You know I can't do that."

They had arrived at the curtain entryway to Erik's tent. The tent was the same, but more people were in it this time. More women had come, and more food was placed around the few pieces of furniture the tent held. Erik was upset once again when he saw the teens enter his place.

"Leave," Erik told them, drinking another glass of wine.

"No, Erik, we have to talk," Aya told him.

"I don't care."

"I do," Rose said to him, creating a ball of red fire and causing it to gleam into his dark eyes.

"I don't care even more now."

"Ashbel will be here soon, to talk to you about how horribly you are treating your people," Aya told him as a threat, snapping her dark fingers in his face.

"So you entered my tent to warn me with your empty threats and waste my time with your meaningless words. Great planning! You lot should be on your way to Ravens by now, shouldn't you?"

Rose paused, about to step closer to the rotten old man. Her heart fluttered wildly when she heard of the place.

"Ravens, what do you know about Ravens?"

Erik stood up from his sad little chair and waddled his fat body over to face Rose, looking at the blue he had once tried to hide.

"Everything you can read in a book," he spat, pushing his nose into her skin.

Rose looked in astonishment at the man. He had slowly guided himself to the opening of the tent, found the curtain door with his fingers, and opened it so widely that the door was no longer there. He smiled an ever-so-cruel smile at the people around him, who only wished to help him.

"Like I said," Erik said, exhaling, his smile widening, "leave!"

Rose tried to argue, but the rest of the group quickly left the room, with nothing to show for the time spent in his tent of contempt. Their desperation and ambition to make the world a better place were obviously not shared with everyone, especially those who lived their whole lives being mean to all.

"Is Ashbel really coming?" questioned LeRoy. He was restless when it came to the big red monster. He wanted to thank Ashbel for his advice when it came to Rose. He wished he could be with Rose until the day he died, to care for her in the place she wanted to run away to, and to be anywhere she was.

"Of course," Aya told him while aggressively jumping onto Lords. Her hair was freshly combed, and it swayed when she settled onto the back of the stallion.

They started traveling to Ravens, the town they were so anxious to visit. Rose worried about how much thinking Aya was really putting into all their plans. Rose saw Aya becoming sloppy and her palms becoming sweaty. The trees here in Nava were permanently covered in snow. They were always glazed in the winter and drizzled in the summer. Rose loved the way the golden sun felt on her white skin. She felt less alone with the trees surrounding her every pulse and with the bark inhaling her every exhale.

"Aya?" Rose questioned. Her perfect chin perked up when she heard the innocent sound of her name being called. Her silver eyes caught Rose's blue ones. Their calm air tracked with their lips as they spoke. "What all is known about Ravens?"

Aya smiled softly. Her horse walked slower so she could be heard better by Rose. Aya's dimples showed as she laughed her way into the sentence, saying, "Oh, Rose, there truly isn't much. Erik was in a bad mood."

"Jason told me about a well. Where is that?" Rose asked.

"In Ravens."

Rose smiled. "Let's start there," she told her. She was rather happy with herself and the way she smarted herself into the conversation. "Tell me more about the well."

"It's hidden, far out of reach. It hasn't been used in years."

"Where would one find it?"

"You aren't seriously thinking of washing away your identity, are you, Rosie?"

Rose was quick to respond, nearly talking over her close friend, "No, absolutely not. I'm just worried about how easily the king could find it and pour the water on an army of Reds."

Aya laughed because of the stupidity of the question. "There isn't enough water for that."

"Well, someone had to have enchanted the water. What if that person enchanted more? Maybe lakes or oceans worth of water!"

The horses trotted slightly faster as they entered a narrow path. Rose was still focused on all her fears, wanting to think through every problem they could face. After all, Rose thought, they were only teenagers who had never fought before in a real fight. They were moody teens who were fighting out of fear and loneliness and lacked both courage and nerve.

"Rosie," Aya began, her soft smile reappearing, "whoever made that water the horrible substance it is today lived centuries ago. The chances they are still breathing air are slim to none."

Rose sighed through a deep breath. "Right, but once again, where can we find this well?"

UBEL

Rose jumped off her horse at the first sight of the Veella River. Her feet carried her straight to the river, which ran through Ceptem, Remular, and Nava. The locals in Remular and Nava called the major portions of this river the Veella River. Because the river turned black once it entered Ceptem, the locals in Ceptem called it the Black River. Out of caution, the travelers were using back roads instead of the popular trail following the Veella River. The king had sent his special military unit, the Kings Knights, to guard the trail in hopes of catching or killing Rose if she traveled north into Nava.

The water from the Veella River was so cold against Rose's soft red lips. Drinking the water, the kids and their horses were completely refreshed. They hadn't drunk in a day and had barely eaten because they were rushing to get to the northernmost part of Nava in the smallest amount of time. Jason made sure that no time was wasted during this most risky leg of their journey.

"You thirsty, Rosie?" Jason taunted. His smirk lit up his face, and his perfect dimples glistened in the sunlight. The sun was just beginning to set and the moon was beginning to rise as the teens arrived in the town of Ravens. Rose shook her head in annoyance at her big brother, smiling deep down in her core. LeRoy and Jason had been sharing a horse, so Jason was also sharing her annoyance. While LeRoy was nice and important to Rose, Jason had grown annoyed because LeRoy was always talkative and unrealistically optimistic, at least to Jason's way of looking at the world. Then again, it was an awful lot to ask having two teenage men share a horse for a day or two.

Once again, Rose turned her red lips to face the cold water and sipped it down her throat. She felt satisfied as the liquid ran down into her stomach, refreshing both the Red genes that Rose was born with and the Purple infection that Rose had chosen. Since leaving the village of the lost children, Rose felt like she was continuing a downward spiral in her veins and in her head between Red and Purple.

Jason sat next to her and drank with her. He also filled several bottles to the brim with the pure water that the Veella River offered. She took in the view of the water, watching as the cold froze every nearby lake while the water in the Veella kept running. This river was vital and gave sustenance to every civilized country in the world. Except for the quirk about its color, the river stayed the same, never changing in every climate. Rose loved how beautiful and reliable the Veella River was.

"Is everyone's thirst quenched?" Aya asked, looking into the toughened eyes of her friends.

Rose smiled, moving her thin body upward and onto the back of Bealfire. She nodded toward her closest friend, making Aya aware that she was ready to move on. The rest of the team agreed and mounted their horses to continue their journey to Ravens.

"Is the Veella water also enchanted?" Rose asked Jason, who told her all the stories she knew growing up.

Jason chuckled. His face lit up every time she talked about their past and particularly about their journey to the Red Islands. LeRoy was watching the way they talked. He seemed to enjoy how powerful the sibling relationship was and how gloriously Rose looked when she talked to her brother.

"No, Rose, the water in the Veella is not enchanted."

"I don't remember it from when we walked through these woods."

"We would have been too scared to walk so in the open like we are now."

"We were so young," Rose told him.

Birds were tweeting their final songs for the day as the group trotted on. The slight scent of sweat and dirty horses could be smelled in the area. The breeze was sharper as they rode farther north. The damp smell of the snow surrounding them and of the evergreen trees was also in the air, along with dust and mist.

"Are you nervous to go back home?" Jason asked Rose, watching her twitch and tear up when they continued their conversation about their history.

"If we were going home, we would be heading south, not north," Rose answered.

"What's south?" LeRoy asked. "I thought you both were born in Ravens?"

Rose smiled up at the boy, whose dorkiness was incomparable. "We weren't loved there. We weren't listened to there or respected. It was barely a home."

"We lived with our aunt and cousins in the Red Islands for a year. We left to pursue our dreams and to murder the king," Jason joked, and Rose laughed.

"What was that like?" LeRoy asked, his interest shocking Rose. In all honesty, she hadn't thought much about the cabin she used to live in or the little children that would run around the halls of the house and sometimes pick berries with her.

He would love it there, Rose thought. *He would love Aunt Liza's cooking, and he might even find Celia attractive.*

"I had a lake not too far away from the cabin. The woods would move around to my every command. The water would ripple whenever I wanted, and the deer would come up to me and I would pet them."

My lake.

"Maybe once a month, hunters would enter the woods in search of a good catch, but I never let them into my woods."

Rose thought of the days when she would fall asleep next to her little lake. How her aunt would scold her afterward when Rose would walk back into the house covered in dirt and grass stains. Her aunt would give her the same lecture about being more ladylike and how she would never marry a quiet man with those kinds of scars on her hands and legs. Rose remembered watching the birds in the sky, observing the way they would fly, wishing to be up flying with them.

"I shared a room with my cousin Celia. She was my closest friend. She had these brown eyes that I could never not stare into," Rose described. "She had long blond hair. She was good with hair, and most days she would braid mine."

"She sounds pretty cool," LeRoy told her, watching Rose's eyes widen as she agreed with him. He listened to her continue her innocent rant about her home in the Red Islands. He watched her skinny hands move when she made gestures. He watched as she played with her bronze hair when she talked of the gardens she would pretend to be in.

"Liza would make these warm dinners for the family. She would buy bread and meats in the markets that would open at the beginning of the week. She would place one bowl of sugar in the center of the table, and my little cousins would reach their tiny hands out to try to dip their fingers in before Liza would notice. She would force us all to eat berries and veggies at every meal. Of course, I had no problem with that, and sometimes she would force me to eat a small amount of ham or beef to ensure I was getting all the nutrients I needed to grow big and strong. At least that was how Aunt Liza would put it."

"That seems so beautiful," LeRoy told her, enjoying the rare moments that Rose was in pure bliss.

"Yes, it was beautiful," Rose said, hesitating, her smile fading, "and I killed them."

Jason paused in his laughter, and so did LeRoy. They turned back and saw that Bealfire had stopped his steady movement, and Rose had also given up on moving forward.

"Rose...," Jason tried to begin.

Her eyes focused on the ground as she began to collect the danger she had brought upon her loved ones. She thought of all the pain they must have felt before she killed them. How the king must have personally tortured them for housing her.

"Rose, you don't know that," Jason reassured her.

"But I do."

They died because of me, Rose thought. *They died protecting me.*

"I have to go," Rose told them as she kicked her horse so hard he jumped forward, running so far in the distance that in seconds she passed Aya. She blocked out the shouts of her name from Aya, Jason, and LeRoy, trying to run as far ahead as she could.

They'll catch up eventually, she thought deeply to herself.

Bealfire was quickly worn out after galloping for just ten minutes, even though he had been walking for most of the day. Rose's head was spinning in every way it could. Her heart was in such a good place. She was falling in love. She was happy. She was confident. She was coming to accept her mission to replace the king. She remembered the one time in her life when everything felt just right. The only time besides the present when she could breathe normally. She killed the people that allowed her to breathe safely, the people who had a bed for two children running from the law.

She felt so distraught. She missed them. She felt guilty for not thinking of them when she was happy, for not letting them feel happy too. Her horse stopped running. Bealfire was tired, and so was Rose. She allowed gravity to pull her body down to the ground, and then the beautiful horse ran over to a small creek and ate the blueberries that grew from the bushes along the sides of the water.

Rose sat on the dirt ground, her body trembling in fear of what kind of person she was becoming. The person she wanted to be was a person who would have remembered the way Celia smiled and the smell of Aunt Liza's cooking. She tried to remember the way the house looked, the way the wooden stairs wound up into the second floor, but her vision had grown hazy.

A low holler for help came from the near woods. Rose heard it and wandered deep off the path, following the sound of the cries. Her blue eyes scanned all the trees and leaves for the being from which the cries for help originated, while her pale ears acted like radar homing locators.

"Help! Help? Help!" the mysterious voice called. Rose came nearer and nearer to the source of the sounds. She wandered until she found the source.

A tall boy with brown hair and dark black eyes was tied to a tree with sharp and tan ropes. The cries became scratchy as Rose grew closer to the boy. His hair was cut and tangled. He had obviously been beaten, and his eyes looked pained and detached. The shirt the boy was wearing was bloodstained and shredded in certain places.

"I'm here! Hey! It's okay! Help's here," Rose told him as she went behind the thick tree to which he was tied. Her warm hands created the perfect temperature; she used the Red heat from her veins to melt the strands of the rope, freeing the mysterious boy from the captivity of the tree.

"Thank you," he told her as Rose noticed his pale lips. His black eyes seemed to notice her red lips quickly, yet he still smiled up at her when she used her fire to cut the rope.

Rose nodded, appreciating the appreciation. Her hands leaned into his arm to help him stand back up. He was much taller than Rose, perhaps the height of Jason. He had the same messy hair of her dear brother but looked slightly *darker*. A slight scattering in the leaves was heard, but Rose didn't bother to take her eyes off the boy she had just rescued from danger and the dark eyes he held in his face.

"I'm Ubel," he told her, taking her hand to kiss the upside of her palm. "Do you have a name?"

"Rose," she told him, blushing at his gesture, "Mensch."

"Oh, you must be royalty!"

"No! Absolutely not. Why would you say that?" Rose asked in shock, looking in his somewhat-pleased and sculpted face.

"You have a last name. Only lords and ladies have those," Ubel said to educate her. He was touching the different scabs he had on his chest and sides, revealing the toned abs he had under the light-green shirt on his body.

"I never really thought about that," Rose told him honestly. Factually, she knew her friends didn't introduce themselves with a last name. Perhaps she and her brother were the only ones with a full name.

"Maybe it's nothing," Ubel said, attempting to find agreement. They began walking together back to the path where Bealfire was waiting for Rose.

"Are you going to tell me why you were tied to a tree, or are you going to pretend like that didn't happen too?" Rose asked him with a smirk on her face. She arched her trimmed eyebrows.

Ubel laughed, showing his crooked teeth before he told her the story of why his limbs nearly lost their circulation.

"I was walking, just like we are now, when these big men in heavy fur coats jumped me. They took all my coins and letters. Then they got into this big argument about what to do with me, and they decided to tie me to that tree to make sure I wouldn't follow them and make trouble for them. I guess I am lucky they didn't just kill me."

"That's cruel!" Rose exclaimed, her hands reaching out to the cuts on his body, supporting him while he walked closer to her. She sat him down on a rock as they waited together for Rose's friends to find them.

Eventually, Aya was spotted leading the group on the path, right to the rock where Ubel was drifting in and out of sleep. He looked less frightening to Rose without the black eyes gleaming at her. His skin was dirty and cut. His nose was sharp, and his lips were pale and small. To Rose, he could almost be attractive, but those eyes were mesmerizing, in all the wrong ways.

"Rose! There you are! What was that back there? Everyone was so worried!" Aya called out from the top of Lords. Her dark black hair covered her silver eyes. Her dark skin was almost camouflaged in the moonlight.

"Can we not talk about me? This boy, Ubel, is badly hurt. He was beaten by thugs over there in the woods."

The whole group jumped off their horses, relieved to have found Rose and concerned about the injuries to the new boy. Aya judged the look of his face but ignored herself. She rushed to Ubel's aid. He was still breathing loosely, and his eyes were barely opened. She did her best to clean and bandage all his sores and cuts. Massaging the shoulders and rubbing the back of the boy, who seemed so tense he couldn't walk. Her hands worked wonders on the boy, speeding up his recovery.

Ubel coughed up a little blood that was trapped in his throat as he awoke. His dark eyes squinted. His jawline stretched, making the cuts on his face grow. The left of his face was worse than the right. Slap marks covered most of his cheek, his pale lips were scabbed, and his arms were bruised. Rose took pity on the boy for being taken advantage of by bandits, much like the muggings Red Lips often suffered.

"Ride with me, Ubel. We will find a safe place to rest for the night," Rose suggested to him, her skinny hands gesturing to the back of Bealfire.

LeRoy, who was already envious of the attention the mystery boy was receiving, confronted the idea of the boy riding with Rose aggressively. "No, Rose, I'll ride with you. The boy can ride with Jason."

Rose laughed at her recent popularity with the two boys. Going along, Rose and LeRoy rode Bealfire and Jason and Ubel rode Liza. The group spent the next hour trying to find a good place to camp for the night.

The moon wasn't very visible that night, leaving their eyes without good moonlight to guide themselves on the path. Rose used her powers as much as she could to move the trees out of their way, pushing all the roots and branches away from the horses' hooves. Their eyes were weary from the long day's travels, and they were less focused on searching for openings.

"Guys, I think I see something!" Rose called from the lead of the line of horses. Her eyes were set on something close ahead of the group.

A small building was set in the middle of the woods, with a large opening of green grass surrounding the rust of the house's metal foundation. From a distance, it looked like a dark hunting shack that hadn't been cared for in many years. As they grew closer, they saw that it was a red-trimmed barn that had a freshly cut lawn but also had an exterior badly in need of repair and repainting.

Rose saw that none of the windows were filled with the yellow glow of candles and the doors were sealed shut by logs. They rode their horses up to the small hill that led to the barn house. Rose and Aya were the first to walk up to the door and see up close how the door was not meant to be opened. It was a large building that only had one door. Rose saw the white railing on the facing of the red wood. She sighed. It was no use, and they were going to have to sleep outside on the grass. There would be no comfortable bed of hay for her group tonight. The owners of the barn, apparently long gone, had seen to it before leaving.

It suddenly got warmer. Rose turned back to face the door, where she found Aya playing with her blue fire and burning the wood away from the door, causing the entrance to open for them. The blue fire was a great light in the darkness, with the black sky. How perfect it was seeing Aya use the powers she so loved to display.

"We will sleep in the hay and shelter the horses," Aya told everyone. "We leave in the morning."

Everyone walked inside. There were two rooms, both filled with sawdust and hay residue. The first room, or main room, had a large open area with old machinery in it to mow the lawn or to rustle cattle. Bags and bags worth of seeds were draped over false fences along the sides of the inner barn. Nothing was well lit in the room the seven kids entered, so those who could make fire guided the rest around the room, careful not to light the barn on fire. The group quickly decided that they would all sleep in the main room.

The second room west of the first was a straight hall of old stables with individual stalls. There was a manger in the central area, with dry hay, which they agreed would be perfect for their horses. Andrew left to start walking the horses into the barn and nourishment while Rose and LeRoy continued exploring the barn. As Rose walked, she carefully guided herself and LeRoy, checking out each individual stable for security.

"I don't think anyone will be coming to kill us for trespassing tonight," LeRoy said as they walked through the deserted barn. Rose agreed. If anyone did own the place, they weren't doing much of a job taking care of the barn. Toward the end of the long hallway was a third room. This would have been called the trophy room. In it there were animal traps hanging on a wall and animal-skin rugs on the floor. Rose gasped at the horror on the wall, seeing all the dried bloodstains within the metal traps. LeRoy looked in awe at the different materials used for gathering the fur of *precious* animals.

"My father and I used to hunt, but never like this," he said. There was a trap that had long claws on the side and sharp teeth on the other side. If an animal were to hop inside, they would be chomped to death by the teeth. If the sharp teeth did not kill the animal, the long claws would. Rose was mortified by the death trap. Rose gasped again when she made eye contact with the beautiful rabbit skin, raccoon skin, and squirrel skin that lay on the floor under the traps. Most of the skins had been torn and were missing pieces of the fur. Some had holes on the back of them, which LeRoy hoped he would not have to explain to Rose.

Rose and LeRoy decided to walk back, far away from the old stables and the horror-filled animal traps. They met the tired eyes of Aya before checking on the rest of their group and then back to the horses. The horses were still eating hay in the old stables, happy to be under shelter. Rose, LeRoy, and Aya arrived in the main room just in time to hear snores from the others, who were wiped out from the travels. Aya, Rose, and LeRoy all were unable to sleep for the first hour, thinking of how far they had come in the past months of traveling throughout the world. Rose had found the world to be an increasingly cruel place. The thoughts that haunted Rose when she was awake continued to nag at her while she was sleeping, or at least lying there, trying to sleep. Rose dreamed about the king and all the wicked and cruel things he had done. Seeing so many of his acts of wickedness in her nightmares scared Rose. He was such an evil man and needed to be replaced. This thought of a new option, just replacing the king, gave Rose enough comfort to actually fall asleep.

Rose had been asleep for less than an hour when she began hearing the screams. At first, she believed them to be in her head from Red Lips being tortured by the king, or perhaps from Liza for protecting Rose. They were so real Rose found herself sitting up and looking around. This only made matters worse, because she immediately smelled smoke.

Then Rose saw fire. The wood and dried straw made perfect fuel for the burning purple flame. Rose moved around, her bronze hair sticking to her red-hot, sweaty face. Her hands shook the bodies of her friends as she watched the angry purple flame spread closer and closer along the west wall of the main room. Rose shook the dreaming body of Aya first, then Aya saw it too. She saw the ugly fire rise high into the ceiling, slightly burning the wood above them.

Rose then touched the cold neck of her brother, while Aya ran to tap the brown hair of LeRoy. Jason woke up with a start, his eyes widening when he saw the purple inferno growing. By this time, Camilla and Andrew were both awake from coughing. The lack of oxygen and the abundance of soot-filled smoke were really straining their lungs harshly. Their throats filled with soot, and their eyes clouded with smoke. All the while, the screams continued. Rose looked at Aya, and Aya at Rose, as they realized that it was the horses that were screaming. Sounds of cries and discomfort could be heard from each horse, almost like they were from a person. Rose tried to go to the entryway between the main room and the stables, but the stable area was just too hot and smoky.

Rose searched frantically for the dark eyes of Ubel, all while she gathered the few bags of things they had, but his eyes were missing. Rose and Aya searched everywhere inside the barn for any sign of him. Different pillars from the barn began to buckle and explode. The purple fire had now collected most of the western wall and was climbing across the ceiling over to the eastern wall.

"Rose!" called her brother, Jason, from outside the barn. He was worried sick for her and Aya, as they were still trapped inside the barn as the roof began to collapse.

"Jason!" she called back with a large cough. She was trying to run, hand in hand with Aya. They had accepted that if Ubel was still in the building, his life was no longer their concern.

They darted as fast and carefully as they could, breathing as slowly and as few times as their lungs would allow them. More logs made their way to the ground from the ceiling. Most of them were burned to a crisp, but some had small fires still attached to them. Rose and Aya leaped over as many as their strong legs would take them. Their skin would never burn, but their eyes would fog, their throats would fill with soot, and their lungs needed oxygen to keep them both conscious. They screamed together when a large part of the roof exploded over their heads, throwing flaming debris everywhere and nearly crushing the life out of the two girls. Rose's legs were in such pain that during the final leap out the door, her abs were pushing, not her calves. The skin surrounding the bones and muscle of her legs was shredded.

"Rose!" yelled Jason for a final time as she collapsed to the ground with Aya once they were outside the burning barn. Jason held Rose in his arms, grateful she had made it out alive.

"Guys," Andrew said, looking back at the red barn, staring at the purple fire as it consumed the structure and their horses.

Each horse had a different cry as the fire hit their flesh. The horses could not understand why this was happening to them. The purple consumed their eyes and brains, while the fire roasted their hearts. Their soft fur turned to ashes as they disintegrated to the ground. The sounds of pain filled the forest.

Bealfire and another horse they could not see continued shrieking in misery. The children wailed as they watched their beloved animals die. All of Nava must have heard it. Bealfire, Lords, Xenia, Liza, and Bear would be nothing but burnt bones come morning. The smell of cooked meat filled the early-morning air. Rose screamed in agony as she thought of the burning body of Ubel hidden somewhere inside the barn.

Jason was the first to realize the urgency of the situation outside the barn. At its peak, the fire became an inferno, shooting flames high into the air. The echoes from the horses' screams would have reached far into the distance. In the early-morning light, the thick smoke from the wretched barn, which had been a death trap for Ubel, would bring lookers and military guards very quickly. They could not afford to stay here much longer if they hoped to not get captured or to not fight again this very morning. They must begin walking or running immediately and put distance between themselves and the fire.

Jason and LeRoy carried the heaviest of the bags that they had been able to save from the fire. Rose was still lost in her own thoughts, so Aya continued to pair up with her as a walking buddy. Jason took the lead, and LeRoy trailed to pick up stragglers and protect the group from attacks, with the other four in the middle.

"We have to get moving now," Jason implored the group as the final structures within the barn exploded, sending splinters of wood into anything soft that got in their way. Rose remembered seeing this same scene before in the vision with Erik. Now was a time for action and motion, so she put her legs into gear and began pushing forward. The team of misfits kept moving for a whole day before daring to stop and make a campsite for the night. Jason insisted on burying the firepit to reduce the chances they would be discovered. The night ended peacefully and, more important, uneventfully.

The next morning, they continued marching on, without horses, just as it was in the early days of their journey. By the first hour of moving their feet collectively, they were all sore and frustrated with the endless walking. The next hour, they were soaked in sweat from the clothes on their backs and the items they carried in their clammy palms. The sun wasn't hot, the clouds covered the rays, and the breeze chilled their necks as they walked on.

Rose missed her horse. In her mind, Rose weighed Bealfire against the soft bed back in the cabin at the Red Islands. She missed them both so very much, but it was possible that, at this moment, she missed Bealfire more. She walked on with the rest of the group. They stopped at the Veella occasionally to quench their thirsts. When the Veella continued north, the team of misfits had to part company and continue heading east. Rose's heart pounded faster and faster in her chest as her team of misfits approached closer and closer to Ravens.

Rose had found that her powers to move natural objects in the forest worked again here, so she continued influencing the shrubs and trees to make this part of the journey easier on her team. She was still mourning the life of her dearest new friend, Ubel. The team had talked about how the fire could have started, with Rose looking for a way to blame herself. Aya had reminded Rose that the fire that burned down the barn was purple fire and not red or blue, which were the fire colors for both Rose and Aya. Unless the laws of physics had changed, neither one of them could have started the fire. It did not make sense that someone with purple fire in their veins would set the fire and then not wait to see or even capture any of them that were able to escape. They all agreed that it was the horses that saved their lives, warning the team with their screams and their sacrifice.

The sky was lighter now, the sun straight above their heads. The air felt warmer, but there was still snow on the ground. Rose heated her body to keep herself comfortable, hand in hand with LeRoy, their fingers intertwined. So he stayed warm too. Her heat transferred into the body of the boy with the attitude, filling him with warmth and comfort. Every so often, his thumb would press upon her pale flesh, rubbing against her bones, to remind her that he was here to help her. The beauty in their affection was how dangerous it was. They had seen time and again how everything could go wrong so quickly. They celebrated their difference, which made them stronger together.

Camilla and Jason were touching the same way Rose and LeRoy were. Their hands also belonged with the other. Camilla's heat filled Jason up, warming him with her touch. The cold didn't bother her as much,

They all walked collectively toward the mystery of Ravens. The sounds of their feet marching against the white snow was overpowered by the loud sounds of crows croaking and wild boars squealing. Birds, those who didn't travel south for the warm weather, flew high above and chirped every so often. Their wings glided and soared, until the sharp breezes came and they needed to huddle in their nests. Rose watched the birds shiver and whine when she moved the trees out of their path. The birds feared their noises and were surprised by all the shaking and shifting within their habitat. Rose watched them relax again when the trees stopped moving. When the team passed, the birds would whine again when the trees moved back into their original places.

"I'm frightening the birds," Rose whispered into LeRoy's tan ear, their hands still secure with the other's. He shivered at her cold breath but smiled back down at her, caressing her cheek with his strong fingers.

"So what?"

Rose glared with disdain at his smirk. She was displeased with his disinterest, but then again, Rose was upsetting herself over something she couldn't help.

"Rosie, what would you like me to do about the birds?"

Rose looked into his brown eyes and became distracted by how dreamy they were. She spoke softly. "Do you know why it is called Ravens? I haven't seen a single raven fly above our heads."

LeRoy laughed once again. He held the hand of his love much tighter now, forcing her to walk much closer to him.

"No clue."

Aya walked next to Andrew toward the front of the line and ahead of Rose and LeRoy. They talked with conviction about the old times and different strategies of attack on the king's armies. The longer they talked, the closer they came to the center of Ravens. Aya was making a point about the need for military discipline when she heard a slight hustling in the woods. As the turned her head, she saw the sight of a miracle.

Ubel, with his dark black eyes, was resting his dark head on a dead tree on a small hill ahead of them. His sad eyes were closed shut, so their scariness didn't put off Rose or Aya. Aya ran toward his limp body, prepared to treat his wounds. Rose saw exactly what Aya saw and rushed to Ubel's side as well.

Rose tapped him lightly with the pads of her fingers to bring him back to consciousness. He awoke loudly, shifting his head vigorously from side to side, stealing glances at the two girls. His eyes were just as dark as two days before, when the cabin had burned down. Aya quickly offered that he must have escaped right when the fire began, and Ubel nodded that she was right.

Aya searched his body for burn marks or infected scratches from the ropes he had been tied in several days after the mugging. She took pride in her abilities, because the cuts seemed to have healed quite nicely and there were no burn marks. Aya ran her fingers up and down his spine and along the veins on his arms so his body temperature rose and stabilized. Aya sensed the pain and discouragement he felt in his mind, what with all the cramping and changing his body had been through. Rose touched the most knotted parts of his body and untangled them with ease, graciously feeling the most sensitive parts of his back, while Aya treated his bones. He was frightened but maintained the same smirk to which they had grown accustomed.

He appreciated the hugs and smiles he received from all the kids in the group. He held Rose close when she touched the arms on his muscular body.

As they gathered their belongings, the group of misfits continued. The path of Ravens wasn't very far, and they could reach the old family house by nightfall. They walked into the depth of the woods, eyeing all the trees and bushes that decorated their surroundings. Rose continued to move all the trees out of the path of her friends, her own feet right next to LeRoy's. Ubel walked halfway between Rose and Aya, deep in thought but interested in any conversation. Rose and LeRoy's fingers stayed intertwined, and they swayed their arms slightly.

Ubel's heavy presence had darkened the mood, which was already tense, as they walked to the front door of a small cabin in the middle of the pine trees. It was a dark log cabin with overgrown vines climbing up the outside walls, causing scars to form. The cuts in the wood needed repair, the weeds that grew outside were tall, and there were untrimmed bushes near broken windows. It was like whoever lived inside had stopped caring a long time ago.

Aya and Jason led the group to the familiar door. They observed the broken frame and shattered glass on the ground. They winced at the small knocker with the label reading, The Mensch House.

"For royals, this isn't much of a palace," Ubel voiced, then hushed himself, apparently realizing that he had added to the stress of the moment.

Rose and Jason ignored his comment as they walked closer to the door. Ever since Rose had learned that her mother was alive, her mind had been playing out this reunion scene. There were so many different ways the greeting might go. Then again, Katrina might not even be here. She stood in front of Jason, feeling his uneven and strained breaths ease down her neck.

The moon was their only light as they knocked on the door slowly and waited for the sounds of someone walking toward the door. Jason watched Rose, as did most of the group, but he was the only one to smile at her when she looked back. His hands slid down her spine, and he pulled her closer to himself. Their eyes looked sadly at their childhood home.

"It was happier last time I was here," she whispered into his ear. They could hear footsteps slowly moving toward the front of the house.

Jason chuckled softly. "No, it wasn't."

The doorknob opened cautiously. Through the glass pane, Rose and Jason saw the body of an older woman with brown hair and gray roots. Her skin had worry marks, and there were small wrinkles around her mouth. She had a small face, but the skin stretched it out. Her small hands reached out to meet those of Rose, who stood directly ahead of her body, and caressed the young skin on her fingers. Seconds later, they were in each other's arms, each gripping the other's shoulder, their warmth comforting each other. Katrina's tears fell fast as she held her daughter tight. They fell fast again when she pulled Jason down to meet her eyes before pushing herself onto his muscular body. Her lips peppered his head with loving kisses. Her hands touched the arms of her son, older now and maturing into a man.

The low howl of wolves farther in the woods echoed in the trees next to the house. Crickets chirped loudly, but the sounds of boots against squeaky wooden floorboards dominated. Aya, Jason, Rose, Camilla, LeRoy, and Ubel were welcomed to the old sofa in the middle of the front room. The sofa had a bounce because of the old springs on the inside of the cushion. The pillows had small scratches, and light balls of feathers were gathered at their feet.

They all fit, though it was uncomfortable. They were treated with a few cups of water to go around, to sip on as they watched Katrina pace around the room, pretending to find something she had lost. Rose saw a few circular tables on the floor in a different room. Broken glass was spread out throughout the rooms. They had been told to watch their steps as they walked in, in caution, toward the sharp edges of the glass. Rose observed the different doors leading to the different bedrooms in the home. In her mind, Rose tried to remember which door led to which bedroom. She saw the candle wax melt and fall onto the ground as Katrina desperately lit a few of the scattered tall ones to give light to the dark room.

Once the available candles were illuminated and *properly* located, Katrina sat down on the wooden chair closest to the group of the sofa, the closest one that had all four legs. Her old body sat lazily as she smiled awkwardly at the children. Rose stared deeply into her eyes, wondering how Rose once thought her mother was the most beautiful woman she had ever known. Rose stared at the expired powder that layered her mother's skin, the pink gloss on her pale lips, and the weak tea leaves in the cup with her tea. Katrina's old hands shook when she guided the teacup toward her mouth.

"What are you doing here?" Katrina asked after a few moments of silence.

"Ekon told us you were still alive," Rose told her. "We decided to come looking for you."

Katrina's face flushed red, and then she coughed deeply, clearing her throat when she heard her husband's name.

"When did you speak with Ekon?"

"At Dragons Nest," Aya told her politely.

"How is Ashbel doing?"

"He is fine. How are you, Mother?" Jason said, leaning closer to her frightened body. His eyes met hers again. Their hair shared a color, brown; their smiles shared the same shape, and their noses both had the same angle.

Katrina stared intently at the group of kids that stared back at her. Her body shuddered when she tried to find the words to speak to them. Her long brown hair slid to cover her eyes when she began to talk. Katrina's voice was soft at first, but it gained its confidence.

"I've been better," she began. "I have missed my children."

"We thought you were dead," Rose informed her. "We thought you had been killed in an attack at this very house. We thought you and Dad both died, but that was a lie. What other lies are you going to tell us?"

"Rose," LeRoy whispered, his hands trying to restrain Rose's knee before she said something more that she would regret. She leaned deeper into his touch, resting her back on his soft chest as her breathing returned normal.

"Rose, I never asked for any of this to happen," Katrina informed her, but Rose already knew that. Rose already knew that Katrina chose to rid herself of her red lips, that she had a glitch in her genes, and that Rose was born with the traits of a Red. Rose had believed that Katrina had died protecting her from the king's men, who were ordered to kill her, except Katrina didn't die. She hid and left her children to fend for themselves at such a young age.

"Liza told me you were good," Rose continued, changing the subject.

"Where's Liza?" Katrina asked excitedly. She missed her sister dearly.

"Dead, because of me."

Katrina's eyes closed for another moment of silence. She was dreading the thought of her dearest sister's lifeless body. She was imagining the young woman from Nava who married the poor man from the Red Islands. The woman who told her to exchange her red lips for pale ones and a normal life.

"Why did you return to this house?" Rose questioned. She had many questions.

"The memories of you and your brother live here. It made me feel better, and that way, you would always know where to find me if you wanted to."

"How did you know I would want to find you?"

Katrina hesitated. "Ashbel visits often to tell me about you. He tells me of your accomplishments. I was so proud when he told me of your first fire. He told me of your life with Liza, and your life too, Jason. Sometimes Ashbel would let me hear your voice, but it sounds much better in person, Rosie."

Rose looked up at her mother. It made sense that Ashbel would do that, look after his good friend, the mother of the strongest Red.

"Did you know what Ekon was? Who he was?" Jason asked.

Her eyes saddened. "Jason, of all people, you must remember that Ekon and I started out very differently from what we became. The four of us had very happy times here in this house, playing games and telling stories. Do you remember how we taught Rosie to walk in this very room?"

"Not really," Rose responded.

"I do remember some smiling," admitted Jason. "But the memories are so fuzzy because it was such a long time ago. An awful lot has happened to us, Mother."

"Rose, when you were sixteen months old, the town doctor was very concerned," continued Katrina, undaunted. "You were still crawling and refused to stand to walk. You had such horrible balance that the doctor thought something might have happened during the pregnancy or the delivery. Anyway, Ekon and I used to sit in this room with you, about five feet apart. I would hold your hands and help you stand, and then Ekon would get your attention and coax you to come to him. You started off by just sort of diving at him. Then he would help you stand and I would get you to come back to me. As you got better at walking, we would move farther and farther apart, until we were sitting at the very ends of this room. We did this for hours at a time. Jason, you would sit on that same couch and applaud, and laugh, after every turn."

"I do remember the look of joy on your face and the look of pride on Ekon's face, but I have never really understood the context," Rose reflected. "What I remember the most is a lot of yelling and fights between the two of you."

"You know, I do remember the four of us laughing and playing cards," Jason added. "Then I remember our father having to be away a lot, and you would tell us it was because of work. The last two years here were so difficult, with Dad unhappy for whatever reason and the two of you always fighting."

"Your father was a good man who took a job that turned out to be very different from what we thought it would be. At that time, we were going through a lot of stress in our marriage and needed the money," Katrina explained. "Ekon became less available and more upset, and we just grew apart, as many couples do. We really loved each other, and I never saw the end coming until I saw him walking up to the house with a small army of men, when he came to kill us."

Aya listened closely as she replayed the memory of his flesh burning and melting at the feet of four dragons. She remembered the cries and pleas of his raspy voice, and Rose's screams from outside the haunted walls of that chamber.

"So what now?" Rose asked Katrina.

"You can stay the night, or longer, if you need," Katrina volunteered awkwardly. "I wish I had prepared better for this, but then we all are called to reckon for our past."

Rose nodded. She was uncomfortable to even be around the ruins of her childhood home. It was different from what she expected. She wanted a mother who was living a better life and who had moved on from the trauma of the loss of her children. Instead, she found a greasy old woman who resided in the tragic memories of the few years she lived her fairy-tale life.

Rose and Jason stood up and walked toward a white door at the back of the house. It led into a small room that once had two small beds, a wardrobe, and paintings hung all over the ceiling and the walls. Now, the beds had begun to fall apart. The wardrobe had been smashed to pieces, most likely by the men who were looking for them. The paintings were ripped and cluttered along the floor. All the different designs the two of them had done throughout their first years were gone.

Rose and Jason walked slowly through their messy room. They maneuvered around the stranded pieces as they walked toward their shared toy box. Jason opened the lid of the white wooden box that had carved-in clowns and animals on the top. Their eyes teared up as they sorted through their dolls and plush toys. Jason pulled out his soldiers with their fake swords and armor. Rose adored her princess dress, which had fake jewels and glitter on the cheap fabric.

"I wish I had more memories of playing with any of these toys." Rose laughed, tears filling her eyes. She touched the dress one more time before she closed the lid for the last time. It hurt too much to look at the lonely toys.

They walked out of the room together and into the room of their parents. It had one single bed and one single dresser. It was all white, so pure, and yet poorly matched for such a destructive family.

"Liza told us that Katrina was beautiful, that she was so kind and so good, and that she would have made a perfect mother. But this home is nothing like the home in the Red Islands. It is filled with lies and torture. How did Liza not know?" Rose pondered out loud.

"Maybe she did," Jason told her as he opened each drawer one at a time, looking for signs of life. A fly or moths would head out every other drawer, but Jason could not find what he was looking for, maybe because he was just searching his memories, trying to remember why something so good could become so bad.

The master bedroom had broken windows and shattered furniture, leaving splinters of wood and shards of glass on the ground. Shredded curtains and clothes were interspersed on the ground as well. The bed wasn't made. The pillows were scattered about the bed, and the covers were gathered in a wad at the foot of it. The carpet that once sat in the center of the room to make it feel less empty was dust covered and torn at the edges from being eaten aggressively by rodents. The air was dry and heavy. The memories of this room haunted Rose.

They walked outside, back into the hall, and then back into the room with the sofa and wooden chairs. The group was scattered throughout the room, and Katrina had wandered into the kitchen. LeRoy was looking around at all the broken glass, thinking how it might have looked before the windows and vases broke. Aya was sitting on the sofa, playing with her blue fire in her hand. Her hand switched above and below her mouth to see if she could still create fire while her lips ceased being red in color.

Andrew and Camilla talked indistinctly while they walked around the room in a circle, forgetting there were other people around them. Ubel had been watching Jason and Rose walk around the other rooms in their house and stayed as far away from Katrina as he could. He sat near the entryway on a broken wooden chair at one of the tables he had turned over so it stood right side up.

Katrina gathered the group into the kitchen for a late supper. They *feasted* on dry bread and some fresh water from a stream not too far from the house. It was quiet, with no one wanting to talk during the meal. Everyone was rather spent and tired from walking all the way to Ravens. So they ate in silence, a safe silence that comforted the rest of the group.

Rose quickly ate her bread, gulped her drink, and then stared at her dirty knife and fork until the rest of the group was finished. She watched Jason pick apart his bread and shove different pieces into his mouth. She saw Aya bite directly into her bread. Underneath all her pain, Rose was so happy to see her mother again. A part of Rose wanted to forgive her mom for everything she had done. Another part her wanted to make peace with the past, which, strangely, was at odds with Rose's need to understand why and puzzle over what had happened. The part of Rose that wasn't purple had forgiven Katrina.

Katrina passed around the butter for the second piece of bread that everyone began eating. She only had enough for everyone to use it once, but they were all thankful to gain flavor with their meager provisions.

It was nothing like the meals at Liza's home, but it was something. It was better than leaves and brown water from the forest. Rose finished that meal fast, too, and so did Jason. The sun was starting to show through the windows, and no one had gotten any sleep. They wanted to rest their eyes before the bright ball of fire was shining in their eyes.

"Thank you," Rose said to Katrina before walking back into her clutter-filled room and crashing onto her small bed. Her body could fit if she scrunched it into a tight ball and kept her toes curled toward herself and not facing down. It wasn't comfortable.

As the rest of the teens were preparing to find places to sleep in, Ubel approached Jason and said, "No disrespect meant to you and your mother, but I think I'd rather sleep under a shady tree than in here."

"Suit yourself," Jason responded.

A little while later, Jason walked into their childhood bedroom and curled up on his bed, his feet sticking out over its foot. The quilt barely covered his torso, and the pillow did not offer much support for his head. It was made for children with children's bodies.

"Good night, Jason," Rose said. For the first time, she felt safe, with him close to her. She nuzzled herself between the covers and drifted off to sleep before she could hear his soft response.

"Good night, Rose. I love you."

CAMILLA

The bedroom floor was dirty and dust filled. Bugs crawled on the wooden boards that were filled with exhausted teens. Rose and Jason slept in their childhood beds. Aya slept on a stuffed doll rumored to be Rose's. Camilla rested her head on Aya's stomach. LeRoy's head was against the wooden frame of Rose's bed, and Andrew's head was the same on the side of Jason's bed. They were all sleeping soundly, though their bodies were beginning to ache. They had been so tired that they managed to sleep through the better part of the day, with the sun already beginning to set. The trees appeared lighter under the first moonbeams. The house seemed as presentable as it could ever be.

Ubel stood above the group, looking intently at the bodies of his friends. His black eyes glanced at the bodies of Jason and Andrew, then rested upon the pale body of Rose. His hair was greasy and shaggy. His clothes reeked of body odor and dirt. He watched until Rose began to stir, then he went back outside to resume his nap. Eventually, they all woke up to sore bones and aching shoulders. Their heads were groggy, and they needed to get blood flowing to improve circulation. Ubel offered to go out and pick them some berries, while the rest of the teens snacked on whatever they could find in the pantry. It was not until their rustling around resulted in banging that Katrina took notice and came out of her bedroom. It was like Katrina did not want the day to begin, although it was already late in the evening.

Rose, who was excited to leave her childhood home, dreaded the idea of seeing her mother for the last time. Slyly, Rose slipped into the bedroom her mother had just left as her mother began feeding the other teens. Rose found herself looking around her mother and father's room once more. Her pale fingers caressed the windowpane and cleaned a line of dust. Her lips mouthed little nothings as she wandered around the room. Her bronze hair was freshly braided by Camilla, who had joined Rose in the master bedroom. Camilla had been asking Rose for permission to braid it for some time now, and Rose had been feeling a need for distraction. Camilla was sitting on the bed, after she spent time making the braid, and she smiled up at the moon as it rose farther into the sky.

A finger began tapping on the open door. "May I enter?"

It was Katrina.

Rose nodded at her mother. Her wrinkled body slowly walked toward Rose, and she sat down next to her on the bed. Camilla sensed that they needed some private time and left the room on her own accord. Katrina looked much older yet very similar to Rose, although physically, Rose took strongly after Ekon. Katrina and Rose shared a bright light, but Katrina's had run out of fuel a long time ago.

Their hands fit into the other's. Until they didn't. Katrina gathered herself and pulled out a small wooden jewelry box she had carried in. The box was a light-brown color, with one single false diamond as a clip in the center. Katrina's hands carefully opened the box to reveal jewels of all kind. Ten unique pieces of jewelry were crammed into the small box, and Katrina pulled each one out one by one.

An obsidian rock was molded into the center of a silver necklace. They both laughed as Katrina put a small topaz tiara upon Rose's head. Katrina put an emerald ring on Rose's pale finger, the same hand as the rose gold bracelet that Liza's family had given her. A copper chain was placed on the bed. Rose stared at the ugly piece of fashion. Katrina showed Rose a ruby diadem, and then a quartz stone, a gold ring, a diamond earring, and a red-stone crown in rapid succession. Lastly, Katrina held a tight hand around the body of a solid crystal that came from the depths of the ocean. It sparkled in the sunlight and was rather big. Katrina shared the full contents of the small box, bedazzling Rose in reflected light.

"What are all these beauties?" Rose asked in awe. Her hands were growing heavy from holding all the treasures.

"The twelve jewels of Remular. Well, at least ten of them. You have the eleventh one on your wrist already."

"Liza gave it to me," Rose told her as she touched the gift she had been wearing around her wrist for months now.

"So what about the last jewel?" Rose inquired. "You only told me about eleven."

"When I was expecting you, Aya was merely an infant living in Dragons Nest. The day the dragons came to tell me about you, I gave them the final ring as a gift for the princess. It was a dragon ring. The silver dragon circled around your finger. It was rather cool. I felt powerful when I would wear it and make my fire."

"So Aya has it?" Rose confirmed.

"I assume so," she agreed.

"And these jewels are mine to keep?" Rose asked as she removed the jewels and replaced them in the small wooden box. She locked the false diamond, and the box was sealed.

"I suppose. The jewels have been in our family for generations. They belong to us and are the reason we have our last name," said Katrina, smiling at her daughter.

"So we are royals?"

"Distantly, yes. We don't have cousins that are lords of the king, but we were once good friends of the royal family," answered Katrina, a trickle of sweat coming down the side of her face.

"Jason once told me that whoever possesses the stones holds claim to the throne," Rose began.

Cutting Rose off, as if pressed for time, Katrina replied, "The more reason to march down to Remular and sit on that throne."

"I won't. Jason will," Rose confided in her.

"The people believe in *you*, Rose, not anyone else," Katrina finished nervously and kissed Rose's forehead.

"What happened to you?" Rose asked, standing up to leave the bedroom with her mother.

"The day you fled with Jason, I was trapped and had to make a choice," Katrina explained, beginning to shake, closing her eyes to focus. "A daughter needs her mother, but I have lived out the last few years hoping that you would grow strong enough. Ekon still loved me, but he had his orders." Katrina looked frightened and was just able to gurgle out, "I love you. Please be careful."

"What did Ekon do?" Rose asked as she turned back to see her mother's horrific transformation. A small bomb dropped onto the ground, and Rose heard the light clicking sound above Katrina's sobs. Rose began yelling for Jason and Aya. She ran out with the box, gripping her mother's limp arm, trying to pull her outside the room that was about to explode. Katrina refused to move, her legs pushing against Rose's every pull. They were both swimming in tears as Katrina began melting into the ground, and from the inside of her grew a monster, much like the ones at Ashbelle. The monster began attacking and snapping at Rose's fingers, and Rose screamed. Rose ran faster than she had ever before, finding the helping hands of Jason and Aya in the front room. They called out the names of LeRoy, Camilla, Andrew, and Ubel. The beeping became louder, and the screaming continued. The teens all followed outside the cabin and fell into the grass as the bomb went off, sending the house exploding into pits of fire.

Coughing and wheezing filled the ears of the group as they watched the house burn to its final ashes. Rose cried on the ground with the jewels in her hand as she watched her house collapse, refusing to close her eyes. She sat and watched another home destroyed. She was now an orphan. Rose thought she was before, but now it was official. The day with her mother took a toll on Rose, leaving her feeling as out of control as ever.

It was Aya that reminded the team that they must move on or risk being captured. So they left, gathering what they could, and marched south of Ravens to Remular. Rose was puzzled about what had happened but quickly agreed to put distance between themselves and the childhood home. LeRoy comforted Rose as best as he could. Holding her hand as they walked was the only thing he could do to make things normal. He listened to the sounds of her whimpers and sniffles when she would think about her mother. When Rose quieted, LeRoy focused on any strange sounds that might come from the woods, wanting to protect the team from intruders.

Aya, as usual, led the group, so when she stopped suddenly, the group was immediately curious as to why.

Jason, who stood close to her, was the first to notice her feet losing momentum. She questioned her, "Why'd you stop?"

"The well is near here!" she said excitedly. "I've always wanted to see the well!"

Jason scoffed. "We have to keep moving, Aya. Don't make us go see that horrible place."

"Maybe it would be a good idea," Camilla interjected, her smile sinking into her dimples. Camilla's red hair covered her pale neck, and her soft hands touched Jason's growing beard. "We need a distraction before we go to Remular, to lighten the mood."

"I would love to get in a bit of mischief with some trolls," LeRoy commented with much enthusiasm, his eyes wide and bright.

Rose, who was still traumatized by her mother and father, couldn't bear to lose one of her friends to the trolls. "Absolutely not!"

Rose and LeRoy touched noses before they all agreed that maybe fighting practice and some distractions wouldn't be a *horrible* idea. Rose was still cautious about it. She held LeRoy's fingers much tighter, but she was in no condition to argue. Bad thoughts returned to Rose, and she wondered how many more people that she loved would need to die. She feared the deaths of LeRoy, Aya, and Jason. Her head felt like it would explode, which Rose almost found comforting.

Aya led the group to a small path that was moss covered and bloodstained. Trolls had taken many lives from those who would abandon the Red gene.

"Where are the trolls?" Ubel and LeRoy asked together. Rose and Aya were beginning to answer when loud thumps echoed throughout the deep forest. The group walked faster, deeper down the path, leaving their footprints in the white snow. The trees wouldn't shift for Rose. Of course they wouldn't. This wasn't her woods. These were the trolls' woods. Then, in the woods, they saw the ugliest of trolls.

The path led them to a small bridge. On the other side they could see the beginnings of a large stone wall.

Four or five grumbling giants guarded the skinny, weak, and eroding pass. They had sticks for hair and rocks for noses. Their eyes were as jet-back as Ubel's, and their noses were dripping with yellow wax. They mumbled cruel words as they strutted hugely toward the group of children. The biggest one began speaking, but Aya quickly cut him off with her words.

"I am Aya, princess of Dragons Nest, and these are my friends. We demand you let us through, please," she quietly added. Her short hair swayed in the light breeze. Her dark skin glowed in the sunlight, which captured her well-toned body.

The trolls began to laugh at her words, then mocked her with a crude tongue. The biggest one, who was meaning to speak earlier, squatted his large body down to meet her eye. "Don't care. Leave now. Don't have time for this."

"Sir, please," Aya pleaded. She was desperate to do something fun with Rose.

"No."

"Why?"

"Because—"

"That's no answer!" Aya exclaimed after nearly giving up. She was a princess, after all, and was not accustomed to being turned down.

"I said no!" the troll roared.

He was beginning to turn around toward his ugly troll friends when LeRoy shouted, "Let us pass, you blockhead!"

LeRoy's arm was chucking stones and rocks at the back of the troll's head. Specks of blood came squirting out as it was being abused by the minerals. LeRoy kept them coming, until the cry of pain came from the troll, then its friends stood up and ran over to the group. They carried clubs. Large wooden clubs that they could swing over their entire shoulder. They were smaller than the troll who was being attacked with rocks, but they still looked mean.

LeRoy ran out of rocks, and his voice grew tired of the jeering. As he threw the final rock, the gang of trolls swung their bat at him so roughly he flew a few yards into a nearby tree, bruising his forehead.

Rose, who had heard the crack of his head, gathered so much fire in her hands that she could melt the trolls' eyes without even touching them. Her fists of flame burned into the skin of many trolls. She ran to LeRoy's aid and carried him safely across the bridge to the side by the well. Rose then ran back across, her hair tucked behind her face in the braid, and assisted Aya and Andrew as they fought off the trolls.

Clashes of blue, red, and green fire meeting the green of the trolls' skin filled the air. Groans of pain swam into the ears of the three as they continued to melt the clubs and the sticks that the trolls would grab off the ground.

"Fire! Fire! Fire!" one of them yelled before it ran away with a burning arm. A second troll fell to the ground because of a burned foot. The others darted away into the woods, leaving the group of Reds with the dying body of the biggest, ugliest troll.

"Do you mind if we pass now?" Ubel asked with sass, smirking at the blood streaming out of his head.

LeRoy sat up from where he was sitting and watched the troll take his final breaths. He was saddened as he watched all the life leave the troll's eyes.

"The well is dangerous. Beware," the troll said, grasping at the air with his dry throat. Rose saw the rocks that stuck to the back of his head, drilling holes into his skull. Then Rose looked at LeRoy, horrified that he killed the troll.

Aya, Ubel, Rose, Andrew, and Camilla, along with Jason, walked carefully across the small pass. A far drop into a deep, dark cave was what lay underneath the bridge. Once Rose crossed the bridge, she shooed away LeRoy's arms and stared back at the body of the troll, remembering the words of warning he had given them.

What is so dangerous about the well? she thought. *Why would it hurt something that didn't want to be hurt?*

Rose and Aya walked together up the stone wall, carefully taking themselves up the steep staircase that seemed to wind up to the sky. The stone wall spiraled and had moss growing in the cracks of the wall. It made sense that, being a well, the inside of the wall was a deep, deep hole. They climbed until they had nowhere else to climb as they reached the top.

The roof of the stone wall was a large flat slab of stone brick with a circular hole in the middle of it. The deep circular hole fell off into the depths of the well, no doubt to the enchanted water. Rose guided herself over to the place where her mother lost the ability to control fire and where her aunt gained the ability to do horrible things. Rose could see the water at the bottom of the well.

The water was tragically clear, and Rose saw her reflection perfectly. She found herself cringing at the way she appeared in the rippling water. Aya stood beside Rose, and they watched themselves move in the poisoned water.

"So perfect for something so disgusting," Rose said to herself, yet Aya heard her loud and clear.

"For some Reds, it's the easiest answer," suggested Aya, whose smile released the tension between the two of them.

"How?" Rose began, her blue eyes sinking into Aya's clear ones. "How can Reds do this?"

"For some, the genes aren't enough to keep them away from doing unreasonable things. Your mother, for instance, the well took away everything good about her but kept the gene so it could be passed to you. Your aunt lost her genes, but not everything that was positive about her," Aya softly said.

Rose hesitated and admitted, "I'm not sure that the well took away all the good in my mother." Rose remembered how Katrina warned Rose before she turned. Rose looked back into the water that so terrified her. Her braid was now in a knotted mess, with different strands of her bronze hair coming undone from the tight twist Camilla tied in her hair. Her strong legs walked closer toward the water, her face nearly inches from the bewitched liquid.

"Rosie," Aya called to her, watching her as she drew closer to the water. Her hands reached out and grabbed the shoulders of her closest friend.

"If I go in, then maybe it will keep my good traits like it did my aunt!"

Aya watched Rose's shaking body tell her the words with such shock and utter disappointment that her own tears streamed down her face, and fast.

"Rose, don't do this," Aya warned her.

"Rose is right," Camilla interrupted, her curving body waltzing over to meet Aya's white eyes. "We should dunk ourselves in the well."

"Are you listening to yourselves?" Jason said loudly, shaking his head at the women he loved. His muscular hand reached out to take the pale palm of Camilla, as she was now standing right above the water. Camilla, green eyes and red hair, smiled softly before stepping back closer to where she thought would be the safest place for her.

"Jason," Camilla whispered, "if I weren't a Red, monsters wouldn't be trying to kill us constantly. I would be back home! We could go back home together!" She wasn't fighting her impulse, as Aya had expected. Camilla had accepted her choice to leave behind her magic.

Andrew was twitching as he was questioning his owns existence and masculinity with his red lips. His protective instincts were also questioning the depth of the fall and the dangers of jumping into the well.

The sun was falling, and the golden light shone on Camilla's pale skin. Her feet were slowly edging her body closer and closer to the hole, while her head was begging her to submerge herself and submit to the wonders of the magical water.

Camilla, the Red Lips with green fire, continued to walk slowly toward the well water, until she fell in backward. Her perfect fingers were the last to be submerged. They were still reaching out for Jason's strong hands to pull her back from the edge when her body sank underneath the clear water, where no one could see her. Andrew ran and dived toward her, falling right in after her and creating a small splash of water. The water crashed against the green vines that grew along the cracks, blackening and killing them. Both the twins had jumped into the dangerous waters. Their green fire was put out, and the red light of the Ceptem children burned no more.

After moments of terror for Jason, LeRoy, Rose, Aya, and Ubel, the twins' hands were seen pulling themselves out from the evil waters. Their tan skin and weak muscles pulled themselves up, slowly. The water drenched the red shirts and leather pants they were both wearing, drenched the dark red hair that covered their heads.

Camilla tripped and trembled as she trotted into Jason's arms, her body fitting into his muscular Nomad arms. He touched her pale lips and stared deeply into the hazel eyes on her tan face. He held her close, and Andrew, too, as they coughed up the final sprits of water from their throats.

"Down two," Aya whispered into Rose's ear as she walked away from the tragic well.

Rose and Aya gripped hands and felt the warmth of each other's fire through their palms as they walked down the eroding staircase.

"What did we just do?" Rose heard Camilla say from behind them, her voice much deeper now.

*****

It took many days for everyone to realize that they officially were outnumbered. The pain Camilla and Andrew had caused in those few days was enough to torture Aya and Rose. They needed the green fire they'd lost. They needed the skill they'd left behind that dreaded evening in Ravens. They needed the passion they once had for the Red Lip gene. They were nearly out of Nava. The trail they had been following had grown smaller, and the amount of food they could find was scarce. They would feast their skinny bodies on berries, leaves, and rocks, chewing their own nails when they began to starve.

As night fell, Rose found herself once again struggling with the ringing and the knocking of the Purple fighting to get in her veins. The visit with her mother was supposed to help confirm Rose's purpose but had had the opposite effect. The rest of the team had already huddled around the firepit Jason and LeRoy had built, settling in for the night. In her head, Rose played Katrina's last words over and over, trying to find meaning. Katrina had to make a choice. Rose had to grow strong enough. Ekon still loved Katrina, but he had his orders.

Katrina had to make a choice. Rose had to grow strong. Ekon still loved Katrina, but he had his orders.

Fortunately for Rose, Jason shook her shoulder, woke her up, and said, “Rose, you were talking in your sleep. Are you okay?”

“I guess I cannot stop myself, brother,” Rose explained.

“What were you saying?” Jason asked. “It sounded like you were talking about our parents.”

“Something has been bothering me since Mom exploded and turned into a monster,” Rose admitted with a start. “What a horrible sentence to ever have to see.”

“I cannot say that I envy your experience seeing that happen to Mom,” Jason admitted with a shy smile, “but I have been bothered by memories about that day as well.”

“Before Mom died,” Rose began, “she told me that she had to make a choice the night we fled. I had to grow strong enough. Ekon still loved her, but he had his orders. What do you think all that meant?”

“Did you at least get an ‘I love you’ or something better than that as her last words?” Jason inquired. “It would be rough if Mom’s last words were about herself.”

“Yes, Mom told me, ‘I love you. Be careful,’” Rose answered.

“Well, that is more than I got. Just some stale bread,” Jason reflected out loud. Then he added, “But then I had a few really good years with both our parents when they were young lovers.”

“I’ll trade you,” Rose responded playfully. “Why do you think they grew apart?”

“That’s easy,” Jason retorted. “Dad’s work got in the way.”

“What kind of work did Dad do?” Rose asked.

“I am not certain,” Jason started. “But from time to time, the king would send soldiers with horses to come pick Dad up, and then he would be gone for weeks at a time.”

“Dad worked the king?” responded Rose.

“Dad worked for the king,” Rose realized.

“So when Mom told you Dad loved her but he had his orders, those orders would have been directly from the king,” Jason realized.

"The same as the orders Dad had when he planned that horrible attack at Ashbelle," Rose thought out loud, her mind speeding up.

"And the same monsters were in Ashbelle as the monster that came out of Mom," Jason added, getting excited himself.

"I bet Dad had something to do with the monster that came out of Mom!" Rose added.

"I'll do you one better!" Jason started. "I bet Dad put that monster in Mom the night we fled instead of killing her!"

"How wicked is that?" Rose said, realizing it. "Dad told me Mom was alive at his trial, knowing I would go back to see her and fall into his trap! He was trying to kill me."

"But that is what is killing me, Rose," Jason responded. "Mom and Dad were in love and had a good marriage when I was young. How did they go wrong?"

"Think about it, Jason," Rose professed. "If our dad was the guy the king sent to do things like what happened in Ashbelle, how could he stay a good person? Just being around the king ruins people."

"That is why the king has to die," Jason said, realizing it as well. "You have to kill the king, Rose."

"I have to kill the king," Rose repeated.

Rose

Remular was near, which to Rose meant that the fight was near. She would have to practice aggressively to murder the strongest king in history. No one had ever accomplished what she was going to do. None of the Red Lips had believed in someone as much as they now believed in her. Rose was surrounded by dangerous thought and fears. She started wondering what would bring the greatest disappointment and loss. Was Rose more afraid of failure, humiliation, or death? And then, why fear any of them? Because if she failed, she would almost certainly be humiliated and die. The one new comfort Rose had going for herself was that she was no longer evaluating whether or not to kill the king. Rose had seen firsthand and now was convinced that capturing the man and imprisoning him or some fate other than death would lead to the ruin of even more people. Rose was certain.

"Rosie," Aya said as they walked next to each other, getting closer to the edge of Nava, "I have an idea."

"Is it a way to get out of killing your evil father?" Rose joked, knowing well it wasn't an idea for that.

"No," Aya said, laughing. "I have an idea for Camilla and Andrew."

Rose's smile left her pale face, and her red lips straightened. She hadn't thought about the twins since they fell into the well. She didn't want to think about the choice they had made. She refused to think about the love Jason and Camilla shared. It was odd that they laughed at their crude jokes and that they made their own odd gestures. Why would Jason want a life with *her*?

"Please tell."

*****

Aya led the group through her ring of fire in the middle of the forest, which led into the nest for the dragons. Once they had all entered safely, Aya, with Rose following behind, walked into the large throne room where Rose had first met her. The large chamber looked exactly the same, with the four thrones, the large throne for Aya, the vines, the story, the paint in the halls, and the bare brown walls.

Rose heard slight bickering coming from the thrones, where she saw the scales of the dragons. She saw the large wineglasses of Erik, listening closely as the group walked toward the talking. She quickly began to understand that Erik was finally being punished for his treatment of the Blue people.

The bickering got quieter as their footsteps grew nearer. The dragons finally finished their points and changed subjects to acknowledge the group of kids. Rose and Aya, the only Reds left, stood in front of the rest. The duo was the only one to make eye contact with the dragons, except Erik, who wanted to look and laugh at everyone.

"Welcome," Ashbel greeted with his deep, dramatic voice. "How has Nava treated you?"

"My mother turned into a monster and tried to kill me and my friends. So we've been better."

"That damaged the souls of two of your friends, I see," Ashbel said calmly, glancing at the twins.

"Sadly, yes, it's been hard on all of us," Aya told him apolitically. Her hands swayed in front of her body, while her feet twisted in shame.

"Whose idea was it to take the group to the most tempting place known to Reds?" Erik asked with a sly smile on his face as he sipped another large gulp of deep-red wine in his golden chalice.

"Mine," Aya admitted, her head hanging low now.

"That was horrible judgment, Aya. I expected better from you," Ashbel said, judging her. Aya felt humiliated and sorry for her action. She didn't believe it to be a bad idea at that time.

"You take two emotionally damaged and traumatized children and bring them to the one place they can rid themselves of pain!" Erik laughed. "Are you allowed to be surprised by the outcome? How's that Purple doing? Close to your veins yet?"

Rose stepped closer to the little fat man, gathering her red fire in the sweaty palm of her left hand. Her braid was nearly gone now. The bronze strands fell in front of her blue eyes, but she could still make out the body of Erik, king of the Forgotten Children.

"Rosie, I trust you enjoyed yourself at that barn, just like I taught you." Erik smiled again, spilling his wine on a blue robe he had managed to tie around his fat waist.

Rose scoffed, refusing to be goaded by Erik's cruel words, thinking of the example she would need to show and be for Camilla and Andrew. Her red shirt and cloth pants warmed her body as she stood in the cold presence of Erik. Her eyes looked fiercely at his vile bruised lips.

"Ashbel," Aya restarted, her dark hands beginning to pet his scaly body lovingly. "We came to ask you a favor."

"Ask away."

"Would you please temporarily return the green fire of their past selves to the Nomad versions of Camilla and Jason?"

Vulcan laughed as Ashbel said, "No."

"Why not? In this very room, I've seen you satisfy this same request from others at times that were less important than right now!"

"I can only give them their fire back if they desire to have it back. From what we have observed, these two adore their life as Nomads just as they are."

"I disagree. They are just scared," Rose stated, her purple fire fighting against everything she had learned while being with her friends in the woods, particularly against her red fire.

"It would be easier to befriend a Forgotten Child than turn a devil back to an angel," Erik joked, obviously drunk on his wine.

"Would it be painful?" Camilla questioned, her face showing that she just might be willing to try.

"Yes. Candice must infect you with her blood, then I will occupy your immune system will fire long enough for the infection to recreate the blockage around your animal brain."

"Would I be able to return to being a Nomad?"

"Inevitably," Ashbel answered.

Camilla had a sudden qualm, but she nodded slowly. She walked closer to her brother. The two of them looked so similar at that moment. Andrew shook his head, refusing his sister's request. This wasn't his war. This wasn't his sister's war. This was Camilla desiring happiness for her lover. Camilla was going to do it for Jason.

"Just like that?" Rose confirmed, her hands collecting Camilla's fingers in her own, consuming all her pain in one touch.

Camilla nodded, then explained her love for Jason, her love for Rose, the passion she once had for her fire, and the talent she had with her green burn. She missed it.

"Step into the center of the room." Ashbel guided her body, carrying itself over to the center of the large room. Her fingers fidgeted at her side.

Her curved tan body began to float a few feet above the ground where she had been standing. Her feet tucked themselves one behind the other, and her arms fell loosely and limply by her sides. Camilla's back supported her whole body as she rose higher into the air. Ashbel's eyes watched her with worry and admiration as his claws moved her body closer to the group.

"Camilla, do you consent?"

She nodded slowly before bowing her head to the dragon king. "Yes."

Her body began to shake, starting with her toes. The slow trigger of her fidgeting grew into her knees, and then her hips began thrusting forward vigorously. She began to cry out in fear when her hands were not only shaking but glowing as well. Next, her head was shoved to each side, forward, backward, to her left and right. Green lights circled her whole form, spinning around her from head to toe, hip to hip, spinning around her head, twisting up her arms and down her spine. The lights were piercing to the eyes, and Rose had to close them so she wouldn't go blind. Andrew was watching with hesitation. He had had to save her once and hoped he wouldn't have to save her again. Jason was standing beside Ashbel, watching his as his claws controlled the shaking. It seemed like Ashbel was controlling Camilla's fear. Candice, who stood beside Ashbel, played with her long sharp claws and pushed the green glow around her body, controlling its location and speed as it was dancing around Camilla's body.

The brighter the green light glowed, the more it appeared like fire and the more it seemed to attract heat. Camilla's Nomad skin wasn't immune to the burn of the flame's touch. She screamed longer and louder when the green touched her skin, and when it did, her skin lost its color. The tan slowly turned pale each time the fire touched her perfect skin. She screeched when it touched her face. It burned off the layer of Nomad on her skin, peeling the dead cells off her body.

The maroon in her hair quickly fell out of her head, leaving her bald for a short minute. It then quickly grew back, with the luscious cherry locks that were originally attached to her head. She began to feel lighter when the fire left her body. The glow returned to the sky and then was reflected back down to the ground. Camilla's body hung from the nothingness. Her hair streamed down her back, with gravity pushing down her limbs and turning her body to face the cave's floor. The fire returned to her hands, sinking deep into the pads of her fingers, the palms of her hands, and the veins in her wrist. It twisted in and out of her arm, running through each blood line and forcing its power into her. The fire climbed all the way up to her shoulders, until it sank deeply into her bones, and then it disappeared.

Camilla breathed deeply, trying to believe it was over, but it wasn't. The final push of her green fire went directly to her pale lips. The scream she released due to the pain was the worst one Rose had ever heard. It was so loud and piercing that Rose worried about breaking an eardrum. The green fire stabbed Camilla's lips so deeply she bled out green blood. The liquid fire streamed down her chin.

Another sharp scream erupted from Camilla as the fire dyed her lips red. The same bright shade of red she wore before she submerged herself into the waters at the well. The fire and pain were over, and the shaking stopped. The heavy weight released Camilla, and her feet returned to the ground once again. Camilla's knees snapped to the ground, and the group ran up to meet her and hold her.

"Camilla, are you all right?" Rose asked as she massaged her shoulders and ran her fingers through her hair.

Camilla's mouth was sore from the fire. Her throat was tired from screaming in agony. A moment later, Camilla was able to collect the nerves in her neck enough to nod softly. Jason and Andrew held her up, until Camilla gained more consciousness. They guided Camilla onto Ashbel's throne so she could rest her body. Her pale body curled up in a tight ball, and she drifted mercifully into a soft sleep, her muscles very sore.

"Not what I expected to happen today!" Erik exclaimed, his far hands flying in the air, his drunk mouth mumbling curse words and then gulping more of the wine.

"What are you doing here?" Aya asked, her body shifting to face the little Blue man.

"Getting lectured by my oldest friend," he answered, smiling boldly at Ashbel. "It seems that I've been a horrible King," Erik continued, whining.

"Erik has graciously offered to have the Forgotten Children fight for you in the war that is rapidly approaching us."

Erik nodded, but he was really nodding at his drink before he chugged all of it down his throat. Rose smiled graciously at his generosity. She was pleased, and she thought, perhaps they could win. The Forgotten Children were known for their brutality and their ferocity. It was a blessing that they were willing to fight for the Reds. The Forgotten Children were usually very independent. Rose became apprehensive. She would be the cause of many deaths, with many fathers, husbands, and brothers joining the fight and perhaps never coming home. Just as what happened to her beloved Celia and Liza, the little girls who would never truly know their father.

"And you?" Aya asked. "Will you be at the battle?"

Ashbel touched her soft skin with his sharp claw, calming her nerves. She felt safety in his touch.

"Yes, Aya. I wouldn't miss it."

She smiled.

"As for the other dragons, it's up to them," he told her, loudly enough for the others to hear. Rose understood that it was suicide with the promise to be hurt and a death wish. It was a real wonder that Camilla now suffered having her fire returned and took on the responsibilities of a Red.

"I will travel to the towns around the world, asking for volunteers and building your army, Rose," Ashbel told her. *Her* army.

"Thank you, Ashbel," Rose told him.

"Thank you, Rose."

Aya opened the portal once more for them to leave Dragons Nest. They all left, with Ubel leaving last. They returned to exactly the same place where they were earlier in the day. They were on the edge of Nava, entering Remular, leading for Remular City, where the king lived.

"You are feeling better?" Roe asked Camilla hopefully after they began walking.

"Much," she replied, her high cheekbones blushing. "I did it for you."

"I know."

"I love your brother very much."

"You are going to make an amazing queen," Rose told her, "with or without red lips."

"You believe so?"

"I know so."

They walked into the clear fields of Remular together, Camilla showing her all the things she could do with her fire. Playing tricks, telling jokes, sharing memories, and planning parties she would have in the castle. The sun was setting, and night was just beginning. The new day would arrive soon enough. The week was beginning perhaps to be the longest week of Rose's life. Rose thought of her whole life while looking at the full moon and counting the stars. She dragged her hands across the tall grass, which was covered in a layer of snow.

It was December now, and the wind was getting sharp and cold. Rose warmed her body with the fire that rested within her blood, her hand reaching out to Ubel, warming him with her touch. His sad skin winced at her sudden touch but melted into her warmth.

JASON

"Did everyone sleep well?" Jason asked. His arm was around Camilla, his voice deep and tired.

Everyone mumbled an answer. Each person's was different. Watching everything Camilla had gone through to get her fire back to fight in the coming battle had really changed Rose's feelings about Camila. Rose was surprised when she found herself smiling at the affection her brother and Camilla were displaying. Rose began to accept the real love and commitment the couple shared. Rose missed LeRoy's touch, and she missed even more his smile and his easy way of making her smile. Their relationship had not been the same after the way he murdered the troll and the way she had condemned him. Rose had been very cautious around LeRoy after that because he was capable of things that Rose couldn't do. She feared things she couldn't feel and control. Rose did not understand LeRoy and everything he could feel, but she knew he would always protect her.

Andrew was sitting alone in the garden of a random Nomad who lived on the path to Remular City. The garden was filled with tomatoes, grapes, apple trees, and peppers. It was fenced in with white wood wall, over which Andrew easily jumped. Andrew had no difficulties stealing from the locals, figuring it was necessary to *support the war effort*. Ubel arrived, and the two of them collected as much fresh food as they could. They even smashed a few flowers for fun, then they feasted. The pair then returned to camp and shared their plunder with the rest of the group. The group enjoyed the fresh food and carried on light conversation between munching and crunching. The attack for Remular City was still a few days away, only because of the distance and the fact that their horses had been lost in the barn fire. Rose reflected on Erik's comments and thought it was just mean of him to remind her of that barn when they had been at Dragons Nest. Rose missed her horse, remembering how Bealfire saved their lives by warning them about the fire. Aya missed Lords, and Jason missed Liza. Rose and Ubel were touched again. He was cold, and she was willing to share her fire. She was willing to feel his awkward and sad touch. She enjoyed his scent, as it was both strong and mysterious.

"What were the letters?" Rose asked Ubel, showing an interest in him and trying to contribute to the polite banter within the group. Ubel withdrew his hand, with the sudden interest causing him to get goose bumps down his neck.

"What letters?" he stuttered.

"The thugs?" Rose began, and Ubel arched his eyebrows and tilted his head thoughtfully. Rose continued, "They took your letters. When I found you in the woods, you told me the thugs took your letters. Whom were you writing to?"

Ubel took a deep breath, seeming to enjoy the hearty and crisp air from the mountains and the winter forest. The oxygen was freshly made by the nearby trees. His dark hair was pushed ahead of his black eyes, and his shoulders hunched together. As they continued walking, his pace slowed, as he took smaller steps, which Rose found strange. Ubel was different from the rest of the group, which Rose found interesting.

"Oh," he said after a while, "I write to my father."

Rose smiled. She wished she could go back in time and talk to her father again and see how the love story developed between her father and mother. The happy image of her parents courting was dashed by the memory of the trap her father had sent Rose into right before he was punished in Dragons Nest. Rose's red lips moved again.

"Who's your father?" she asked.

"It doesn't matter who. It's how long," Ubel continued, seeking the warmth of Rose's hand again. "Haven't seen him in a while, or my brother."

Rose quietly listened to some of the stories he told her about his brother and the mischief they got into when they were younger, but he never shared a name. Rose enjoyed how mysterious Ubel was. She relished listening to him answer her questions with questions, teaching her valuable lessons about how to have a proper social life.

He's very smart, Rose thought. *He would be a great adviser for Jason.*

Her warmth began burning him, so she let go. At the loss of his touch, she felt cold again.

"Let's make camp here and rest for the day. My feet are exhausted," Aya declared. She carried a small backpack filled with the group's gear, including the jewelry box from Katrina, the contents of which Rose had not yet shown to the group of misfits. The backpack also contained some clothes that hadn't burned in the fires. Aya's shoulders were tired from carrying the load.

"I agree. I could use a rest," Rose proclaimed to the group, but Jason's voice, like that of a parent, interjected before Rose was able to relax on the soft grass.

"No, Rosie. You need to train."

"I think that's a great idea," Aya added before she closed her eyes. "You could use it."

Rose groaned. Her face was pink from the cold, and her muscles were sore from walking. Ever since learning how to make fire, Rose had always enjoyed looking for ways to display her special talent. Her fire desired to burn, and she knew it. She gathered herself, awoke her tingling legs, and began to stretch.

"Will you help me?" Rose asked Aya innocently, shaking her dark shoulders.

Aya nodded, thinking she could use the practice and that she wanted to spend more time with Rose. Aya, Rose, and Camilla walked into the open field not too far from their path and began rubbing their warm palms together vigorously. After they had created small sparks in their fingertips, they scratched their calves with their nails until their calves were bloodred, with the fire burning from their flesh like a series of shields. Together they burned one fire above their eyes, with green, blue, and red pushing against one another, fighting for dominance. They slowly let go, until their fire found their way back to their fists, waiting for its rightful master to manipulate the flame. Aya shouted directions as the trio moved forward in unison, pushing fire out of their hands while maintaining their fire shields with every step they took. Behind them, their calves were exhaling sparks, melting the grass below their feet.

Aya, quite the drill instructor, then forced them to run for twenty minutes while keeping a ball of fire alive in both palms. Rose outran Camilla by far, but every now and then Rose would lose focus and her flame would die, leaving her hand cold. Rose would get exasperated, her face turning red, as she would have to restart. Then Rose and Camilla were astounded as Aya showed off her fire skills. Rose's jaw dropped as the skilled Aya burned blue fire from her tongue, a trick only Aya could manage when she was inspired. Rose, Aya, and Camilla finished their training with a rather-difficult formation. After running with fire, they launched a series of punches and kicks into the air, with bright flames leaving their bodies. As always, the last routine was always dueling with Aya. They were all very tired, and Rose was not surprised that she herself continued struggling with balance. This had become a focal point of the duel training with Aya, teaching Rose how to achieve better balance.

"Breathe," Aya directed them. Aya instructed them to put their hands above their heads, with one foot at a proper angle in front of them and their eyes closed. Rose tried desperately to breathe, not wanting to let her friends down by failing the drill. It seemed like every time she inhaled, she was pushed backward and would fall to the ground. To make matters worse, nearly every time Rose exhaled, she would trip over one of her feet awkwardly. Aya coached Rose that she needed to find her center and bring air in and out of her core.

"Rosie," Aya said calmly, "breathe."

Rose held her breath for as long as she could so she would look like she was controlling her body. Her two friends never seemed to struggle with balance; even Camilla, with her fire just returned, rarely *misstepped*. Rose exhaled and then lost her footing, collapsing forward. Her fire left both her hands and her feet. Her body found its way onto the soft and forgiving ground.

"Are you nervous?" Aya asked, sitting down next to Rose, who had her eyes still closed.

"Yes, a little bit."

"Do you know what this reminds me of?" Aya inquired, looking over at Rose with a beautiful smirk on her red lips. Her hair was pulled back, so her eyes were beaming. Rose loved looking into Aya's clear eyes, so Rose quickly faced her friend, while Camilla approached to join the conversation

"Enlighten me," Rose said.

"Do you remember one of the first times we met, when I showed you one of the battles my father had won?" Aya asked Rose.

"With the cannons?" Rose's voice was shaking.

"Yes, with the cannons," Aya affirmed and continued coaching.

Rose nodded, her hands taking control of Aya's, leading her fingers into her lap. Rose lazily traced the shapes of her bitten nails as she listened to the rest of Aya's story. It was almost night again, and the moon arrived like an old friend, reminding the trio of girls just how long they had been training. They would reach Remular City soon. The sky displayed its innocence, with the birds singing their final songs, while the forest showed its purity through the small and beautiful but random patches of snow glistening peacefully in the soft moonlight. Camilla had taken a seat, completing the circle with Rose and Aya. Camilla listened to Aya's storytelling with such focus, desiring to know more about Rose and Aya. Camilla loved these moments and conversations between the young women.

Aya continued, "I told you before about my first interaction with purple fire and how my brothers managed to get ahold of it."

Rose nodded, so Aya continued, "Would you like to hear another story?"

"Yes."

"You might not enjoy this one as much," Aya warned.

"Thanks for the warning, but I can handle it. It can't be worse than some parts of my life already." Rose smiled, reassuring Aya that Rose would manage.

Aya began, slowing the pace of her words. "The dragon realm is the oldest thing known to man. It is an existence between dragons and Nomads, and now Red Lips. All dragons die eventually, but not our dragons. Our four dragons are the dragon realm, the owners of unimaginable power. They need a way to channel their power and to ground them to this life forever. Your family is that channel."

Rose's heart beat faster.

"A long time ago, your family proved themselves worthy to Ashbel. Ashbel decided your family, Rose, was worthy to generate the chosen one and worthy to stay alive forever as a line of powerful Red Lips," Aya continued. "This special connection lasted until the Nomads lost their dignity and their worth to the dragons. Disheartened, the dragons decided to attach their lives to one soul and to just one life, yours."

Rose couldn't breathe.

"When you die, Rose, the dragons will die with you. The gene will discontinue, and the world will continue with its final Red Lips. No new Red Lips will be born."

"So if the dragons are just doomed to die when I die and the Red Lips will eventually perish as a race, then why are we fighting for them? Why save the Red Lips and Nomads from the king?" Rose asked, fear rippling through her body.

"To prove," Aya answered calmly, "the true potential of this world, a very deserving place, without dragons and the influence of Red Lips. We are fighting to restart life here and to remind the people of the world of their inherent goodness."

Rose wished she were dreaming. Rose hoped against hope that this wasn't true, but she knew Aya would never lie. Tears streamed down Rose's cheeks, onto her chin, and then down the front of her neck. Camilla gripped her strong arm and massaged it slowly. Camilla leaned her head closer to Rose's heart, listening to the pumping, which came both fast and loud. Aya sat in silence, fighting against her own instincts to embrace her best friend. Aya wondered in her mind how to comfort someone carrying so much responsibility who was filled with so much pain.

"Why would you tell me this?" Rose said after regaining the courage to talk to Aya. Rose had become quite the vision, her hair sticking to her tearstains and her sweat and tears drenching her red shirt.

"So you don't decide to die on me," Aya told her, smiling down at her. "If one of us has to, let it be me."

"No one has to," said Rose, lifting her head to see Aya. Aya's eyes strained to look back into Rose's blue ones.

"But someone does have to die," Aya shared, folding her hands gracefully into her own lap. She seemed to regret the word she had just spoken as she continued, "There is a prophecy that during the battle that results in my father's death, a child of royal blood opposing the king will also die. Don't think I didn't see those jewels in the box. If it is true that those jewels belong to your family, that makes you part of the royal family."

"So I am destined to die?"

"I wish I could lie to you and tell you that we could win this fight without any of our own blood shed," Aya's voice continued, losing its confidence with this series of revelations that shook Aya to her core and broke her.

"And you tell me this to scare me?"

"To inspire you!"

"To inspire me with my own death?" Rose whispered.

"It might not be you!" Aya shouted. "It could be me!"

Rose thought for a while, both thoughts terrifying her. The image of holding the decaying body of Aya in Rose's arms was unsettling. Equally traumatizing was the vision of Aya holding Rose's own lifeless body in the center of a bloody battlefield, with snowfall entering into Rose's still nose.

"Your brothers!" Rose realized, thinking out loud. "Your brothers are of pure royal blood."

Aya scoffed. "Why would my father kill either of his sons? They are all on the same side and against us."

"If they were to die, just one of them, then perhaps we could satisfy the prophecy, without you or I having to die," Rose said, Purple thoughts filling her head.

"Are you suggesting I kill my brothers?"

"No," Rose said quickly, but it was exactly what she was thinking. "We just need to find a way to make your father kill them."

"Kill who?" a familiar voice asked, the dark long hair covering his black eyes. His shoulders dangled in front of his neck, and his veiny arms reached out to lift both Aya and Rose off the ground. Camilla had to pick herself up.

"We were just," Rose began, "plotting."

Ubel laughed, a cold smile washing over his face.

"LeRoy wanted to know where you were. Jason and LeRoy are worried. So is Andrew," Ubel said, his voice hesitating before mentioning each name. He smiled when he realized he had successfully remembered all of them. Rose's smile left her face. She remembered that she hadn't talked to LeRoy in a while, not since the death of the troll.

Rose reluctantly walked back to her boys. They were gathered around a small fire that they had made using sticks instead of their hands. They had taken the opportunity, being devoid of their female counterparts, to discuss the many and varied topics most young men found uniquely interesting. When they noticed the girls walking toward them, they adeptly changed to more *sensitive* topics.

Camilla snuggled herself into Jason's arms, his hands running through her thick red hair, becoming very quiet. Aya had taken a seat next to Andrew, who was next to Jason, yet Aya kept her distance. Rose and Ubel settled in on the ground next to LeRoy, with Rose in the middle.

"When will we arrive?" Rose asked, trying unsuccessfully to make eye contact. No one immediately responded. They were all somewhat daunted by the realization that the battle culminating their long journey was nearing on the horizon. For the longest moment, no one answered.

"If we go straight to the castle, it could be tomorrow," Aya finally admitted.

"When will the free Reds, Nomads, and perhaps the Forgotten Children who wish to fight arrive? And what about the dragons?" Rose inquired, continuing her preparation.

"Whenever we want them to be. My ring will let the dragons know when we are there," Aya said, holding up the twelfth jewel of Remular, spinning it lightly around her finger.

“Will it be cold?” Camilla asked, rubbing Jason’s freezing hands with her own.

“Yes, it will be cold. It’s December!” Andrew responded disdainfully, his hands flying into the air in frustration. He was tired, he was hungry, and he was wet.

“No need to shout and draw attention to us,” Jason said to educate them.

Rose and Aya agreed. They warmed Andrew up with their fires and then continued talking of their plans. They all ate small bites of leaves and berries, and then they prepared for bed.

Rose sat in the soft dirt near the orange fire, her hair tangled in a messy bun, her muscles sore but trained, and her eyelids fluttering open and close.

“Rose,” squeaked LeRoy’s voice, “please follow me.”

Rose stared up and looked deeply into his eyes. His hand was extended out toward her. His bushy hair was a mess, and he had obviously been restless when he could have been relaxing and asleep. He smiled lightly at her when she took his hand. LeRoy’s hand felt safer than they did holding Ubel’s. It was more homely, and Rose knew LeRoy was her protector. They walked with their hands closely intertwined deep into the field, near where the girls had trained earlier in the evening. It was painfully close to where Rose learned that she couldn’t die but that she was supposed to die. The grass was high, and the flowers that grew in some areas were either dying or covered in snowflakes. The night breeze was sharp and cold. LeRoy, dressed in his normal shirt and pants, was cold, so Rose warmed him by spreading her fire around both of them.

“Why are we walking back here?” Rose asked after a moment of silence.

LeRoy responded, turning to look into her blue eyes, “To be alone.”

“Why would we need to be alone?”

He inched closer to her.

“Rose,” LeRoy began, “I am sorry that I am not a perfect man. I am sorry that I can feel things you can’t, and I am sorry that I act on those impulses.”

Rose gripped both of his cold hands into her own, caressing every curve and line on his palms. She listened as he quietly spoke to her.

"Whatever happens in the next few days, I want you to know that I trust you and I believe in you. You are strong enough to fight the king, to win, and to sit on the throne, even though you fear it."

His hands touched her bronze hair, slowly collecting her in his arms. Her face beamed in the dark of the night as she felt her head rest upon his shoulder. He smelled of sweat and fire, but it was comforting. She thought gratefully about how very fortunate she was to have him hold her so close.

"Rose," LeRoy continued, gathering her attention, "you won't die in the battle."

Rose's skinny and pale fingers ran through his bushy brown hair before she nodded slowly back at him. She trusted him too.

"I promise that I will fight for you," he told her.

She smiled.

"I promise I will find a way to protect you."

Rose began to cry, but for the first time in a very long time, they were happy tears. The tears were not coming because of pain or worry or even the loneliness Rose constantly felt because she was different. The tears flowed from the love she felt for LeRoy.

"I promise to support and protect you through every evil the world throws at you. I promise to help guide us through the hate, all the hate and misunderstanding."

"I promise," he concluded, "to let others see your light, forever."

Rose mumbled something that sounded like his name, but LeRoy didn't care what she had to say, only what he wanted her to hear. He felt her warmth run chaotically through her body as he touched her back and her hair. He enjoyed feeling her melt with his touch.

"These are my promises to you," he expressed, maintaining full eye contact tearfully, "because I love you."

Rose stared back into his gleaming eyes as he finished his romantic testimonial. Her smile grew so large it touched her cheeks.

"I love you, Rose Mensch, more than words can describe. You deserve someone who is more like you, so kind and generous, so selfless and productive. I can't always be that man, but I can give you my love, if you will have it."

"I love you, LeRoy Amoson," she testified to LeRoy before pressing their lips together in an emotional reflection of their love. Their lips connected in a way that wasn't there when he had first touched her lips that one day in the water. This kiss was a kiss of two young adults in love, who were so terrified of their future but could not escape from their true and deep *feelings*. They both felt all the anxieties and tried to banish them away, if just for a moment, with each other's mouths. They felt the ache in their bodies and shared it in this intimate way, with so much passion that they reacted physically. *That kiss...*

"You needed me to walk all the way over here to tell me all this?" Rose whispered after their lips parted.

"Well, I also wanted to tell you that I don't like Ubel and I was worried he would hear me and try to beat me to death," LeRoy joked, though somewhat seriously.

"I find him very interesting!" Rose defended.

"Yes, very interested in *you*!" LeRoy told her. "I don't trust him."

Rose laughed at his jealously. She wondered what that felt like. Was it like the distrust she had felt with Camilla or the anxiety she felt when she had to share Aya with everyone else? She would never know, unless she let the Purple enter her veins. Then she would really understand and feel all these foreign emotions.

"I trust him," Rose argued, squeezing LeRoy's hand hard. LeRoy laughed his way into another kiss with Rose, interrupting her and keeping her from sharing why she decided to trust Ubel so much. He didn't want to listen to her say another word about any other man. LeRoy wanted to hear and feel Rose's heart beating faster every time he spoke.

"Are you going to be able to sleep?" LeRoy asked genuinely.

"Well, I probably should try," Rose responded. She missed his constant worry.

"Good night, Rosie."

"Good night, LeRoy."

The next day, they all woke up with their backs sore and heads hurting from the rocks and sticks stabbing them all through the night, even through the soft coat of snow. The sun had barely risen, but it gave enough light that they could continue their journey on the path safely. Rose and Aya walked into the woods near the prairie to collect more berries in preparation for the trip to Remular City. Everyone ate the fruit slowly, wasting time and not rushing to see the journey completed.

They gathered the few items they had and began walking back on the path, leaving footprints in the snow as they passed. It had snowed during the night. The wind was piecing their eyes, washing over their lashes with undeniable force. They dragged their feet along, most of them holding the hand of another person to ensure the safety of themselves as they walked through the rough morning. Later in the afternoon, the wind was kinder to them, pushing against their backs.

"How much longer?" LeRoy whined, his hands intimately intertwined with Rose's hands.

Aya answered, her nails digging into Andrew's palms, "Hasn't changed much since the last time you asked. There are still hours to go."

A large groan escaped LeRoy's throat, and Rose couldn't help but laugh. Her heart was beating rather fast, her hands produced much more sweat, and her face lost the few pigments she had. She needed to find humor in the small things, because she was so anxious.

LeRoy wasn't wondering how close they were and needed to voice it every few moments. He knew it would entertain Rose. He would rather sacrifice himself to Aya's mercy than see Rose in fear. He knew she would smile and occasionally laugh, that her hands would loosen their tight grip around his wrist, and that perhaps she would wipe the sweat from her eyes.

The sun was now directly above the small group, guiding them to the fight of their lives. It seemed to take longer to rise without their horses trotting along every path and without Rose moving the trees to clear their way. The snow was thawing slowly under their feet, and their boots clenched onto the muddy puddles left behind by the thawing snow.

"Jason," Rose called, stopping her body and releasing herself from LeRoy's hand to wait for her brother to match her position. He was constantly behind her, trailing the group as they would walk. Rose waiting for him had become a common activity. She often could predict how long it would take him to reach her.

"Don't you think his hands will get cold?" Jason remarked, obviously meaning her constant holding of LeRoy's hand.

"He will be fine," Rose told him.

"What about Ubel? He seems to have lost his partner."

"I asked him first, but he rejected me. He told her he would be warm enough without my hand."

Jason mumbled a response, but Rose didn't seem to care what he had said. Instead, she jumped to the reason she had called his name originally.

"I have been meaning to ask you," Rose began, her voice still shaking and her muscles still sore from sleeping on the ground. "Will you give a speech at your coronation?"

Jason, who himself was walking with a limp due in part to their recent sleeping arrangements, laughed.

"I don't understand your amusement," Rose said, seriousness controlling her face. "All good kings give speeches."

"I can't believe you are still set on me ruling!" Jason told her, a smile on his pale lips. "I would have thought you would change your mind after knowing there is no life to go back to in Nava."

"I will just have to make one," Rose told him.

"And I guess I will have to find comfort in my large palace with my many servants and my feasts and parties," Jason said, sighing greatly.

"Oh, pity." Rose smiled.

"You must come to our parties, Rose. I have already planned out our first one," Camilla said excitedly, her cheeks blushing crimson. A golden crown would fit her red hair perfectly. Of the different jewels she would wear around her neck, most would be emeralds, Rose imagined, to commemorate her green fire.

Rose nodded, thinking of just one party. She would have to wear a dress; maybe Camilla would braid her hair.

Rose's mane had fallen out of the clean braid it was in all those days ago, back in Nava, and she had not remembered to ask for Camilla to do it again. She couldn't imagine fighting a battle and having her hair in her eyes. It would be unprofessional. Aya had taught her what that meant.

"Jason," Rose said after a comfortable silence, his head perking up, "you haven't answered my question."

"Yes, please remind me what that vitally important question was."

"Will you give a speech at your coronation?"

"Well, all good kings give speeches, don't they?" Jason asked her.

Rose smiled, knowing he took that fact from her, so she nodded. She lost her jitters as she resumed her friendly conversation with him, asking about all the different things he would say in his great speech. He would answer only in the way he knew she would want him to answer, just so she would be pleased with her decision to hand over the throne to him.

Rose eventually wandered back up to her dearest LeRoy, grabbing his hand and then strutting along beside him. The sun had barely moved from the center of the sky since Rose last checked. The gray in the sky had gotten lighter as the path they were walking on had grown muddier.

Aya and Rose could see the outlines of the great castle and tall buildings growing nearer and nearer from where they were and off in the horizon. The prairie was coming to an end, with the forest beginning to dominate the vegetation. The darkness of the trees covered their view as well as their being viewed. They were hours away from the city still, but now they could see it. They could see the city where the king lived.

"How do we know he is even there?" Rose asked, her eyebrows cocking up at Aya.

"Ashbel's reporters have stated that he is at home," Aya told Rose, patting her shoulder softly.

"Ashbel has reporters?"

"Yes, little spies that work for him in the city," Aya informed her.

"Why don't they just kill the king?"

"Because," Aya told her, "if they killed him, then who would rule next? Who would enforce equality among the Reds? What lesson would be gained? It has to be you."

Rose agreed, though she didn't really want to. She wanted to believe that there was someone else who had to die or to kill, but everything was coming back to her.

"What is the king's plan?" Rose inquired.

"He wants to kill the Reds, take their power, become a more powerful ruler over the dragons, and rule a world without good or bad, just hate and fear."

Rose tried to absorb as much of that as she could. Aya briefed it so well. She couldn't even bare to think about all the damage he would create if he cleansed the world of Reds. The evil he would perpetrate without the balance of good was daunting.

"Has there ever been a good king?" Rose asked in good humor, thinking of the long line of Nomad rulers.

Aya laughed as she looked behind herself to see the rest of her friends. She smiled as she watched LeRoy shiver behind them and Ubel talk indistinctly to Andrew. She didn't smile at Ubel.

She smiled at Jason, who was still holding Camilla's hand, her long hair resting at her hips. She feared for the lives of these people. Aya knew best the extremes in behavior that the king had displayed to protect his power.

The darkness of the green trees overwhelmed the eyes of the teenagers. They breathed in gasps of heavily scented air, then they exhaled, feeding the trees. They walked along a nonexistent path, maneuvering their bodies through the trees and bushes. As they walked toward the city, every so often they would see buildings through the tops of the trees.

The group of teenagers walked together until they could see the castle and the city from a more complete vantage point. They observed it and tried to relax in the calm before the storm. Remular City was a very large city, with thousands of sandstone buildings running in straight lines until they touched the hill upon which the large castle rested. They could see the different colors of clothes, banners, and lights hanging from high ropes above the buildings and homes. They could make out the different balconies and porches bulging from the walls of the homes. Rose's eyes focused on the large castle, with different pillars and halls, stairwells, and rooms, exterior and interior. She thought deeply about running through the rooms of the castle and chasing down the evil man. Just the thought exhausted her more than she could imagine. She was pulled away from the opening by Aya's warm hand as she demanded they move back farther into the woods. Even though the inevitable battle would begin soon, she was also in no hurry to start the battle prematurely.

Rose was dragged through a copse of trees and tripped over a few sticks before she understood that the memory of the city was all she had left. She had long left Aya's grip. She now held on to the cold hand of LeRoy, submerging herself into him. He coyly massaged the skin and muscles on her fingers, rubbing against the skin with a loving intent.

Aya led them into the depth of the forest. The sun was setting, and they had spent the whole day walking, without stopping. They were all tired. Aya burned a light-blue fire in her palm to see where she was walking and to guide her friends. It was the end of the woods. They were visible to the city and could hear the bustle and see the bright and lively city. Aya was the first to see the large walls that was wrought around the city for protection. Ubel was the last to take in this sight. The wall was strong and thick. It hadn't needed to be guarded, as it was a guard. Different doors and gates were scattered along the border, but a whole army and dragon's couldn't fit in perfectly.

Rose gasped, although she knew they were ready. She was certain that the city was filled with Red-loathing Nomads who would kill any fire-controlling girl on sight. She was certain each Nomad that lived in the city had been manipulated by the king into a frenzy and to the point that they were willing to fight his war for him. Sooner rather than later, Rose and Aya were going to have to tell whatever army they would have how they were going to attack and get Rose into the palace.

"In the morning we fight," Rose told everyone after they had seated themselves in a circle. Igniting a fire was too dangerous, for fear that the smoke would give them away, so they relaxed in the dark, their skin burning against the cold snow.

Everyone grumbled a cheer.

"We will march into the city and burn it to the ground!" shouted a tired Andrew.

Loud disagreements rushed out of the mouths of the rest of the group, including Ubel, who had been unnaturally vocal during the prior conversation.

"What is wrong with burning down the city?" Andrew genuinely questioned.

Rose grew wide-eyed and dizzy, her morals seeping through her veins.

"We don't want millions of innocents to die," Aya snapped.

"Even if those millions of innocent people wouldn't hesitate to see you die first?"

Aya choked on her own words, but Rose quickly responded, "Yes."

"What a depressing way to kill yourself," Andrew told her.

"You need to calm down," LeRoy told him, his small body rushing to protect Rose.

"I don't want to see Camilla die. If she does, we will know who is to blame. The girls are too scared to protect their friends."

"You're tired," Aya said calmly, trying not to make Andrew even more heated.

"Even if he isn't, he's right," Rose said after gathering her courage. "What losses are we willing to endure during this battle?"

"The ones that are reasonable," Aya answered, her face growing stern and strong.

"What if they kill me?" Rose said, waiting for her response, an example of Purple getting closer to her veins.

"Then we lose and we go home. We wait for Reds to no longer exist. We blow up the world. I don't know!"

"We continue fighting," Rose corrected. "We fight until the king drops dead, even if it means more casualties. I won't lose."

"Rose," Aya said softly, her dark arm resting along Rose's pale one, "you can't possibly mean that?"

Rose thought for a while, thinking of the consequences of each answer and the reasons she would say anything. Rose collected herself, smiled, and then breathed out.

"No," Rose said. "Equality for both Nomads and Reds, right?"

"Right."

The quick steps of someone shifting around was heard above Aya's words after she agreed, causing them to investigate their surroundings to find the source of the noise. They walked around the bushes, searching for the cause of the disturbance. Rose looked behind a wall of bushes, just in time to see the black hair of Ubel running toward the gated walls of Remular. He was shouting words, unknown to Rose or Aya, until he disappeared into the city of power. He ran so desperately and was careless about how loud he was. He shuffled his feet behind him, his clothes trailing behind him. Rose stood immoveable as the last sight of Ubel vanished through a gate in the walls of Remular City. At the time of Ubel's sudden departure, the group of teenagers had been located in the forest just east of the walls of Remular City. As a precaution, they broke camp and followed the walls of the city all the way around to a location directly west of the city inside the forest, with the Veella River behind their new campsite. What sleep the teens were able to get that night was disturbed early in the morning by the distressful sounds of angry bells pounding from the city, and then the more welcomed screeches of dragons in the sky.

ROSE

During the night, thousands of Nomads arrived by boat from the Veella River and began filling the woods behind the new campsite the teens had created. Rose and Aya became more confident in their potential for success as each new volunteer arrived. Rose dispatched Andrew to help organize these Nomad volunteers, with specific instructions to take half of the Nomads and surround the city walls, while leaving the other half of the Nomads to support the main attack. When the four dragons elegantly arrived, Rose called a meeting to review the battle plan with the dragons, Aya, and Jason. Rose began by drawing a near-circle on the ground to represent the walls of Remular City, and then Rose drew a smaller circle about halfway between the center of the city and the western most segment of the outer walls.

Rose began her first battle briefing by taking a deep breath and looking each of her dear friends in the eye. Rose commanded, "Today, you are a critical part of our necessary efforts to reshape this world for the better. Aya and I are humbled by your support. I have drawn on the ground here a rough image of the walls of Remular City." Rose pointed to the outer circle. Rose then continued, "And the real prize for today's battle, the king's castle." She then pointed to the inner circle.

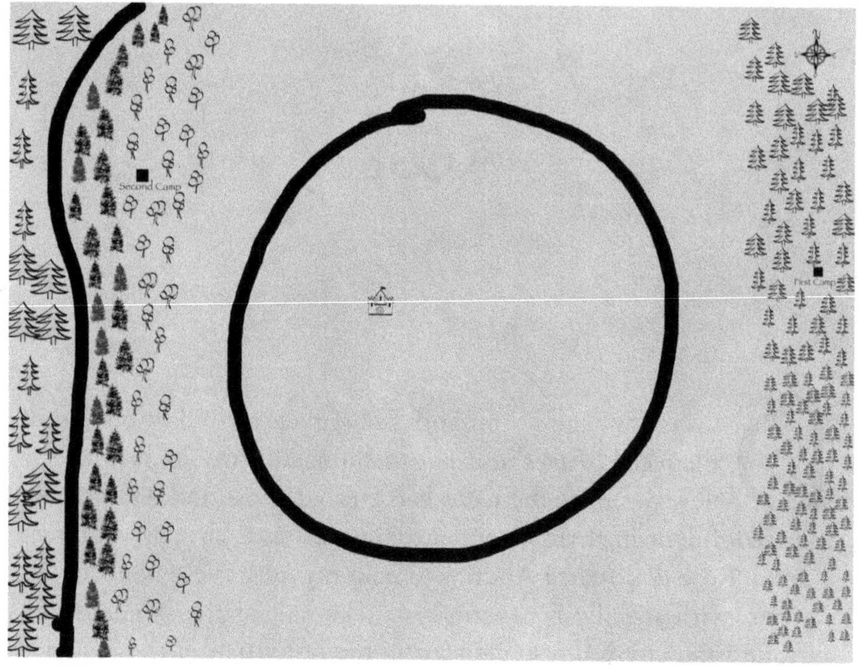

Rose continued her briefing as professionally as she could. "Our most important mission today is to get me to the castle so that I can find and kill the king. Our secondary mission is to destroy the loyalists who remain within the king's army after seeing the full force and lethality of the army we have brought to this battle. The sooner the soldiers in the king's army become more afraid of us than the king, the sooner many of them will flee, reducing the number of people who must die on both sides of this battle. We will begin the battle with air attacks by the dragons on the walls ringing the city and on any cannon batteries that the dragons can locate. You, brave dragons, will remove the comfort and protection that the king's army might take from the walls and destroy the most lethal part of the king's army, his cannons. As you are doing this, please try to be safe and to be thorough. Please make certain to destroy one entire wall section in each of the primary directions and as many cannons as you can locate. Do not worry so much about troop locations during this first part of your attack. We want to let the army soldiers have a choice whether or not to fight with the king after they have seen the audacity and strength of our forces. After this first phase is completed, begin destroying the entire wall currently in front of us. The western walls and the path from the western wall to the castle must be cleared of cannons and defenses, including soldiers, to the very best of your abilities. Once that path is cleared, clear a ring around the castle that our ground troops can occupy once we reach that target. Once the air portion of our attack is completed, we will form up our ground army in the clearing between our current position in the forest and the western wall, which will have been destroyed. Edan, Vulcan, and Candice will form a large equilateral triangle, with Edan on the point facing nearest to the city wall. In the space between the three dragons, half of the Nomad volunteers that remain for the main attack will be located. Jason, you will command and lead the Nomad army, with responsibilities to protect the dragons from ground skirmish troops and to protect the rear of the battle formation as you advance. This will allow the three dragons in the formation to burn every obstacle in their path as they move forward through the walls and toward the king's castle. Aya will be located in the front with Edan, helping direct the dragons forward as efficiently and quickly as possible. As I mentioned earlier, I have already sent Andrew to organize a perimeter around the rest of the city, to prevent the king from escaping his just punishment. If the dragons motivate the proper behavior in the soldiers, many, if not most of them, will decide to flee the city and surrender to the Nomad army that has formed a perimeter around the city."

Rose continued her briefing. "Ashbel, as the battle formation with the three dragons begins advancing, you will pick me up and fly me to the castle. Once we arrive at the castle, you will drop me off on one of the towers, from where I will go about seeking and killing the king. Ashbel, as the battle formation continues their march through the city, burning the resistance that the king's army might organize, it will be your job to scout and disrupt any organized activities you can identify. In the best case, the ground formation will arrive at the castle just after I have killed the king. When the ground formation arrives at the castle, it will become your responsibility to form a perimeter around the castle to prevent enemy troops from entering and to destroy any members of the king's army within the perimeter who still wish to resist."

Rose looked her dear friends one by one in the eyes again, saying, "If something happens to me, you must continue the fight until the king is dead. Aya will take over my responsibilities as your leader, so follow her. Just know that I am not going to let you down. What questions do you have for me?"

The group of leaders was solemn and committed. The instructions and individual responsibilities were simple enough and clear. Each leader nodded at Rose and Aya and then began organizing their gear and their people for the mission. Ashbel had already briefed the Nomad volunteers on the rules agreed for the battle, so the four dragons relocated back into the field to decide how best to assign roles and locations for the aerial attack that would begin the battle.

Rose scrambled around her little circle as she mentally prepared herself for the battle to come. Aya and Jason shared the battle plan with the Nomads loudly, trying to reassure them that their role was a support role helping the dragons focus on clearing their path forward. Andrew had returned from positioning the Nomads in a perimeter around the great city. The morning sun was rising above the city so peacefully. Rose could only think about how the world will have changed when the sun would set that evening and rise again the next morning. She just might not be here to watch that glorious dawn arrive. Rose was at peace with her choices and grateful for the group that was following her. In a strange way, Rose was uncomfortable with while prepared for the judgments she would face for what she knew she had to do.

Andrew and Camilla were talking quietly while her green fire performed tricks and spun around her fingers. Jason was throwing sharp sticks into the bark of trees, while LeRoy threw fake punches into the air. Aya had given up on talking and began shouting at everyone to gather their things and begin positioning themselves at the edge of the woods. Rose was somewhat excited to see the aerial show of the dragons, which would start the battle. Rose saw the last of the fruitless trees, the small bushes, and the weeds growing at the feet of the wood. They marched forward, some standing together, some standing behind others. Rose stood next to Aya, her feet mirroring the stomping of Aya's boots. They splashed into the small puddles of the wet mud from the decaying snow. Surprisingly, there was still some pure snow that clung on leaves and other elevated structures.

The four dragons met in the clouds centered above Remular City. They had climbed into the clouds at a distance so that their presence there was not observed. Ashbel nodded, and each began a high-speed dive toward the wall sections ninety degrees apart. The move they each performed next in perfect harmony was agreed for both its ferocity and for the sheer terror it would invoke in the king's army. Each dragon dived hard and spewed a huge ball of fire, destroying some cannons on the wall segments. Just in time, the dragons unfurled their wings to catch enough wind to slow their speed enough so they would not crash into the ground. As the dragons slowed and got closer to the ground, they identified the most senior soldier in their view and grabbed him in the claws of their feet. They then took their prisoners up with them into the sky and paused above the locations where they had collected their prizes. They then dropped their soldiers and allowed gravity to pass judgment.

From the ground, the scene was shocking, to say the least. The soldiers had been preparing for a ground battle, with many of their ranks feeling secure behind the protection of their walls. Very few soldiers noticed the dragons approaching from above until they spewed their fireballs, making clear that anyone without strong overhead protection might be next. The sight, but more horrifically the sound, of the dragons taking prisoners back up into the sky was traumatizing. The four soldiers captured, including one lieutenant and three senior sergeants, screamed for help all the way up into the sky. When the dragons and their prisoners passed out of view into the clouds, the air was silent for a moment, which seemed to last and last and last. Just as hope began to mount that the worst was over, the king's army heard the faint screams of the captive leaders, who had begun their descent back to the ground. It became apparent by the lieutenant's silence that he had quickly vomited, perhaps as a reflex to the fear of falling, and then choked on his vomit and died during the early part of his fall. The three battle-tested and professional sergeants managed to scream like little children all the way until they hit and bounced off the ground. The landings of the four soldiers created a rain of body parts and fluids that coated those around the areas where the four soldiers returned.

Next, the dragons proceeded to attack the city walls and the cannons in their sectors. Each dragon had assigned a quarter of the city where they were to burn a large hole through the outer wall and then focus on any armaments, like cannons, they could identify and light them on fire.

The soldiers protecting the walls saw the beginnings of the wall burn to ash. It started on their left, the sandstone crumbling to nothing, then it spread to where they were standing, then to their right. The heat of the fire nearly burned their eyes. Smoke and desolation filled Remular's sky. The people in the city struggled to find places that offered protection. Some stayed in their homes, while others tried to flee the city entirely, holding the hands of their children as they saw Ashbel burn down their protection.

Where clusters of soldiers were identified, the dragons allowed the soldiers to decide their own fates, except for the soldiers in the western sector. For whatever reason, the largest concentration of army soldiers was quickly identified near the eastern walls of the city. Vulcan kept an eye on the soldiers while focusing on armaments and cannons. Any soldier attempting to engage Vulcan or any of the other dragons was quickly lit on fire and left to run. After the four dragons completed their sectors, they formed a line and began clearing everything in sight from the giant hole in the western wall that Ashbel had created all the way to the castle. The initial strafing runs made clear the dragon's intent, so any person foolish enough to remain in the path was deemed a combatant. After a wide swath was created for the ground assault, the dragons focused on clearing a perimeter around the castle, setting dozens of the king's best soldiers on fire. Once this mission was completed, the dragons returned to the agreed position on the ground, facing the western wall.

A large roar, actually a chorus of roars, echoed from the fields west of the city. Ashbel, Candice, Edan, and Vulcan announced the ground attack with a roar that shook the ground and made clear the resolve of the forces attacking the king within the city.

Rose nodded her approval as the large shadow that was Ashbel flew overhead and came to rest in the clearing west of what had been the city's western wall. Ashbel, with his grand red fire and his great red scales trailing down his back, gave Rose a wink while trying to control the satisfaction he had with the efforts of the other three dragons.

"So this is happening?" Rose asked Aya, her blue eyes looking into the majestic, clear eyes that rested below her eyelashes.

"It will be over before you know it," Aya told her, gripping her wrist affectionately. Rose smiled, enjoying the support of Aya's touch. Aya ran a hand through her short black hair.

Camilla had braided Rose's bronze hair. Rose had dressed in her long leather pants, her loose red shirt tied at her side in a knot. Aya and Camilla were dressed nearly identically to Rose. They did this so the king would never know which one was Rose if the king dared to show his face in the city.

After the aerial portion of the attack was completed, chaos reigned inside the city, with both soldiers and civilians uncertain about what would happen next. During the aerial phase, when the dragons were clearing the path from the western wall to the king's castle, the senior officers in charge of the troops organized near the eastern wall forced their soldiers on threat of death to march across the city to the area just south of the large hole in the great wall. Civilians and soldiers alike began fleeing the city and surrendering to the Nomads in the woods around the city.

Rose left the comfort of her friend Aya and walked tardily toward Ashbel's large body. She reached out a friendly hand to his forehead, petting his scaly skin, feeling his warmth underneath his tough layer. He let out a huff before lifting his chin at her, ignoring the loud shouts of his name from nearby Nomads.

"Rosie," he said, "little one."

"Ashbel." She bowed.

"You made it?" he questioned, his eyes blinking at her whole form.

"Was this the plan all along? To end in a battle?"

His yellow eyes looked directly at her, his solemn figure breathing in her sweaty scent through is large nostrils as he pronounced, "The plan was never anything we knew you couldn't handle."

Rose chuckled at his plan. She leaned into his temple and kissed it slowly, her lips lingering for only a moment. This time she was taking in his ghastly scent of fire and fear.

The second loud bell rang from the city. From afar, they saw the tower. It kept the same sandstone high into the clouds, nearly overpowering the castle. Rose then knew it had begun, the terrors of war, the lust for blood. She let go of his head and walked back over to her dearest friend, Aya, and next to her was Camilla. They saw, through the dust, the large army that had marched from the eastern wall and was now emerging through the hole in the western wall that the dragons had burned down. There was a majesty to the way these soldiers, with their armor, swords, helmets, and capes, continued marching toward Rose's army in its triangular formation. Their leaders rode horses, while the resolve of the soldiers reflected both anger and passion.

"Don't die," LeRoy whispered into Rose's ear, making her tingle slightly. She smiled back up at him, kissing his hand, which he had slid into her for a few seconds of safety.

"You too."

Rose felt his presence leave her side, but Aya stayed the same. They watched as the army grew closer to them. She could see hundreds of them; she could see their numbers outgrowing her wildest nightmare.

Suddenly, faint screeches and yelps of victory echoed and wailed. It took Rose and Aya a moment to locate the origin of the cries. They came from behind the teenagers, from the woods. Rose's confidence shook, and she was on the verge of tears, her pulse beating in her throat. She tried to think how the king's army could have outflanked her own army or what demons they had gotten to kill her. The demons grew in size, number, and ferocity in her own mind as the noise approached.

Rose's eyes clenched shut as she heard the bushes and leaves thrown to the side behind her. This was the end. It was only a matter of seconds before she felt the breathing of something much closer to the ground on her feet. She opened her eyes to see the ugly faces of children with blue skin running mad up and down the hill, but not into the city. She saw the twigs poke out of their heads. Their horrible, demented eyes stared back at her, and only then did she see the bruised blue lips of the Forgotten Children. They were biting and screaming at one another. They had purple fire pouring from their eyes and long sharp fingers. Rose laughed as she remembered Erik's commitment to try to convince the Forgotten Children to join her army. The man himself then emerged from the woods. He was in a different and spotlessly clean robe. He held a large staff in his right hand, with the chief's crown topping his bald head. His large nose and ghoulish smile faced Rose.

"I live for dramatic entrances," Erik told her with a pleased smile. "But I do hate war," he added.

"What's that like?" Rose asked him.

"What? Hate? Oh, you'll find out!" Erik told her, his grin spreading along his greasy face.

Rose laughed at the Forgotten Children frolicking around in the clearing at her toes, climbing into the firepits that were once a strong wall. Rose then heard the stomping of feet again, louder, but much more controlled in their marching.

"Who else did you bring?"

Erik laughed.

Out of the forest came a powerful army of bruised-lipped Reds and Reds who had the cherry pigment on their lips. Each one played with blue or green fire in their palms, some even holding swords or sticks in their other hands. Trolls and ogres who were treated kindly by Ashbel stood awkwardly towering over the Reds. Rose gasped a heavy gasp as she tried to count how many there were. Ashbel really must have been convincing.

"Enough," Erik answered after watching her face light up at his support. He chuckled softly.

"How marvelous it is to be yourself, wouldn't you say so?" Erik pondered out loud.

"No one else I would rather be," Rose whispered.

Vulcan, Edan, and Candice roared, breaking up the happy reunion and reminding Rose of the king's army, which had formed in front of Rose's army. The dragons wasted no time before looking over at Rose, who had grown paler from the overwhelming love.

"They know only to join the fight on your voice," Vulcan said eagerly, his blue scales glistening under the winter sun.

Rose walked out into the clearing toward the king's army. Her feet took their time. She moved her way through the field, collecting all her bravery and ambition before she took her final steps. She was now standing innocently in front of the king's army, which approached from the edge of the city. The king's soldiers had watched as all the Reds escaped from the woods. They had the honor of looking Rose in the eye. She smiled honestly at them as she focused on the their army, whose loud armor was clanking against the shields they were forced to hold, their reflection clear in the windows of some homes.

Rose turned to the three brilliant and beautiful dragons in the triangular attack formation and said, "Burn them!"

Edan, Candice, and Vulcan launched a torrent of fire then quickly spanned the gap between their own positions and the approaching king's army. The fire turned the metal in the soldiers' armor and swords into a plastic fluid that burned their own flesh. Exposed flesh blackened and melted, exposing bones underneath the flesh. The advance halted, and those soldiers who could still move chose to move away from the opposing army with the dragons. The three dragons paused, having successfully accomplished Rose's simple request.

Rose began running toward the king's army, her hands at her chest, her hair dancing against her back and her feet bouncing off the ground. She screamed a holler that could be heard from the farthest island in the Forgotten Ocean. Her throat burned after it. Her peaceful ears could hear the battle cries of Aya and the Forgotten Children as they ran straight through the burned remains of the king's army.

Rose met with few soldiers, burning their swords to the handle easily. She yelped as she jumped high into the air, being caught by Ashbel and lifted onto his great, scaly back. Ashbel had taken to the air as Rose began her run and now was lifting higher and higher into the air with every beat of his wings. Rose secured herself onto him, preparing for a bumpy ride. The triangular dragon formation with Jason and his Nomad army was joined by the new arrivals. They began their march forward to the king's palace. Rose saw Aya fight and punch different men and burn their faces and hands. She saw the three dragons occasionally spit fire at groups of the king's soldiers who lacked the sense to understand that they had already lost. Ashbel continued directly forward in the sky, carrying Rose to her destiny inside the castle.

AYA

Aya listened and watched intently as the king's army emerged from the hole in the city wall created by the dragons' aerial attack. Her heart had halted when she saw the size of the king's army, only to be relieved by the purging fire issued by the three dragons. Once she heard Rose's war cry, Aya ran toward the hole in the city wall. Aya could see that their battle plan had resulted in the king's army being stripped off their best armaments, their cannons, and outranged in the battle. The three dragons with the ground assault could burn opposing soldiers at a greater range than the soldiers could throw spears or shoot arrows, both of which had a low probability of hurting the dragons. Aya worried about Rose and wanted desperately to make sure she would be safe and to back her up, but Rose was just too fast.

Aya swung her hand lazily at a few opposing soldiers that were moving to attack Rose from behind. Aya's unquenchable fire attached to the soldiers, causing their arms to blacken, their eyes to grow wide in surprise, and their throats to issue bloodcurdling cries from the intense pain it caused their flesh. Aya thought to herself and almost said out loud, *So how's that choice of working for my father working out for you? Is your life turning out to be everything you reckoned it would become? I hope you have a moment before you pass out and die from my winnowing fire to realize the mistakes you have made and repent.*

Aya's heart pounded fiercely in her chest when she saw Rose being carried away by Ashbel. Aya knew that Rose was going to be in the castle soon, searching for the king. A nagging fear entered

Aya's mind. Her father had always found ways to survive the sorts of attacks Rose was attempting. Even though the ground battle would end soon, with the castle surrounded, Rose needed help. The prophecy foretold that if the king died today, one of them was going to die as well.

Aya pulled herself out of her trance as she came head-to-head with a sword swung in rage at her neck. Aya's hand grasped the blade, melting the hot iron into a puddle of boiling liquid, before she kicked the guard in the nose, causing blood to drip endlessly from his nose. Jason, who fought next to Aya, was using a sword he had won from an earlier combat to fight off oncoming opponents. His skill was a pleasant surprise, although these opponents were exhausted from being marched from the other side of the city at the beginning of the attack and then demoralized by watching their ranks purged by fire. Jason would swing, hit, slice, and mark most of the soldiers that came his way, but he seemed to struggle with keeping his adrenaline up.

"You need water?" Aya asked as she ran toward her friend, carefully assessing his needs. He was thirsty and out of breath.

She warmed his throat up with her hands, wrapping her skilled fingers loosely around his neck, easing the sharp dryness that ached his throat. He coughed and was able to collect himself.

Aya left Jason to his own healing. Her nagging thought about Rose in the castle returned. She looked quickly back at her advancing army, anchored by the three dragons, and felt that they had the battle well in hand. Aya thought, *Rose will need me in the castle. I need to run ahead and get there as quickly as I can to save her.* Aya managed to sprint her way through a crowd of angry city dwellers who were stalking Aya's every move. They gripped and tugged at her hair and took out knives and sliced her arms. Aya managed to get through the crowd and looked back to see Camilla run behind her. Camilla used her green fire skillfully to elevate herself above those who tried to harm her. She delicately landed and ran toward Aya, breathing slowly, just as Aya had taught her.

"You all right?" Camilla asked, her hands burning a flame in a palm as they ran farther into the city.

"I'm just trying to get to Rose," Aya told her, fighting off another angry mob of people.

"She can handle herself," Camilla tried to explain. She was cramping badly as they continued to run. Camilla found herself trying to run, talk, and not kill innocent people as others tried to kill her. Some city dwellers had bags of rock, and others hard and sharp objects. They were throwing these projectiles at Rose's army from the tops of different buildings.

"We love our king!" they would shout as they chucked the bags at them. Some throws would hit hard if they landed, while others would be soft and bounce off her but would smell horrible.

Aya tried not to mind them as she ran through the endless path of people. They would charge back at her with their most grimacing faces, axes in their hand, evil pouring out of their eyes. A man with gray in his hair, wrinkles on his face, and shaggy skin dripping from his bones ran, as best as he could, with a large sword aimed for her face. She pushed back on him, causing him to trip to the ground. She extended an arm out for the sword, then wielded it as she charged at a mob of men just like the one who was coughing on the ground.

She traced the hair of the first man, who paused right in front of her clear eyes to try to punch her confidence right out of her. Her skilled legs marched over to the second man, jabbing the sword deep into his foot, blood pouring out of the flesh. He screamed in pain. Aya flinched at the sight. Bits of bones were swimming out into his puddle. She gathered her fire in his hands, elevated it to the face of the third man, burning his forehead harshly, until it stained red. He yelped, calling out desperately for water or ice for his wound. The final man, who had been hesitant to fight her originally, had reluctantly lifted his foot to her face in an attempt to knock her unconscious. Aya grabbed mercilessly onto his weak ankle, twisting it around so he lost his balance and landed on the hard ground, cracking his nose. His blood flowed into a pool of blood from the man with the sword in his foot.

"Sorry," Aya whispered in a voice that no one heard. She truly was sorry. She didn't want to be violent, but her head was throbbing, and she needed to get to Rose.

She paused for breath before continuing her run to the castle. When she continued, her fists soon met a soldier with a spear in his hand. He yelled angrily as he aimed the spear at her stomach with all the force he could muster. She gripped the end of the spear, then melted it as it slid toward her, the melted iron dripping off Aya's fingers, painlessly, and then attaching to the soldier's hands and body, burning his clothes and then his flesh on its path to the ground.

"I'm sure you are trying your best," Aya told him, bringing her hands to match his face, his eyes burning at her touch. She wondered, for a short time, what it would feel like to find pain in fire. Her leather-padded knee met his stomach. He collapsed into her, and then she dropped him to the ground. He whimpered.

"Rose?" he asked, trying to sit himself up, wincing at his mouth, moving his new burns and scars.

"You wish," she told him.

Another soldier, this one much taller and more muscular, ran up to Aya. His deep voice growled something strange. His glove-covered hands tried to circle her dark neck. She reached out first, taking her blue fire and melting every inch of his armor right off his back. His naked body was vulnerable, and the citizens in the streets began laughing at him. Fearing for themselves, the citizens ran away from Aya, giving her a wide berth. Aya easily broke the soldier's grasp and sighed, as she had grown tired of war. Aya began running through the crowd of bystanders and toward the sandstone castle.

Camilla had gotten distracted with helping young children find safety inside different homes. She also gathered the elderly into small groups and showed them the safest way out of the city. Camilla tried following along the path Aya had taken but realized she could do more good right where she was. Camilla turned her head to see different homes burning and the dying bodies of city dwellers, both men and women.

The dragon formation was now marching through the city toward the castle. The path had effectively been flattened by the aerial assault, but it was still uncomfortable for the dragons. They were so large compared to the path that the triangular formation became more of a single-file line, with Edan in the front and Nomads, Forgotten

Children, and others continuing to protect the feet of the dragons from skirmishing attackers. The dragons had great difficulty turning their heads to target fire at attackers from the sides and especially from behind. At the same time, the intensity of the city's defense had significantly dwindled. The resistance that remained quickly was becoming onlookers, even some children who jeered at the invading army from outside their homes, using common slurs against the army of Red Lips. Camilla watched as some of the people left their homes to evacuate the city through the burned wall.

Camilla paused for a moment, realizing that an important element of the battle plan had been abandoned. If Aya and Camilla were so far forward of the dragons, the team members with the best fire skills were far away from the dragons. She thought, *Who is handling the battle if you are up here?* Camilla's body stopped, and she had to sit down to gather her thoughts. *Who is helping Jason?*

Camilla began running in the opposite direction, leading herself back to the battle. She didn't even look back. She ran faster than before, with a newfound motivation to get to where her lover was and protect Jason.

Aya continued along the brick road that would lead her to the castle. Soon the sounds of the battle were beyond her ears. Though the fires were not spreading very quickly, many of the homes would need to be rebuilt, and most of the people would need to move, perhaps to Ceptem. Aya did not pace herself, fearing what Rose would find in the castle. *Rose needs me,* Aya thought. Aya was handling the situation as best as she could. Her ankle tattoo reminded her of the Purple infection and burned against her skin.

Aya looked up into the air and saw Ashbel, her old friend, who had been more of a father to Aya than her biological father. His shadow was visible on the ground, and she was able to catch glimpses of him through the buildings. Rose was not on his back.

Aya smiled up at her favorite creatures as she warmed her body with her own fire. Seeing that Rose was already at the castle just heightened Aya's anxiety, and she began running toward the castle once again. Once she turned her head, she heard the dramatic roar of Ashbel once again as he protected the advancing army from the air.

Ashbel belched another fireball at troops that were hiding along the route of advance, hoping to surprise Edan and the rest of Rose's army. Aya thought to herself as she was running, *Some people just never learn.*

The sun was almost at its peak as Aya darted simply into the castle in which she was supposed to grow up. Aya beamed at the banners celebrating military victories hanging along the walls, the stone statues lining the first set of stairs, the paintings of the family, and the guards whining and hugging their burnt bodies on the ground. To Aya's amazement, the castle gates were wide-open, the doors were unlocked, and the stairs were unguarded. The many and various rooms of the castle were not even closed. The king must have been aware of their return and their presence near his city. Eerily, it was as if he wanted them to walk into his home and he wanted to meet Rose. Maybe he wanted to meet Aya too.

The sandstone inside the walls was dyed gray, with different other colors that accented the walls. Aya noticed but didn't particularly care. She darted up the stairs two at a time to try to match the pace Rose would have taken as she would have run up the stairs. Aya followed the wails of men as she climbed, desperately trying to find Rose. Aya was trying to reach Rose to protect her, and even perhaps to accept the mortal danger in her place. Aya was of a single mind until she found a room. Her room. The stairs had led her directly into her own bedroom. This was the room that she had slept in for a mere few nights before her father chucked her off her own balcony.

"I have my own magic too," Samuel said behind her, his dark eyes scanning her body, observing her every move. He drew closer to her, his delicate feet carrying himself toward her, his golden cloak covering his body and trailing behind him.

"You have grown so much since you were once in that bed," he told her, gesturing to the pink bassinette in the middle of the large room. The canopy draped over the head of the baby basket, with little stuffed cows and pigs in the corner and a sweet little blanket lazily tossed in the center.

"You mean I have gotten heavier," Aya retorted, gesturing her hand, mirroring the gesture he had made, but with hers toward the glass doors of the balcony.

They stood together for a short moment, Aya soon realizing that he was stalling for time. Her father offered a charismatic smile that was just evil.

"Where is Rose?" Aya's face tensed as she mentioned Rose to her father.

"Wandering around the castle, I assume, looking for me."

"So all the dying men? That was to lead me here?" Aya said, waiting for his cruel plan to be claimed. As she guessed, it was all done by her father to get her into her childhood room, far away from Rose.

"You will die today," Aya spat at him, her short black hair covering her eyes as she jerked forward to get in his face. Strangely, his black hair matched the color of her own. They grappled lightly, leaning into each other.

"I hope so," Samuel said with a smile. "You will then be king."

"I won't ever be your successor."

"After I kill your friend," he tried to begin, but Aya, ever so obsessively, cut him off her with her sharp tongue.

"Don't you dare hurt her!"

"I won't," he said. "She'll kill herself once she sees all the damage she's created. Once she sees all the death she caused!"

"That's your plan?" Aya asked, squinting her silver eyes at him, trying to take him all in.

He smiled again, looking back into her eyes.

"You're very beautiful, you know. It would be such a shame if I had to slice off that pretty face of yours." They continued circling each other in the center of the room.

"Your threats mean nothing to me," Aya informed him, her own smile forming on her face. Her white teeth brightened her dark face. Her own power energized her whole body. Her own wishes were fulfilled as she attacked his arm viperously. She twisted and burned the hair right off his skin. His eyes watered in pain as her blue fire rotted his skin.

"I see that what your mother and brothers put in you is still there," he coughed out, wincing in pain.

"Still the same shameful daughter you threw from the tower?" She gripped tighter.

Her father was now screaming as the fire cut deeply into the flesh on his arm. The fire cut deeply enough that Aya could see the bone, before the streams of blood filled the wound. He pleaded with her to let go. She did, knowing it was Rose who would have to kill him. Rose would have to render his body lifeless.

"This isn't my room," she snarled into his ear before she left the room ironically filled with baby toys and pink princess dolls.

Aya heard him scream in frustration after she slammed the old door shut. She ran back down the stairs to follow another path to find Rose. Then they could go together to find the king. She saw fire outside the windows.

ROSE

Rose always loved birds. She always wished she were flying in the clouds above everything else. But now she was displeased to be above everything. She was frustrated to be gliding through the majestic morning sky, feeling the chill of the winter clouds, and to be resting on the warm scales of Ashbel. Rose wished she were fighting on the ground with her army, but she knew her life's mission was inside the castle.

"Put me down," Rose pleaded before lightly kicking Ashbel's side.

"You would rather run to the castle? I thought you would be more grateful," Ashbel told her, disappointment in his voice.

"I am, but what if my friends need me?"

"Did you not see the way your army dispatched the king's army outside the city walls?" Ashbel answered her, continuing, "You delivered a fine battle plan. Let's stick to your plan."

Rose thought of all the battle she would be missing but then realized that she only had one job. She must kill the king and not die. She didn't want to lose her focus on that one thing. She lightly patted the side of the body she had so impatiently kicked. Rose rested her head on Ashbel's neck, waiting for them to land on one of the many turrets of the castle.

Rose opened her eyes when she was on top of one of the towers of the large sandstone castle. There were towers on every corner of the castle, with balconies overcrowding every bedroom. White banners hung from the top of the castle's highest elevation, stretching to the dirt ground at the base of the castle's gate. The brown roofing decorated the palace. The blue-and-white stained glass colored the windows, creating an enchanted view of the world. To Rose, the castle didn't feel like an evil place. There were plants dangling from certain windows, adding life to the structure and mesmerizing her blue eyes.

Rose could smell the king's scent and the taste of his malicious perfume.

Ashbel was prudent with Rose's delicate body as he landed on the tower on the top of the castle. Thistles guarded the thick wooden door, with their tight thorns waiting to impale the purest skin. Rose waited for Ashbel to claw down the door, opening it with some force. He threw aside the door, opening the inside of the castle to Rose. She took her first steps into the house of horrors, so beautifully decorated. Rose felt the pressure of Ashbel's uneven breaths dripping down her spine.

"I will wait until you enter the castle, and move down a ways to ensure you entered safely," Ashbel told her from outside on the tower, his voice encouraging Rose with confidence.

"Thank you," Rose told him, her body now farther down the stairwell. She could still hear the shouts of her army marching forward to the castle. As Rose reached the landing at the bottom of the long stairwell, she saw many closed doors to the great and common rooms of the castle. She picked one door and pulled together her strong-arm strength and pried it open. Rose groaned slightly from the effort because of the door's weight and was rewarded with a spectacular view of the grand room. Her eyes turned behind her, to look up the long stairwell, to see the faint image of Ashbel's eye through the door at the top.

"Do well, Rose. Good luck," Ashbel bade her, his large red wings stirring in the sky as he flew effortlessly into the air.

Rose closed the door behind her rather quickly, until it slammed, blocking out the morning sun. The room was dimly lit with candles lining the hall that was first opened to her. The room was barren of banners, having wooden statues of soldiers dressed in full armor instead. There were no furnishings, except the chair, which was a golden throne, far in the back, on the center of a stage. The seat was heavily pillowed and fit for comfort. The gold was newly polished. The bright candles that lit the stage had fresh wax.

Rose walked daintily to the chair, fingering the material on the seat, her muddy boots leaving dirt on the steps.

Jason's throne, she thought quietly.

She walked around the chair, into a far room with no lighting, and began climbing the steps up into a northern tower. The steps were steep and crooked the farther she ascended. The light of the candles in the throne room ceased to help Rose see. She relied on the small windows to aid her sight.

Rose was winded, but Rose remained staid, searching for the king. Rose fed herself thoughts of ending his reign. She entered a small room filled with more small rooms. There were chains hanging from the walls and benches bolted tightly to the shared walls between the cells. She choked in her own throat as she tasted the sweat of the hovels, the feeling of uneasiness twisting her stomach. The air was heavy and drew sweat from Rose, coating her lungs with dust.

"Rose?" whimpered a familiar voice. The voice belonged to the brown-eyed and long-brown-haired woman from the painted room.

Myra was standing on her bench, her feet chained to a long rope of metal. Her cheeks were red and tearstained. Blood streamed down her nose, and her neck was bruised from a beating. The life was slowly draining from her heart.

"Myra?" exclaimed Rose, her hands banging against the locked cell door. Rose's fingers desperately tried to reach through the gaps and drag her through.

"Rose? Rose! Yes, it's me!"

"What happened to you?" Rose questioned, eyeing her scars and ripped dresses, the garments she was barely wearing.

"Samuel, the king, he found out about me, about my gifts to you," she explained, her voice trembling.

Rose shook her head. She felt Myra's pain and wished her to be okay, to be safer. Rose's eyes scanned the room for a key to the chains that imprisoned Myra. Instead, Rose found a rope of knotted rags hanging from a gap in the ceiling, the rest gathered around Myra's red neck. Rose watched, her heart beating loudly in her ears, as Myra whispered gibberish, mumbling words and nonwords.

"Where is he?" Rose fought the tears in her eyes.

"Where is who, dear?"

"The king?"

"Samuel, dear?" Myra corrected, her brown eyes widening.

"Yes, Samuel. Where is he?" Rose agreed, her pale hands gripping the cell pillars tightly, fidgeting against the metal door.

Myra whispered an answer that was not auditable.

"Myra," Rose called, slightly louder now.

She spoke again, her feet pounding against the bench, to make her words, once again passing Rose's ears.

"Myra, what has he done to you?" Rose solicitously demanded.

Myra began laughing, her red lips appearing on her mouth. Myra smiled, then laughed coyly, then broke out into a cackle. She loudly exclaimed her amusement, making Rose listen for a long time. Her laugh was unbearable to Rose's ears, nearly mocking Rose.

"You," Myra said, "you bitch!"

"What?" Rose inquired softly.

Myra continued cursing, yelling every word off the top of her mind, shouting them, slurring them, combining them, until she ran out of breath.

"You told me you would kill me!"

Rose gagged on her own tongue.

"You promised to murder me! Now you are going to make me do it myself!" Myra screamed.

Rose tried to argue with Myra. She tried to plead with her and to convince her that Rose could protect Myra. She would be safe.

"No one is safe," Myra finished. "Not while he's here."

Rose realized it then. "This was all to distract me, to keep me away from the king!" Rose accused. She hadn't even thought of her purpose to murder the king and end the war. Rose wondered what horrible sorts of things were happening while she was here with Myra, where the king wanted Rose to be. It was time to stop playing the king's game by the king's rules.

Myra laughed again, the pain slipping through her eyes. Red tears fell through her lashes. Myra jumped off the bench. Rose screamed at her not to, but her body began struggling to breathe. Rose pounded on the cell door, then Myra let herself fall to the ground. Rose watched Myra's life leave her body.

She was gone, perished, dead. Myra's lifeless body hung from the ceiling of the farthest cell. The sun was now almost directly above their heads, and Rose whimpered on the ground as Myra spit out blue foam, her eyes draining themselves of blood, her vessels popping. The last of Myra's red fire spilled out her veins, until she fought no more. Rose needed to leave and to find a way out. The door behind her led her back into the throne room.

On the golden throne was the muscular body of a black-haired, black-eyed smirking boy. When the king's court was in session, the boy loved ripping out the tongues of misbehaving jesters. On his head was a silver crown, with red jewels on the sharp edges and thorns poking out of the rim.

"Rose," he said. It made her sick hearing her name being called.

"Ubel," she responded.

The silence was piercing.

"Rose!" Aya's distorted voice echoed through the halls.

"Aya!"

"Rose?"

They met. Their eyes shared the pain of their individual experiences that day with each other. They wanted to embrace and feel the safety of each other's arms. There was the important matter of the boy who was sitting on the throne.

The door was opened again. The sun beamed into the room, and a cold breeze drifted across the tense scene. Outside, there were bright colors from the sky, the fire and smoke from burning houses within the city, and the sounds of agony in the battle.

"I hoped I would see you again," Ubel slyly said, his feet swaying off the chair, his hands running through his hair.

"You told them we were here?" Aya questioned. He nodded.

"You work for the king?" Rose asked, her skinny body wandering closer to him. She was remembering all the times she had allowed herself to touch him and how she had shared her treasured fire with him.

"I am his son," he told them.

"Aamon?" Aya asked sheepishly. She felt like a fool.

"No, Draven, actually. You killed Aamon."

Rose remembered the fire, the feeling of loss she had for Ubel's supposed death.

"Then who is Ubel?" Rose finally asked.

He laughed. "You are so stupid! No one is Ubel! We shared a person, my brother and I, to grow closer to you, but then you killed him. You killed my brother!"

"Don't raise your voice to our guest, Draven," the low, chill voice behind them said. The perfectly dressed king wearing a long-sleeved robe waltzed closer to them. The angst of his presence haunted the room.

The four of them gathered together. They watched one another's movements closely. *This is it, the end,* Rose thought.

"Rose, he has magic. Be careful," Aya whispered.

"Which one of us?" Draven asked maliciously, his ruthless smirk growing on his face again.

Draven's hand reached out to flex his palm. The low glow of the purple fire manifested into his hand, growing so quickly it toppled the spikes of his hair.

"The Purple curtain," Aya whispered.

"We were given this fire as a gift. Though, sadly, we never learned to control it. It is rather beautiful."

"I suppose I will have to rip your lips off, then?" Aya spat, her own purple fire heating her brain.

"No, Aya. Ashbel wouldn't be so pleased with that nasty tongue," Samuel lectured, his hands waving all around his robe, shifting and spinning royally as he talked.

"Rose," Aya called to her, her blue fire growing in her fingers. The passion was swimming through her veins, just the same as with Rose.

They watched one another again. Rose's eyes imprinted on the movements of Samuel, mirroring them as he breathed.

Aya waited intently as she cocked an eyebrow at her brother. Her heart sank after learning about their blood relationship and learning that one of her brothers had died.

Rose leaned in, bracing herself for the first attack on the king, matching his pace, hitting him with every burn she had. Aya attempted to do the same to Draven, but he launched his own fireball at Aya. Their purple and blue fires mixed, drying out the oxygen in the air.

Rose dragged the king into the corner of the room. His punches and kicks missed her fast legs.

"You're fast." He sighed. "But you have horrible balance." He jabbed into her side, feeling the roughness of her abs, pushing her down on the ground. He growled and got on top of her. He then slapped her soft skin and drew blood from her nose.

She extended a hand, burning the upper half of his face. The hair above his eyes fell in a bloody clump to the clean floor. He gasped, an eye dangling loose from his skull. Spurts of blood spilled all around, staining the ground.

Aya fought her brother aggressively. He had managed to wound Aya with several cuts and bruises by using his strong arms. Aya had given up on using her fire, knowing that it wouldn't hurt him and that his fire would hurt her. Her face was covered in sweat as she slammed him into the golden throne. Aya's hand grabbed Draven's head and banged it repeatedly against the back of the throne.

"It was you," she said, catching her breath as she held him tightly against the bar.

"What was me?" he gasped.

"You burned down the cabin!"

"That was Aamon, but he was so clumsy. He must have gotten lost in the fire." He laughed. His teeth were bleeding, and the gums swelling. The red on his lips was washing away in the stream of blood coming from his mouth. Draven continued laughing.

"You are a monster!" she told him.

"Runs in the family."

Aya pounced on his head, hard, knocking him out with a shot punch. She dragged him by the hair away from the throne. He was still amused, laughing hysterically as she punched him in the groin.

He grabbed a dagger that was hidden deep in his leather pants and was nearly about to stab her in the chin. His body froze, and a frame of purple fire bounced along his body, freezing him in his place.

"You don't have the permission to kill," Aya whispered into his ears. He gagged. Aya was collapsing his lungs, slowly.

"But I do," she continued to say, touching her tattoo, which was covered in dried blood and dirt. Her feet positioned on the brown ground of the throne room. She took the knife out of his hands and threw it lazily on the ground. Aya then closed in on his face with a series of aggressive punches.

Her knuckles grazed his face, marching up and down his jawline. Aya caved in Draven's skull around his eyes, denting his forehead. He refused to scream, to cry, or to plead. He just laughed. Draven laughed as Aya dug her nails deep into his face, clawing his skin and scarring his cheeks.

She punched him again, this time knocking the life out of him. He lay alone on the ground, spitting up blood. Aya found peace in watching him close his eyes in that final sleep, her final brother, dead, the prophecy fulfilled.

"Aya," Rose called. Her body had been toppled by the king. His left eye was rolling on the ground. His blood covered her red shirt.

Aya quickly ran to her aid, shoving him off Rose's body and launching a raging blue fire at his face and hands. Rose pushed the king's stomach with her foot, heating it with so much fire it punctured the gown he was wearing, rotting more flesh off his body. Aya, Draven's blood still on her hands, punched her father's face, hard.

"Aya, leave! Help Jason!" Rose commanded her, her hands spitting fire out at the king, making him tumble over the throne. Blood covered the throne.

Aya hesitantly left the throne room, leaving Rose alone with the king. His eyes filled with hate.

"You are much stronger than I thought you would be," the king admitted to Rose. He shared the grin Ubel once had displayed.

"Why aren't you fighting back?"

"My sons are dead. I have nothing left."

"Why did you hurt Myra?" Rose asked, applying pressure to his chest, her hand growing hotter by the moment.

"She helped you. She wanted me off the throne," he responded.

"You needed to be off the throne. Ashbel would have done it more brutally without me!" Rose shouted, her hand slamming her burning hands higher up the king's chest.

"Those dragons are mine! They belong me!" Samuel retorted enthusiastically. His voice began to drain.

"Nothing belongs to you."

"Evil owns everything," he commanded. The king then added, "Just wait. I will show you by taking even more important things from you this very day. In time, you may well realize that we are the same."

The golden jewels hanging around his neck were dripping in red. Rose stuttered over her own words, giving him an opportunity to kick her off him. Her body collapsed to the ground, and she coughed from the impact.

"I own you," pronounced the king before grabbing a sword from one of the mannequins near him and aiming it at her head.

Rose, quick to think, grabbed the knife that was at her side and slid it up into his chest. The sword dropped to his side. Blood and organs spilled from the gaping hole in the king's side. He fell to her feet. Rose began to grasp the finality of what she had just done. His body curled at her toes. The golden robe be had dressed himself in had peeled off his figure. His tan skin rested uneasily as she pushed him over onto his back so that Rose could look into his lifeless brown eyes.

She took the knife out of his chest and inserted it into his brain, causing more blood to spill from his body. The pieces of brain matter that had been cut off from the rest of his head swam out into the beginning of a pond of red blood.

Rose smiled deeply to herself as she looked down at Samuel's body. As she smiled, she felt a qualm enter her stomach and a new electricity burn through her veins. Purple fire shot out of her fingers and legs. The gas of purple filled the air. The intoxicating feeling of power rushed through Rose's mind as the purple centered itself around her heart and cozied itself into her veins.

"Rose!" Aya yelled from the entrance of the castle, now the castle of the Reds. Aya saw Draven's and Samuel's bodies on the ground and the purple aura around herself.

"Rose, you must come out here!"

Rose followed Aya out the front of the castle to see the battle, the chaotic ruins of a city filling their eyes. There were buildings on fire and cries from confused children. The duo ran west toward their army, which was just arriving in the circle around the castle. Edan was the first to arrive, looking tired from all the fire he had coughed up during the march to the castle. Nearby, Ashbel was hovering in the sky, prepared to address any sudden uprising or challenge from the king's defeated army. Rose's eyes met with Ashbel's as he flew valiantly in the sky, acknowledging each other's success.

It came as most surprises occur, suddenly, ferociously, and without warning. As Rose's army began surrounding the castle to claim it for their own, a lone artillery battery of eight cannons came to life. The Red leg artillery men in the battery were the finest and most professional cannon cockers in the king's army. They took pride in their precision and in the confidence the king often placed in them. They had been instructed to hide their armaments and position, which was well-chosen on a three-story building having views of both the sky and the grounds around the castle.

The captain commanding the battery of men shouted, "Target in the sky, two thousand meters. Special munitions. Dragon in the open. Fire on my command."

The captain's command set of synchronized motion at all eight of the cannons within the battery. Within thirty seconds, the position leader at each of the eight cannons had a raised hand, indicating readiness. When all hands were in the air, the captain shouted, "Fire!"

The shouts of angry men clouded Rose's thoughts and her response time. She watched paralyzed as the sound of the cannons to the right and at some distance caught her attention. Moments later, Rose saw the artillery shells move through the air and find their target. Most of the eight rounds missed, but one found Ashbel's head and a second hit the great dragon in the chest, stopping his aged heart. The great dragon tumbled backward from the sky, falling to the ground on the city's outer wall.

A second and third blast from the special cannon battery shot into the air, knocking down Ashbel's red wings and beginning to mutilate his corpse. The wings fell into a crumble of stones where the great city wall had once stood. The old stones pierced into the dragon's back as another cannonball penetrated deeply into Ashbel's thorax, spilling his heart and other organs onto the ground around him. The artillery rounds that missed Ashbel exploded unforgivingly into nearby buildings and structures, causing one of the buildings to become unstable and collapse into another building like dominoes.

It was Candice who was the first to react. She launched herself into the air, moving to the south after hearing the first cannon barrage. Her intuition informed her actions even before Ashbel's body hit the ground. She quickly located the artillery battery and approached from the air behind it. A straight line could be drawn between her approach then through the artillery battery and to the location where Ashbel had been hit. Candice's first belch of fire into the artillery position was sudden, ferocious, and without warning. Secondary explosions from gunpowder and other munitions hurled shrapnel into the surrounding area as Candice circled for another attack. Candice continued strafing the position until there was no motion there.

Ashbel's red blood disgorged under the pile that his body had made. There were wounds all along his arm from the impact. His yellow eyes were shut, with no will to reawaken. Rose screeched, and Aya did as well. They had run to his location on instinct after he fell from the sky. Their hands traveled all along his vast belly, begging for him to rise.

The firing of the cannons served as a cue for a second military operation. A squad of the most elite of the king's special forces had been instructed to hide in the city during the attack. After the aerial attack completed, the team of ten men located in an untouched building just north of the line of destroyed buildings from the western wall to the castle. The team was near enough to both the castle and the attack route of Rose's army that they could observe the actions in both locations. Their orders were to attack and kill the general commanding the army and any of the leadership near the general. They had been told that the general would likely be a woman or even a pair of women, which did not give any of these men any qualms. They served at the king's pleasure and found pleasing the king quite rewarding.

The team observed as Edan approached the castle. The army general on the ground was quite obvious, barking orders to the skirmish troops at the feet of the dragon. When the second dragon, the female dragon, launched into the air, the professional killers knew this would be their best opportunity. They quickly fanned out and launched their attack, slicing through skirmish troops on their way to accomplishing their mission.

Jason saw some motion to his left just after hearing Candice behind him take flight. He was about to order some of his men to address the disturbance when, all too quickly, two of the attackers engaged Jason. While Jason had enjoyed some combat success in the battle, these men were just too fast.

On instinct, Rose ran as fast as her body would take her. She sprinted through the crowds of people, the fires that were beginning to spread into the streets, jumping easily over the broken plants and doors. She darted into the courtyard, her heart beating quickly, trying to find her brother again. *I will show you by taking even more important things from you this very day.*

Rose ran intently, finding the king's special unit as it attacked her brother.

One soldier had a knife in his hand and had cut off Jason's lips, making them bloodred. Another had punched Jason's eyes swollen shut. A third had ripped out his hair. Rose gasped at the brutality, and her Purple intensified. As the full view of the counterattack came into Rose's focus, she could see that other men were menacing LeRoy and Red Lips. Camilla was approaching from behind the attackers along with Aya. Rose wished she were dreaming as she watched Jason's body fall suddenly to the ground. Camilla watched in horror as blood streamed out of Jason's mouth. Camilla saw his eyes close once his head hit the hard gravel.

"The traitor!" the soldiers mocked.

Rose screamed as she tried to run faster. She began to trip over her own feet and fell hard into the dirt. She was crying as she crawled over to him. Aya began to pull the soldiers off Jason.

"Your king is dead!" Rose hollered. She and Aya, tears still streaming down their sore cheeks, darted emotionally toward the ten-man squad that had wrought so much damage and killed Jason. The Rose's and Aya's hands, once drenched with sweat, now burned with their great fire. They marched onto the men who had continued slaughtering Rose's army. As the death squad watched the girls intently, the trained professional soldiers prepared, with swords and knives drawn, to kill the girls. Rose and Aya began to throw heavy purges of red and blue fires. The fire swarmed the girls' beautiful bodies and colored their hair. They screamed as the duo's strong arms extended to face the men who were professional killers. Rose passionately let her fire rage as it managed itself onto the bodies of the men. At first, the special forces soldiers did not scream. When the screams began, they began in earnest and were accompanied by agonizing yelps. They screamed at the horror of being burned alive and feeling their skin be denigrated and burned. Rose found it refreshing.

As the fires of vengeance from Rose and Aya purged the battlefield of the ten attackers, Camilla held on to Jason, crying onto his shoulder.

The men were dead, and the fire continued to burn their limbs. They lay as waste in a pile near Jason. Rose and Aya were satisfied and then sad as they ran back over to their dear friend Camilla.

Rose, covered in ash, trembled as she joined Camilla in holding tightly onto her brother. Rose noticed his clothes were burned and torn, his shoes had fallen into pieces of leather, and his hair was spread throughout the courtyard.

She saw the last of him and cradled his body into her own.

Aya ran behind them. They witnessed her anger rage as fire out of her hands. She felt her muscles throb in her arms and the cuts swell out in her chest. Camilla was heartbroken and in denial. She kept waiting for Jason to open his eyes and tell a joke about something stupid that would just cut Camilla up. Her heartbeat slowed as she caressed his head, especially the bald patches the soldiers had made. She began accepting the finality of their actions.

The three girls walked together into the courtyard and began watching the people, looking out for the faces of their friends. The quickly identified the bright-red hair of Andrew and the brown hair of LeRoy.

"Aya, we won. Don't they know?" Rose asked, her body filled with energy.

Aya shook her head rapidly, utterly abandoning the idea of ending the war peacefully. Many deaths had happened on both sides. The Forgotten Children had been somewhat reckless, throwing themselves through the walls of buildings. Often enough, destroying building walls would have a cascading effect, breaking down the supports and collapsing the buildings on nearby Nomads.

Aya and Rose watched with terrible guilt as the three dragons stood on the farthest side of the city, carrying injured Nomads on their backs, away from the rotten fire. The fire burned, raged, and intimidated.

"They shall never love us," Rose whispered into the nothingness of the smoky air.

Aya agreed. They gripped each other's hands, feeling the warmth of their fires spread into their bodies. Rose saw that some of the Nomads had bright-red noses and that their fingers were beginning to freeze. The December war was cold, and the frigid breeze did not contribute to the comfort of the innocent people.

The pair walked with serenity dripping down their spines, their feet aching and their heads throbbing. Rose's perfect blue eyes now had a bit of purple in them. Her hair had fallen out of its braid, her nails, those she had not bitten off, covered with dirt and blood.

They walked into the bedlam, their heads facing the ash on the ground, the soot in the grass, the broken homes and glass scattered around the city. Rose eyed Camilla's long red hair as she tackled a soldier to the ground. The green fire in her hands liquified his armor into magma.

Vulcan, Edan, and Candice gathered the rest of Rose's army, taking them quickly out of the city. The Nomads shut themselves into their homes. Other Nomads were busy trying to stop fires that were still burning in their own homes. Rose and Aya walked back into the city, carrying the large red heart of Ashbel in their hands, feeling its veins and vessels. Rose began imagining that his heart was still pumping blood, driving life through her beasty friend.

They walked in the dirt, back to the castle, to ensure there were no more cannon rounds firing into the sky. They pushed the rocks and crumbled walls out of their way with their toes as they walked.

Camilla had run back to be with Jason. She touched her chest and collapsed to the ground next to him with a thud. She could see nothing but the dark clouds above her and red shirt and bloodstained skin that layered Jason.

"My king," Rose said, whimpering, as she saw Camilla with Jason. Camilla began to kiss him, kissing his forehead delicately as she cried onto his dirty skin. She held him tightly, though he was too heavy for her to let him rest on her lap. She sobbed continuously, feeling a stabbing pain for her lost lover.

The city was in ash, the sky filled with smoke, and the sun was now directly above their heads. The feeling of the midday warmth glazed Rose's and Aya's skin. Ashbel's heart was in her hands, the body of her dead brother in the arms of Andrew. The team of teenagers tied up different soldiers to posts and began walking back to the front of the city.

They were in no hurry to meet the rest of their army, Rose especially. She had lost her two closest friends within minutes. The memory of the unbearable loss was still fresh in her brain. The pain was beyond words. She was surprised she could walk, that she could gather the strength it took to hold herself up, but occasionally she would trip over her feet. Rose though, *Jason always reminded me that I have horrible balance.*

Rose's hand was tightly intertwined with those of LeRoy, who had met them after being flown to the castle by Vulcan. He held her, palming her thumb as they walked.

Camilla was still crying on Aya's shoulder, her red hair draped over her face. Camilla never strayed that far from Andrew, who struggled mightily as he carried Jason's body.

"It will be the shortest battle in history," Candice told her as they embraced in a tight moment.

"You mean we could have lost more?" Rose simply said, her heart aching more than her feet or her head.

"The Forgotten Children have been safely escorted back to the Blue Forest, and the Reds have been flown back to their homes," Erik told her after these things had taken place. They had sat for hours under a tree, massaging one another's shoulders, fixing their hair, chatting happily, waiting for further instructions.

Rose was alone. She would have wanted to help Jason prep for his speech, for his coronation, and to make a crown of leaves for him to practice. It felt different now that she had killed someone, that she had carried out the horrible deed, and that Samuel's blood was on her hands. Her tattoo had faded away. It left a scar to remind her of what she had done, the same way that Aya's had transformed.

Rose had cried, tears streaming down her face. Her heart felt empty, and there was a brokenness in her form. She could look at Jason if she wanted to. His body was getting so much love from people who didn't even know him. That hurt more.

Aya gathered her courage and convinced herself to sit next to her best friend, her black hair and dark head resting on Rose's shoulder. They sat together for a long while before Aya spoke.

"Someone is going to have to be king," Aya told her.

"Ask Camilla."

"She's too heartbroken."

"Andrew maybe?" Rose tried to tell Aya.

Aya found amusement in her refusal to cooperate with her.

"It has to be you." Aya giggled.

"Absolutely not."

"You have the jewels!"

"I also have purple fire now! We can't risk it!"

"We will get through that together, Rosie, but right now we need a king, and we all want it to be you," Aya reminded her.

LeRoy and Camilla peeked their heads through one of the nearby shrubs. Camilla's face was still tearstained. They all gathered around the tree where Rose was sitting in what had been her own private misery. Andrew followed behind them, bowing his head down to her.

Aya reached for Rose's pale hand and lifted her to her feet. Afterward, she knelt at her feet, kissing her toes, staining her knees green from the grass. After her, Camilla and Andrew both closed their eyes and touched their noses to the grass before Rose. Finally, LeRoy kissed her hand then slowly fell to his knees beside her, lowering his tan head. Rose then stood tall under the tree.

The castle was filled with the lords and ladies who reigned in hidden castles around the city. They were all dressed in red gowns and suits, their children in pink dresses, and their maids wore red bows in their hairs. The city was bustling with activity after the war. They quickly had moved forward and begun to rebuild. The children were singing happier songs, and their parents were beginning to accept the new ways of life—some at least. They had all brought their owns gifts and food for the banquet. They had been so generous to wrap everything in red, to dye everything red, and to repurpose the old red things that they had been forced to throw out by the old king.

Most of the city dwellers had hung red banners outside their doors and displayed red roses for the special occasion. The scene was cheering happily outside their homes. The whole city had filled with people waiting outside the doors of the sandstone castle. They were holding their children above their heads so they could get a glimpse of the goings-on on this marvelous occasion.

Inside the castle, Rose had freshly decorated the throne room. The carpet welcoming guests was bright red. The streamers hanging from the ceiling were also red. The fires that burned the wax of the candles celebrated every color of the dragons.

Light was coming in from every window, and it triangulated spectacularly on the throne in the center of the large room that awaited Rose's touch. The throne was still golden, but the bloodstains of the late king and prince had been properly removed by careful hands. In fact, every memory of Samuel had been promptly removed from the palace as soon as Rose announced the beginning of her reign. Rose could hear the chants and sounds of praise from inside the throne room. Aya stood beside her.

Rose was dressed in a red gown with golden lace and black trim. Rose's hair was pulled tightly in a braid that Camilla had done. Rose's skin smelled of roses, and the powder on her face also smelled of rose. The gloss on her lips tasted of sugar.

Aya irreverently wore her combat boots with the white fur around them, along with a red skirt and matching blouse. As they entered the great room, Aya guided Rose to the throne. They delicately held hands and exchanged knowing smiles as they walked the path of the red carpet. Rose set her groomed body, still slightly bruised, on the solid golden throne.

Around Rose's wrist was the rose gold chain Liza had given her, around her neck was the obsidian necklace her mother had gifted her, and around her finger were the tight tail and body of the dragon ring. The rest of the jewels were spread among Camilla and Aya, with even LeRoy sporting a piece of rock.

Rose, who could see the people looking proudly upon her, smiled gently when the red-stone tiara was laid on her head. Rose felt the tiara on her bronze hair giving her formal power.

She leaned back against the throne, resting her back on the warm gold.

Aya, who stood at Rose's right, smiled down at her friend as she walked down the steps of the stage and bowed her head at Rose again.

"I always knew it was to be you," Aya mouthed before lowering herself to the soft floor of the throne room in the palace. Her knees rested on the red carpet, her combed-back hair covering her face as she proudly dropped her head.

Camilla, who had stood to Rose's left, was dressed in a long green dress, her curly red hair dazzling with jewels and glitter. Walking behind Aya, Camilla bowed her head down before kneeling at Rose's side.

Andrew and LeRoy, the lords and ladies, the noblemen and noblewomen then bowed too. They focused their eyes on the ground instead of trembling in the presence of the great Rose Mensch.

The people then, row behind row behind row, in front of and behind the castle, guided themselves to the ground and lowered their heads. Behind them, the Forgotten Children, being tame, lowered their prickly heads.

The dragons, the three remaining, mightily sank their heads into their chests, bending their long necks.

All eyes then turned to Erik, who was in the grand room with Aya but had grown distracted by the taste of the royal wine and had forgotten to bow his head. When he remembered, he did so earnestly. He smiled proudly at her, taking in her power, thanking her for leading the Reds into such a victorious battle, even at the price she had to pay.

Rose looked out into the sun, right above their heads, and watched as her people handed over the power of the throne to her. She now held the power of the king.

Rose lifted herself off the ground, getting familiar with the weight of her dress. She extended her hand out for Aya to grasp, then Camilla, then the whole of the city rose back to their feet.

Rose, hand in hand with Aya, walked out into the courtyard of the castle and looked out into the happy city. Inspections had required many of the building to be toppled, but there was so much construction. The rebirth was so beautiful.

She smiled sheepishly, her blush turning redder.

All this for a killer, she thought to herself. *Perhaps they will fall out of love with me.*

"Reds and Nomads," Rose began, and they quieted down their cheering, "my dearest friends."

Aya smiled, her hand still intertwined with Rose's, though she had stepped farther back. Erik came and stood next to Aya. They listened to Rose in a comfortable silence, the winter sun in their eyes.

"I want things to be different. I want things to be right," Rose said loudly, her voice projecting above all the people in Remular City.

"I see my role not as a king but as a leader to guide every person to a better life in this, our world. I plan to look out for the lives of each and every person and to make this kingdom a better kingdom.

"I don't wish to remind you of the horrors of the previous king. He damaged so many of the people that he was supposed to love and protect. I will promise to serve you no matter what and to put *you* first."

The people clapped loudly.

"Aya," Rose continued, gesturing for her dearest friend to stand next to her, "my closet friend, the beautiful princess, I name you Aya, king of Dragons Nest."

Aya smiled as Rose handed her the dragon ring, sliding it onto her dark skinny finger. Aya's white eyes beamed down on her body. They embraced once more before Aya walked behind her while the crowd cheered again.

"The world, as you know, has been around for centuries. No one has yet to deserve it. Then my brother, Jason, came along. He was kind, passionate, generous, honorable, and courageous. He deserved the world, even at its worst times. But he was taken from us." Rose trembled. "So I have decided to give the world to Jason. From this day forward, the world will be known as Jade, in honor of my late brother."

The city shook with all the cries of joy and happiness that radiated throughout the streets and alleys.

"Citizens of Jade, arise for you king!" exclaimed Aya with so much love in her voice that she could barely exhale afterward.

"All hail King Rose!"

Rose felt the brokenness of her heart slowly growing back together. She felt the power of the purple energy surge in her fingertips. She felt the urge to *feel* become stronger. She felt safe in her castle, though the people whom she shared the halls with were foreign to her. She found the vibe to be a positive one. She was happy. She was happy to rule. She was home.

*****

"You all right?" Aya asked her as they stood on the balcony of her master bedroom, overlooking the prosperous city of Remular.

"I feel as if you are always asking me that question," Rose told her. "Let me ask you it for once."

The girls giggled as they watched the sun set over the trees of the forest. The ombre mixtures of red, orange, and yellow in the sky, the black of the trees, with the smoke of fires in the houses clouding the air. They smelled freshly prepared ham served on a glass dish outside the room, in a hall where the rest of the people were, where Rose was supposed to be.

"I am doing fine," Aya whispered through a smile.

Rose ran her fingers through her short black hair, tasting the gloss as she licked her lips.

"When do you return to Dragons Nest?"

"Soon," Aya informed her, "unless you need me here."

"I do," Rose said, smiling, "but they need you there too."

"Erik will be here," Aya joked, knowing well that it was no comfort for Rose that Erik was staying in the palace.

"How is he handling Samuel's death?" Rose pondered, knowing of their strained relationship.

"As well as he can. He doubted you, but I know he believes in you and is thankful for you."

"I hope so."

They listened and watched as the sun set over the city.

"What will your first act as king be?" Aya asked after she sipped a glass of wine from a tray inside Rose's room, which was decorated with vines and grapes.

"To rule," Rose pronounced, "properly."

"You imagine you'll manage?"

"Yes, I think I will."

They laughed again. A gentle knock was heard on the door before Camilla, LeRoy, and Andrew popped their heads into the king's room to celebrate the taking of the throne. They gathered together on the balcony, remembering things they did on their journey, like biting their nails. After a good laugh and a few more sips of wine, the private party ended. They joined the dinner party in the grand hall. Afterward, the sun would set. The day was over, and a new day would arise.

EPILOGUE

ROSE

Aya and Rose walked up the dreamy hill of the Red Islands. They chatted about the times Rose and Jason had raced up that same hill. Rose remembered the times she had won and the few times Jason had almost won.

Their hearts were beating in sync as they saw the remains of the homey cabin, which was ripped to shreds by Samuel's army. The door was busted down, and all the windows were smashed to pieces, with the glass lying on the ground of both sides of the walls. The kitchen was a mess. The sofas in the main room were ripped and torn. The stairs were still intact and led to many rooms, also violently savaged.

Rose and Aya spent hours looking into the mess the soldiers had made, observing the final pieces of her happiest memories destroyed. The fireplace, where she had burned her first real fire, was torn apart brick by brick, and the logs that once burned in it were splinters. The brush that Celia had left on the counter had her blond hair still stuck in its pegs, but the handle had broken off and separated. The brush had been thrown lazily to the ground below the large table. The chairs were overturned, and so was the table. It looked no better than Katrina's house, although it hadn't been blown to shreds.

Rose wore her new crown on her head, with leather pants and a loose-fitting red shirt. Aya wore the same, along with the dragon ring around her finger.

Rose's hair was in a tight braid. Before they left, Camilla had taught Rose how to do it herself. Camilla hadn't been heard from since she left the city the morning after Rose's coronation, and neither had Andrew. They were probably trying to manage a normal life without Jason, just as Rose was trying to do. Rose would think of him before she made any royal decision, picturing his approach to every problem.

A loud crack echoed. Rose had stepped on a piece of glass from the windowpane. Her skinny fingers lifted it to her blue eyes as she carefully inspected the sharp edges, glancing at the different colors it produced in the light.

"Do you want to go see your old room?" asked Aya as her feet started climbing the first step, anticipating moving up to the second floor.

Rose nodded, and they walked right into the old room. Rose's and Celia's beds had been slashed by swords. Their dresser and chairs were turned over, with clothes falling out of each drawer. Celia's white dresses lay wrinkled in the center of the room. Celia's blue and floral dresses were tossed in the corners of the room.

Rose imagined the determination in the soldiers' eyes as they looked aggressively for the rest of her family. The anger they felt when they didn't find Rose.

"Like the townspeople said, their bodies were found in their rooms, dead, and then taken away," Rose mumbled to herself. "It was no use coming here to see for ourselves."

"Yes, it was," Aya told her calmly. Her voice smoothed the anxiety Rose had about seeing Celia's lifeless body on the ground. The bodies had been cared for and interred long before the arrival of Rose and Aya.

"You needed this."

"I wish I didn't and that they were still here." Rose sniffled through her pale nose. The powder was still on her cheeks and eyes from a ceremony the prior morning, before Vulcan flew them to the Red Islands.

"I bet they wish they could have seen you sit on that throne for the first time, wearing your crown for the first time."